THE WORLD
AND ALL
THAT IT HOLDS

THE WORLD
AND ALL
THAT IT HOLDS

ALEKSANDAR HEMON

MCD

FARRAR, STRAUS AND GIROUX   NEW YORK

MCD

Farrar, Straus and Giroux

120 Broadway, New York 10271

Printed in the United States of America

First edition, 2023

Library of Congress Cataloging-in-Publication Data

Names: Hemon, Aleksandar, 1964– author.

Title: The world and all that it holds / Aleksandar Hemon.

Description: First edition. | New York : MCD/Farrar, Straus and Giroux, 2023.

Identifiers: LCCN 2022043724 | ISBN 9780374287702 (hardcover)

Subjects: LCGFT: Novels.

Classification: LCC PS3608.E48 W67 2023 | DDC 813/.6—dc23/eng/20220912

LC record available at https://lccn.loc.gov/2022043724

Designed by Gretchen Achilles

For my daughters, Ella, Isabel (R.I.P.), and Esther

For refugees of the world

Three kinds of dreams are fulfilled: a morning dream, a dream that a friend has about one, and a dream that is interpreted in the midst of a dream. Some say: Also, a dream that is repeated.

—BABYLONIAN TALMUD, Tractate Berakhot

If he is mine, why is he with others?
Since he's not here, to what "there" did he go?

—JALĀL AL-DĪN RŪMĪ,
"Where Did the Handsome Beloved Go?"

CONTENTS

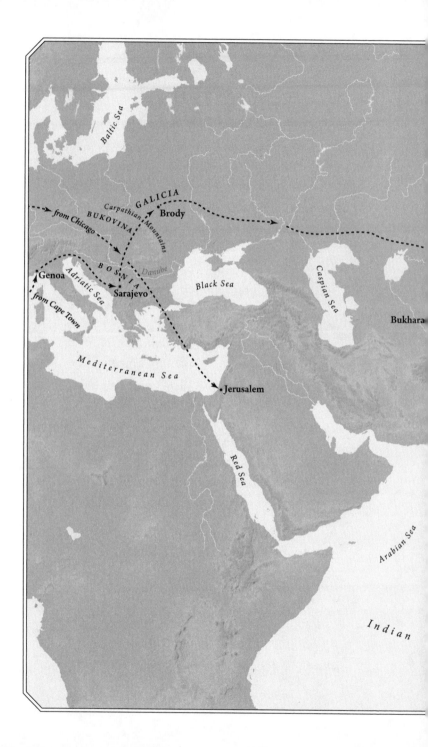

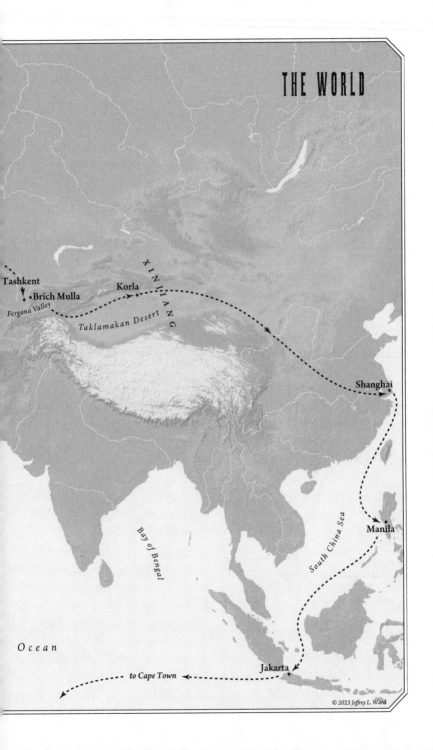

THE WORLD

Tashkent
Brich Mulla
Fergana Valley
Korla
XINJIANG
Taklamakan Desert
Shanghai
Bay of Bengal
South China Sea
Manila
Ocean
Jakarta
to Cape Town

© 2023 Jeffrey L. Ward

PART I

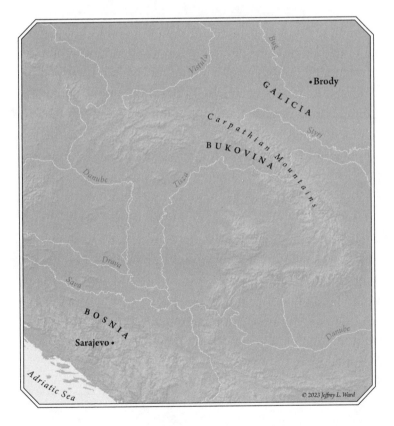

SARAJEVO, 1914

THE HOLY ONE kept creating worlds and destroying them, creating worlds and destroying them, and then, just before giving up, He finally came up with this one. And it could be much worse, this world and all that it holds, as I certainly know how to get my hands on some interesting stuff around here. Let's see: LAPIS INFERNALIS, LAUDANUM, next to it, LAVENDER.

Pinto took the laudanum off the shelf, knocking over the lavender tin, which miraculously did not break open when it hit the floor. He released a drop of laudanum onto a sugar lump, watched the brown stain bloom, then placed it in his mouth. While the sugar and bitterness dissolved on his tongue, he picked up the lavender, dipped his nose into the tin, and inhaled—vast Mediterranean flower fields stretched inside him, the blue sea lapping at his soul, a turquoise sky and swallows floating above it all, the laudanum sailing on his blood all the way to his mind, and then beyond. To all the things created at twilight on the Šabat eve, the

Lord wisely added laudanum, just to help make everything more beautiful and bearable.

Now was Rafael Pinto much better prepared for the Archduke Franz Ferdinand von Österreich-Este, Heir Apparent to the Habsburg Empire and Inspector General of the Imperial Armed Forces, and for the whole spectacle he was bringing to Sarajevo just to see how we live here. We live rather well, Your Highness, I must say, provided there is enough laudanum and lavender on hand, thank You very much for Your kind concern. And since this is an enterprise of providing remedy for the body as much as for the soul, we're sure to have plenty of whatever we might need, long live the Emperor, the Lord be praised, and bless You too.

After a drab, rainy week, the morning was sunny and the light broke through the windows as never before, rearranging the checkered floor into unprecedented patterns. The sugar was now completely dissolved but the bitterness lingered, tickling his tongue. God wrapped Himself in white garments, and the radiance of His majesty illuminated the world, and right here on the floor of the Apotheke Pinto we can now behold a little patch of one of those very garments. There might be a poem for me to write about the light shifting and altering the visible: God's Garments, it could be called. But then, who would ever care about any of it, no one cares about light and what it does to the soul, not here in this city behind God's back.

Ever since Vienna, Pinto had been writing poetry in German; he wrote in Bosnian too, but only about Sarajevo. He even tried to write in Spanjol, but that always felt like his Nono was writing it, everything always sounding like an ancient proverb: Bonita de mijel, koransiko de fijel; Kazati i veras al anijo mi lo diras, and so on. Whereas light is everywhere and nowhere. It exists, but never by itself, always a garment, just as God is knowable only in the imperfection of His Creation. Even darkness is clothed in light; light makes itself present by its own absence. We carry the darkness inside and return it to the light when we die. That could sound good in German. Im Inneren tragen wir das Licht, da wir, wann wir sterben, zurückgeben der Finsternis.

He put the laudanum and lavender up on the shelf. The opiatic ease set in, slowly, like a deep breath, while he studied the floor smeared with shadows from letters in the window. APOTHEKE PINTO. He should finally get rid of all the silly herbs Padri Avram had bought from peasants and collected for decades. Padri had insisted that all that junk be moved from the old drogerija in the Čaršija and put up alongside the actual medicine, which he had derisively called the patranjas. But, moved though they may have been, all those obscure, old-fashioned herbs were now dry and dead, their ancient, cumbersome Turkish names (amber kabugi; bejturan; logla-ruhi) sticking out in the neat alphabetical order of the patranjas, which Pinto had established after the move. He didn't even know what they were for, those magic herbs. In the old place, only Padri knew where to find things and what the principles of classification were—the drogerija had really represented the interiority of Padri's head, all the books and the prikantes and segulot and basme on the shelves, and the burnt-sugar scent of the halva he had with coffee, crawling against the ceiling, the clouds of tobacco smoke as dense as his thoughts. Those ancient peasants of his still came by the Apotheke sometimes, clad in their sheep-stink clothes and animal-hide footwear, with their random ripe boils marring their mountain veneer, with their untold diseases, gnarled bones, and rotten teeth. They'd enter and look around as if they'd just disembarked from a ramshackle time machine, disoriented by the camphor smell and the serene medicinal quiet and the marble floor, awed by Emperor

Franz Joseph's baroque backenbart in the picture they could not fail to see. Only Nono Solomon's picture on the opposite wall, dating from the last century, assured them they actually were where they were meant to be: they recognized Nono's fez, his furrowed brow and stately white beard, even his kaftan adorned with a medal on his chest, pinned once upon a time by none other than a representative of the Sultan Abdul Hamid himself. The peasants would ask for the old Jewish hećim, and Pinto would have to tell them that the old hećim was dead and gone, and that he—Doktor Rafo to them—was now the rightful heir of this medicinal little empire and that the only herb he would ever be interested in buying from them was lavender. But there was little lavender in the grim mountains around Sarajevo, so the peasants returned unrewarded to their thick and ancient forests, where they lived and copulated with wild beasts, and never came back to the Apotheke Pinto, which was just as well. Because we now lived in a brand-new century, progress was everywhere to behold, the future was endless, like a sea—nobody could see the end of it. No one cared about bejturan anymore. Amber kabugi was probably something that summoned ghosts or killed witches and vilas, made your teeth fall out, caused a never-ending erection. Well, that wouldn't be half as bad.

The morning had started with a cannon salvo, welcoming to our beloved Godforsaken city the Archduke Franz Ferdinand von Österreich-Este, Heir Apparent to the Habsburg Empire and Inspector General of the Imperial Armed Forces, accompanied by Her Highness the Duchess. Now there was another boom, an extra welcome to His and Her Highness. (Only later that day would Pinto find out that the boom had been caused by a hand grenade a hapless young assassin had hurled at the Archduke's car. I can confirm, from personal experience, that we are always late to the history in which we live.) Across the street, Hadži-Besim had hung the imperial banner above his tobacco shop as per Governor's order, and presently stood under it, his thumbs stuck in the vest pockets, the top of his claret fez nearly touching the black-and-yellow rag with the stiff Austrian eagle in the center. But the colors were pleasingly aligned, and the smooth rotundity of Hadži-Besim's stomach was just as pleasant. Laudanum helps the world be snug inside God's garments. Pinto realized he should've put the banner above the door as well; he was planning to, never got around to it; there were so many banners all over the city, nobody would notice the absence of his. Nono Solomon and the Emperor frowned at him from their opposite walls, rebuking him with their aged and stolid wisdom for his negligence, and for many other things as well; they watched him all the time, the mighty old men. This was a century of progress; great things were coming our way. Remember the future! The Archduke Franz Ferdinand von Österreich-Este, Heir Apparent to the Habsburg Empire, himself came to Sarajevo to see how we live, and tell us how we can live even better.

And there he was now, the Archduke, like a prince straight out of a fairy tale, banging on the pharmacy's door, more specifically on the A in APOTHEKE PINTO, ignoring the sign that said it was closed. Behold the famous steel-blue eyes and the upturned hussar's mustache now pressed against the glass as He peers inside! What would His Highness want from Pinto's humble self? What could one Rafael Pinto ever offer to the Heir Apparent, other than his unlimited and undying loyalty, his joy at casting his gaze on His Imperial countenance? He hurried over to unlock the door, slowing down and stepping around—just in case—the recondite reticulation of the light and the shadow. Light changes the world, yet it stays the same, ever warm inside

God's garments. Das Licht ändert die Welt und jedoch bleibt sie gleich, auf ewig warm unter Gottes Gewänder.

The Archduke was not the Archduke at all, though he certainly entered like one, as if everything before him belonged to him, importing venerable mothball residues in his ceremonial Rittmeister uniform, a sash across the chest like a perfectly made bed, the meticulously shaven and powdered face, and the wax in the symmetrically pointed mustache, and his splendorous helmet with a perfumed horsehair hackle, and a tinge of sweat underneath it all—he smelled, all of him, like the Vienna Pinto had known so well, like the very first day of the century of progress, he smelled like something that accelerated Pinto's heartbeat and made his palms sweat. He rubbed them against his sides.

The Rittmeister's saber cackled against the stairs as he stepped down. He took off his helmet to execute a perfect about-face. A decision behind his own thought, Pinto still held the door open. The heat and the din of a distraught pigeon flock, of an anxious crowd, rushed inside. Bitte! said Pinto, and closed the door, locked it too. Bleib mein schlagendes Herz.

The heat was unbearable, the Rittmeister said, dabbing his forehead with a whitest handkerchief, just horrid and unbearable, and he desperately needed some kind of powder for his insufferable headache. And he also wondered why there was no Royal banner above the entrance. He spoke to Pinto with a curt Viennese accent; there was the shadow of an A on his sashed belly; stars glittered on his uniform's collar. His eyes had a melancholy, consumptive sheen, so Pinto was compelled to consider his widening pupils, until the Rittmeister averted his gaze, a breath too late. His lips were cracked and he licked the upper one. The tip of his tongue touched his mustache.

As for the banner, Pinto said, bowing, he humbly begged for

forgiveness—too much excitement in expectation of this glorious day evidently got in the way. He would be glad to rectify his error promptly, but before that, with Herr Rittmeister's kind permission, he should rather hasten to fetch the powder that would almost certainly alleviate Herr Rittmeister's headache. The Rittmeister clicked his heels and nodded in appreciation. Erect he stood in the center of the light field, as if accustomed to being admired.

It all rushes back to Pinto, that joyous time in Vienna when his jetzer hara reigned: the glances exchanged on the promenade along the Danube, in the crowded student cafés; the tinglingly surreptitious touches in the hoi polloi theaters; the poetry quotes encoded with desire, flaring out in the middle of a carefully innocuous conversation; the mischievous emergence of the very same dimples on the face of one Hauptmann Freund as he offered his passionate and false opinions on women, on Sacher torte, on Schubert, on love, on laudanum, on Oberst Redl, even—daringly—on Herr Pinto's exotic facial features expressing capacity for passion, until Rafael shut him up with a kiss. Gute Nacht und Guten Morgen, Hauptmann Freund!

Oh, we could live so much better!

Behind the counter Pinto crushes with his trembling hands the ingredients into the powder, recalling a future moment—the moment he'll be caressing, as if inadvertently, the Rittmeister's hand, thereby transmitting the currents of his passion. The Rittmeister has repositioned himself to stand before Nono Solomon's photograph, his chin upturned in wonder as though he had never seen a Sefaradi, which he probably hadn't. He would not be able to connect Pinto—fezless in his suit and cravat, a gold chain across his stomach, and, despite his swarthy face, European as can be—with the sepia sheen of the Ottoman past and

Nono's biblical frown. Who created Heaven and Earth, who installed this thunderous heart inside my chest?

Pinto envisions grabbing the Rittmeister's hand and then pulling him deeper into the back room to grab his hanino face and kiss him, the full submission to the impulse: sliding the sash aside, the manly chest, the infernal depths of the body, touching his already stiff pata, the heart bursting with pleasure. They would be safe—no one is going to come in, the pharmacy is closed, the door is locked, it is Sunday, and the whole world is busy with kowtowing to the Archduke Franz Ferdinand von Österreich-Este, Heir Apparent to the Habsburg Empire and Inspector General of the Imperial Armed Forces. Who would care to see der Kuss in the dark back room of the Apotheke? Even the Holy One, who is everywhere and nowhere, might wish to look away when I press my lips against his. What is in your heart about your fellow man is likely to be in his heart about you. Šalom, jetzer hara!

Pinto finishes the powder, pours it onto a paper sheet, spilling it all over, then collecting into a heap to scoop it with the paper edge, folds it slowly, as if presenting a way to perform a magic trick. He hands the triangular envelope to the Rittmeister, who may have noticed the tremor in Pinto's hand. Their fingers touch, their eyes meet.

Naturally, nothing happens.

May I ask you for a glass of water? the Rittmeister says.

Rosenwasser? Pinto offers.

The Rittmeister pours the powder into his mouth; his Adam's apple bobs as he downs the rose water. A faint nick on the tip of his chin; his mustache is perfect. He looks toward the ceiling as he downs the rose water, empties the whole glass, and then sighs with what seems to be pleasure. There could be a future in which the Rittmeister faces a mirror, gorgeous in his undershirt and his tight rider's pants, the suspenders hanging down his thighs to his knees. Pinto conjures up the morning in a Viennese room—the shaving soap and cigarette smoke, and a rose in a glass at the bedside, still fresh from last night; crumpled bedsheets; on the wall, a painting of a path winding into a dark forest. His name is Kaspar, Pinto determines. Kaspar von Kurtzenberger. Guten Morgen, Kaspar! he will say. Guten Morgen, Rafael! Kaspar will say. Did you sleep well? Not at all, mein Lieber. I spent the night listening to your beating heart.

Dankeschön! says Kaspar. He returns the empty glass to Pinto, and then dabs his lips with the pristine handkerchief.

Bitte! whispers Rafael, his throat dry and tight.

Before Pinto can unlock and open the door, the Rittmeister stops, his gloved hand on the pommel of his saber, to consider Rafael as if he had one more thing to say. He says nothing, his gaze long and deep, waiting for something to happen or reveal itself. Now is the time to step up and kiss him farewell. Their eyes lock; his eyes are in fact green. The Rittmeister smiles, without exposing his teeth, dimples forming above the very peaks of his waxed mustache.

Before he could make any decision, Pinto rises on the tips of his toes, and kisses the Rittmeister right at the border between his mustache and his lip. It tastes of rose water and tobacco, of wax and sugar. The Rittmeister moves his face away from Pinto's, not to escape him but to look at him with bemused surprise. He glances outside to see if anyone has seen what happened, but everyone outside is looking in the direction from which the Archduke is supposed to come; the only sound is distant cheers. Jetzer hara has taken over, and Pinto has no thoughts that are not dizeu; his pata hardens. He still has the glass in his hand, he is still aware

of the world beyond the Apotheke, but all of it is distant and receding. Pinto kisses the Rittmeister again, and this time Kaspar
opens his mouth, and Pinto takes in his rose breath. This is crazy;
he's never done anything like this, and he knows how dangerous
it is, and yet he can't stop. The man's lips are soft; the kiss is quick
but gentle, and in the time it takes, in the muscled hardness of
the Rittmeister's chest, there is an entire possible life.

Kaspar, Pinto says, and presses his cheek against the Rittmeister's chest. Kaspar.

It is only then the Rittmeister steps back, as if what happened
did not happen, and asks, Was ist das?, and everything is dispelled. Pinto has no answer, can't produce a single word, so he
steps back too, the dance is finished. He bows to Kaspar, who
wipes his mouth, clicks his heels, and leaves, leaving open the
door behind him.

Pinto is not moving, gasping for air, as if he just caught up
with the madness of the previous moment. Now he yearns,
yearns for that which is forbidden to man. Das Licht ändert die
Welt und jedoch bleibt sie gleich. The light swirls the dust motes
in the air and shivers among the black and white squares on the
floor, re-spelling everything into a new meaning, as though his
mind has contracted deeper into itself and left a void for whatever was going to happen next. He is dizzy, his knees are weak;
outside, the cheers are coming closer. What now?

He could lock the door and retreat into the depth of the
Apotheke, into his life and past, and spend some time touching
himself and thinking of Kaspar, who would thus become nothing but a story that he would repeat to himself, recollecting all
the details that he could: the smell, the green eyes, the kiss, the
taste of his lips. Or he could go after Kaspar, offer to take him
around the city after all the Archduke fuss is over, show him the

Čaršija and its ancient stores and temples, purchase some rahat lokum so that he could see sugar dusting on his mustache. They would stroll, and share secrets, and Pinto would take him to a back room at Hadži-Šaban's kahvana, where they could have a few drinks together, let their lips do the talking, no one would bother them. But before Pinto can do anything or go anywhere, he'll have to have another little drop of laudanum just to slow down his galloping heart. Laudanum will take care of everything.

As Pinto locked the door behind, he noticed that not only had he put up the black-and-yellow banner, but he had also put up the Bosnian red-and-yellow one; it was just that the banners were entangled and not unfurled—he reached to fix them, and a rush of colors dropped down upon him. A bright day, this, the kiss tingling on his lips, all colors aligning, summer light garmenting everything. He followed the Rittmeister down Franz Jozef Street, all the way to the Appel Quay, with no idea what he would do if Herr Rittmeister Kaspar von Kurtzenberger were actually to turn to him, look him in the eye, and say: Ich folge dir, wo immer du hinghest, Herr Apotheker!

Still, returning to the ongoing world was a magnificent thing to do, this splendid rolling forward into the future in obeisance to his heart and desire, away from—or deeper into—his own life, into a brilliant reticulation of unknown outcomes, toward Kaspar. To the place my heart must learn to love, there my feet take me. He could see the hackle on the helmet passing over the crowd—Kaspar was very tall—and he stopped at the corner. If he could find a pathway to him, he could say: Herr Rittmeister, it gives me enormous pleasure to inform you that the royal banner is presently proudly fluttering above the door of Apotheke Pinto. And if you would like me to show you our humble city and its Čaršija, just say a word and I am yours. Or I could make you a cup of Bosnian coffee in the back of my Apotheke, where it is quiet and no one would bother us. Just say a word. A clamor emerged from the crowd that suggested that something was unfolding, but Pinto just kept pushing deeper into it, until he was forced to stop.

There were two men now between him and the Rittmeister, at least one of them reeking of woodsmoke. There was an odd, mangy dog there too, pushing its way among people, as if on a mission. The Rittmeister stuck out in the crowd with his gorgeous uniform, lit up from inside by his heroic beauty. Pinto wanted him to turn around, see him in his wake, see him carried forth by dizeu. From behind, Pinto perceived the shining skin on Kaspar's shaven cheek, and the point of his left mustache marking the spot where the dimple would be, and the straight horizontal hairline at the top of his neck. He envisioned two moves—parting the men, addressing the Rittmeister—that could get him close enough to inhale his rose scent; instead he inhaled the rancid smoke-and-sweat reek of the men before him. One of them was clearly an edepsiz, overgrown hair sprouting from under his filthy, loose collar. The dog must've been his. Off the other one's shoulder an accordion hung like a dead animal, one key missing on the keyboard.

A car as big as a locomotive turned sharply from the Appel Quay and halted right before the Rittmeister, and Pinto instantly identified on the back seat the real Archduke, a helmet with peacock feathers over a gold collar with three silvers stars, and the Duchess in a dress so white it might have been fashioned from God's garment itself, an even whiter hat with a veil, a bouquet of blue and white and yellow flowers in her arms. (History recorded that it was a gift from a Muslim girl, which for some reason brings tears to my eyes.) It appeared to him that Her Majesty smiled at Kaspar through the veil, as though recognizing him, while he bowed his head to her, and again Pinto's heart raced ahead, and he had to take a deep breath lest he faint.

To the right of Pinto, a short young man, his hair also unkempt, a thin, strained mustache above his lip, his eyes sickly, pulled out a pistol. For a moment, no one could do anything nor move, even the dog stared at him in bafflement, while all of the reality hinged on that incongruous detail of a barrel pointed directly at Their Imperial Highnesses. The Rittmeister's face tightened in stupefaction, the whole of it: the eyebrows and the mouth and the eyes somehow constricted and became bigger at the same time. The edepsiz reached for the young man's gun—tiny tufts of hair on his fingers between his knuckles—and would've grabbed it if the other man hadn't bumped him aside with his accordion, whereupon the shots rang, louder than a cannon salvo, and then the world exploded.

Rej muertu gera no fazi, the Sarajevo Sefaradim liked to say. A dead king does not make war, but a dead Heir Apparent to the Habsburg Empire and Inspector General of the Imperial Armed Forces does indeed. Within a few weeks, Pinto would be conscripted into the Imperial Army along with tens of thousands of other Bosnians. He would climb the slope of time while idling in endless meal lines, or while performing meaningless drills drenched in sweat. He would repeatedly recollect that precise moment just before the century of progress had disintegrated into these desperate days, and consider how differently everything would've turned out for everyone, particularly Their Royal Highnesses, if the man with the accordion hadn't shoved the edepsiz, who would've then managed to grab the pistol and stop the young assassin. He wouldn't be here now, constantly banging the rifle butt against his shins, nor would he be enduring dumb peasant jokes about his dark Arab face, about Jews and their avarice, nor listening nightly to Osman's sawmill snore from the bunk above him, nor would he have left Manuči in tears and ripping her hair out as she remembered the future in which she never saw her only son again. Had the edepsiz grabbed the assassin's pistol, Pinto thought time and again, he would've kissed Kaspar again, and—who knows?—maybe would've spent a few days with him, drinking tea and making love, and then, in some gorgeous future, they would live in Vienna, take their morning coffee at Café Olimpia, read the newspapers to each other, worry about European politics and live together in an endless world.

Yet, even before his basic training was over and his regiment deployed to invade Serbia, Pinto understood that there was no sense in fantasizing about different outcomes: everything that happens is always the only thing that could happen; everything before this moment leads to this moment. Still, for the rest of his days he would remember the Rittmeister, who—Pinto would one day swear on his daughter's life—looked at him from the heart of the melee not so much in terrible panic, nor in comprehension of what had just taken place, but in dreadful sadness, as though he knew that the bond between the two of them was severed never to be repaired. The Rittmeister raised his saber, which glinted in the sun for an instant, and swung down onto the tumult of bodies swallowing the young assassin, thereby vanishing from Pinto's life.

After the shots exploded, the Archduke and the Duchess sat motionless in their places, and it seemed that they were not hit, that nothing at all had happened, whereupon the Duchess fell face-down toward Her husband. Pinto would later claim that he was so close to the car that he saw the blood bubbles on the Arch-duke's lips and heard him saying: It's nothing . . . it's nothing, until his voice finally trailed off. Pinto would speak, to those few who cared to listen, of the Archduke's face distorted with fear, for His Highness must have begun to realize that he was facing the great void itself, the endless nothing—la gran eskuridad, as Manuči used to say—a living mind can neither enter nor escape; he would speak of the death rattle in His Highness's throat creat-ing one final pink bubble, which then, simply, popped.

But I read Lieutenant Colonel Count Harrach's testimony, however, where he claims that the car, driven by one Leopold Šojka, had no reverse gear (for old cars, like time, could only go forward), so it had to be pushed back out onto the Appel Quay and then hurried forth at a great speed, away from the assassin, and, incidentally, away from Pinto. Her Highness slid off her seat with her face between the Archduke's knees as he cried: Soferl, Soferl, don't die. Live for our children. Whereupon Count Harrach grabbed the Archduke by the collar to stop his head from sinking forward and asked: Is Your Highness in great pain? His Highness responded, Es ist nichts . . . es ist nichts, at least six or seven times and then gave up his soul, by which time the car had arrived at the Governor's residence.

Rafael Pinto, in other words, couldn't have seen much of what he would so eagerly pack into his tale. Which is to say that for his narrative purposes he froze the moment, preventing the car from getting back onto the Appel Quay; their Highnesses' sink-ing before him into la gran eskuridad was thus entirely his inven-tion. Nonetheless, for a few other Bosnians in the barracks, Pinto staged and restaged the tragic scene, usually late at night and in a careful whisper, since describing the bathetic circumstances in which the Archduke Franz Ferdinand von Österreich-Este, Heir Apparent to the Habsburg Empire, had perished amounted to blasphemy. Pinto's small soldat audience was invariably held captive by his rendition of the dawn of the war and the midnight of their lives, of the exact moment, no longer than what passes between heartbeats, that broke the world in two, into the before and the after. Some of the Bosnians even wept, exhausted already by their unimaginable future.

GALICIA, 1916

ONLY THE HOLY ONE knows what the smell of the world was right after the Creation, but this must be what it smells like right at its end, this odor of everything being finally undone: deep-grave clay, disintegrating socks, dead rodents, shit buckets, sickness, blood, men without home and water, the rich stench of the shallow trench. Pinto kept fidgeting and turning, each motion making him more restless. Dando bueltas por la kama, komo l'peše en la mar, ah komo l'peše en la mar.

Osman was still awake, in case he needed to attend to Hauptmann Zuckermann, who was tossing on his bed in the Deckung the soldiers had dug out for him and then reinforced with hard-to-find pieces of wood. Tucked into the Untertritt, Osman was talking to Drkenda and Smail Tokmak, who stretched on their backs, smoking the tobacco residues scraped from the bottom of their pockets. A candle's light trembled on Osman's face, ever smooth, even if there never was enough water for a proper shave. His mustache was always trimmed, as though he'd discovered a way to resist the undoing of everything.

The first time Pinto saw Osman, he was delivering some story to an audience of Bosnian soldats; he sat on the upper bunk, his bare feet dangling, one of his socks brandishing a hole through which his big toe peeked, like a potato escaping a sack. They had all been just mobilized; their uniforms were still crisp and smelled of warehouse and mothballs; yet Osman's foot had already torn a hole in his sock. The vigilant toe was somehow part of his exuberance, what with his waving his hands, and pointing at imaginary spaces and objects featured in the story. Pinto could not hear what he was saying, but he could watch Osman's mouth, and his trimmed mustache, and the acrobatics of his eyebrows, his bulging his eyes to act out surprise, his flashing a gratuitous grin to make some point or another. He would occasionally look toward Pinto lounging on the far horizon of his narrative domain and smile in a way that appeared to be only for him. And when he laughed, he laughed with such abandon—from his heart, as they say—that the soldats laughed along with him too, and could not stop for a while. That laughter Pinto would never forget, even when, in the end, Osman was no longer laughing. Pinto longed to join the group, hear Osman's story, his voice, be close to the salvo of his laughter, but he couldn't make himself get up from his dark lower-bunk lair and walk over in the middle of the story and interrupt it. Later, when the story was done, and someone offered a few sips of rakija to Osman as recompense for his storytelling, he came over to Pinto to offer him a drink. Pinto accepted only in the hope that a residue of the taste of Osman's lips would be left on the canteen's mouth. He thanked Osman, who said that he'd had better rakija in his life, but none was as sweet as this one. He was going to say another thing, but before he could utter anything, Osman was pulled away by the Bosnians, who wanted more from him.

And now, in the trench, Osman was again telling a story, as he always had and would, delivering it as if no one had ever heard it before. Even the stories about himself, about his orphan childhood, about all the people he knew in the Čaršija, Osman told as though for the first time, as though he had just heard them from someone and could not wait to share.

Once upon a time, Osman said in a low, amused voice, in a hovel up in the hills above Sarajevo, there lived Husref, a poor hamal, who had nothing but a wife, a fez, and holes in the seat of his pants.

Drkenda and Smail Tokmak grunted to report they had successfully pictured Husref the hamal in his hovel with holes in the seat of his pants. Like children, they were, eager for a story.

One night, Husref is in bed with his wife, Merima, and they hear a cannon fire from the fortress. Merima is startled, scared, yelps, What's this? Why's the cannon thundering in the middle of the night? Husref says, There's been a rebellion in Sarajevo. The agas and beys and the rich people rose against the sultan. But they were caught and thrown into the dungeon. Yesterday, the executioners arrived from Stamboul with a satchel full of silken cords the sultan sent for the condemned. Each of them is to be strangled with their own cord.

Drkenda and Smail Tokmak gasped and wheezed, as though their own cords were tickling their very necks. Drkenda had been shot in the arm by a Russian sniper, and would've bled to death if Pinto hadn't acted quickly, tied a rope around his biceps, and tightened it with a stick to stop the bleeding. He helped Smail Tokmak write letters home, embellish them in a way that made Smail see himself differently, better, even if he had no idea whether anyone read those letters, let alone what they said. Smail knew and loved the story Osman was telling; he had insisted that Pinto write it in the letter, because he'd thought his wife and the village reader who read it to her would like it.

And now, Osman whispered, the executioners are strangling them, one by one, and the fortress cannon fires each time the soul of a condemned person leaves his body. Each blast is a soul departing. Merima asks, Who are those people, Allah have mercy on their mothers? Husref the hamal answers, They're the leading men of Sarajevo: the Morići brothers; Hadži Paša and his brother Ibrahim; the mighty Hajdar Paša; many others—the rich and the powerful of the Čaršija. Strangled with a silken cord, one after another.

Osman ceased talking, for his story was about to end—he'd told it to Drkenda and Smail Tokmak many times before, back in Bukovina, and before that in Serbia, maybe even that first time Pinto saw him—and he knew that deferring the closure would increase their pleasure. His voice was breathy, and Pinto saw the flame's reflection flicker on his lips.

Merima says nothing, and then she pulls the jorgan over the two of them and says, Thank good Allah you are a nothing and a nobody.

Drkenda and Smail Tokmak chuckled, not only because they liked the story, but also because it ended as they'd expected yet again—thus everything was just as it was supposed to be. Thank good God you are a nothing and a nobody, Osman repeated, and they all laughed at their own safe insignificance. And then Osman lowered his voice even more and uttered something that made Drkenda and Smail Tokmak fall silent. Pinto was reluctant to move; he wanted to hear what Osman was now saying, but he could no longer understand him. Osman was there but not there, his voice disembodied, his sounds now devoid of shape and meaning.

Padri Avram used to stay up late and read the Atora aloud. While Simha, being older and a girl, had had her own chamber, Pinto had slept in his parents' bedroom, behind a blanket that served as a curtain. He'd see the shadow of his father flickering on the blanket, humming in Hebrew: They arrived at the place to which God's voice guided him. Abraham built an altar there. Terrified, Pinto would see Abraham lay out the wood, bind his son, Isak, and place him on the altar. He would feel the scorching heat of Israel, and the prickly wood, and the fear, and the ropes chafing at his wrists. The room smelled of the receding fire and the melting wax, of the wool rugs, of the drogerija herbs remembered by Padri Avram's clothes. And when Abraham picked up the knife to slay his son, Pinto's heart would cramp in horror. But he was as afraid of making a sound as Isak must have been of Abraham, and he gnawed on his knucklebone and swallowed his tears and waited for Padri Avram to reach the point of relief, the moment when the Lord mercifully stops Abraham from slaughtering his own son. For the rest of the sleepless night, Pinto would blasphemously try to grasp why God would torment a child with such impunity, and why the Atora said little about Isak's fear, or about his tears, or about his being forever thereafter terrified of his father. Over time, he learned to undo the meaning of the words, to listen only to their incantatory music, as though Padri was singing a song, which would put Pinto to sleep.

And then there had been days when Padri Avram would read the Atora not whispering at all. He would thunder instead at the dumbfounded Rafo. What does it mean: God also created the one over against the other? What does it mean? Little Rafo would whimper, stutter, rummage desperately all over his mind to come up with the correct interpretation of the verse. But nothing would come to him, nothing but the stinging tears, which would infuriate Padri even more. For everything God created, He created its counterpart: He created mountains and He created hills! He created seas and He created rivers! He created me and He created you! You! You: a know-nothing, a pišabaljandu! What sins have I committed to deserve you! What are my sins? Tell me!

Yet when Rafo returned home from Vienna with a diploma under his arm, wearing instead of a fez a bohemian fedora and a commodious student suit, his speech liberally interspersed with Latin and German words, Padri Avram embraced him, and sat him by his side, his hand proudly squeezing Rafo's shoulder to the point of pain. He'd present him to the solemn jury of elderly teos in kaftans who'd dropped by to see the miracle of a son educated in the far-off capital of the Empire. And Rafo did speak to them like a worldly scholar, like the doctor of pharmaceutical sciences that he was, expounding with pronounced ease on ideas he could tell they couldn't commence to understand but dared not admit it. They slurped coffee dregs from their fildžani, glancing at Padri Avram in jealousy and admiration. In the lanky foreign man who came back, they barely recognized the Rafo who had left as a lanky Bilave boy, and they knew he'd have access to a world they knew nothing about except that it might exist and that it was big and brand-new. And there was a world they could not imagine existing, and if they could, they would be terrified. Still, Manuči kept baking sweets, exhausting her entire repertoire to offer them along with the bottomless džezvas of coffee Simha kept serving. She put out the rose petal preserve, which he had spent his childhood longing for as it sat high up on top of an armoire. There was even a konvite for Rafo, which culminated with Padri Avram actually singing, while the tipsy Sinjor Papučo hit all the wrong notes on his saz. Nočes, nočes, buenas nočes, sang Sinjor Padri, violating in his beautiful biblical baritone some prohibitive tenet or another, the damnable abandon in the tremulous pitch of his now unthundering voice. Nočes son d'enamorar, ah, nočes son d'enamorar.

The Lord's punishment was promptly inflicted the following morning: Padri Avram did not wake up, his lips pale and tight as if all night he had been holding back some angry word. No one could remember when it was that they could no longer hear his earsplitting snoring; they asked themselves guiltily what would have happened had they awoken him when he turned quiet; they added more guilt to their already thick ledgers. Before long all of Bilave was shedding tears, Manuči and countless tijas wailed and clapped their hands in the other room, while Rafo sat on the minder, entering a daze that would last for the entire šiva, and then for some time beyond. The tijas made the same sweets and džezvas of coffee, and the same kaftaned men now arrived to sit šiva, not touching the sweets, refusing the coffee, offering obscure ways to help. They showed concern for the speechless Rafo too, his Viennese suit presently buried in some distant trunk. They all knew that Rafo's future in the big new world was now indefinitely canceled, as it was his indisputable filial duty to take over his father's drogerija. Mercilessly, they pointed out to him that none of his scholarly Viennese tricks could ever slow down dying, let alone stop it, because the Lord held in His almighty hand an itinerary for each of us. They wanted him to accept that his knowledge of fancy oils and powders fell well short of knowledge of the mysteries of actual life and actual death, let alone of Heaven and Earth. Sucking on their čibuks, they recalled how after our father Abraham had left us at a good ripe age, all the kings and sages stood in line and said: Alas for the world that has lost its leader! And they praised the Lord that had blessed Abraham's son, Isak. For his part, Rafo felt painfully unblessed and, with his sweating hands in his lap, drained his eyes with silent tears. Padri mio, komo lo voj a dešar.

After Padri Avram's death, Pinto started hearing a voice now cursing and blaming him for Padri's being snatched away so suddenly, now warning him that even during the time of man's mourning jetzer hara might overcome him and lead him to sin against nature. And so he'd revisit all the words spoken and unspoken between Padri Avram and himself, all that could've been said but had instead been dispersed in increments of silence throughout their lives. There must've been a moment when Padri Avram's heart recognized the abomination his head had refused to see in Rafo, the moment after which it was left with no choice but to burst. Thunders were created, to straighten out the crookedness of the heart, to extinct the jetzer hara. The same voice told him that it was better if Padri was dead, because now Pinto's shame could die too, because now Padri could no longer be killed by Pinto's abomination. And he would never meet Osman.

Having finished his story, Osman came over to lie down next to Pinto, as if he'd heard his voiceless beckoning. He pressed himself close so they could feel each other's bodies, the warmth that protected them from the cold void. Years later, in the frigid night desert, Pinto would long for the thickness of Osman's chest, for his smell: onion breath and soldat armpit and sweet mustache pomade, and he'd recall this beautiful nobody waiting for Drkenda and Smail Tokmak to start snoring before he pressed himself even closer so he could wedge his face between Pinto's head and shoulder and search for a path to his belt. Osman slipped his hand inside Pinto's pants, and touched his hard pata, then held it as if not knowing what to do with it. Except he did know what to do with it, and he did it. Pinto gasped, and let the air out slowly, afraid that the two other men might wake up, but Osman kissed him as if to revive him, deftly caressing Pinto's pata, making it grow harder.

They had made love like this before: in a trench, in the woods, on a haystack, in the barracks bathhouse, where everyone was naked anyway. The first time, the night after he'd offered him a drink, shortly before they were sent to war in Serbia, Osman simply slipped into his bunk after everyone else in the barracks had fallen asleep. He nudged Pinto for space, and when Pinto moved over, he put his arm across his chest, and his face against his neck, as if to sniff him. They had touched as if inadvertently, locked eyes, and smiled at each other, which inescapably made the hair on the back of Pinto's neck bristle. But before Osman had slipped into his bunk, everything could've been denied, interpreted as excessive soldat friendship, as a joke, a misunderstanding. That first time, however, there could be no misinterpretation of Osman's moving his hand onto Pinto's stomach, then kissing his temple as Pinto, petrified with possibilities, stared at the underside of the upper bunk, where various soldat names were carved in. He then turned to face and kiss Osman, and, while the innocent Bosnians snored and grunted around them, they touched all the parts of each other they could reach without undressing. When the windows paled with a new day, and Osman returned to his bed, Pinto stayed awake embalmed in the haze that follows pleasure, and spent the time before they all had to rise worrying that Osman would avoid him, maybe even hate him for what they'd done, denying that it had even happened.

But he found courage later that day to approach Osman and

say, How come you never tell me any stories? To which Osman said, We are bound to spend a lot of time together. I'll tell you every story I know. Before the day was out, Osman traded his bunk and moved above Pinto, and would slip down night after night, until their unit was deployed to Serbia. They slept together in holes in the ground, shared their food and water. Osman was a plain Jäger, Pinto a Sanitätssoldat, or, as everyone in the company called him, the hećim—never Doktor Rafo. When they got separated in a battle, or Pinto stayed behind in the field hospital, a cannonball of worry would grind his intestines until Osman returned unharmed. There was a day in Serbia when Osman got separated from the patrol he was in, and Pinto nearly lost his mind, searching through the pile of corpses readied to be burned, unwrapping the mauled face of a soldier who had a hole in his sock to discover it was not Osman. And when he came back the following day, limping and using his rifle as a staff, Pinto wept, pressing his face against Osman's chest.

By the time they made it to the trenches of Galicia Osman's telling stories to Pinto was no longer necessary for their coupling. There was no way of denying what was presently happening either. Whatever world and imperial army surrounded them tonight receded into the long darkness, so Pinto could turn his face to Osman and open his mouth to receive his tongue. Drkenda suddenly sat up, and the two lovers froze, holding their breaths, until he looked around in some kind of confusion, the edepsiz that he was, shouted at his dream enemy a promise that he would fuck his dead mother, and lay back down. He's dreaming, Osman whispered. So am I, Pinto said.

There had to be other soldats who knew what Osman and Pinto were doing, as there must've been others who did it too, and still others for whom two men fucking was so unimaginable they wouldn't believe it possible even if it was to be happening right before their very eyes. At first, Osman was more cautious than Pinto, because he claimed he wanted to get married after the war and have children, to acquire what all normal people, he said, called a proper life. But after war devoured all they'd known and were sure of, all of the peaceful future they could imagine, it was Osman who always sought excuses to get away from other soldats so he could touch and kiss Pinto, get inside him to come in groans and grunts and screams that scared forest animals and attracted curious peasant children they had to bribe with dry bread and cigarettes to stay silent. And it was Osman who suggested that they share the Untertritt with Drkenda and Smail Tokmak, not only because they were endlessly loyal, but also because it was obvious that they would never believe their ears and eyes, even if they saw Pinto and Osman fucking. The four of them were a family now—Osman and Pinto the parents, the two peasants their not-so-bright children.

Padri Avram used to mount Manuči in the middle of the night, safe in his conviction that their children would be asleep. But Rafo had often been awoken by Padri Avram's growls and belches to listen to Manuči's silence and worry about her, about what was happening to her. Once he even got up and peeked from behind the curtain that separated him from his parents' bed, and witnessed Padri's hump bouncing on top of Manuči, her gnashing her teeth to stem a cry, grimacing in pain, until she saw him and gave him an eye signal to make himself scarce before Padri beat him senseless. Rafo retreated to his bed, where, all night, he considered the possibility that the true reason Abraham was so willing to kill his son was because he had borne witness to Abraham violating his mother.

Slowly, Osman pushed down Pinto's pata, and then pulled

it, and then faster, and firmer, nibbling his earlobe, as Pinto got even harder and grabbed his hair, thick and wiry, brittle with filth, and he bit into his shoulder, into the dust and the sweat soaking his long-unwashed shirt, still snorting like a bull, unable to quiet himself, panting in short coughs, until he finally came in Osman's hand. Now you, Osman said, wiping his palm against Pinto's belly. He felt, and loved, the stickiness on his stomach, the weight of Osman's hand, and knew that he would, without hesitation, sign whatever contract the Lord might offer if he could stay in this Untertritt until it was his or Osman's time to die.

The first thing Pinto saw under the morning's relentless sun was the empty stork nest high above the trench, a slim tree holding it up on the tips of its verdant fingers. He stepped carefully over Drkenda, fast asleep as if his throat had been cut, and then over Smail Tokmak, who lay crooked like an arthritic thumb. He dug a book out of his medical pouch, and ripped a page to roll a cigarette; the smoke in his lungs was as thick as gruel. Before the war, he used to smoke fine, dandy cigarettes, which burnt steadily and felt feathery in the mouth. Hadži-Besim ordered them from Vienna, and after the shipment had arrived they'd always smoke a few together, gossiping about other merchants, watching passersby, discussing the matters of the wide world—what the British King would do, what the Russian Czar would decide, whether America cared—as though they were living at its very center, and not in Sarajevo, a city where God said good night and never came back in the morning. What was smoked at the front line could hardly be called tobacco, as it surely contained sawdust and straw and clipped nails; it was rolled up in book pages, since there was nothing else, and it tasted of ink and ashes and war. Smail Tokmak would crawl under barbed wire, dodge sniper bullets to dig through the pockets of a rotting corpse, hoping to find some real tobacco. Every cigarette had the flavor of being the last one. Let me just finish my smoke and then I'll be ready to receive a bullet in my forehead.

This one tasted like a woodstove, and Pinto put it out—the day was already too hot, he was already too thirsty. Osman was already up and gone, leaving but an indentation in the reed mat on which they slept. Had he kissed him before he left, or was it part of a dream? In some other world, in some other life, Pinto might've prayed in the morning, prayed his šaharit, prayed to be relieved of his abhorrent passion. But the only prayer that came to his mind now was to the Lord to let him keep Osman for the rest of time, for his voice to be the last thing he would hear before slipping into la gran eskuridad. At the bottom of his pouch there was a tempting vial of morphine, but he decided to wait—morphine made his mouth dry, and that God-awful cigarette made it even worse. A father said to his son: Don't leap over a sewer, don't pull your teeth, don't provoke serpents, don't fall into the habit of taking drugs. Three out of four, that was still rather good. What kind of a son provoked serpents anyway?

Osman was bent over a chair occupied by Hauptmann Zuckermann, trimming his mustache, humming, as he did whenever he needed to be careful. And he had to concentrate around Hauptmann Zuckermann, who paid more attention to his mustache, attire, and possum collar than to the war they were supposed to be winning for the Emperor. The Hauptmann had been recently deployed to the 1st Bosnian Regiment, where his demeanor loudly bespoke his conviction that his present posting was but an unjust penalty, and that it should end as soon as justice prevailed. The war that to the Bosnians was murderous fate, to him was an inconvenience; behind his back they called him Šerbe. For his part, he commanded his 16th Company with contempt and neglect, uninterested in anything other than returning alive to whatever he'd come from. In that respect, he was not unlike any of his soldats, except they had to attend to the daily business of being and staying alive, while he attended to his possum collar as if it were a pet.

There had been a time early on when Hauptmann Zuckermann reminded Pinto of the Rittmeister, when he could see in his handsome military haughtiness a memory of his brief encounter with Kaspar. But after a month or two of submersion in the petty filth of war, Hauptmann Zuckermann lost his Viennese sheen and became as dusty and discomfited as everybody else, so Pinto could no longer recall the Rittmeister face—now it was the worn-out Hauptmann Zuckermann who had drunk Rosenwasser in the Apotheke; it was he who now smirked at Pinto from the dusty murk. Pinto could not bear to look at his face, because it reminded him that what he remembered as that which had been was in fact mutable and ever vanishing.

For more than a year now, 16th Company had been stuck in Galicia, shuttling between the various encampments and trenches that had all been shoddily forged in the same infernal workshop. Galicia: the fetor; the tormentful weather; the dust converted into mud by rain, only to be distilled into another generation of dust; the barbed wire stitching a landscape flat and dull as a sheet of tin. God's garment here was a hair shirt. Some backenbarted general, somewhere in Vienna or Warsaw, or in some resplendent deep-rear Deckung, had frowned over the map representing this waterless wasteland pocked with villages bearing names he could never pronounce, and decided it was worth losing a regiment or ten to keep it away from the

Russians, who for some unfathomable reason wanted it for themselves.

The Company's position was in a feeble forest where trees grew slanted, as though about to totter forth and fall, providing merely a semblance of shade under the scorching sun. Early in their deployment in Galicia, the men died like flies, particularly the pampered city boys who could not bear the boredom and blistered feet and infections and bullet-torn flesh, so they threw themselves at death, as if it would cure it all. A year later, everything had managed to settle into a bearable routine whereby all they did was devise ways to unstick themselves from the molasses of time. Like beasts, they fully woke up and emerged from the darkness only to eat and shit. Most of the soldiers left were the bašibozuk: the Drkendas and Tokmaks—wily and well-nigh unkillable, skilled at improvisation, theft, and survival. In the trenches they thrived whenever nothing happened, and nothing happened all the time, and also very slowly. By now, the only ones who'd get killed were the few idiots who in their tedium planned heroic deeds, or those who foolishly followed the occasional morphine-crazed corporal into a suicidal raid. The rest kept away from those imbeciles, letting the war naturally cull such a breed. Back in the Carpathian Mountains, they had once run into the blind company, where all the soldats afflicted with trachoma had been transferred: the poor ones at the head of the column could still see a little, while those at the tail end could not know where they were or where they might be going. The blind company wandered around in the rear, expecting to be sent home or to the hospital, until they were massacred by an artillery attack, fluttering about in the shrapnel storm like beheaded flies, unable to find cover because they could see no cover. There should also be a regiment of fools, Osman had once said, where all those would-be heroes could enjoy the war together for a week or so, before their cretin brains were spilled into the dust. Luckily, their Hauptmann Šerbe was staunchly committed to keeping himself and his possum collar as alive as possible.

Pinto was thirsty, but had to wait until breakfast, when tepid, turgid water, no doubt home to fecund nations of intestinal bugs, would be distributed. There had been a sneaky snowstorm at the end of May, but all of the thaw had run off because underneath the dark forest soil there was only sand and clay. Much of June they had spent hoping for rain and meaninglessly digging for water, but caught and found none. Osman stubbornly dry-shaved, scraping hair off his face like sediment, his cheeks streaked with dotted lines of blood, resembling untranscribed Morse code.

That nest up there belonged to a black stork. Pinto had watched it sit patiently in the nest through the spring. He had never seen a black stork, never a beak so red; the Sarajevo storks were white, with yolk-yellow beaks, simple and ungraceful like a child's drawing. In May, he'd seen the black stork return from hunting to loom over its chicks and drop frogs and baby snakes into their gaping beaks; the snowstorm could have killed them, but the mother stork sat in the nest enduring it all for the sake of her chicks. And then a drunken Hungarian from the 32nd Budapest Regiment positioned on the other side of the woods shot up the nest, for no reason other than boredom. The stork crashed through the trees in leaf and fell, awkward and angular, on a barbed-wire obstacle, where it rotted for days and weeks, its beak open like a pair of scissors. For everything God created, He created its counterpart: for the stork, he created a Hungarian. What happened to the chicks, Pinto couldn't tell. The Hebrew word for stork was also the word for kindness: hasidah. It could be that all the evil in this world came from the leftovers of the worlds that the Lord had righteously destroyed.

Osman saw him and winked at him, and Pinto grinned back. Pinto had never seen Osman cry, even if he'd caught him staring at a floating dust speck with a frown of despair. The man never used up the mirth innate in his oval face, in the flush on his cherub cheeks, in the trimness of his mustache. Ever since he'd first landed in Pinto's bunk, he relied on the same bright disposition, conspicuous in the doldrums of putrescence and hunger. And he had a knack for fixing problems. En kada dado un marafet. In every finger another talent: patching the clothes; closing the hole in a boot; sharpening his razor with a rock; telling the stories; stroking Pinto's pata as if it were his own; kissing him with the exactly right combination of strength and tenderness.

They'd clung together on their way through Serbia, then through the Carpathian campaign. Pinto lanced Osman's boils, shared bread and Deckung with him, while Osman defended him from the soldats who practiced the age-old custom of bullying a Jew. Once he'd smacked a certain Zovko, having caught him rummaging through Pinto's stuff in search of the gold coins which, Zovko insisted, all the Ćifuti, being avaricious, always possessed. Zovko then cursed Osman's Muslim mother, stopping only when Osman stuffed his mouth with dirt. They'd had to watch their backs for a while, as Zovko was the kind of man who would shoot them from behind and blame the Russians. But then Zovko himself was shot by a Russian sniper and endured, just before he died, the ignominy of Pinto the Ćifut compressing the hole in his chest to stop the air from leaving his lungs.

Osman was good as bread—buenu komu il pan—never angry, never whining, never smoking. An orphan, he used to scrape a living as a kid running errands for store owners in the Čaršija, fetching for them ašče, coffee, and lokum. The stingy, strict efendijas taught him to read, paid him in books; the others teased him in every language they could speak; others still made him do things no child should ever have done. He also worked for bakšiš at Hadži-Šaban's kahvana, where he swept the floors, crushed coffee beans, and loaded the nargile, and, sometimes, lit up pellets of opium—afijun, they called it in Sarajevo—in the back rooms. Eventually, he'd sell halva and gurabije from a cart, pushing it all over town, advertising his wares in all the different tongues people used in the Čaršija. Padri Avram too used to buy halva from him, always trying to bargain, just for fun, but Osman would never yield, always grinning, bartering in rudimentary Spanjol. He'd sold a lot of halva, saved money, and begun to consider getting married, and then the Archduke and his wife were shot.

And he'd known everyone in the Čaršija. Following the days of mayhem and bloodshed, when the soldats spent days leaning on their rifles as if on crutches, or cowered hopelessly under a rain-laden tarpaulin stretched among three sticks, Osman would unfurl stories featuring his characters from the Čaršija and Hadži-Šaban's kahvana: the lame Mujo who'd get drunk and hear voices telling him that his father was a paša, and not a hamal who had to go up and down the hills carrying baskets of bricks and coal on his back; and Prljo who never cut his nails and never said a word, but glared lecherously at the uncovered women, and would get beaten for it but still couldn't stop; and the wise Hafiz Ahmet who could recite long passages from the Kuran over coffee at Hadži-Šaban's, or sometimes a single poem, featuring heroes and maidens, for hours, even days, on end; and the horny Kemal who arranged to be carried in a sack inside Mehmed-beg's courtyard to see his daughter wash her face; Hrvoje the student

who would fall in love with a girl he saw at the Bentbaša promenade once a month, and would climb Jekovac monthly in order
to throw himself off the cliff, but would be talked out of it by
his friends; and Hadži-Resko Šupak who sat outside his slipper
shop all day, slurped coffee, and berated passersby—Look at the
shape of your head! You're walking like a camel! Your snout is
all smudged with gravy! May you choke on your pače!—and few
customers would ever stop by his store, which would make him
angrier and berate people even more. Each time Osman showed
them what the camel walk looked like, the soldats of 16th Company heehawed with laughter, the joke never getting old. If a man
is liked by his fellow man, he is liked by God.

In the Carpathians, the Company had been decimated by
cholera, the infected soldats hived in a hollow sawmill so as to
die away from the rest. Pinto the hećim attended to them, while
Osman accompanied him to provide stories and consolation.
Voiding themselves to death, the soldats would struggle to keep
their eyes open as Osman unfurled the tale of a paša who gave
a bride leaving Sarajevo to get married a chest full of diamonds
and gold—because, the paša said, she would lose and forget so
much away from her city. And to a bride who was arriving to the
city to meet the groom he gave but a handkerchief, for her gift
was a lifetime in Sarajevo. Osman would sometimes manage to
convince the dying soldats they'd soon be home, and they whimpered in excitement, their eyes glassy with hope and dehydra-
tion. Soon Pinto had become sick too, unaware of anything but
his own weakness and Osman levitating above him like a gorgeous ministering melek, dripping water from his fez onto his
parched lips, telling him things he couldn't understand, singing
songs he couldn't recognize, somehow never getting sick himself. In his hallucinations, Pinto was served coffee by Osman

at Hadži-Šaban's, or wandered the Čaršija sitting unsteadily on his shoulders, Osman's hands gripping Pinto's ankles. After he'd made it through the fever, Pinto found bruise rings around his ankles. Show me the rule whereby You guide the world. The Lord replied: You cannot fathom my rules.

More than half of the Regiment perished in the Carpathians. Some of the soldats survived the epidemic only to find themselves in Bukovina, where the miraculously recovered Pinto would huddle over their blood-spurting wounds, or he would pile back the shattered bones into the mangled body so that the whole soldier could be carted off to a mass grave. Good men dissolved into slimy flesh in his bloody hands: Nezirović, Lukić, Čuljak, Čeh, Tanović. Blum, the only other Jew in the regiment, got a bullet into his open mouth and choked on his own blood. Blum was observant, but the Holy One had failed to sustain him. The Holy One heals, or He doesn't. Usually doesn't, because why would He? God is always the same, yet people have to change, and they all eventually change from alive to dead.

Osman straightened up and clicked his heels—although there was no actual click as his boots were in tatters—to indicate that the grooming operation was completed, his face beaming as if something of value and importance had been accomplished. Hauptmann Zuckermann lazily opened his eyes to face the mirror and regard himself in it.

In Spanjol, stork was lejlek, which is a Turkish word. In Bosnian: roda; Storch in German. Pinto used to walk down from Bilave on his way to the Apotheke, and see a nest on top of a chimney. In the spring, he'd see a bird sitting on it, watching him as he passed below it. Of all the things the Holy One created in His world, Sinjor Rabin used to tell the children studying the Atora, He did not create a single thing that is useless. Sinjor

Rabin had also taught that everything that existed on dry land existed also in the sea, except for the weasel. Rafo could never understand what the problem with the weasel was. Why did the Lord decide against the sea weasel? Pinto would want to know whatever happened with the sea weasel, and Sinjor Rabin would call him a sofu and promptly make him stand in the corner, and then send a note to Padri Avram, who would beat his son with a measuring rod, until he'd promised he would never ask stupid questions again, or even utter the word weasel.

Walking to the Apotheke, his mind infested with all the languages, Pinto would on different days recall a different name for the stork, which was thus always the same and then also not. Sometimes, it was hasidah, often roda, but it would be lejlek in his father tongue, after he'd recall how Sinjor Padri had used to dress him down for not studying the Atora, for caring more about his attire and cigarettes than the word of God, for being rude to customers by not looking up from his Austrian books while they were trying to talk to him, for disrespecting the elders and their wisdom, for daring to be so different from everything his Padri had imagined and hoped for. Kali bivir a la moda, he railed. Sometimes, Rafo couldn't even understand what Padri was saying, his anger relegating his vocabulary to the earlier centuries where fulminant prophets and absolute prohibitions reigned. On such days, the lejlek would glare at him from its perch as if it had flown from fifteenth-century Espanja in order to judge him in Sarajevo. There had been a time before the war when he'd wanted to write a poem about the stork, something perhaps that would've echoed Baudelaire, whom he'd read in German, but he'd aborted his attempt after realizing that the only proper way to do it would be to deploy all the words for the stork he possessed—and maybe even some he didn't. Hasidah, roda, lejlek, Storch, maybe even the French word, whatever it was. Once upon a time, everyone on earth had the same language and the same words. Now there were a lot of disparate words for each of the things the Holy One created, and it was because the maredo had asked stupid questions and had not kept their faces close to the ground.

Who was it that made the house for birds, who fed them? Who taught the baby storks to open their beaks for a frog? Who singled out the poor weasel? Who taught man to open his mouth and speak? Who put the chatter of voices into Pinto's head, and everywhere outside it, and why do the voices and the words never stop? You cannot fathom my rules.

Since the war had begun, Pinto had been fully cured of the desire to write poetry. Once you had to scrub brains off your hands, once you saw a man shit himself to death, once you put your finger inside a man's neck up to your second knuckle to stop him from bleeding to death, the passion for poetry evaporates like a tear in the sun. He couldn't even make himself write a letter to Manuči, who must've ripped out all of her hair by now, and surely wouldn't have slept since the day the Archduke had been shot; he couldn't even find words to let her know he was still alive. The Lord said: Let us, then, go down and confound their speech, so that nobody shall understand. Who put morphine in man's medical pouch and gave him an ever-throbbing dizeu? Who placed Osman next to him every night? Who did all that, and why?

The top of the tree with the stork nest suddenly vanished—it was there and then it wasn't, a patch of blindingly turquoise sky in its stead.

For less than an instant before the shell hit the ground and threw up a storm of soil and wood and flesh, Pinto was perfectly thoughtless.

Another shell immediately followed, shearing the top of another tree, and someone's boot flew past Pinto, who could no longer hear, or say, anything, and who started running, as though there could be a place to run to and hide. Everything was set in motion, like coffee beans spilling into the fire out of the roasting cylinder, nothing was where it had been a moment ago. Osman was on top of Hauptmann Zuckermann; clumps and splinters and limbs rained onto them; the soldats scrambled for shelter as the Russian artillery pounded the copse, the shrapnel spraying the sprinting bodies, taking them off their dire trajectories. Before he threw himself to the ground, Pinto saw Osman making the terrified Hauptmann Zuckermann crawl to the edge of the shallow trench, then shoving him into it like a sack. He didn't dare look up, but sensed the shrapnel all around him shredding flesh like rags, tearing the trees apart, undoing the shapes of objects, ripping through the garment of what had been itself just a moment ago. He heard nothing except the throbbing heart in his temples, but guessed there was a momentary lull and got up on all fours to run toward the trench with his nose down, like a badger. He landed on someone or something that didn't move, his mouth filled up with dirt and he spat it out, which must've meant he was alive. Osman was dragging Hauptmann Zuckermann toward an Untertritt, his possum collar now trailing behind him like a tail. A shell hit close and lifted Pinto from the bottom of the trench to drop him at the feet of Osman, who yelled at him something he couldn't hear. He touched his own face and pulled out a finger-sized splinter from his cheek, whence a spring of blood emerged to be soaked up by the dust on his face. He lay immobilized by the shock, as clouds of clay and blood and wood descended upon everyone and nothing could be seen or heard. This is the time to die, now everything required for dying is in place and none of it is useless. His heart was galloping, but toward nothing and then beyond; where was the fear? He was absent from his own mind, but not from his being; blood ran down his cheek and neck, he was not dead yet. He touched his body to see if there were any other bleeding holes. Another detonation ripped the wickered sides of the trench and something crashed onto Pinto's head. The Holy One kept creating worlds and destroying them, creating worlds and destroying them, until He created this one, and now He was intent on destroying this one just as well. The worlds that preceded ours and were destroyed were like the sparks that scatter and die away when the blacksmith strikes the iron with the hammer. So here we are, the sparks, all in our place, everything in its place, dying away, as the darkness abandons light and returns to its beginnings, komo l'peše en la mar, ah komo l'peše en la mar.

It was none other than Major Moser-Ethering who observed, in a foreword to one of his many memoirs, that every war is made of hard and heavy days, scattered like rocks in the rush of time, not at all unlike life. It's only after the end, if there is ever an end, he writes, that those who have lived through a war string such days into concatenations of history, so that they could claim to know what happened, and when, and how, and why, so that the undoing is undone and everything hurries back to having a form, solid and named, everything gets back to a shape that might make up for everything that vanished forever. There can be no world without history, he concludes; the question is who writes it, and whoever writes it shapes the world, which cannot exist without a shape. I happen to agree with the Major.

What Pinto and Osman experienced on that day in June 1916

is now remembered, if indeed that's what history does, as the beginning of the Brusilov Offensive. Back then, the two of them, or any of the nothings and nobodies whose bodies were to be destroyed, had no name for it, for it needed no name since it was simply what it was. The Brusilov Offensive broke the Empire's back, killed more than a million nameless soldats, Drkenda and Smail Tokmak among them, and left a lasting scar on Pinto's right cheek.

When Pinto came to, Osman was yawning at him, while the sky ducked behind wisps of smoke and shattered clouds. The only thing he could hear was a sourceless screeching, and there was Osman pointing at himself and then toward somewhere beyond the trenches. Is there anything left out there? Where is there? Shells were showering the elsewhere, for Pinto felt the concussions carried by earth and pulsing through his flesh. Osman lifted him to show he had to start moving, and he did walk over the bodies and piles of dirt and helmets and an arm with a rolled-up sleeve, still holding a canteen from which water dripped onto the clay. Without stopping, Pinto picked up the canteen, kicking the arm out of their way, the fingers still clutching a memory of what had been held. He offered the canteen to Osman, who considered it as though it were part of some malicious ruse, then poured warm water onto his desiccated lips and drank, spewing out the dust to no avail.

Pinto tripped over a body that looked like Hauptmann Zuckermann's, except for the crater in his abdomen, the muscles contracting in death, the intestines roiling in blood. A piece of shrapnel must have entered through his back and torn his belly apart. Bauchschuss—a bullet in the stomach, a word Pinto fully comprehended the first week in Serbia. Another mute shell hurled someone's rucksack at Hauptmann Zuckermann, landing on his head, to which he did not react, except for the snake-ball of intestines spilling out of the hollow. Kopfschuss is a bullet in the head. Herzschuss must be a bullet in the heart. Mundschuss killed Blum. What a beautiful language German is. Anything can be said. Death makes you impervious to dying. In war, as in the universe, every single thing is in some way useful. Except your mind right now. Kopfschuss. Sinnschuss. Smail Tokmak rolled over the edge into the trench and landed facedown and was obviously and completely dead, what with the top of his head missing, as though it had come off with his cap.

Osman let Pinto go ahead of himself; they had to be careful not to step on Hauptmann Zuckermann's writhing bowels, or Smail Tokmak's brains. For all Pinto knew there could be an army of rabid Russians hollering on their way to slit their throats; whatever was happening was happening beyond his ken. Everything was shaking and trembling, yet soundlessly—on his departure, the world had nothing to say to him, just this choral nothingness screeching in his ears. Because you hear so many voices, do not imagine that there are many gods in Heaven. Osman rushed him along toward some other place, some distant presumed elsewhere, continuously opening his mouth at Pinto, trying to utter something, when another explosion dismembered everything. Yes. Weltschuss.

His mouth was full of clay, and his eyes and ears too. Behold the fire and the wood, but where is the lamb? Am I the lamb? He felt the weight of soil on his face and arms, and it was only because it took him a moment to realize he was not dead that he didn't make a sound or twitch when a boot stepped on his hip and then another one on his chest, and then both boots and their weight were gone. When he raised his head out of the dirt he was burrowed in and cleaned his eyes enough to look around, he saw the soiled gray neck of a Russian frisking another dead man, cutting through the uniform to get to whatever was in the man's inner pockets. Pinto put his head back down and closed his eyes, careful not to inhale and exhale too much, desperate to silence his breathing. Now he was unburied, undead; the Russian might either notice the difference, or just decide to pilfer his body. The most prudent, the safest thing to do now would be to die. Weep not for the dead, for death makes them impervious to dying.

The Russian kicked the dirt off Pinto's body, and pressed his stomach with his knee to cut through his jacket with a blade. Pinto gasped and opened his eyes to see a Cossack face right above his: the horseshoe mustache and the forehead crisscrossed with scars, and a smirk on his face as he realized that Pinto was alive and therefore killable, and Pinto threw a weak punch at the Cossack, who grabbed his hand with ease and twisted it away from his face, and then there was a razor sliding across the Cossack's throat to slit his jugular, and an effusion of blood spraying Osman's hand, Pinto's face, and the soil, and there was surprise in the dimming blue eyes, the Cossack frowning as though his own death was a trespass that could now never be rectified. Osman let the body drop and wiped the bloody blade against the Russian's uniform; tears were pushing their way through the dirt on his cheeks.

All day long the thundering Russian artillery chased and decimated the Imperial Army. Osman and Pinto knew there would be more cleansing units coming in behind the first wave of attack to capture the survivors and slaughter the wounded. They hid tucked in a hole under a corpse whose face was shrapnel-minced beyond human semblance. But the Brusilov blow turned out to be so crushing, the advance so exultantly rapid, the Imperial Forces so panicked, that the second wave of Russians sped through the enemy positions dropping hand grenades randomly, shooting at the bodies just in case, spending little time to plunder, confident that the greater spoils were ahead, in the deeper rear, in the richer future.

Still, the two men did not dare get out from under the corpse until dark. Osman managed to sleep, but Pinto was startled out of his soundless waking nightmare because he could suddenly hear something; unable to move, he listened to the gurgling sound of someone's lungs drowning in blood. It was somewhere far, but also too close, and he could hear nothing else. He considered crawling out from under the faceless corpse to seek the soldat and end his suffering on this earth with a hand pressed over that gasping mouth. Come to Galicia and see how considerate the Holy One is of human dignity. Come and see how much He loves us. You cannot fathom my rules, God said to Moses. I should've taken the morphine earlier, for I would've been at ease now, while waiting for something to occur. But the morphine was gone; somewhere in this battlefield was his pouch, with his unfinished letter to Manuči and a book called *Der Tod in Venedig*, ravaged for cigarettes, a vial of morphine, a promise of peace. His cheek hurt, but it had stopped bleeding, the dust had dampened the flow. He felt the plug of dirt in the wound and could see from under the corpse that twilight was spreading into the visible corner of the sky. They say twilight is like a drop of blood placed on the tip of a sword—the instant it takes the drop to divide into two parts, that is how long twilight lasts. The gurgling stopped, and Osman woke up.

"Are you alive?" Osman whispered. There was no sound in Pinto's ears, only Osman's voice inside his head. He hadn't regained his hearing; he must have imagined the death rattle. All that was left was Osman's voice and the thumping in the ground.

No, Pinto said. You?

The corpse was heavy on Pinto, pressing his shoulder, which hurt; he grunted, but could not hear himself. The Lord used to slay in justice, and in mercy bring back to life, but not anymore.

The shelling continued through the dusk, moving away from them, each blast a soul escaping from a corpse through the reverberating earth, and then it seemed to have finally stopped. Now Pinto heard Osman singing in a deep, abdominal voice, warm and whispery, clearly at home inside his skull. Pinto knew the song, except Osman sang it in Bosnian rather than, as Manuči had, in Spanjol. She'd be peeling apples for a pie or rolling out the dough on the table, singing: Jo paso por la tu guerta. Tu estavas en la puerta. Te saludi. Te fuites. Esto no me se aresenta. I passed by your garden. You stood at the door. I greeted you, you ran away. I can't understand. There was an apple tree in their garden; he was strictly forbidden to pick any off the branches; he liked the snap of the branch releasing the apple.

How do you know that song? Pinto asked.

"Everyone knows that song," Osman said.

Everyone is everywhere. La gran eskuridad. There was no longer everyone, there was no one, there was no one left, not one, except Osman.

They stayed in hiding until the moon rose and then left the sky to deepen the darkness; no Russians came across them. They unburrowed themselves from under the stiff corpse, and only as they crawled farther away from it in and out of shell craters did they realize that it had already started stinking. Weep for the mourners not for the soul that has gone home. The trench was rife with cadavers, scattered like apples under the tree, already rotting, the stench growing thick as snot. Pinto still could hear nothing, and now even Osman's voice became silent. There were scratching and digging sounds all around them, he could see that on Osman's face, which grimaced in torment at what he must have been hearing. Pinto imagined dogs and storks and rats and badgers, the unspeakable creatures, gouging eyes with their claws, gnawing on exposed ribs. When they saw a ravenous gaze pointed at them from the depth of the shadow, they decided to get out of the trench. They crawled out and continued on their bellies, until a flare went up in the distance, creating a shadow of a dog, or something like a dog, right ahead of them at the edge of the woods. Every motion hurt, and Pinto's cheek was burning with pain. He crept to a stiff corpse, then snailed over it, feeling the hump of the bloated intestines, the edge of a dislocated hip. The reek and dust reentered his mouth and nose and he retched and was about to cough, but did not dare, so he rolled on his back to breathe.

The moonless firmament was speckled with stars and there was the Great Bear, and some other constellations he could not begin to name; the whole setup looked ludicrous in its ostentatiousness. Osman had once told a story about Meho Kulampara, who'd dress up in the most splendorous silk clothes and ride his shiny Vienna-imported bicycle up and down Bentbaša. What was the reason for the sky's luster, for the whole celestial arrangement? Meho was what the Sefaradim called kulu alegri—a happy ass—the same name the rough and tough Bilave boys had more than once thrown at Pinto. Meho rode his wheels just to show everyone how beautiful he believed he was. Every once in a while Meho's drunken father would emerge from Hadži-Šaban's and smack him around, leaving welts all over his face, once breaking his nose, and then Meho would not be seen for months, but then he'd be back and out on his bicycle again. Pinto could not move: weight and pain descended upon him, as though the sky were a lead blanket, pressing all his limbs and his chest, and he could not breathe, and did not even want to. Something stirred inside the cadaver next to him, maybe the rot gas bubbling up. That thing, that thing used to be a man, trying to reach some point whence he could extend his life for a little longer, the life which theretofore consisted of nothing but a desire to live. Everything that lives wants to keep on living. But why? Why not die right now? Why keep going? Where could we possibly go? What was there to get to? To la gran eskuridad above their heads splayed with splendor? Esto ne me se aresenta. His shoulder hurt, and his cheek, and his stomach, and all of the body's three hundred parts, including his soul, a clump of clay.

Osman spoke: "Did He not find you an orphan and shelter you?" Pinto rolled back on his stomach to look around. Osman was nowhere near: Pinto could see his shadow squatting behind a tree at the edge of the forest, far away, waving at him to encourage him to move. "He will help you. Come on." Who could He actually be? He would be whoever or whatever carried Osman's voice across the distance to speak to Pinto from between the hairs of his head, which now stood up so straight he was reminded that he'd once had a cap and it had been gone for days. There are times when the world and the fullness thereof cannot contain the glory of Creation, and then there are times when He, having taken off a man's cap, speaks to the man from between the hairs of his head. You cannot fathom my rules.

* * *

They spent the next day hiding in a forest where there had been no deployment, no military, no camp. But the forest floor had been trodden upon by many passing feet, and they followed the tracks to a tree against which a soldat in his green Honved uniform was leaning with a bullet hole, like a birthmark, below his Adam's apple. Kehlenschuss. In his right hand, he had a canteen, opened—he must have died drinking, the water pouring out the hole in his throat. Osman snatched the canteen, took a gulp, then offered it to Pinto, who emptied the rest into his mouth, his tongue so dry the warm water evaporated on contact. The soldier's rucksack was next to him, his left hand on top of it verily covered with a regiment of ants, its advance units moving up to scour the abundant blood field on his chest, his eyes wide open and dry, the vacated gaze stuck to the tip of his left boot as if contemplating its baffling and arbitrary permanence.

Inside the soldat's rucksack Pinto found a petrified piece of bread, brushed off the few expeditionary ants and split it to share with Osman. Rolling the bread shards in their mouths, further looking for water, they dug up from the rucksack's bottom a letter. It was in Hungarian, but a picture of a young woman was inside it, her hand on her hip, her bosom thrust out, her name—Zsófia—signed in a curly script on the back side, below the stamp of a photo studio in Hódmezővásárhely. Her mouth was closed, but it was clear that behind the lips was a wistful smile, as though she had been reliving a kiss received just before the soldat would be ushered onto the train and she would wave her tear-soaked handkerchief at his vanishing. Osman put the picture in his chest pocket and tapped it, as if to show its proper resting place was right against his heart, and said something Pinto couldn't hear.

In that moment Pinto remembered a future in which Osman would be elsewhere, away from him, as he had not been since they'd met. He would not be near him to smell his war reek, nor watch him shave without water, or hear him in the middle of the night smacking his lips, touching his cheek to stop him from snoring. If they were to make it alive out of this war, they would probably have to come apart, go back to their previous lives, and might end up in different places, maybe even different countries, writing letters and postcards to tell each other that so much missing had accrued in their bodies that their bellies hurt.

Osman was facing him still, talking, saying something that the howl of love and future longing in Pinto's head made incomprehensible. He watched Osman's lips, still wet from the water, open and close, but there was no voice. Osman said again something Pinto could not hear. Pinto loved the way the upper lip wrinkled his mustache and his eyes brightened when he smiled, the way he nodded when he said something he thought was important. Osman's face was flush, beautiful, dirty, with specks of what must've been the Cossack's blood on his chin, a dry leaf of grass woven into his mustache. In those capacious, flushed cheeks, in the mirth that sparkled incessantly in his eyes, in the smirk that slanted his mouth barely noticeably so that he always seemed on the verge of kidding, Pinto could see the only way in which his life could contain any joy. He clutched the hem of Osman's collar and pulled him in for a kiss. Their mouths were dry; it felt like licking the inside of a tin cup. But if he could have ever married Osman, Pinto would tell Rahela many years later, that kiss would've been the crushed glass.

They slept on the forest floor, thick with dried leaves, until Pinto, yet again tossing and turning, threw his arm across Osman's body and woke him up. There was more light than there ought to have been; a great fire lit up the sky, and they reckoned that must have been Brody burning. There's your God's garment. They should find the Russian rear, Pinto read from Osman's lips, and surrender. Combat troops would kill them, but in the rear some clerk or cook could get a leave for capturing them. If we're lucky we will run into someone who has not gone fully mad from killing.

They hid in a ditch at the entrance to a village, watching the road for hours until they were sure that the last Cossacks had ridden away. When they entered the village, Pinto spotted a man in a black kaftan leaning against a door, but as they got closer, he saw that the man's chin touched his chest, his sidecurls drooping, in a way that was possible only if his throat had been cut through and his head was dangling on a strip of skin. His hands were nailed to the doorframe, his tallit at his feet, soaked in blood, the tzitzit still white and resembling skeleton fingers. All along the main street, bodies were strewn: women with legs spread, their skirts pulled over their faces. They saw a child with a smashed head, the torn cheek covered with a tumult of feasting flies. Osman's face was white as a sheet, but he kept walking through the mayhem as if through a market, stopping to consider the dead. Inside Pinto's head, the enormous hum erased all thought and spawned nausea. He wandered away from the main street and through an open gate into a courtyard where there was nothing but a dying dog, unable to lift his head, just shifting its already glazed eyes to look at Pinto. Someone must have kicked it, and hard, for there was a huge indentation in its rib cage. At the far end of the yard, there was a bush of blooming roses covered with snow, except it was not snow, but down—all around him down was floating, reluctant to land. He stepped into the house, its small kitchen, where there was a fire in the stove, and there was a pot on it; he lifted the lid, and saw it was full of dark blood-like liquid, and he barfed onto the floor that was a field of smashed pottery.

He found an unbroken pitcher with water, picked up a chair, and sat down to drink. Here, a Jewish family would've eaten together, their Padri would've read from their Atora before the meal, and the children would've squabbled over who would get to offer their bowl to him first to distribute the kasha. Pinto remembered what his life was once like, and not its festive days, nor Seder, nor those wondrous afternoons when the shade the mountains threw onto Sarajevo made the edges of everything softer and everyone kinder. What he remembered were the spring mornings when he was so warm under the jorgan and the room outside was so cold that he deferred getting out of his bed, and just listened to the din of dishes in the kitchen, and smelled Manuči's bread swelling in the oven.

He spotted a movement in the corner of a window, and frantically scouted the kitchen for a place to hide, when he recognized what was a child's face stricken with fear. For a moment, their gazes locked, and then the child vanished, and he ran to the window to see a girl in rags, with stork legs, running away from him and then behind an ambar, inside which he could see a bare foot on the floor covered with spilled grains, the rest of the body invisible behind the door ajar. He wanted to follow the girl, but could not run, and by the time he got to the ambar and looked at what was beyond it—a hillock of manure, a field of weed—the girl was gone. A little hanuma she was, like Sara, Sinjor Mair's little daughter, who had freckles unevenly shared between her cheeks, so that one of her eyes always looked bigger. He peeked inside the ambar, and saw that the foot belonged to what must've been the girl's mother: her legs spread, bent at the knees as if broken, her dress rent, her scratch-marked breasts drooping to the sides. Her face was not covered, not at all: she looked up over her forehead, for her throat was carved open and gaped like a second mouth. Pinto found a rag and put it over her face.

He left the house weeping, which he hadn't done once since the beginning of the war: not when he'd left his home, not when they'd marched to war, not when the first man—one Pronek—had died in his arms in Serbia. His wounded cheek hurt with tears, and he saw that the dog was dead now, and when he walked out on the street, he saw Osman kneeling with his head lowered in submission, the mouth of a Russian rifle pressed against the back of his head.

PART II

Syr Darya

Brich Mulla

Tashkent

Fergana Valley

Bukhara

Amu Darya

© 2023 Jeffrey L. Ward

TASHKENT, 1918

WAS THERE ANYONE in the world who didn't know that Alija Ðerzelez was perfectly bald, that his scalp was as smooth as a baby's ass? Whenever he went to the forest to fetch wood, Alija would leave early and return late in order to dodge the agile children of Sarajevo who'd always set up an ambush and throw rocks at him, chanting, Ćelo! Ćelo! Dođi mi na sijelo!

Alija was a servant of a rich bey's wife. He carried water for the hanuma, fed her fowl, picked her apples, beat her rugs, stuffed her pillows with freshly plucked down. She was as beautiful as the moon, but Alija was just a destitute, hairless nobody and would've surely been thrown into the darkest dungeon of Sarajevo if he were ever to disrespect the bey, who was powerful and round as a barrel. Alija just did what she needed him to get done, stole glances at her forearms, her neck, her bosom, and pined.

At the word bosom, Hasan raised his hands up to his chest, palms up as if praying. The soldats stared at the hands shaping the hanuma's imaginary breasts. Pinto sensed the gravity of their memories, of the women and the breasts they had held once upon a time. And there were among them also those—some of them children still—who may have never even seen, let alone touched, a disrobed woman before they had been carted off to fight in a doomed war. Here and now, they could be recollecting only their own old fantasies, or the memories of stories they had once heard.

Pinto had once stolen glances too, but only to look at Osman's hirsute forearms, his neck, the fine line of his jaw, the exact border between the shaved skin and his thick mustache. He liked to watch his chest rise when he slept next to him. They had always had to hide to make love, they would never take all of their clothes off, ready to run or pretend they were just wrestling. Only once, in Serbia, when they got naked to swim, could Pinto clearly see Osman's muscles and ribs and a zigzag scar on his back, like lightning. And the tapestry of hair on his thighs, and his flaccid pata, which Osman called ćuna. But he could not touch him then, because there were all the other naked soldiers around, slapping each other's asses, pointing at the difference between the circumcised ćunas and the uncircumcised ones, protecting one another from desire by way of making up stories about far-away fantastic women they claimed to have fucked.

The only time Pinto had seen a naked woman was when Binjoki had taken a herd of Bilave boys to Isabegov hamam, where Sefaradi women took their tevila; the boys climbed on the roof to find a crack through which they could only see a woman's shoulder and the tip of her breast; Binjoki claimed it was Hanuča's, but who could ever be able to say. None of the boys, other than Binjoki, had ever seen anything like that. Pinto was terrified that Padri Avram would find out and flay him alive. He never found out, but he did flay him anyway for some other transgression Pinto had committed.

Hasan shook his hands to suggest the bosom's ample weight. The hopelessly aroused Bosnians fidgeted in the prison's murk, weighed down by a possibility that what might never have happened indeed might never happen again. Imagining the hanuma, a few of them would be stroking themselves tonight, or each other, if they were lucky.

Osman would've relished telling the part about Alija's sneaking glances, but he wouldn't waste his words, let alone his hands, to describe the hanuma's concealed body. Her face, maybe, its luminance when exposed to the daylight in the garden, or the hue of her blushing cheeks when she caught Alija looking at her. Osman used to glance at Pinto too, back in the barracks when they were fresh soldats, their faces still unvarnished by sun and dust and degradation. Pinto had always understood what the quickness of Osman's gaze meant, and would blush, just like the hanuma had in Osman's story; his cheeks and ears would flame up and he knew that the fire he was on could be seen, and he would burn even more, and kept away from Osman, the luminous hanino. Until Osman had lain down next to him that night in the barracks, and there was no longer a way to escape, and everything was as it was supposed to be. If a man is liked by his fellow man, he is liked by God.

Well, Hasan went on, Alija trekked one morning all the way up to Vučja luka to forage for wood. He never cut trees or chopped young branches, because Allah had not made the world to be meddled with and everything in it to be spoiled. Every living thing wanted to keep on living so it could fulfill the purpose it was meant to have—everything in the world existed for a reason, even if we couldn't always know what the reason might be.

Thus was Alija collecting sticks when he heard a child cry. He followed the wail and discovered a tiny newborn baby, squirming in the hot sun. What could such a small creature be doing alone in the forest, exposed to the merciless sun? Alija felt so sorry for the child that he cut a leafy branch and placed it above the child's head to give it shade. The child calmed down, turned quiet. He went back to collecting wood, but every once in a while he'd check on the child, now sleeping peacefully. Suddenly, a woman all in white appeared beside the child; her swarthy face couldn't have been any more radiant, her long black hair flowed all the way down her back—Alija instantly realized she was a vila. She asked, Was it you who made the shade for my daughter? And Alija said, Yes, so that the sun will not burn her and she can sleep in peace. The vila said, Ask for whatever you wish, and I will grant it to you. Alija thought about it, and said, What I would like is to be strong and brave. Very well, the vila said, come and suck on my nipple. She unbuttoned her vest and lifted her shirt—Hasan lifted his filthy, tattered shirt to offer his flaccid tit—and showed him her full breasts and nipples. Alija did what he was told, drank her warm milk. Then the vila said, Do you see that big rock over there? This was a large rock, which twenty healthy young men could not have moved a hair's breadth. She said, Now go and lift it. Alija lifted the rock just a little from the ground. The vila said, Come here and suck a little more, and he suckled at her other breast. Then he picked up the rock and threw it like a pebble.

Hasan extended his arm, and pointed at the window, over the rows of supine soldats, as if to conjure up the rock's trajectory. Osman used to make that very same motion whenever he had told the story of Alija and the vila. Yet Hasan's move was not graceful at all; he was but a second-rate apprentice, still struggling to learn how to tell the story the way it was supposed to be told. All the same, the Bosnians followed the trajectory in unison; thus they bore witness yet again to the vila gifting Alija Đerzelez incredible strength, to his becoming the great hero they had always known. They could also see the other soldats, who didn't speak Bosnian, or were too sick and dying to be interested in stories or memories. And they could also see the soiled, disintegrating boots of a Russian guard outside the window as he leaned against the porch pillar to doze standing up. They could see that there was no way out of this damned hole. They could see the nothing, the vastness of la gran eskuridad.

Alija thanked the vila, who kissed him on the forehead, and then he headed home carrying on his shoulders a pile of sticks as tall as a minaret. The children watched him with new awe as he passed them on his way home, not one daring to assault him. He unloaded the sticks before the hanuma and said, As long as I live, you'll never be cold again.

Osman always looked toward Pinto when Alija made his promise, and Pinto would bite the inside of his lip until it bled so as not to grin at him. Back in Galicia, Osman had whispered those same words into Pinto's ear, his arm across his chest, as they lay under a tattered, lousey blanket not long enough to cover their feet. The side Osman was not pressing himself against was cold, while the Osman side was warm and alive, Pinto's every hair and patch of skin rising to meet him. He sang into Pinto's ear, his voice breathy and moist: Bejturan se uz ružu savija, vilu ljubi Đerzelez Alija. Vilu ljubi svu noć na konaku, po mjesecu i mutnu oblaku. The way he pronounced the soft end of noć. You would never want the noć to end.

People say that Alija kept the hanuma warm for a long time,

Hasan said, and was done. He gave them nothing to take away, to ponder or remember—the story just made them despondent, so they sat there slouching, under the weight of their daily despair.

Whereas Osman would've delivered that story as if he'd been the one who'd told it first, as if he had been Alija himself. Osman danced it: he swung to face the nonexistent nook whence the child's cry came; he leaned forward coming upon the discovery; he reshuffled objects and events with his birdlike hands; he shaped the ravine and the child in it, his slender fingers straightening to mark the length of the baby; he chopped an invisible branch with the blade of his palm; he placed the branch above her head; he bent down as he sucked at the vila's nipple; he dropped the bundle of sticks at the hanuma's feet; he caressed her body and it exuded warmth, all of her silk unfolded, her legs intertwined with Alija's under the rose-scented jorgan. And the bey, oblivious to it all, wasted his rich life on becoming more pious, fat, and important, and Osman outlined his belly, and his vain, empty heart, and the soldats would laugh, rejoicing that Alija enjoyed so well the world they could no longer live in, but still strived to imagine. Osman would sing the song about Alija and the vila to Pinto, breathing into his ear. Wormwood creeps along the rose, Đerzelez Alija makes love to a vila. To a vila, all night long in bed, in the moonlight and the murky cloud. Sarajevo was but a dream, the hanuma went on living her warm, eternal life, never running out of kindling, or Alija's desire. But where is my Osman now? Where did he go?

The body is strong, but the world always ends up crushing it. Being imprisoned did its damage, but Pinto's body ached with missing Osman: his joints were inflamed, his feet swollen, his flanks felt scalded, and in his stomach pit a rock the size of the one Alija had flung kept grinding whatever was left of his vacant intestines. Glory be to Him who created all the pairs of things that the earth produces, as well as themselves and other things they do not know about. Where did he go without me? Am I still his vila?

Once Osman had gone, the other Bosnians never mentioned him, never talked to Pinto about him, or about anything else for that matter. Osman's space among them closed up after he was no longer there. It was Hasan who now told Osman's stories; it was Zaim who took his wooden spoon. Pinto was Osman's widow, someone who must suffer alone, someone destined to spend in sickness and isolation what little life he had left. Now he was a Ćifut again, the only one among them, and when it was his turn to be gone they would remember him for nothing else.

Yet even without Osman no one challenged Pinto's claim to a spot on the dirt floor whence, if he lay prone on his straw mat, he could see a patch of the sky. He would stare at the sky all day, and often at night. Los sjelos kero pur papel, la mar kero pur tinta. He'd occasionally catch a piece of the moon; one night he woke up to see a tip of the crescent slide across the corner of the window until it slipped out. There was sometimes a gaggle of stars, a fragment of a constellation. I want the sky as my paper, and the sea as my ink. Another time he saw a muster of storks flitting, like a sudden memory, across the framed sky patch. There were swallows too, and once there was a lightning bolt that was never followed by a boom of thunder. The vila cried from the cloud: No one will ever have as much pleasure, my Alija, as you and I. The sun never overtook the moon; the night never outran the day; the lice kept on burrowing deeper into him. To what there did he go?

Osman had knelt under the muzzle of a Russian rifle. Pinto could see, even now, the tightening of the Russian's finger on the trigger, his unshaven face and his eyes dark as coal. It was clear that he was about to kill Osman, who was, incredibly, smiling, as if the whole thing was ending exactly as he had known it would. The other Russians stood around, some drinking from their canteens, some wiping their bloody bayonets. Pinto hurled himself at Osman to grab him from under the Russian's rifle and cover him with his body; the Russians laughed at Pinto's cries and tears. It could be that they had simply become tired of killing, or that they had found Pinto's despair amusing, or, who knows, they may have even been touched by his willingness to die for his friend—whatever it was, they had shot neither him nor Osman. They laughed instead at their pathetic embrace in the blood and mud of the massacre. The Russian who had pressed the rifle against Osman's pate gun-butted Pinto in the neck, and when Osman put his left hand on it to protect him, broke Osman's wrist. But they survived, the wormwood and the rose.

Once upon a time, Pinto had believed, like all the soldats on their way to war, that they would be either dead or returning home once the war was over. It was going to turn out one way or the other for them, life or death, home or not. But no soldat, least of all Pinto, could ever have imagined they would be rotting in a frigid Russian jail in Turkestan. None of them had even heard of Tashkent before reaching the collection camp in Kiev where the Russians processed prisoners of war, stripped them of all possessions, and kept them alive half-heartedly. It was going to be Siberia, they were told as a detachment of vicious, drunken Cossacks whipped them into what the history would remember as teplushki—train cars with coffin-like bunks and a stove that was supposed to keep them from freezing to death. They spent the long weeks crossing the steppe and dreading the endless Siberian winter, its icy tentacles already crawling up their scabrous limbs. For days and days, they could see nothing other than the patches of ashen sky passing over their heads. The train stopped every now and then so that the dead could be dumped out and buckets of fetid water be provided to those unlucky enough to be still alive. Once or twice, there was bread and rotting cabbage to buy, but nobody had any money, so the closer to Tashkent they got—still believing they were on their way to their freezing death in Siberia—the weaker and more apathetic they were.

Osman spent the entire journey by Pinto's side, killing the misshapen time with weak-voiced stories for the weary soldats. Somewhere in the endless steppe, days after a morsel of food passed anyone's lips, he told them about Nasrudin Hodža teaching his ass to live without food, cutting its meals in half each day—and just as the ass finally learned how to live on no food at all, it died. The Bosnians chuckled, in spite of their infirmity, against their despair. The other soldats wanted to know what the funny story was about, but neither Osman nor any other Bosnian had any language or strength to translate it properly, so Pinto retold it in German and it was not funny at all.

After a while, Osman's stories dried out; all he would do was sleep, and Pinto knew that he was ill. Soon Osman had red spots all over his face and body and was fading and feverish, losing his mind in no time. How many towns have we destroyed! he would suddenly scream. How many countries! Our punishment came to them by night or while they napped in the afternoon! He would howl and rock like a Hasid while draining himself over a feculent bucket in the teplushka corner: This is not good! Not good! How wrong we were! Don't let me die wrong! He would sob over someone he called his bride—she was his only joy, he suckled on her tits, she was faithfully waiting for him in Sarajevo, she had an embroidered handkerchief he had gifted her. He would sing raspingly a song wherein he begged the bride to visit his mezar after he was killed, while she asked how she would recognize his grave. Who can ever know what their grave will look like? He would grab Pinto's face with his unhurt right hand, a delirious sheen in his eyes, and tell the bride how the Russians had put a bullet in the back of his head, how Pinto had defeated the Russians, charged and scattered them like sticks, and then raised Osman from the dead, healed his wounds. Because he was a melek—and he would press Pinto's hand to where the bullet hole would've been, and Pinto would stroke the back of his head until he calmed down. But the calm would be brief; he would soon rave again about the handkerchief, about the hollow in his bride's neck, about the pearl button protecting her bosom. Holding up a pinch of nothing between his fingers, he demanded that Pinto take a good look at that button, to look at it, to look at how beautiful that pearl button was. Yes, it was beautiful, Pinto would say, he had never seen anything as beautiful as that pearl button. Finally, exhausted by delirium, Osman would lean uneasily on Pinto's shoulder to burn it with his febrile cheek, and mumble, He created man from a clot of blood. He created man from a clot of blood. When the train stopped again, Pinto would have only a sip of water before pouring the rest down Osman's throat, as if it could scorch the disease out of him, aware that the Russian might have been giving them infected water all along. Osman's curls stuck flat to his temples, his mustache like a wet brush. Fear is strong but typhoid fever makes it stronger: The soldats thought Osman would die, and soon after him Pinto too, so they maintained a distance from the bunk where the two slept together, not talking to them at all, willing to forget they had been alive until they thought their end was near and started edging toward their scant possessions: their boots, their buttons, Osman's single fingerless mitten, covering his injured hand. Pinto kept himself awake and had to kick away a Pole who was interested in Osman's mitten. How wrong we were! Osman abruptly screamed into the typhoid air, sitting up to smash his forehead against the bunk, while Pinto held him down, and all the other prisoners now wriggled a finger breadth farther away from them.

By the time they realized they were not heading to Siberia, there was much more space in the teplushka, as many emaciated corpses had been discarded in deep anonymous ditches along the way. Osman's head was now covered in scratches, bruises, and scars, a detailed map of his febrile nightmares; but his wrist somehow was healing. Pinto kept his hand on Osman's forehead in a vain hope his touch might cool it, singing what Manuči used to sing to the sick little Rafo: Anderleto, mi Anderleto, mi kerido i namorado. As the train pulled into what would be Tashkent, Osman opened his eyes to look up at his man and attempt a frail smile. Aj, mi kerido i namorado. That which my lips know they shall speak in purity. Ever a beautiful man, a hinozu, Osman was; that smile could break many a heart, take down empires, sink a thousand ships. That lovely face, like a moon, where did he go? The vila cried from Heaven: No one will have as much pleasure, my Osman, as you and I have had.

Manuči used to drown mice, and the little Rafo would stand over the pail weeping at the sight of a mouse clawing the walls. He'd beg her to let it go; he'd offer to carry the pail out of Bilave and all the way down to Mejtaš and release the mouse there, far away from their house. But she would never let him do it, and the mouse would hopelessly and incessantly struggle to climb the pail walls until it drowned. Long after its corpse turned mealy on the garbage heap, Pinto would still hear the scraping, even while playing klis out on the street, even in the middle of the night, even in the temple on Šabat. He knew it was possible that the mouse would never die, or that it would never escape the bucket, scratching and scraping, just as it was possible that the Lord could undo the world in which such a thing could take place to create a better one, with at least one mouse that could break out of Manuči's pail and live. Everything that lives wants to keep on living, but all that really means is that everything is always deferring death until the moment of death. A wise man spent his life searching for a way to live without perishing, and just as he found it, he perished.

Osman and Pinto survived the teplushka only to find themselves dying in Tashkent, a place that had not fully existed in the world until they disembarked the train and saw the ochre mud-wall prison building, and the minarets beyond, and the sky above it all, just before they were shoved into the murk of the jail, where the freezing wind searched for every crack in the wall, where the rats and lice sought shelter from the cold under their straw mats.

Osman had barely, and miraculously, survived; reduced to a slender bag of bones and organs, he slept for days, waking up only when Pinto made him eat and drink water; his wrist healed, but it was curled inward, like a hook. Pinto would keep him warm through the winter by snuggling against him, alert to his grunts and gasps, to his remaining alive. At night, the wind failed to muffle the sound of the soldats tossing and turning as if on a grill, hacking and moaning, but all Pinto would hear was the steadiness of Osman's breath, the swelling and deflating of his chest. Sometimes Osman would suddenly shake and shiver and Pinto would embrace him and squeeze him tightly as if wrangling a šejtan, and then would wait, tight as a spring, for whatever form of death was passing through Osman, for Pinto would never let it stay with them. When our love is strong, we can lie on the edge of a sword, or we can lie on a vermin-infested straw mat and avoid dying until the war is over and something else, something better, replaces it.

Pinto nearly killed Hasan when he caught him stripping off the rags that served as Osman's socks. He stuck a thumb into Hasan's eye, even as Hasan was pounding him in the head, until others separated them. The rags had been made from Pinto's shirt; he had torn it into strips to wrap Osman's feet. Occasionally, Pinto would unwrap them: sores and pustules; nails fallen off, a few of the remaining ones nacreous, ready to come off as well. Pinto would rub and stroke Osman's toes and soles, patches of his sickly skin peeling off, and he would be overwhelmed with love for that man, hardly present and so weak that he could not keep his eyes open. To the place my heart loves, there these feet lead me, to the place inside him, to his soul.

By the spring, Pinto had become used to the wind, and would wake up whenever the windrush whistling stopped. Which was why he heard, turning his better ear to the source of the sound, the door slamming open, and a swarm of men bursting in, shouting in Russian, kicking the soldats with their boots and gun butts. Osman remained silent and motionless, as if they could pretend not to be there. They heard the cracking of the bones, the splitting of the flesh, the painful yelps. The raiders grabbed a few soldats, who grasped on to others, on to the door, on to the doorposts, wailing as they were yanked out. The door slammed shut and soon rifle salvos broke through the wind, followed by the pocks of pistol fire. And then the crunching of dirt as the corpses were hauled away, and the thuds of the bodies thrown onto a cart that would carry them to an afterlife in some Turkestan ditch. The Heavens are the heavens for the Lord and it is the earth that He hath given to the children of men to kill as they wish, whenever they wish, however much they wish. Nobody dared move or make any sound; they just listened to death and silence outside, to the somber hum of la gran eskuridad.

The rumors of a revolution in Russia had reached them, of the Czar chased out of his palace, of cities burning. The soldats had expected that it would sooner or later come to Tashkent, for no misfortune had ever failed to find them before. Nobody quite figured what that revolution would actually look like, what it would turn out to be after it had rolled across the steppe, how it could make its cursed way to this jail. Osman comforted the soldats by telling them the story about Merima and Husref the Nobody. Thank good Allah we are nothings and nobodies, he would tell them, but they were not convinced their worthlessness could save them. And after the raid and the liquidation, they knew revolution would kill them. All the nothings and nobodies now watched the door night after night.

Pinto positioned his better ear to listen for the sounds that made it through the wind, as if his sheer attention could stop the evil from breaking in. He would eventually hear the revolutionaries' boots shuffling across the yard just before the door flew open again. They carried a couple of lanterns, and the darkness was suddenly a riot of fluttering, screaming shadows. This time a revolutionary rushed to Osman, ripped off his blanket, and was lifting him by the scruff of his neck like a puppy to be drowned. Pinto punched at the soldier, who kicked him in the stomach without any fury or anger, a matter of simple protocol. Pinto dropped to the ground to groan in pain; the soldier dragged Osman out; the door was locked. Pinto wanted to go after Osman, to whatever horrible thing they were going to subject him to, but he could catch no breath, and his body would not obey, and by the time he reached the door to bang feebly on it, there was no one on the other side, and Osman was gone. The shots never came, but the taken soldats never returned either. Osman was gone.

For days afterward, few of the soldats could sleep, many praying again, some all the time. Pinto floated in a discombobulated state where everything was real and not, where he might have still been at home in Sarajevo but not, where there was war and death but not, where he was alive but not. Yet in no iteration of his nightmare did he forget that Osman was gone, that his space was empty. One night he looked out from his torment, and saw Kerim, thoroughly toothless from scurvy, trembling from the wind and trepidation, his gaze fixed to the door, reading like a Holy Book its shabby wood with its knot spots and cracks. Pinto got up to sit next to him, which Kerim didn't even notice, continuing to shake, even if Pinto covered both of them insufficiently with his blanket. For the rest of the night, and for many nights after that, Kerim and Pinto would listen to the boots kicking up the dirt in the yard and then stomping down the stairs even when they were not. If the boots got close to the door, Kerim would wake everyone up as if they'd have time, or place, or desire, to escape, while Pinto squeezed his shoulders in a meaningless gesture of solidarity. He brings the living out of the dead and the dead out of the living, Kerim kept saying, slurring the words like a toddler. The living out of the dead and the dead out of the living. The soldats would at first wobble and rumble in somnolent panic, but when it turned out that the footsteps belonged to no one, they'd sit back down, disoriented and terrified. Kerim would look toward Pinto, as if to confirm that when death came it should take them both, then sobbed tearlessly. Pinto would squeeze his emaciated shoulder to confirm he too was ready to go.

And here was Pinto now, still alive, and alone. Kerim was gone. Osman was gone. To what there did they go? All the blue was absent too, the sky vacant, the wind even colder. He thought he saw a snowflake, but it could have been ash, or a fleeing soul, or nothing. When the wind goes forth from the Holy One, it endeavors to destroy the world. He scratched his hair and beard, absentmindedly crushing a few lice. But the Holy One slows the wind down with mountains and breaks it up with hills. He commands it, Take care not to harm My creatures, and the wind obeys. Often doesn't.

There had been a time when Pinto envisioned returning with Osman to Sarajevo—what their way home from Tashkent could be, he couldn't begin to know. He had imagined Manuči meeting Osman for the first time. He had seen Osman and himself walking up the streets of Bilave, and how he would impress him with the stories of il hanizitju and its old Jews, with knowing the names of all those feral children, of the exact same kind that threw rocks at Alija Đerzelez, and sending them home to tell all their parents that Rafo Pinto had come back home after the war. That one there with a smeared face is Alfi who never forgets anything, Pinto would tell Osman. The little fool knows the names and birthdays of all the people in the neighborhood, knows the Atora by heart. And here's the old Papučo whose daughter ran off with an Austrian and ended up in a brothel in Graz after he'd left her, as everyone always knew he would. Do you know about the time Sinjor Papo went to Stolac to place a stone on Rabin Danon's grave, but never made it there because he got stuck in a kahvana in Mostar, where he spent all his money to have some beautiful Emina sing all night at his ear? And he would explain to Osman who Rabin Danon had been; how he'd known it was his time to die so he'd set out to walk to Palestine and die there, but had never made it past Stolac; and how the Sarajevo Sefaradim liked to say that a Jew is always on his way home, but never makes it there.

Manuči would like Osman, she would relish his smile, his stories. Kel hanizu! she would say. What a handsome man! She would serve him coffee with rose rahat lokum, and listen to his stories, happy that Rafo had found himself such a good friend, even if he was a Muslim. Manuči would press her hands against her chest as Osman told her how the two of them had lived through the slaughter in Galicia, and then survived the jail in Tashkent, and how it had taken them years to find their way back to Sarajevo. She would cry as he described how the muddy jail floor would frost up when the nights got frigid, and how they had kept each other warm and alive. She would see how much they loved each other, Rafo and Osman, but she would never recognize the presence of toeva, could never imagine the miškav zahar, never believe they were lovers. I want to reveal my secrets, the secrets of my soul. Sekretos kero deskuvrir, sekretos de mi alma. This man is my kismet, Manuči, I love him more than I love myself. And now he's gone. Where did he go without me?

He should write to Manuči. He will write to her, as soon as it gets a little warmer and he finds some paper and a pencil. As soon as he is strong enough to sit up. Dear Manuči, I am as well as I hope you to be. My man is gone, before you got to meet him. There is nothing left here, the endless wind and a patch of the sky, piles of corpses swelling like cotton puffs. Meine Mutter hat viele gülden Gewänder.

In Vienna, before the war, a century ago, Pinto had gone to

poetry readings in peripheral cafés and gasthauses, where fetching but unkempt students vociferated against obscure elder poets and the unconscionable damage those charlatans inflicted upon the spirit of the German language. Maybe that Vienna, like Sodom, like his soul, was now obliterated, along with all those ruddy-cheeked poets and their curls and eyelashes, and their desire-laden bodies. Most of them, except maybe the tubercular ones, ended up in the trenches, where all poetry inevitably ended. Where are they now?

My mother has many golden robes, they are made of God's garment. She would be spending her lonely days as if her Rafo was still alive somewhere, praying and imagining the unimaginable places in which the Lord might be good and kind to him. All of the world is, or soon it will become, la gran eskuridad. She had no idea how much her son longed to die right now, how ready he was to go to the next place, to finally reach the nowhere. Among the dead I am free. Madre mija, si mi muero, hazanim no kero jo, so non doze mansevikos. It must be that there were no men left in Bilave, except the oldest of the Jews, Sinjor Papučo or Sinjor Samuel, both further bent from keeping their noses stuck inside the Atora, no longer able to walk before anyone's coffin, eager to face the Lord they had loved so well, to pray for those left festering in their earthly lives. El ki seja dovadži. And what if Manuči was already dead, if she was praying for him at His feet, if she was the one keeping him alive despite his wishes? He had no news about her, or about anyone in Sarajevo. It was too late to write to her even if he could. He was already dead, just waiting for the door to open so he could step straight into the heart of la gran eskuridad. Osman was already there, because he was not here. Weep for the mourners, not for the soul that has already gone home.

What if Sarajevo perished too, and no one and nothing was left? What if the city had been burnt to the ground by some rabid army or another, not a stone left upon a stone? There is no reason to believe that the world, let alone a city, is a lasting endeavor. Worlds perish, why shouldn't cities perish too? It could well be that there is nothing outside of what I can see in the present moment, what is now framed within my window; it could be that the Holy One relentlessly erases all that is outside of what I can see, wipes out the traces of my past being, imprisoning me in this endless present. If He keeps creating worlds and destroying them, creating worlds and destroying them, then this one too might be at any moment flattened like a rotten egg. The worlds that preceded this one and were destroyed were like the sparks that scatter and die away when the blacksmith strikes the iron. It could be that this herd of defeated half-dead soldats is all that is left of humanity—no more Jews, no more Austrians, just a few Russian guards, and Dumitru and Milan, and the ghost of the insane Kerim, and me, and no Osman, all of us perishing but still not quite perished. God has no beginning and no end, but to create He has to open up space that is not Himself so He enters deeper into Himself and opens up a void, la gran eskuridad, into which we were spilled, alive, to die.

And look at us now. He has abandoned us here to feed lice, to be thrashed and killed by the Russians, to be eaten by fever, to long for death that would unite me with the man I love. Manuči would've adored Osman. All a world needed to justify its existence is the presence of Osman, his body, smile, and stories. He spread his light among us like a candle. I have seen people's heads explode like a pomegranate; I have seen soldats draining themselves to death into shit buckets, giggling all along as if being in on the joke; I have seen people pulled by their feet into la gran eskuridad. I have no explanation nor reason for being alive, other than Osman, my kulu alegri. Eternal life means living in an endless present. But Osman is gone.

The bald Bosnian Alija who doesn't like to cut trees except to make shade for children. Who was he, really? How did he die? Did he mourn the hanuma to his own death after she had perished? Or did he charge at an army in order to get himself killed and thus end his long suffering, only for his cursed power to stop him from dying? Did he ascend into the moonlight and the murky cloud to be with the vila? If you can imagine death, you should be able to die. If you can imagine a life, that life could be lived, and if it could be lived, it could be unlived too, it could be lost. Why would the Holy One go out of His way to create unless He was intent on destroying what He had created, sooner or later? Why can't He let me go? The Lord sent me Osman only to take him away. I should go too. Let me go. As the gardener so the garden.

Pinto was startled when the door flew open. All the soldats cried at once, and pressed themselves against the far wall to shiver like chickens before slaughter, eyes locked on the daylit doorframe. The wind rushed in, and they would've been cold had they not already been so terrified. They hid behind one another, pushing the weak ones toward the front of the throng to be taken if someone needed to be taken. They cried, and cursed, called for their mothers, trying to find a position as far away as possible from the opening into which they'd be sucked to die. Pinto did nothing. This was it then, the time had come: when the Russians came in he would submit himself, to being tortured and shot. He sat up to welcome the blessed guard who would hurl his corpse into la gran eskuridad.

But nobody came in, nothing happened. It took a while for

the soldats to dare to sit down, still staying away from the door because they believed that beyond the door was their end. No boots came down the stairs; no guard came in to take anyone away; nor did they deliver the vomit soup, nor the wooden bread. The soldats were restless and scared, turned toward the door like sunflowers. Pinto watched their hesitation, and their fear and their pathetic desire to be free, and alive, and he pitied them. The sky looked different now: there was more of it, but it was also farther, and more indifferent. Los sjelos ker pur murir.

"Come out," Osman said, "I want to see you. I want to kiss you." The voice was mirthful, as if kidding, just as it was that first night in the barracks. "As long as I live," Osman said, "you will never be cold again." Pinto looked around to see if Osman was somehow back in the jail—it was his body that turned, in fact, for he knew Osman would not be there, just as he knew that Osman's talking to him meant that he was alive, elsewhere, outside. He was not distraught by the presence of Osman's voice and the absence of Osman; all he felt was a rush of weakness as though his body was being emptied of blood, and of death; his knees buckled, his neck thinned so that keeping his head up was suddenly hard. The door gaped at him, the sunlit darkness beyond it throbbing with possibilities. "Come out. There is only one guard here, and he's packing to leave," Osman said. He hadn't heard Osman's voice inside his head since Galicia, because they had not been apart. And now there it was again, that warm, plush timbre, that breath that tickled his ear and so easily turned into a kiss. The soldats fidgeted, stomped their feet, waiting for something to reveal itself. "It's very nice outside," Osman said. "There is food. There are good people. You will never be cold again."

Nobody moved, because no one else could hear him and Pinto now saw what Osman must have been seeing and hearing at the same time: minarets and muezzin calls; houses of clay and straw, dust devils spinning in narrow streets; wild poppies covering the flat roofs like a purple carpet, and there were poplars too, and blooming locust and almond trees, and swallows and turtledoves, and barking, skinny dogs, and beyond it all the tall mountains stood against the sky, their peaks snow-covered and sharp, illuminated by the setting sun. "Here I am, Rafo," Osman said. "Come out. It is a beautiful day outside. I'm waiting for you. I can't wait to hold you in my arms."

Pinto stepped out into the blinding day and kept tottering forth, until he fell on his knees to blink at the ubiquitous light. When you enter a town, follow its customs. Someone helped him stand up, but it wasn't Osman because this man smelled different—sweat and vinegar and saffron—and they walked together through curtains of heat and coruscation. Troubles dim your eyes, but liberty blinds you. The stranger who was helping him along kept talking cheerfully in some obscure language, as if he were making it up on the spot. Pinto could see nothing but the light, and it had different hues and shades. The evil in this world is the leftover from the worlds destroyed. He had thrown himself at Osman to snatch him away from under the Russian muzzle. He saw luminescent motion in the corner of his blitzed eye and it seemed to him that it was made by some whirling dervishes who also sang and chanted, but when he got closer he could only recognize the familiar outline of hungry soldats huddling. He had lain on top of Osman as the Russian dropped the butt of his gun on his hand. Then the light changed, turned narrower, and Pinto was on a street, crowded with bodies flowing past him, as around a rock in a creek. In the jail they had all been pickled in spacelessness, not moving because there was nowhere to go, and now warm and whirling bodies rubbed against his, bumped into it. The stranger talking to him was laughing at something, with someone, and they talked past Pinto. There were men in splendorous dresses and turbans, like sultans in a fairy tale. There was a row of heads stuck on poles, but they turned out to be astrakhan hats. He ran into an enormous snorting beast that stank like a dead horse and was angry. The stranger led him around the camel by his hand, like a child. A man offered him a gourd and Pinto took it but didn't know what to do with it until the man showed him how to suck smoke out of it, so Pinto did and it was not tobacco but something else, something that rushed blood into his head. Because you hear so many voices do not imagine that there are many gods in Heaven. Where was Osman's voice, it was drowned out by this terrible noise of the unfettered world. Who is this that has revealed my secrets to mankind? In the jail, death sat in the corner, humming and moaning and festering, and you always knew where it was. Everyone positioned themselves at an angle in relation to it, not turned away and not staring at it. Here on the street, life rushed through and caused pain and noise, and it was hard to tell where it was coming from or where it was going. There were veiled women and there were barefoot children prancing like squirrels. Recite and thy Lord is the most bountiful. He created Man from a clot of blood. They turned into a narrow street, and then into a passage so tight that they had to squeeze through it sideways, so Pinto could see the stranger's profile and his nose and lips against the light and he was willing to kiss those lips even if they didn't belong to Osman. Where was Osman? To what there did he go? The stranger was still talking, untroubled by Pinto's incomprehension. Is there a language no one in the world can understand? A language spoken by one man alone, or maybe even none? All the gurgling and growling and chuckling and grunting and lip smacking the edepsiz stranger was producing. Why couldn't he understand it? Where did my beloved go? The stranger stood at a door, not knocking, and the door opened. Jo paso por la tu guerta, tu estavas en la puerta. And then Pinto was in bed, unable to lift his head, and Osman was by his side with his crooked hand on Pinto's forehead, speaking to a man in a Viennese suit in a language Pinto understood but could not name. Osman said: Here is my Rafo. And the other man said, My name is Isak Abramovich. Welcome back to the world, Rafo, such as it is.

TASHKENT, 1919

OSMAN STROKED Pinto's cheek with his knuckles, as if to check if his scar was properly healed. Pinto's beard was wispy and unevenly spread—there was a bare patch on his right cheek, where Osman liked to plant a kiss. Osman's touch tickled Pinto, but he said nothing.

You're very beautiful, Osman said.

So are you, Pinto said. More and more every day. One day you'll be so handsome I am going to lose my mind.

Well, we're already past that, Osman said, and kissed him again.

When I was a kid, I wanted to be a tree in a garden, Pinto said. They say, as the gardener, so the garden. I say, as the garden, so the tree. This garden is not too bad. I could be happy in a garden like this.

Isak Abramovich's garden was thick with prickly flower bushes and plants. A couple of pomegranate trees stood guard at the far end. Along the wall, there was overgrown wormwood surrounding a rampant rosebush, which throbbed with the scent. Osman and Pinto sat smoking on a couple of low stools right by a copse of tomato stalks. The tomatoes were small and green in daytime, but at night they swelled and darkened, so they now looked like shiny steel balls, or dark eyeballs. Over the tomatoes loomed large sunflower heads, folded in for their sunless sleep.

I find it funny that we are hiding in the garden, like school-boys, Pinto said. A perfect place for a first kiss.

The Kuran says there will be a high wall between Heaven and Hell made of earth and sand, Osman said. Atop the wall will stand the wretched souls and they will call out to the people in the garden: May peace be with you!

I wouldn't care to listen to the wretched souls, but it would be nice to be living in peace, with you. This garden might be as close as we ever get to that.

Who was it that built the wall between Heaven and Hell, and why? Pinto refrained from asking because he didn't want to spoil the moment by being a sofu. Whoever it was, He did a good job with this night and the stars, which Osman was presently admir-ing, releasing cigarette smoke slowly, out of the side of his mouth, as if not to obscure the view. Things were clear and simple to Osman: the sky was beautiful; food was good; love was good; touching your beloved was even better; one day, peace would be upon us; the future was bound to be better or at least as good as now; God was kind, He made us, and everything around us, and everything for us, including the wall between Heaven and Hell. Pinto gave Osman a kiss on his shaven cheek.

Everything I've ever had, everything I've ever been, the whole world, I've always hidden and carried inside me, Pinto said. When you are right here, and I can touch you, it all comes out with ease, like a breath. But the other day I woke up in the middle of the night and you were not next to me, and for a moment I thought you were just a dream and I wanted to die. It was only after I smelled you on the pillow that I knew you were real.

I know. You told me all that when I came back.

I almost died. Don't ever leave me.

I'll always be here.

Where were you? Pinto asked. Osman made a couple of cigarette smoke rings, but said nothing.

I was going to go out to look for you, Pinto said. Then I worried you might come home and find it empty. And then what would I do? I don't know where I would go to look for you.

I came back to you. I always do. It doesn't matter what I do. I do what I have to do. Why do you have to torture yourself like that?

Manuči used to say that between the Garden of Eden and Gehenna there is no more than the breadth of a hand. If we could somehow expand it into a proper garden and never leave, well, that would be life.

Life is when you're alive, wherever you may be, Osman said. What more do you need? Every soul is certain to taste death. But before that it's all life, all the time. Where there is life, there is no death. Everything that lives wants to keep living. When death comes, that's the end of life. That's it. I am here, then I am not here, but maybe elsewhere, in a better place.

Osman had a particular way of nodding right after he said something he deemed significant: he would nod twice, then tip his head to the right and raise his eyebrows. This time, two parallel plumes of smoke came out of his nostrils as well. He also put his hand at the back of Pinto's head, where it sat, warm, life pulsating in it. He pressed his lips against Pinto's thick, wiry hair.

It is dark in here, Pinto said, and tapped himself on the temple. La gran eskuridad.

There's no darkness in there, Osman said. You have a soul, that's the candle. The candle never burns itself out. If it did, a man would just be organs pickled in blood.

I disagree, Pinto said. I disagree. It is dark in here.

Then look up at the stars.

I am looking up at the stars. It's still dark inside.

Did you start taking morphine again? Osman asked.

No, Pinto said.

Fine, Osman said. I believe you.

As you should, Pinto said.

Above their heads, the Milky Way was thick like sugar, and one or two falling stars streaked across the dark patches beyond it. The moon hung low above the roofs, indifferent to the spectacle, and to the people watching it. A single shot broke the nocturnal silence, and suddenly all the dogs of Tashkent were barking. Yet they were far away, elsewhere, outside the walls of the garden.

I don't want to go anywhere, Pinto said. I don't ever want to go anywhere. I want to stay here.

You don't want to go home to Sarajevo?

You're my home.

I am not. I have nothing. You have your family.

I don't know what they would say.

About what?

About us.

They would say nothing. We would tell them we are friends and they would ask no more questions.

You don't know them.

I know you. I know the stories you told me.

We would lie?

Well, we are friends.

Friends don't fuck.

You haven't had many friends, have you?

All I want is to fall asleep with you, and wake up with you. Every night, every day. And not worry what other people say. Or about kids throwing rocks at me.

We could find a small house, Osman said. Somewhere up in the hills—in Alifakovac, or even higher up, in Hrid, and live as friends. We'll have a walled garden, maybe with two rooms.

I want to sleep with you.

Okay. We'll sleep together.

Everyone will see we love each other.

Maybe. But a terrible disaster has taken place everywhere. Things have changed. Maybe in Sarajevo people will be better than they used to be. Maybe they are all kinder now. Maybe they'll pretend they don't see.

When we walk around here no one is looking at us.

They took walks in the evenings, through the narrow alleys between walls and houses of baked clay and straw, then in the shade of tall, slender poplars lining the boulevards, along the irrigation canals used to water them when the Saar was high enough. They would stroll all the way to Kauffmann Square, to the shady trees, a few of which were cut, and the overgrown flower beds, some dug up for the soil, or to bury a corpse. After years of army, war, and imprisonment, just to go for a stroll was exhilarating. Sometimes, the dust refracted the sunset, so the square would be enfolded in golden fog, and Pinto and Osman would move through it as through a dream. Occasionally a soldier, or even a civilian, would salute Osman, and Pinto couldn't figure out whether it was Osman's rather worn and dusty uniform, or his Cheka authority, which was not quite visible to Pinto, that made them salute. In the center of the square was a statue of some Russian general, who looked important and cruel, even while coated in thick dust and turtledove shit.

That is not true, Osman said. They're all looking at us to see if we are spies.

Still, they don't care if we sleep together, Pinto said.

You can't know that.

One day in May, when everything was lush and blooming and the irrigation canals were full, they walked past the White Palace all the way to the Saar, where they took their clothes off and dunked each other in the murky, cold water. Later they lay naked on the bank, with their naked legs intertwined. A pair of turtledoves in a tree branch above watched them, cooing, as in a poem. They heard guns from the town, but it was only a couple of shots, probably an execution. They made out, but the sun was down, and their patas were so shrunken from the cold they could not make love. Still, it was the most beautiful evening they had ever had.

We cannot stay here, Osman said.

Why not?

We are not from here.

We are not from anywhere.

We are from Bosnia, from Sarajevo. I want to go home.

You are my home. I am your home. Am I your home?

Home is where people notice when you are not there.

Who is going to notice we're not there.

Somebody will. Besides, I don't want to die here. When you're dead, there is no home anywhere.

I've just never been happier in my life. In the midst of a cursed revolution, in the middle of nowhere, I am happy like a little girl. I keep waiting for the sky to crash, for everything to end, but I am so happy that I can sometimes imagine staying happy for a long time.

Nothing lasts forever.

That is a terrible thing to say at this moment.

After Osman had come back home the other night, he fell asleep right away, and Pinto, awake through the sunrise, watched his face until it was lit up by the dawn. Pinto had no idea where Osman had been or what he had done that day. He imagined him galloping on a horse, pursuing bandits, shooting from his hip; sometimes he would envision, against his will, Osman being shot and tumbling off the horse, but then would quickly shut down the thought. He knew that Osman had to arrest people, interrogate them; he probably beat them, but Pinto could not imagine that he would torture or execute them—Osman was the kindest man in the world. But there was no way of knowing. Sometimes, he would come back home with his eyes empty, and would just go to bed without a word.

Pinto listened to Osman's breathing and an occasional incomprehensible word he squeezed out of whatever dream, or nightmare, Osman was in. Pinto did not want to leave Osman's side, that old cot, or that room, or Tashkent, before the end of his life. It was hard to recall how he had managed to live without Osman before; even harder to see how he would survive without him. Osman just went about the business of staying alive as if it were his daily chore. He had walked right into the Bolshevik midst and announced himself: Here I am! He had volunteered to join the Cheka, because he reckoned that it would give them time to figure out how to get back home to Sarajevo. Pinto and Osman reached a tacit agreement that whatever he was doing for the Cheka should not be talked about when they were together, and occasionally Pinto would see his face and thoughts darken for a moment, as though the shadow of a bird had passed across his face.

But in this dark garden, under the sugarcoated sky, Osman seemed lit from the inside, like a furnace with a crackling fire in it.

I am going to kiss you, Pinto said, and leaned to reach Osman's lips, teetering on one leg of his stool. Osman's mouth tasted like smoke and the sweets he'd had with his tea. Isak Abramovich stepped out of the light of the door and into the shadow of the garden, startling them, so that Pinto fell off the stool. Osman grabbed the lapels of his coat to break his fall, which caused Pinto to roll on the ground, stopping just before he tumbled into Isak Abramovich, who carried on a tray three glasses and a bronze pitcher, no doubt full of vodka.

What are you two doing?

Oh, nothing, Pinto said from the ground. Talking.

We just open our mouths and words come out, Osman said. And they never go back in.

When you are young, everything is easy, Isak Abramovich said. Svetlana Teodorovna used to say that when you are young, you have no end. As far as you can see, everything is a field that is your life, but you cannot see the end of that field. You cannot see the end.

Pinto rose up before Isak Abramovich, as if done with worshipping him. Isak Abramovich sat down on a large rock that was usually used as a table and placed the tray on the ground. Osman took it upon himself to pour the vodka into the cups, and when Pinto straightened up his stool and sat down, they were facing one another, their knees nearly touching. But Pinto could not look Isak Abramovich in the eye, because he didn't want to find out if he had seen them kissing.

Ever since he woke up in the hospital and Isak Abramovich welcomed him back to the world, Pinto spoke in Bosnian to him, while the good doctor spoke back in Russian. From the beginning, they would pick the words from the other's language and insert them in their sentences and thus they exchanged and learned them. Pinto sometimes clandestinely imported Spanjol, just as Isak Abramovich smuggled in Yiddish words, while Osman added Arabic words he had learned in mosque. Over time, they developed their own pidgin, and they understood one another, no need for any translation.

Back in Kishinev, when I was younger, Isak Abramovich said, and wagged his finger to announce the beginning of a story, I had a friend. A very good friend, Benyamin. Benya. I loved Benya very much. We grew up together, Benya and I. We went swimming together. We read the Torah together. We read all kinds of books, to each other, novels and poetry and whatnot. We loved Tolstoy, because his people blush all the time. Benya was pale, like an angel, with a permanent blush on his cheek and thick, straight eyebrows. I liked to touch his eyebrows, they were like two little brushes. He would put his head in my lap, and I would stroke his forehead, and read to him. People say that a man can only love God and a woman. But I loved him, more than God, far more than any woman, and I never wanted to love anyone else. My father wanted me to get married but I kept avoiding it. I wanted to be with Benya.

Isak Abramovich sat with his back to the house, so that his face was in the dark, but Pinto and Osman could tell that his eyes were full of tears. He poured the entire glass of vodka down his throat, and slammed it down on the tray at his feet as if it had contained bitter potion for his sorrow.

But then, one day, Isak Abramovich went on, a carp spoke in Hebrew from a fishmonger's stall—everyone around the stall heard it, including my mother who happened to be there—saying that a great evil would soon be coming upon us. The carp just opened its mouth and said it, twice, and everyone heard it. And then only a few days later a terrible pogrom took place. The pogromchiks went from Jewish house to Jewish house, killing and stealing. We climbed on the roof of our house and they tried to reach us with hooks on long sticks to bring us down and slaughter us, but they couldn't, because we were hugging the chimney. Finally, they gave up and moved on. But they killed our dog, just because they were in the mood for murder.

What happened to Benya? Osman asked.

The pogromchiks killed him. The police stood by and watched as they killed Benya. He was twenty-eight. They caught him on the street, beat him on the head with sticks and mallets, threw him into a ditch.

What is it that makes people do things like that? Pinto asked, not expecting an answer.

Nothing hurts more than losing a friend, Osman said.

Isak Abramovich refilled their glasses, and said:

The fat carp told us it was coming, but who was going to believe a stupid fish? And the funny thing was, once the carp stopped talking, they sold it. To my mother, of all people, who made soup out of it. It was very good, the carp soup.

Isak Abramovich chuckled, and raised his glass to indicate that the story was over.

To good friends! he announced.

They downed the drink, then grunted to express the burn the vodka made.

Heals the soul, Osman said.

The world is full of souls that need healing, Isak Abramovich said, and poured them another round. But this time they sipped their vodka in silence, looking up at the sky in order not to talk.

Isak Abramovich knew that Pinto's ideal soul-healing potion was morphine because Pinto had outright told him, just as he had confessed that he would be tempted to steal it for himself if he were ever to be allowed to administer it to the patients. I don't want to touch it, Pinto said. It is poison. The armed guards thoroughly searched everyone on the way out, except for Isak Abramovich, whom they patted lightly, because he had run the hospital for many years, and had a kind and calm demeanor that worked even on the Cheka ruffians, and they didn't want to have to liquidate him. For his part, Isak Abramovich didn't want Pinto to get shot, because he liked him and needed him at the hospital. Pinto was Isak Abramovich's only other physician, except for Kaczynski, the dour and reticent Pole who didn't believe in anesthesia and kept the Cheka apprised of the goings-on in the hospital. Pinto, of course, eventually succumbed to temptation and stole a handful of morphine vials. The wise and forgiving Isak Abramovich said nothing about it, just added a lock to the cabinet with the morphine, and kept the keys in his pocket. But he also smuggled out a few small vials of morphine, the extra supplies of which he had long kept hidden through the war and revolution in case of an even greater calamity. He sat Pinto down, with Osman at his side, and told him that he could have those vials if they were to be the last ones. Because if he kept using morphine, Isak Abramovich said, one of them, probably, all of them, were bound to die—from the Bolshevik bullets, from overdose, or from sadness. Osman nodded along as Isak Abramovich was speaking. Pinto took the vials.

He rationed what he had, waited for Osman to go on a mission chasing down counterrevolutionary bandits, and then set out to use the morphine. The first couple of days were heaven, even if its bitterness made him gag, so much so that he overrode his own plan and kept at the drug until he ran out of it. He'd imagined, to the point of hallucination, all the bites and kisses, all the harsh and beautiful ways in which he would make love to the absent Osman, and then he would just levitate above the bed, thoughtless and painless, light as the last breath. Then there were a few horrible, painful days. In their small room with a window facing a mosque where no one ever dared to pray, he pissed and vomited into a bucket, lived through terrible, painful nightmares. Isak Abramovich stopped by to check on him, to see if he was alive, but Pinto would not let him in. When Osman came back, Pinto opened the door, but then sat down on the floor, exhausted, because he hadn't eaten for days. Osman embraced him like a child and held him in his arms, and Pinto cried, and cried for a while, and Osman with him. Through that deluge of tears Pinto kept looking at Osman's boots, caked in dust and mud, his left pinkie toe squeezing its head through a laceration on the left one. Then Osman put him in bed, washed his face, emptied the bucket, kissed him on the forehead, and fell asleep. He woke up the following day, after the Šabat sunset, washed, shaved, and trimmed his mustache. He did not mention what had happened, and just waited for Pinto to clean himself up, for they were going to the Boyms' house to have some tea or raisin wine.

The narrow alleys were watered to keep the dust down, and here and there they were shadowed by noisy, laughing boys who eventually pulled at their sleeves demanding something from them. Osman broke a few cigarettes in half, threw them up, and let the boys fight it out; then they asked for matches to light the cigarettes that were not destroyed in the scuffle. By an irrigation canal they saw a bare-chested Sart washing himself with care and attention, scrubbing his skin as though brushing his horse. He looked them in the eyes as they were passing and said something, laughing, at which Osman laughed as well. What did he say? Pinto asked when they turned the corner. I don't know, Osman said. He just seemed happy.

But when they got to the Boyms', Pinto was still immersed in the aftermath of his nightmares and talked to Isak Abramovich about the despair that overwhelmed him in the middle of the night, the horror of an absent future, of only living in the present, which is constantly degrading. It is hard to see what the point of any of it is, he said. We just live because we are afraid to die. We live out of cowardice. Isak Abramovich refilled Pinto's tumbler with plum wine and told him that he should be happy just to have survived the war, and the camp, and that he had his beloved friend by his side, and if the past can be lived through, so can the future. There has never been a time when there was nothing, Isak Abramovich said. On Monday, Pinto forced himself to get up and make it to the hospital, where cutting off someone's arm or dipping hands into their stomach would distract him enough to forget what his body and mind still craved. After a dreadful week, when every one of Pinto's limbs and organs hurt, his craving finally subsided.

Osman and Pinto kept going to the Boyms' on Saturdays, even when the Bolsheviks imposed an early curfew, because, Pinto realized, Isak Abramovich's wise voice and fatherly demeanor, Klara Isakovna's smiles and curiosity, and even the oversweet raisin wine, were now analgesic. And Osman always enjoyed the vodka, more than he should have. The Boyms' home smelled like warm milk and burnt sugar, even if milk and sugar were hard to come by at the time of the revolution. The smell was somehow exuded by the lace tablecloth, the deflated cushions on the chairs, the tchotchkes crowding the shelves, even by the part of the velvet curtain that was not refashioned for clothes. Everything in the house looked old, like residue of some previous life that was no longer available. Pinto understood that the unchanging quality of the home in which Isak Abramovich and Klara Isakovna lived was a way for them to mourn Svetlana Teodorovna, whose fading photograph stood on the windowsill next to where the piano used to be before the Bolsheviks requisitioned it.

The Pintos' house in Sarajevo looked nothing like the Boyms', what with its divans, sofras, and low stools, stacked thin rugs instead of a carpet; a piano was as unimaginable in the Pintos' house as a locomotive. But the milk-and-sugar smell was just the same. Maybe that was how all Jewish houses smelled, regardless of where they were. Whenever Pinto had a sore throat Manuči would burn sugar in a pot and then add hot milk to it and he would drink it; he loved it so much that his throat was sore much too often. But when the feigned soreness was deemed to have lasted too long, Padri would instruct Manuči to make marshmallow tea, which little Rafo hated, and his throat would abruptly heal. All that had been long ago, in Sarajevo, in a home that was so far away it no longer existed, in the world that had probably been razed.

Then, one day, there was someone else at the Boyms', and his presence somehow changed the smell of the house, not least because this man smoked cigarettes with a harsh, acrid odor. The first time Pinto saw Jozef Lazar at the Boyms', he was sitting across from Klara Isakovna in his faded Imperial uniform, beclouded by thick smoke and Pinto's suspicions. On the table before him lay his soldat's hat brandishing a pale shadow of an eagle on its front. A rush of fear went through Pinto, for it seemed clear to him that the presence of the man who introduced himself as Lazar, Jozef, was going to change everything for the Boyms, and for Pinto and Osman, and that this man was going to be here, around and among them, for a long time. In the way the man's eyes darted sideways, as if looking straight at people was difficult and uncomfortable, Pinto recognized there was more than one version of him. Moreover, Pinto noticed that Lazar, Jozef, read him in a glance, and nodded at him not so much to greet him as to mark the completion of his assessment.

By the time Pinto asked Osman about the guest at the Boyms', he was sure that Jozef Lazar was not an Albanian soldat who was getting French lessons from Klara, but someone whom Isak Abramovich was hiding. There were rumors that a British spy was on the loose in Tashkent, and when Pinto asked outright if Jozef Lazar could be the spy, Osman avoided answering until he finally shushed Pinto by pointing at all the ears sprouting out of the walls, at all the eyes peeking through the windows and keyholes. The two Bosnians shared a small room that contained two beds, though they always slept together in one of them, in an old requisitioned house where the tenants in all the other rooms were former prisoners of war, coming from all over the deceased Empire: Hungarians, Slovenes, Bohemians, Poles, Croats. Osman shook his head to confirm the necessity of silence and restore, tacitly, the understanding that Pinto should never ask him about his work.

Pinto could not sleep, and spent the night now longing for morphine, now imagining the many ways in which everything could go wrong. What they had in this small room, within whose walls they could arrange their life as they wanted, place flowers and tchotchkes in the sunny spots, make love in the morning, and kiss before sleep—all of that, so new and fragile, was now in peril because Lazar, Jozef, was in their life, casting a shadow. Pinto wanted him to go away, and never come back. As soon as Osman opened his eyes in the morning, and smiled at him, Pinto said: I need to know who that Lazar is. No, you don't, Osman said, and put a finger on Pinto's mouth, then stroked his hair, then kissed him, then touched his pata, so Pinto gave up on his inquiry.

That first time Pinto met Lazar, he nodded back at the troubling stranger, concealing his trepidation and unease, whereupon Klara Isakovna said, with her soft Russian inflections, On cesse de s'aimer si quelqu'un ne nous aime. What? Pinto asked, and Lazar exclaimed: Ça c'est véridique!

On their next visit, Pinto declared to Isak Abramovich that Jozef Lazar seemed to be a decent man—pošten čovjek—to which Isak Abramovich responded with a meaningful finger wag. Isak Abramovich understood that Pinto chose not to ask the questions that begged to be asked—who exactly was this Jozef Lazar and what was he doing here at their house? Pinto was not mentioning the rumor about the British spy all of the Cheka was looking for, all over Tashkent, and Isak Abramovich appreciated that just as well.

The first time Pinto saw Osman in Jozef Lazar's presence, he was touching his vodka glass to the stranger's, and Pinto had no doubt that Osman knew exactly who was who and what was what. Later that evening, when Pinto and Osman were alone in their room, he simmered in silence for a while, his face turned to the wall to punish Osman. Finally, he faced him to tell him through clenched teeth that if Osman could not trust him after everything they had gone through together, perhaps there were other things too he was hiding from him.

Listen, Osman said. I do what I have to do to keep us alive and to get us home. I don't like what I do. But I have to do it.

Fine, Pinto said. Are you saying that Jozef Lazar is your work? Is he a spy? Is he the spy they are looking for?

Do you want to lose you head? Osman asked. Do you want me to lose my head? I do what I have to do. What you don't know cannot hurt you.

Yes, but what you know can hurt me. You can hurt me, Pinto said. He can hurt us.

Who is he?

Lazar.

Lazar is just someone who needs help, Osman said. He wants to stay alive, just like us.

I don't just want to be alive, I want to live with you. Other than that, I have no reason to be alive. I am a nothing and a nobody. I don't care about anything or anyone else.

All right then. Let's stay alive, Osman said. Stop asking questions.

Some fifteen years before, Isak Abramovich and the late Svetlana Teodorovna had traveled all the way from Kishinev with Klara the toddler and a piano that had been imported from Vienna, only for the Bolsheviks to drag it out with ropes through the living room window as soon as they took power in Tashkent. The comrades would keep returning to rummage through the drawers full of the late Svetlana Teodorovna's threadbare finery, grope Klara Isakovna, or smash the rest of the unhidden china. But after Osman earned enough standing with his smarts to maneuver among the Cheka spooks and brutes, the Bolsheviks stopped barging in, even if they kept a lazy watcher or two across the street at times—which was really a way, Osman explained, to protect the Boyms from the more dangerous elements. Osman would report to Comrade Stark that the old man seemed to be behaving, doing his work at the hospital, staying away from counterrevolutionaries, spending his time with his young daughter, tending his garden. And if he was to be arrested and liquidated, who would run the hospital?

Osman's job at the Cheka was supposed to be monitoring, infiltrating, and liquidating the Mohammedans resisting the working people building a better, more just world. Osman was to identify and eliminate those who aided or aimed to join the marauding rebels led by a criminal named Irgash. But Comrade Stark knew that before he turned red Osman was a Mohammedan himself so the Cheka watched him closely too, and Osman watched them back. He was not all that interested in monitoring, infiltrating, or liquidating anybody—what he really wanted was to find a way back to Sarajevo, for Pinto and himself. But he had to show the results of his combating reactionary elements, while making friends and allies wherever and however he could, imagining paths back home to Sarajevo.

Sooner or later this sky is going to fall, Osman said one night soon after Pinto had come out of the jail. And whole new constellations are bound to appear. We might be able to read them, and they will take us back home.

I don't know, Pinto said. I really don't know.

What Pinto didn't know, since Osman would not tell him anything, was that Lazar had in fact been hiding in the Boyms' secret tiny, windowless back room, the door to which was behind a movable kitchen cupboard. From the way Isak Abramovich told Pinto that Klara Isakovna learned a lot from their guest, it was clear that his presence was disrupting the Boyms' life too and that Klara Isakovna must've had feelings for the guest, all of which made Pinto surprisingly protective and jealous. For one thing, she was only eighteen, barely a woman. Not so long ago, Pinto was the one whom she had asked to speak German with her, to tell her stories of the strange country he came from, of his family, of his student years in Vienna, of the passionate life and adventures he had had there. He would come by the Boyms' without Osman and they would huddle, he and Klara Isakovna, by the tiled stove, replenishing their tea from the samovar, and talk about the endlessness of elsewhere. She could not stop considering the terrible fact that there was a world out there existing and changing without her—a world, she passionately believed, she could reach only by way of learning a new language. In response, Pinto would recite the only Heine poem he knew by heart, passed on to him in Vienna by a mouthy, drunken student with a delicious curl on his forehead: Ich hatte einst ein schönes Vaterland. Der Eichenbaum wuchs dort so hoch, die Veilchen nickten sanft. Es war ein Traum.

And then it was Jozef Lazar who was making her laugh, and in French too. The evening he saw him for the first time he kept hearing Klara Isakovna's laughter, even in the garden, even as Isak Abramovich reminisced, with Bulochka, his little mutt, in his lap, about a bunny he used to have as a boy in Kishinev; he grabbed Pinto's forearm, as if to stop him from running into the house and breaking up the cozy party. Klara Isakovna could not stop laughing at her own mispronunciation of the phrase amour-propre; she kept saying it over and over, as if it were a punchline of a joke. What was so funny, Pinto wondered, what's so funny about amour-propre?

Bulochka never barked but had a howl that sounded like a child crying. It is possible that inside each living creature there are voices of other living creatures, Pinto said just to say something. He could hear Klara Isakovna take a deep breath, then giggle once again as Jozef Lazar talked about the wit of La Rochefoucauld and described to her how beautiful Paris was, with its palaces, art, cafés, and parks.

When he was at the Boyms', and Lazar was there too, Pinto would always try to eavesdrop on what the stranger was saying to Klara, looking for excuses to place himself in the garden right under the window of the room where they had their classes. When not speaking French, Jozef Lazar spoke broken Russian. But whichever language he used, he never talked about Tirana, allegedly his hometown, nor Galicia, where he claimed to have been captured, nor any place in between. He talked mostly about Paris, never quite explaining what he had been doing there. It bothered Pinto that Jozef Lazar had not come up with a better false identity—Jozef Lazar wasn't even an Albanian name, Pinto was convinced. Whoever Lazar may have been, his true, deceitful self was coming through his demeanor like dye through cotton cloth, what with his verbose, gratuitous poetry quotes in nasal French, and the way he sat in the chair as if on a throne, with his back straight and his shoulders never slouching. His limbs and movements were officer stiff; he appeared incomplete without a rifle or a whip, or both, just as an officer would be.

Pinto had met no Albanians among the soldats he treated at the hospital; no soldat whose broken head he had bandaged or whose wound he had stitched together knew of any Albanians in their units. Pinto asked Osman again, in a whisper, if he knew who the man hiding at the Boyms' was, or whether he was the British spy, and Osman just shook his head.

Why won't you tell me? What do you think I could do or say? Pinto asked. Do you think I will go and tell the Bolsheviks? Or that I would get drunk and babble it out? Or that I would take some morphine and forget where we are and what is happening?

You do not need to know who he is, Osman said. I don't really know who he is. I just know that if he is found out he would be killed, just like Isak Abramovich and Klara would be liquidated, and you and me as well. We would all be shot in the head. I already told you far too much. Do you understand that?

I understand it, but I don't accept it.

Just let him be, Osman said.

I let him be, Pinto said. What am I doing? What can I do? There is nothing I can do but let him be. I just want to know who he is so that I can properly let him be.

Only once during Jozef Lazar's residency at the Boyms' was Pinto left alone with Lazar. They were in the garden, where Jozef Lazar, who never left the house, would get fresh air, and Pinto, jealous as ever, joined him just so he could read him and gather some clues. Shadowy wisps of clouds floated among the stars, like gun smoke. Das Meer hat seine Perlen, der Himmel hat seine Sterne, said Jozef Lazar wistfully and out of the blue, as if recollecting something from a different life. Pinto had never heard him speak German. As far as Pinto knew, he was not even supposed to speak German. Pinto recognized that it was the right moment to ask Jozef Lazar who he really was, what he was doing here, and whether he was the spy the Bolsheviks were looking for. But the night smelled of acacias and woodsmoke, of crisp autumn cold, and the two of them seemed to be alone in all of Tashkent. The silence was overwhelming, raining from the firmament, only the rare and distant dog howls bouncing around town. Pinto just smoked silently next to Jozef Lazar who held an unlit cigarette in his hand as if planning to hold it in perpetuity. Pinto was burning to say that he knew Jozef Lazar was not who he appeared to be, but that his secret was safe with him. He used to declare the same thing to the married men he had met in Vienna. If there were no righteous humans, Padri used to say, the blessings of God would become completely hidden and Creation would cease to exist. And because the sky was above them and the stars kept silently multiplying as the night progressed, Pinto knew there must have been righteous humans somewhere beyond the walls of this Godforsaken garden. So he asked nothing. Eventually, Jozef Lazar got up, said, Bonne soirée!, and went inside. Pinto stayed alone in the garden until Isak Abramovich came out to warn him that nights were cold here and that it would be too easy for Pinto to catch catarrh. Pinto did not move, perched on his little stool, so Isak Abramovich sat next to him.

Did I tell you, Isak Abramovich, Pinto said in response, that the Pintos in Sarajevo live up on a hill, so that when it gets warm and muggy in the valley the air is still fresh up there?

Isak Abramovich must've noticed that Pinto spoke as if he still lived in Sarajevo, as if his being there in Tashkent were but an accident easy to rectify.

In the winter, it sometimes snows up in Bilave, where our house is, while it's raining down in the valley.

Let's go inside, my friend, said Isak Abramovich.

I'll be right in, said Pinto, not moving.

And now Isak Abramovich was looking up at the abundant stars above, as were Osman and Pinto, more vodka in their hands. They had spent so many evenings in this garden, there was no need to talk or say anything. May peace be upon you! the wretched souls shouted at the people in the garden.

My Padri Avram used to say that Heaven is a revolving wheel, Pinto said. Even if you never move from your place, everything around you will change, and the world and all that it holds will be the same and not the same. We could stay right here and just watch the wheel turn. But if we move, if we keep moving, everything will always be only different, and we will never be the same. There had to have been a world where no one was ever at home, where everyone was always going from one place to another. The Lord must've destroyed such a world, and with relish too—for what kind of a place would that have been, a world consisting only of strangers? There would've been no righteous ones there, nothing and nobody older than a day. The people in that world could never be still long enough to see anything. Everything in such a world would've been dimmed by incomprehension.

I have no idea what you're talking about, Isak Abramovich said, his gaze still stuck to the firmament.

See what I have to live with? Osman chuckled and kissed Pinto's forehead.

Just love each other whatever the world you think you might be in, Isak Abramovich said. There is nothing else you can do. And who knows, maybe all this insanity will produce a better world, where everyone could love whoever they want. Stranger things have happened.

Pinto spotted a moving shadow in the far corner of the garden, where there was no source of light other than the dim stars, and no shadow should've been cast. He stood up carefully, gingerly so as not to startle it. The shadow had the shape of a slouching man and was the color of coal dust smeared on the floor. La gran eskuridad, shaped like a man.

Did you see that? he asked the other two.

See what? Osman asked.

Later, he would wonder why he was not scared at all, why he did not think for an instant that the shadow could harm them. Instead, he simply stood up and moved toward the shadow, which then pressed itself against the wall. Isak Abramovich and Osman stayed behind, baffled, exchanging glances, probably suspecting that Pinto had got ahold of morphine from someone else. But there was no door, no way out for the shadow, and Pinto kept advancing toward it, and it panicked and rushed from one end of the wall to the other, never detaching itself from it. Don't be scared, Pinto uttered, and in the same turn understood that he did not need to speak for the shadow to hear his voice. But when he got close, the shadow leaped toward him and attached its feet to his feet, and it was now linked to him, and would not leave him as he ran back and forth from one end of the wall to another.

Rafael Avramovich, you are drunk, what are you doing? Isak Abramovich said, now standing up, his own shadow stretching all the way to Pinto. It's late, it's getting cold. It's time to go inside.

Pinto was facing the shadow, giving it a chance to leap back onto the wall, and then over it, but instead it stretched itself forth to bend at the foot of the wall.

Rafo, let's go inside, Osman said.

Pinto had no choice but to drag the shadow across the garden toward the house. But it never made it inside, dissolving at the threshold.

BRICH MULLA, 1920

MAJOR MOSER-ETHERINGTON surfaced from his excruciating dream and, oblivious to Pinto dabbing his rotting foot with a warm wet rag, spoke as if just continuing the story he had started telling long before.

I left Srinagar, he said, on Lenin's birthday, April 22. Seventeen days to Gilgit, first on boats, then on foot. I skied on the slopes of the Tragbal Pass, and then, after a blizzard that nearly killed us all, I arrived at the Burzil Pass five hours ahead of the next man. In the Pamirs, I shot a few chukars and steinbocks. Few things are more beautiful than the sight of a steinbock tumbling hoof over horns down a steep slope. I used the game to feed the coolies who had run out of food, but one of them died anyway. I crossed the Mintaka Pass, beyond which I dismissed the coolies to use yak transport. I found the Chinese border guards filthy and slovenly. By a fire in a yurt, the Chinese commander told me about a detachment of Cossacks roaming in the area, but he was not sure whether they were White or Red, nor what the difference would be. I ran into the vile Cossacks in Tashkurgan, and luckily they were rabidly anti-Bolshevik, their outrageous hatred fueled with copious amounts of vodka. I crossed the Tort Dawan Pass, then the Kashka Su. On the way, I shot a mountain finch, a bunting, a horned lark, a magpie, and a few ugly, ungodly marmots. I reached Yangu Hissar in early June, where I was welcomed with banners and trumpeters and soldiers raising a dust cloud that nearly choked me to death. Six weeks after leaving Srinagar, I reached Kashgar. There I found Sir Charles Northrop, my old Worcester mate, who served there as His Majesty's Consul. Charlie always called me by my college moniker: Sparky.

You, however, must not call me Sparky, Major Edgar Moser-Ethering said to Pinto, because that's only for my Oxford peers. You may call me Moser, and only Moser, because I don't like the way you murder Ethering with your Balkan pronunciation. Do pronounce Moser like a German word and it should be fine. I am not Jozef Lazar, and will never be Jozef Lazar again, a good name though it was. Just Moser to you.

We're going to have to amputate your toes, Pinto said.

What toes? Moser said, I have no toes. I have skis.

We'll take your skis off, then, Pinto said.

I don't care, Moser said. The snow is all gone anyway.

All gone, Pinto said. All of it.

So Charlie arranged a dinner in my honor, Moser went on, inviting not only Chinese officials, but also the Russian Consul-General—a bearded man in a long Sart khalat and his French-speaking wife, who under the table pressed her hip against mine then placed her hand on my knee. Later, gramophone records with Russian dances were played. I had to dance with the wife, who rambled into my ear about the tediousness of Kashgar, a city more distant from the ocean than any other city on earth, did you know that? The Russians' favorite antidote to the revolution, and to death, and to boredom, and to women, she whispered to me, was vodka, vodka, nothing but vodka. Russian men would rather weep or pass out drunk in each other's arms than touch a woman. Even here in the asshole of the world—she said: le trou du cul du monde, in her derelict Russian accent—even here in the asshole of the world, it is clear that everything will soon end. There's an Irish priest, Father Hendricks, she said, who had one congregant, an Italian, whom he then banned from attending mass, so that he could do it all alone, no sinners present, only God. But I know there is no God in Kashgar, she said. I tried to talk to God, I called God, but there was no response, only mockery, she said, and twirled out of my arms to dance with Charlie. Charlie is not a good dancer, his feet are far too big, and he stepped all over hers. The following day, I got up before she awoke, and shot two doves, a large lark, a ringed plover, a tern, a carrion crow, a stork, and a starling—it was my best day of hunting in a long while. Dead animals, birds or steinbock, always look shocked when you shoot them. You and I can at least expect the oncoming end, but animals suddenly stop being alive, and are always surprised by it. I find that rather amusing; I love seeing that shock. Anyhow, before a game of polo I took part in, I saw the Consul-General's wife—Natalia was her name, I think. No, Natasha!— well, either Natalia or Natasha was glaring angrily at me, and I didn't even bother to nod at her. A woman is a bundle of trouble, my father always says, and he'd know. My father and I, we both prefer hunting to women. In any case, in the middle of the night I woke up Bagrutani, my young Armenian guide, embellished with nature's pride and richest furniture, as the poet said. We hopped on a Triumph motorbike and left Kashgar. We sped like a dream and reached Mingyol in three and a half hours. We crossed the Kizil Dawan, Bagrutani holding on tight to my waist, a very strong grip that man had. We stopped so I could shoot a gazelle, but we could not take it with us, so we left it for the vultures, a flock of which followed us thereafter across the desert. In the Alai mountains, we stayed with a Kyrgyz family and got dreadfully drunk on kumis. Bagrutani snored like a camel. Near Shorbulak, we squeezed through a marble gorge so narrow its walls were polished to a shine. We stopped at the Chinese garrison in Ulugchat in search of gasoline and bought a couple of exorbitantly expensive canisters. The following day, we were in Irkeshtam, where the Russian customs officers entertained us with card playing and homemade vodka. They showed me the skin of a freshly killed bear, still dripping with blood. They also showed me their prized Bolshevik prisoner and offered to let me break him with a mallet. They had nothing to do there, so the Bolshevik was going to be strung up as soon as all of his limbs were thoroughly shattered. Their kindled wrath had to be quenched with blood. When I saw him, they were busy breaking his ankles. I'd heard many men screaming, but those screams were different altogether. Anyway, we crossed the Terek Dawan, where there was thick snow on the ground, and bones of countless animals and men piled high enough on the sides of the road to be visible above the snow. The natives said you could hear the ancestral voices there, prophesying war, whereas I thought that it was the wind whistling through the hollowed-out bones. We came upon some farms at Gulcha: empty barracks, a ditch full of dead children, a snapped telegraph line, a shredded flag on a leaning pole. It was like a painting: the still, sad music of humanity. The vultures were having a ball. I shot a few, and also a stork, and a hedgehog. In Andjian we stayed at a bathless hotel where there was no food; it was not really a hotel, just a building with a roof and straw mats. The town was full of released, desperate Austrian prisoners, none of whom were actually Austrian. Orchestras of Hungarians and Bohemians played in teahouses, Poles and Croats worked as blacksmiths and water carriers, while even the guards outside the Bolshevik command post wore the Imperial uniforms, minus the insignia, minus the German language they refused to speak. There were no Bosnians among them, but then I don't know how I'd have been able to distinguish a Bosnian from any other cube-headed Slav. Did you know that the word slave comes from Slav? It's most obvious, if you've ever met a single Slav, or a single slave—and I've come upon both. I always thought that jewelry comes from Jew. You're a Jew, not a Slav, I know that. You are tawny. You have a scarred face. I will never be able to tell all of those cube-headed people apart, but I know a Jew when I see one. You go about and poison wells, as the poet says. Who doesn't? It is what it is. Anyhow, I spent a few days there, and took Bagrutani to the movie theater to see a film called *Father Sergius*. Bagrutani loved the story of the handsome officer who became a monk; he grabbed my hand when the hero for some reason chopped off his own finger. Bagrutani had very hairy knuckles, and his lofty brows in folds did figure death, and in their smoothness amity and life. I love Marlowe, the old sodomite. But Bagrutani was arrested on the street, and so I got to talk to a Bolshevik Komisar for the first time in my life. The Komisar slammed his Nagant down on his desk with such an exaggerated drama that it was clear he must've seen *Father Sergius* more than once. A man cut off from all his kind he was, as the poet says, and more than half detached from his own nature. Also, horribly ugly, missing a few teeth, his nose bent to the side from some beating he had received, no doubt deservedly. I offered him the Triumph for Bagrutani, but there was nothing that could be done, the Komisar said, as Bagrutani was judged to be a well-known bandit and an enemy of the people. I waited at the station for days before boarding the train, which was then delayed by a sandstorm—tebbad they call it around here. It took a couple of weeks to reach Tashkent. I would've gotten there faster on a camel, but all the camels were requisitioned by the Bolsheviks to be slaughtered for meat. In Tashkent, I disembarked into total chaos. Everyone, and I mean everyone, was out of their minds, as though of hemlock they had drunk. Nothing but fear and fatal steel and flags, my Jewish friend. It was the end of time, all over again, the American Consul-General told me. All he did was pray for a miracle of salvation. He also drank a lot. Americans are muttonheads; they are the recrement of humanity. I ran into another American passing through with a troupe of performing elephants; he had a pet white tiger he fed with camel meat; he also kept a tiny, starved Tibetan man in a cage, because he was supposed to be able to levitate, but the Tibetan was so emaciated and weak that he could not sit up, let alone levitate. I was accosted by a couple of beggars heading east, apparently ecstatic that the world was coming to an end. They carried with them a portrait of Christ and explained to me that the way for the soul to be released from the sorrows of this world and join the sphere of unbegotten God was to make the body that imprisons it pass through every possible condition of earthly life. You should do everything you can down here, they said, commit every sin and crime on earth, and then go to Heaven, the realm of sinlessness, liberated from your mortal body, left behind on earth like a discarded snakeskin. Their patron saint was the young naked man Jesus was with in Gethsemane when he was arrested, I forgot the name. They claimed he was Jesus's lover. Ragged as they were, they offered themselves to me to advance my salvation. Imagine that. Imagine that, my misbegotten god! I am sure that a few Bolshevik bullets have by now released them from their mortal bodies.

Moser finally stopped talking because his fever fully took over; his eyes were aflame, his febrile nostrils pulsating. In the corners of his dry mouth spittle gathered, soaking the edges of his mustache. Tucked inside his face was his ever-moving mouth, like something struggling to escape his thick mosslike beard. He looked nothing like Jozef Lazar, not even close, as if this man here hatched out of the shell of Lazar and then discarded it.

Sahar brought a wooden bowl of melted snow and put it to Moser's lips, and he drank greedily, the water evaporating as soon as it reached his throat. His foot was rotting, a dark red patch moving up from his toes. Pinto pointed at the melted snow and then at the stove to tell her to start boiling the water for the amputation, and she understood. Pinto wondered what Osman was doing at this time. Talking to the Cheka recruits about the Mohammedan religion? Riding into the desert to meet the head of a family that could be bribed away from Irgash? Darning his socks, patching his pants? Sleeping in their bed, dreaming of Pinto? Or keeping company to Klara Isakovna?

Much have I traveled in the realms of gold, Moser continued after Sahar wiped his mouth and picked qurut bits out of his beard. Many goodly states and kingdoms I have seen, but never such madness and mayhem as in Tashkent. It all soon turned crazier and bloodier, and then it got much worse. Can you even begin to imagine what it was like? Do you have any idea? Do you? And who are you anyway? Why are you here? Am I going to die? Am I going to ascend to the realm of sinlessness and leave behind the wondrous architecture of this world? What do you think? What is churning up in your Jewish mind?

Sahar put a pot of water on the stove, added some sticks and sheep turd to the fire, which briefly lit her face with its mazes of wrinkles. There was no way of knowing how old she was. Moser had asked Pinto how old he was and, for a moment, Pinto couldn't remember. He had lived so much life, decades accruing in mere months, years in weeks. Sahar brought another bowl of water and poured it into Moser's mouth, not quenching his thirst. Most of the time Moser spoke in educated German, but then in his delirium would abruptly switch to English, or gibberish French that still sounded like a different kind of English. Sahar did not even look up when he railed; to her, those European languages must've all sounded like febrile gobbledygook.

She will not remember us, Pinto thought. There is nothing about us that matters to her in her life. We're just foreigners carried through by some force, like strange birds dumped by a wind from a distant land. She was helping them because she could not let them die, not because they had any meaning in her life. She would do the same for a wounded bird, or a lamb. Perhaps she was helping because she was afraid that some future punishment by the Europeans would come upon her if she didn't help them. Or it could be because Eshan ordered her to do what he thought ought to be done. But she will never think about the strangers, the two of us, once we are out of her house. And neither she should. Daleko im lijepa kuća, Bosnians say. May their pretty house be far away. If Manuči were hiding strangers, she would be in the kitchen performing duties requested by their presence. If Pinto knew the Tajik language, he could tell Sahar that she didn't need to do what she was doing but that he was grateful. She still would not remember him after he was gone.

Moser lost consciousness, exhausted by his own incessant narration and the throbbing in his dying leg, which stank like a corpse. Yolcha the dog had smelled it first and kept away from the Englishman. Sahar would shake her head and curse at Moser and his leg in Tajik, as if infuriated by the ruthlessness of the illness, by the indelible logic of his dying inch by inch. Foreigners carry death, even if it is their own. Some days before, Eshan had gone to see some legendary Kyrgyz herbalist and get something that could save Moser's leg, or at least his life, and Pinto had hoped he would return in time. But now it was time to amputate. Pinto had to cut the toes in order to slow down the gangrene. And if Eshan didn't come soon, he might have to cut again farther up the leg. Sahar would assist. She would hold the Englishman down, his only anesthetic whatever mead they had left in this place. Then Pinto would solder the wounds with a red-hot iron, and Sahar would pray, or curse. And Moser would have to find a way to live.

Back in the Carpathians, Pinto had incinerated soldats' amputated limbs in a never-ending bonfire. Here were the firestone and the wood; and there were the sheep for the burnt offerings. The thickness of that smoke, the reek of burning human flesh, you can never forget it, it remains in your head, ingrained in your nostrils, forever. A horse was told, Padri Avram used to say, Let us cut off your head, and we will give you a barnful of barley. The wisdom of dead men, all that useless defunct poetry, all that misspent life. God will see to the sheep for His burnt offering, my son. If Moser died, they should build a bonfire and burn him. Otherwise, he would have to be put out to freeze solid, and if he was lucky wolves wouldn't get to him before the ground thawed enough for a grave to be dug. Who knows where his soul might end up, in some Heaven, in some Hell, or in some other place; whatever the case the body, unless it is burned, will stay here to rot.

*　*　*

It is indeed a confirmed historical fact that Major Moser-Ethering left India in April 1918, carrying the orders to reach Tashkent and report back on the extent to which the revolutionary troubles in metropolitan Russia had rippled to Turkestan. He was playing what is still known as the Great Game, and refers to the conflicting ambitions of the Russian and British empires—both wanted more territory, and the territory that is not yours is always beyond the mountains. We know what we know about Major Moser-Ethering because there exist some well-informed books featuring his many clandestine adventures, and it was the Major himself who wrote them. They are what they call page-turners, even if narrated in the contemptuous voice of an Oxford don. And they claim that, by the time the Major reached his destination, it was already too late. The Bolsheviks had removed the earthly crowns of the entire Russian royal family by way of removing their heads, and the armageddon of the revolution became irreversible. At the time of Moser-Ethering's arrival, the Reds held tenuous control in Turkestan, having formed ramshackle military units of prisoners of war. The best (or the worst) of those joined the Cheka and rounded up myriad reactionary elements, not least the Uzbeks, Tajiks, and Kyrgyz who had the temerity to remain Muslim at a time when, under Lenin's leadership, the chains of prejudice and oppression were being cast away. As for the foreigners in Tashkent, they had little choice but to try to continue their lives as they'd lived them before. The brute future had already smashed their doors, requisitioned their goods and property, executed the spies among them in the back alleys, shot the traitors and innocents on the streets.

As soon as Major Moser-Ethering set foot on the streets of Tashkent, the eyes of the Cheka were on him. For his part, he instantly understood that his official papers were not only no longer good but could get him quickly liquidated. In his memoir *Sparking the Fire*, Moser-Ethering wrote, not without delirious British braggadocio, about the many ways in which he had slipped through the paws of the beastly, dumb Bolsheviks burning to arrest him. He could spot agent provocateurs before they said a word to him. He knew to shake off the spooks on his tail by altering the way he walked. Because the Cheka knew he spoke good German he pretended not to know a single word of the language. As a writer, I greatly admire his attention to detail. He learned to put his coat on like a Russian: he lifted it over the left shoulder before the arm was put in. When he finally vanished before their very eyes, he did so by entering a house, changing his clothes and shaving off his mustache with incredible celerity, then going out in the back, jumping over fences to exit through the front door of another house, wearing, like a proper former captive, a worn-out Austrian uniform complete with a hat displaying the Emperor's eagle. He walked past his watchers stupidly smoking in wait for the imperialist spy who would never come out. He then became a Romanian from a Hungarian regiment, as he couldn't speak any Slavic languages other than Russian. Nor could he speak any Hungarian or Romanian for that matter, but there seemed to be few Romanians in Tashkent and he could thus duck behind his wordlessness. He spoke deliberately bad Russian, as if he had learned it only after his imprisonment, exaggerating the foreignness of his accent to conceal his English inflections and make himself as incomprehensible as possible. He clicked his heels and bowed whenever he made eye contact on the street with anyone other than native peasantry. Then he became Jozef Lazar, an Albanian who was captured in Galicia, and then he was hiding in Isak Abramovich's basement. He came out to their tiny walled garden only at night, only after the town's curtains were drawn for the curfew, to stretch his legs and look up at the stars; he once saw a bright orb moving across the night sky only to stop abruptly above the city, as if to consider all the lunacy below. It was only in the garden that he spoke German to Pinto, as if delivering a secret message, which Pinto would not forget for the rest of his life. Das Meer hat seine Perlen, der Himmel hat seine Sterne.

For the Boyms, including Isak Abramovich, Moser was the reticent Albanian who sometimes whispered his gratitude in fine French, and had good but unspoken reasons to keep away from the Cheka. Isak Abramovich followed Osman's instructions and never probed him, never asked him anything. Klara Isakovna, however, was curious about their guest's obscure, distant land. L'Albanie est merveilleuse, he would say, and haltingly describe les montagnes des rêves et les forêts édéniques. What about Count Dracula? Klara Isakovna would ask. Tell me about the vampires. Ils habitent en Romanie, he'd say, pas en Albanie. The Bolsheviks kept scouring the city for Moser, breaking down doors and carting people away in the middle of the night, occasionally and arbitrarily shooting them over a desert ditch. Osman arranged for Moser to head to the mountains in Eshan's arba, enduring horse farts and hoping that the Bolsheviks would not too conscientiously bayonet the bundle of sticks wrapped around him.

Sahar added another handful of dried sheep turds to the fire and lifted the lid on the pots to see if the water was boiling. At this altitude, the water should boil fast, but just about everything was wrong, and who knew if the laws of the world still held up. Everyone believes the sun will rise tomorrow, but no one really knows. The Lord keeps creating the worlds and destroying them without regard for our plans and schedules. You cannot fathom my rules. You go to sleep in one world, wake up in another. It has happened before, it will happen again. Pinto needed to cut off half of Moser's toes, maybe even his leg, to keep him alive in case the sun rose tomorrow, and the day after, and the day after that. Even though it could all be in vain anyway.

The water was boiling, so Sahar put the large, throat-slitting knife into one of the pots. Then she sat down to comb wool, picking and stretching the strands until they were gossamer-like, as if it was her ritual for calming herself down. Occasionally, she dabbed her lips with one of the knot ends of her headscarf. She was a sinewy woman, with spindly fingers and fibrous forearms. She did not cover her face, unlike Sart women, and did not avert her gaze when looking at a man. But she never said anything. Pinto understood that even if they were to share a language she would still be silent; and she would never tell anyone about the two foreigners staying on the bee farm, and she would never mention or remember them. Eshan had left a rifle with her, since Sahar was the one who would use it; she would be the one to shoot, as Pinto could not be relied upon to kill a person, or even a wolf.

When Eshan was around, Sahar barely exchanged any words with him, communicating by way of quick glances. Sometimes she would just know what Eshan wanted. When he drank up all of his tea, she refilled his demitasse. Once Eshan fell asleep at the table, his cheek next to his wooden bowl; she removed his tubeteika as he slept; she had done it before and knew how not to wake him up. It was just as obvious to Pinto that if Eshan ever smacked her she would stab him in the eye; he could tell from the way she grasped the knife handle, her sinews tightening with the grip. Manuči would've never dared to disobey Padri's orders.

When he smacked her, she cried over the stove voicelessly, her tears dripping into the beet soup. Mother's dishes are always the most delicious, she used to say, because they're seasoned with tears.

The fire in Manuči's stove had to keep going too, because what fire desired was to keep on burning, just as everything that lived wanted to keep living, at least until the sun did not rise one morning, or the Lord decided to exterminate every living creature, or maybe just get rid of me and everyone I love. Manuči would be stoking the fire and feeding it with corncobs and dried potato peels; she would never touch the desiccated sheep shit peasants sold to the poor Sarajevo folk who could not afford real wood. She would pour hot water over the stale bread to make popara, no butter to top it off with, but plenty of tears available. She too would now be all sinews and skin, aching and unsoft, holding up her skirt with one hand so it didn't slip off her shrunken hips. Madre mija si mi muero. She would no longer eat much, just enough not to die before her only son returned from the war. Simha must've already married, but she would surely come to see her mother whenever she could, which would never be enough for Manuči, and they would hope and speculate about Rafo, what had happened to him, whether he would find a way to write them a letter. Manuči would sing to ease her loneliness, remembering him when he was a boy, before he went off to Vienna. Halva, sheker ola. Her Rafo, her only boy, wearing a girl's dress and a tukadu to deliver his lines in tija-Laura's play: Si los amijos kajeron, los dedikos kedaron. Even if the rings slip off, there are still the fingers. The few letters he had managed to send before capture had said nothing to her other than that he had been alive at the time of writing—the last one had been sent from Galicia, more than three years earlier. Even if you lose your fingers, they can still hurt and itch.

Moser was wheezing frantically, and the sheep shit was crackling. Pinto was hungry, but he had learned in the war that eating before slicing the putrid flesh and sawing the bones carried some risk. For Sahar, combing wool was a way to prepare for cutting a man, and he didn't want to take her out of her peace. She did not look at him, or say anything, as if everything was entirely clear to her. Pinto did not know if Eshan had explained to her what they would have to do if he was not back in time, or if she just figured it out because it was obvious that Moser's darkening foot, its muscles and tendrils getting more exposed by the gangrene, could not wait until her husband's return.

Eshan had to have been uncomfortable with leaving his wife with a foreign man to go to the herbalist. He knew and trusted Osman, but he also must've had confidence that Sahar would've stabbed Pinto in the eye if he dared disrespect her. They had probably agreed by way of their silent glances that Pinto was innocuous. Or perhaps they could see, in some mountain-man way, that women did not incite lust in Pinto. There was something in the way Eshan moved around him that suggested he had met men like Pinto before; he would face him at an angle, as if to be able to get away from him quickly. Or perhaps to show that he could go either way. Maybe Eshan liked men too. Men liked men even when they were married; men liked men even if they liked women. Sahar looked up at Pinto as if reading his thoughts and he coyly looked down. Eshan was supposed to have already returned. It was clear that Sahar worried that something had happened, that a new setup had taken hold in her world. It was as though she was easing her way into Eshan's absence, still refusing to believe that it could be lasting, that she could be a husbandless wife, but not a widow yet.

At night, as the fire in the stove rose and fell, Pinto imagined living with Osman in a cabin like this, high up in the mountains, far from other people, from their gossip and judgment, from their murderous plans for a perfect future. The cabin would be like their Tashkent room, but better, because there would be no one around. In the winter, they would sleep with their legs entangled; in the summer they would be naked. Clean air, peace, beauty everywhere—they could live a long life here, as long as they kept away from the Bolsheviks. But before that, Moser needed to be kept alive and sent on to Persia or India—wherever he was going to go, he would need his leg.

Hajdemo, Pinto said to Sahar, in Bosnian, as if it could be any different to her from Spanjol or German. She understood and went outside to scoop another bowl of snow and ladled the boiling water into it. The steam rose like a dream, and Pinto offered his hands over a wooden basin for her to pour the water. The water was scalding and Pinto yelped in pain, but her hands did not shake, nor did she flinch. She pulled a clean rag out of the oven and he wiped his hands. She put a log under Moser's foot, then pulled the knife from the boiling water and handed it to Pinto. She lifted the sheet covering Moser's sick foot and a stench of death rose from it. She then pressed Moser's knee down to fix his leg, but he did not move. Death ends all pain. Pinto wielded the knife to slice through the bloated big toe until it hit the bone, and pressed on. Moser yelped and tried to sit up, but Sahar pressed down his torso. Pinto cut the next toe, as Moser beat with his fist against Sahar's back.

The Englishman had been on his way to the next safe hut when he'd slipped and then slid down the slope at the bottom of which was a parapet of tumbled rock. Eshan had to tie a rope to a tree and descend holding on to it to discover that Moser's leg had been broken, the bone sticking out like a stake. Eshan had dragged him up, then carried him on his back to the hut, where he had pushed the bone in with his bare hands, immobilized the leg, and applied some kind of honey ointment. He kept applying it, but the foot had still tumesced, so Pinto had been dispatched from Tashkent to the mountains with a couple of scalpels, and a syringe and a vial of the ever-tempting morphine.

He had cut off scores of limbs as the hećim in the war; many of the soldats had died, some must've made it and could still be alive, some may even have returned to Bosnia. An English-man's leg was not different from a peasant one. His bones were not harder, nor his flesh more resistant to whatever was eating it. Pinto severed the rest of the toes, and they fell into the bowl like marbles, leaving no blood on the log. The big toe rolled out of the bowl and dropped on the floor. It occurred to Pinto that Yolcha might come for the toe, but then he remembered that the dog was outside.

Now he had to give morphine to Moser. Maybe he should let him try to ride out the pain without it first, so Pinto could keep the morphine for later, and if Moser didn't make it, well, mor-phine should never go to waste. It was not easy to cut flesh, even when it was rotten; after the Carpathian campaign he had blisters on his hand from all the cutting. He prepared the syringe. He certainly shouldn't give Moser all the morphine, as Pinto himself could use some later to sleep better. He washed his hands again, as Sahar wrapped the wounds with a woolen bandage doused in honey.

Outside, everything as far as the eye could see was garmented in silent snow. Snijeg pade na behar, na voće. The snow fell on the bloom, on the fruit. Moser talked so much when he was awake and in pain that Pinto enjoyed the quiet whenever he was asleep, as did Sahar. The mountain peaks blunted by snowdrifts appeared as mere curvatures of an endless whiteness, so that the ancient chinar tree down the hill from the hut looked like a mistake, like something that ought to be erased to restore the perfection. Alas for human beings who see but know not what they see, stand but know not on what they stand.

But then a shadow separated itself from the dark trunk of the chinar to trudge through the hip-high snow, and Pinto's heart fluttered in the hope that it could be Osman coming to him. If I were lucky as I am unhappy, and you came into my chambers. But then another black shape followed, a rifle barrel extending from its back, and Pinto recognized the shadows as men advancing uphill. Yolcha was now barking as if possessed. Sahar too looked out the window and saw the men advancing toward them. Pinto could not move, or conceive anything he could do other than wait, but Sahar grabbed the rifle, then pointed with it at the knife. Pinto grabbed it, and waited in cocked silence. She peeked through the window but then quickly ducked back as the men were now close enough to see them. She faced the door, pointing the rifle at it, ready to shoot. Pinto didn't understand what she said in Tajik, but she didn't seem to be afraid at all.

"Snijeg pade na behar, na voće," Osman's voice now sang in Pinto's ear, as it had before. "Neka ljubi ko god koga hoće." Out of la gran eskuridad He had brought forth the song and given light to the world. Let everyone love whomever they want. Pinto could see Sahar's finger twitching on the trigger, he could now hear the crunching of the snow under the strangers' feet. Yolcha was running in circles around the men, not attacking. Moser suddenly grunted in his painful sleep, and the crunching footsteps outside stopped—abruptly, there was silence at the hut's door.

Sahar, the voice outside said, and Sahar exhaled and put the gun down.

Osman's breath was straining between the sung lines, his inhalations and exhalations so familiar to him from having lain in his embrace, his cheek on Osman's chest. Ako neće, nek' se ne nameće. Who says that a man's voice is not as audible by day as it is by night? "Da sam sretan k'o što sam nesretan," Osman sang at Pinto's cheek, "da mi dođeš u moje odaje." Moser whinnied and grunted again, steeped in his own nightmare. The room smelled of pus, wax, and honey, of a feeble turd fire and steam. If Osman's body had accompanied his voice, the song would've been turned into a kiss.

Eshan opened the door and stepped in, his face thickly bearded, the bridge of his nose crimson with frostbite. Behind him, there was a smaller man, fully bundled, his face wrapped in a scarf, and Pinto's heart started dancing even if he knew that could not be Osman. Sahar, Eshan said, and went on talking as she put the gun down. She poured some tea into a couple of wooden bowls, and poured hot water over it. The other man unwrapped his un-Osman face, and took a bowl from Sahar and just kept it in his hands to warm them up. Hunuk ast, the man said, and Eshan and Sahar nodded.

And it was precisely at that moment that Moser opened his eyes still sparkling with fever, unchanged by the amputation, and began railing again as if on cue, Ich verliess Sringar am Geburtstag von Lenin, den 22 April. Siebzehn Tage bis nach Gilgit, zuerst auf etlichen Schiffen, dann zu Fuss.

The Kyrgyz herbalist's name was Aziz. He showed Pinto a round wooden box filled with some kind of dark brown paste, which looked like shit to Pinto. Aziz must've seen disgust and confusion on his face. On a piece of crumpled, unwieldy paper he drew with the burnt end of a stick a picture of a plant: it was tall and slender, the leaves long and narrow, and the flowers like little bells. Okopnik, he said, and pointed at the paste. Okopnik. Aziz stared at him with expectation, even if the plant looked incinerated in some hellish fire, but he had no idea what it was. Aziz shoved the wooden box into Pinto's face until it was awash in a faint shit smell. Okopnik, he said.

In the old drogerija, Padri Avram had shoved boxes of his herbs into his son's face asking him to identify them and tell him what they could be used for. Time and again, Rafo had failed to do what for his father must have been as easy as calling the moon the moon. The only smell he could always recognize was lavender, its sharp, sun-warm, purple scent, but he could not remember what ailments lavender could help cure, other than his perpetually sore heart, and he'd cry and try to guess. Stomach cramps, he'd say. Runny nose, he'd say. It's for shame and sorrow! his father would say, and bang him on the head. Your shame, my sorrow!

Moser stayed asleep even when Eshan unwrapped his foot, which still smelled like overripe yeast and aged maggots. The wounds where the toes had stood were purple, oozing something that was not blood, and was too dark for pus. Aziz spread the paste on a rag and then gestured to Pinto to lift the foot as Eshan stood over Moser's head and placed his hands on his shoulders. So that when Pinto grabbed his heel and lifted the leg, and Moser screamed and attempted to sit up, Eshan pressed his shoulders down, and Aziz placed the rag on his shin first and wrapped it in a downward spiral and around his foot, and the toeless front, and pressed it to spread the paste, while Moser cursed in English and German and French.

Pinto suddenly recalled that there was a small, colored drawing of the plant that Aziz had drawn on a poster hanging off a nail in the shelf in Apotheke Pinto. He had brought the poster from Vienna and there were many plants pictured on it, red and purple and yellow and blue, their Latin names below the images. He had bought it not because he cared about the plants but because it was pretty, because the resplendent abundance of those plants reminded him of Vienna, of the richness and joy of life there. The only plant on the poster he had already known was what Padri called gavez. He used to sell gavez for broken bones, and half of the Čaršija bought it in his drogerija. Pinto had mocked the witchy poultice Padri made from the root and the leaves people applied to their broken arms, or bleeding wounds. He would learn later, in Vienna, that gavez was not a matter of his father's herbal superstition, but that it in fact had a full, serious Latin title of *Symphytum officinale*, that it was called Beinwell in German, and was commonly prescribed by the stiff-collared Austrian doctors to stop excessive menstrual bleeding, and for cuts and infection, and for broken bones, and for many other things. A better son would've told his father what he had learned at the university in Vienna, admitting that Padri had known what was what, but Pinto would never have a chance to tell him because he never sought one.

They wrapped Moser's foot and put it back down, and he passed out. He winced in his sleep, bad blood running up and down his veins. Occasionally, he would shout in a language that was not anything Pinto could recognize and that might not even have existed. God has no needs and we are the needy ones, Osman would say to him, many times. He will substitute other people for us if we turn away from Him, and those people will be nothing like us. They will be worse, or better, but nothing like us at all, and none of them will ever remember us as we were, and if they ever tell stories about us it will be in a language we could never understand.

Klara Isakovich could recite poetry in French; she had once had a French governess who would dish obsolete gossip from Paris, which she had left years before, and would occasionally tell her stories of passion set in reclusive Parisian gardens, featuring fainting madames, adulterous monsieurs, and vials of romantic arsenic. She probably wrote poetry as well, burning passionately with a thirst for being someone else, elsewhere. Klara was curious about the far-off city of Sarajevo; she had only heard about it when the Archduke had been killed. Were you there that day? she had wanted to know. What did you see? Pinto wouldn't have said anything, because it all seemed to have happened a long lifetime ago and none of it mattered anymore, but also because he could sense that Isak Abramovich disapproved of Klara's gratuitous desires, of her burning curiosity. It was Osman who volunteered him, outright bragging about Rafo's presence at the very moment when the world as they had known it was undone. Left with no choice, Pinto would recount the story, culminating in His Highness crying out: Soferl, Soferl, don't die. Live for our children. At which Klara would press the palm of her hand against her chest as if to stop her heart from breaking and say: Oy! Oy! Oy!

Osman would not tell what was Pinto's to tell, even if Pinto had wanted him to, because the story proved that he was present here and now just as he had been present then and there. It fascinated Osman that Pinto could tell stories about himself as he had been in the past, as if they were taking place in a distant land. Sometimes, as they lay next to each other, Osman would ask him to tell the story again, asking questions about the Rittmeister, and the man with an accordion shoving the edepsiz—it aroused him, the telling, so Pinto kept narrating, and their bodies were warm next to each other, and he could hear Osman's breath at his ear, and it was slow and steady, peaceful.

Once, Osman fell asleep before the story ended, so Pinto imagined a future in which he would for Manuči recollect how he had walked out of the jail following Osman's voice, straight into the blinding sunshine that instantly exhausted him. He sat down into the dust of the prison yard and was ready to die; he heard the muezzins' calls from the minarets; the dust was warm; there was a man who helped him get up and who smelled of sweat, tobacco, and, underneath it all, there was a floral scent he could not recognize. But then a word came to him for the flower: šafran, which he could not picture. Neither could he see Osman anywhere, only the shadows of delivered prisoners squinting in disbelief at the sky, then dispersing before the Russians changed their minds. The stranger was laughing. There was a black patch in the dust right before Pinto, which he recognized as dried blood. This is a perfect place to die, he thought, marked just for me. But then Osman emerged from the light to cast his shadow on the ground and lifted him to his feet with such ease that Pinto thought he was already dead, and that what was being raised was his soul. Yet Osman's body was warm and moist, it had strength, and arms, and a scent of sweat that was new, the kind of sweat that came out of a skin washed with soap and water, and the hands gripped Pinto's flanks, the body carried him, and his soul with it. Glory be to Him who created all the pairs of things that the earth produces, as well as themselves and other things they do not know about.

Here I am, Osman had said. Let's go.

Sparky! I'm not Sparky for you! shouted Moser, now asleep. Don't call me Sparky! There were new clumps of dried shit sparkling in the fireplace but Sahar was no longer in the hut.

When Pinto woke up in a hospital bed, and saw the pale, bony face of Isak Abramovich looming as he pressed the flat head of his stethoscope against Pinto's sunken, bare belly, he was convinced that Osman had been a hallucination. Maybe their whole time together had been a dream, maybe Pinto had just wished him into ethereal existence; maybe Osman was his džin, a spirit. The hospital room was full of sick, emaciated men, two in some beds, while one end of the room, crowded like a hive, had only overloaded bunk beds. Welcome back to the world, such as it is. It took Pinto a while to comprehend that the language was Russian, and then German, and then it was nothing, and even then he could not understand. Was sagst du? Pinto asked. Isak Abramovich kept opening his mouth like a fish out of water. Was ist das für ein Ort?

So that when Osman walked into the room, his face shaven and his mustache trimmed as it had been once upon a happier time, wearing a clean mismatched uniform—the green Honved blouse and Rittmeister pants with a red stripe—carrying a watermelon, his body moving nimbly and exuding incongruous health, Pinto howled at Isak Abramovich as though the nightmare of Osman's being there—but not—was his production. It was only when Pinto's beloved knelt by the bed to cut up the watermelon and give him a piece that Pinto believed that he was truly present there. When he tasted the watermelon, juicy, red and sweet, he finally knew that this was the world in which his body lived, and that Osman was alive in it too.

Er ist seit Tagen hier, said Isak Abramovich. Er hat darauf gewartet, dass du aufwachst.

Ich bin jetzt hier, Osman said. Here I am now.

FERGHANA VALLEY, 1921

I'VE SEARCHED FIELDS of pages and forests of indices, read the narratives of wars and great murderous men, of expeditions, revolutions, and colonial exploits, covering much of the vast ground between Sarajevo and Tashkent and beyond, but Osman Karišik attains a shape in historical documents and books only once. He grins and winks at me only from a few chapters in *Sparking the Fire*.

Edgar Moser-Ethering's memoir was published in 1946, at the chilly dawn of the Cold War, when Sparky was busy angling and scheming to become a member of the Cabinet, maybe even Prime Minister and was hence inclined to boost his reputation as a formidable legend of British Intelligence, steeled in guarding the Imperial possessions and fighting the Empire's nefarious enemies, not least the Bolsheviks. Thus he recounts with haughty relish his clever Great Game plays, his frequent crossings of mountains and borders, his subterfuges and disguises in avoiding the Cheka and the NKVD, his outsmarting of brigands and bandits. His elaborate conspiracies are plotted with myriad native and international allies, whose full identities are revealed only if they had since perished or vanished into a different life, and were thus safe from exposure and/or prosecution at the time of publication. Sometimes he goes into what happened to his former foes or allies after they had departed his immediate narrative domain, but usually they just blaze across the pages never to be seen again. Like all formidable spies, Sparky Moser-Ethering was exceptional at ruthlessness, at managing friendship and loyalty by way of selectively forgetting. He has few regrets and no contrition whatsoever, but he does indeed tell many a fabulous story.

In the chapter Hiding in the Plainest of Sights, Moser-Ethering, pursued all over Tashkent by the Bolshevik spooks, descends, through a trapdoor behind a movable cupboard, into the basement of a Russian-Jewish family. They know him only as an Albanian who had somehow served in a Croatian regiment, but they ask few questions, not least because he only seems to speak rudimentary German. He stays with the Boyms for a few weeks, getting out of his lair only at night to catch some fresh air in their secluded garden. One starry night, he meets a handsome Bosnian who works for the Cheka but for whom the scion of the family (Isak Abramovich) had vouchsafed. Moser calls him the Handsome Bosnian, but this is Osman Karišik, marked by his impeccable mustache, oval face, and indelible charm. The Handsome Bosnian tells Moser-Ethering outright that he knows he is the British spy everyone is looking for, and that he could easily turn him in to earn a rewarding promotion. Being a Mohameddan who can read and quote from the Qur'an, the Handsome Bosnian has positioned himself well in the Cheka. He is deemed useful to the Bolsheviks as they aim to recruit the Mohammedans for the cause of the world revolution, since they could eventually provide a bridge to their brethren in the subcontinent, sure to rise against the British rule one day. The Bosnian's real and only agenda, however, is to find a way out of Turkestan and get back home to Sarajevo, of which he speaks with poignant wistfulness. It is clear to the Handsome Bosnian that his utility at the Cheka is limited and that he will sooner or later be disposable. He assures Moser-Ethering that he's willing to help him because he believes that the Englishman could eventually return the favor by helping him get back home. The Englishman prides himself on reading men and quickly grasping the logic of their thinking—he appreciates Osman, and his candor, and understands that he himself has little choice. In the moonlit garden thick with tomatoes and dormant roses, mutual trust is established and an agreement is reached: the Handsome Bosnian shall do his utmost to protect Major Moser-Ethering and help get him out of Tashkent and Turkestan, while Sparky shall aid Osman, in any way he can, in returning home. Lass dies den Beginn einer schönen Freundschaft sein, Moser-Ethering says as they shake hands.

In the chapter To the Mountains, the Handsome Bosnian arranges Moser-Ethering's escape: concealed inside a bundle of sticks in the back of an arba commandeered by a Tajik man by name of Eshan, Sparky slips through Bolshevik checkpoints; in Troitskoe an overeager soldier of the revolution bayonets the bundle, stabbing through Sparky's uniform at the armpit, only grazing the flesh. Moser-Ethering hops between safe houses and huts all over the Ferghana Valley, until he ascends to the mountains to avoid the quidnuncs and snoops. He slips on an icy slope and crashes into a pile of rocks at its bottom, breaking his leg, his shin bone sticking out. He lies low at a snowbound apiary, but his leg gets infected, and the Handsome Bosnian has to dispatch a doctor. The doctor speaks charming Viennese German and has dark features suggesting exotic Jewishness—a description that, its casual racism notwithstanding, fits Rafael Pinto rather perfectly. Pinto (never named as such in Sparky's narrative) amputates his toes and manages to save his leg, but the recovery is slow and difficult. In the chapter Deliverance, the tentacles of spring have crept up the slopes, which means that the Bolsheviks will send out patrols and search parties to comb the mountains as soon as the roads are passable. Moser-Ethering's leg has not fully healed so he can't outrun them again. It is around this time that he develops his legendary limp, which will require him to use an authoritative cane later in his life and career.

In any case, under Sparky's brilliant guidance, the Handsome Bosnian orchestrates an elaborate extrication scheme with a substantial fabular dimension. First, Sparky instructs him to start a rumor, and then spread it in carefully disseminated increments, that Moser-Ethering has been seen all over Tashkent, and is now preparing to leave, as soon as possible, for Bokhara. There he could hunker down under the Emir's protection before heading southwest to the Persian border, beyond which Major-General Ironside and his mighty Royal Forces were stationed. Sparky and the Handsome Bosnian know quite well that the Bolsheviks are not only eager to capture the British spy but also that they're raring to conquer Bokhara, which under the Emir's iron-fist rule—he has already beheaded fifteen Communist spies—sits like a ripe boil in the midst of the territory governed by the proletariat. They also know that the Bolsheviks would not be able to tolerate the possibility of Moser-Ethering's stoking fires in the Emir's belligerent (and large) belly, but neither are they ready to deal with the likely Mohammedan anger if they attack the immured city-state—in short, they must stop Moser-Ethering at all costs before he reaches Bokhara. The rumor of Moser-Ethering heading to Bokhara makes a full circle when it reaches Comrade Stark, the head of the Cheka, and Osman's superior, who predictably consults Comrade Karišik, who in turn assures him that this is without a doubt a rumor circulated by the enemy. The Englishman, Comrade Karišik's sources are confident, is most likely hiding in the mountains above the Ferghana Valley. Now, the Bosnian anticipates Comrade Stark's consulting Comrade Tsirul, his very thick-necked deputy, whose main asset is cheerful brutality in torturing and liquidating the many enemies of the working class and their revolution. Tsirul has long hated the handsome comrade, as he has hated all ass-washing Muslims, and will therefore insist that Moser-Ethering is certain to sneak onto the train to Kagan, a town a mere ten miles away from Bokhara, whence he could make a dash to safety. When Comrade Stark indeed places his trust in Comrade Tsirul, the Bosnian concedes, only to advise him in turn that the British spy will surely expect they'll be setting a trap for him. It is as likely, Comrade Karišik opines, that the spy's allies and supporters among the reactionary elements will create some kind of distraction to help him reach Bokhara. All of that makes perfect sense to Comrade Stark, so he tasks the Bosnian himself with finding out when and how the getaway might happen. I serve the working people, Comrade Karišik responds, saluting Comrade Commander. In the meantime, the Bolsheviks will thicken the train station with their ears and eyes; the train, which is regularly irregular, so to speak, needs to keep going, so as not to discourage the wanted subversive from coming out; the Kagan station too is already full of watchful Bolshevik guards, while the stretch of the road from the station to Bokhara is teeming with mounted patrols.

In his book, Moser-Ethering insists that the stratagem was devised by him, but I'm very tempted to identify Osman's clever touch in the whole setup. While the Bolsheviks focus westward on Bokhara, the Handsome Bosnian and his coconspirators look east instead, toward Kashgar and China. Several moves ahead of the Bolsheviks, Osman takes Klara Isakovna in a requisitioned brichka to a mountain dacha, away from the summer cauldron of Tashkent. Klara Isakovna is large with a child, and Osman makes sure that everyone, including Comrade Stark, thinks that it is he who has been sleeping with her and that the child is in fact his. (Let it be noted that Moser-Ethering spends no words on revealing, or even speculating, on who the father might have been.) On their way, the Handsome Bosnian talks up the guards at various checkpoints, softens their revolutionary resolve with vodka and cigarettes, winks at them as they take a long good look at Klara Isakovna and her large belly so that they can remember her well. It takes a few days to reach Makhram, where she is to wait for Moser-Ethering, now moving pretty well despite his limp, to come down from Eshan's apiary. The Bosnian then heads back, stopping to drink with Comrade Shupskiy, the commander of the Khodjent deployment. The Bosnian feeds Shupskiy's suspicion that Comrade Tsirul is slandering him shamelessly down in Tashkent, claiming he's a spy, and also, you know, a pidor. At the same time, Osman tells Comrade Shupskiy, there are some who claim that Comrade Tsirul is not as committed to Lenin and the Party as he professes to be—sooner or later Tsirul's time of reckoning shall come. Before the Bosnian continues on his way, Comrade Shupskiy kisses him drunkenly, and gratefully, on both cheeks. Back in town, the Bosnian visits with Comrade Stark to report that his Mohammedan sources have reasons to believe that the Englishman will be trying to get out of Tashkent within a couple of days.

Two days later, just as the train to Kagan is leaving the station after the usual hours-long delay, the water tower topples over and a flash flood rushes through the crowd, undoing the checkpoint, so that the passengers not allowed on the train can now force their way through and chase after it. (It ought to be noted that no other source, British or Russian, mentions the toppling of the water tower. It wouldn't have been beyond Sparky to have concealed the real plot by superimposing a cinematically spectacular one onto what really and much less spectacularly happened.) The instantly created mud field slows everyone down, including the Bolsheviks, soaking them and their rifles. Comrade Stark recognizes the sabotage as the anticipated distraction and charges furiously through the mess, screaming orders, pushing the barrel of his Nagant into every suspicious face, shooting into the air, shouting orders to stop the train, which keeps innocently trundling toward the horizon and Bokhara. Comrade Tsirul looks for Comrade Karišik, who is nowhere to be found. Meanwhile, at the other end of town, the Handsome Bosnian and his friend the Jewish Doctor ride out on the brichka, explaining to the checkpoint guards that Comrade Karišik's mistress has delivered a healthy boy (they all drink to it!) and needs urgent medical attention.

It is in the endnotes for this chapter that Moser-Ethering first uses the Handsome Bosnian's full name and speculates that in Sart language, and even in Tajik, his last name—Karishik—would mean something like mixed. The fact that the locals could interpret his name, see it as a mark of his character, and think of him as one of them—that they could read him, as it were—contributed considerably, in Moser-Ethering's opinion, to his already formidable connection with the native Mohammedan population.

Nearly a day behind already, Comrade Tsirul and his crew of liquidators gallop eastward in pursuit of the traitor. In Khodjent they run into a barricade set up by Comrade Shupskiy, convinced that Tsirul is finally coming for him and not willing to surrender without a fight. Comrade Tsirul cannot believe that this pitiful reactionary element and his ragtag band of turncoats dare confront him. A shootout ensues, wounding one of Tsirul's goons, which enrages him even more. Though there are fewer of them, Tsirul's henchmen are far more ruthless and adept at killing. It takes them a couple of hours, but they do dispose of Shupskiy and his hapless unit—Tsirul personally slits Shupskiy's throat, wipes his knife with his very bogatyrka.

In his book, Moser-Ethering recalls arriving at the safe house in Makhram and finding Klara Isakovna panting as if about to deliver, no doubt due to all the excitement she's gone through. He is uncomfortable around a pregnant woman and terrified by the possibility of her giving birth in his presence, but Eshan dismisses his concerns, telling him that females just naturally know what needs to be done and know how to do it—moreover, an experienced Kyrgyz woman will soon be on hand. Still, Moser-Ethering spends the night out on the porch, contemplating the sky, unable to sleep on account of all the maternal moans and grunts, all the womanly spectacle, exacerbated by the horrid black bugs (*Reduvius fedschenkianus*, he meticulously notes) plunging their long sharp beaks into his flesh all over his legs and arms. The following morning, he finds Klara Isakovna sleeping so peacefully that he considers the possibility of her being dead. He can no longer recognize her rotund face, her padded neck, her undone hair, her slight snore. It is as if the real Klara Isakovna is sheathed inside this new, pregnant woman's body and he now has no idea how to reach the actual Klara Isakovna. Submitting to an imp of the perverse, he sneaks up on her to touch her loaded belly, her swollen feet, to smell her hair. She wakes up abruptly, startling him, and goes on groaning. The Jewish Doctor can't arrive soon enough.

The Handsome Bosnian and the Jewish Doctor's brichka reaches Makhram in the afternoon, one of its wheels rattling, well on the verge of falling off (as in the opening of *Dead Souls*, Moser-Ethering remarks offhand). A Bolshevik posse is surely coming up behind them and is likely to reach them within a day. Moser-Ethering is ready to be on his way to the distant Kashgar, but Klara Isakovna's affliction needs to be dealt with first and urgently.

Major Moser-Ethering now regrets leaving the quiet apiary, or not staying higher up in the mountains, away from all this fuss and drama. Klara Isakovna keeps screaming, and the Kyrgyz woman keeps going in and out of the room, as the Major stands on the porch smoking in silence with Osman and Eshan. They hear a distant thunder, and they hope for a mountain storm that could slow down, or even wash away the Bolsheviks. He knows that if the Bolsheviks make it they are all likely to get killed, the unborn child included. He reads Osman's face: the terror of his listening to the unearthly screams, the weight of all the decisions to be made presently. It is high time for them to leave if they are to have any chance of getting away.

But they cannot go yet: the child is refusing to come out. The Kyrgyz woman tells Eshan the baby is upside down and stuck inside. Klara Isakovna bleeds profusely, her torment exacerbated by her fear that she might die away from her home, away from her father, among strangers. Pinto has never delivered a child; in fact, he has not seen a vagina since he dissected a female corpse as a student in Vienna; he has spent his medical career treating men in war, and many of them died. All he can do now is dab

Klara Isakovna's forehead, whisper hollow comforting words to her, and wait for something to resolve itself. The Kyrgyz woman is very helpful but she speaks no Russian, let alone German or some other European language; she is clearly unhappy about the presence of a man in the birth room, and an ignorant one at that, to whom she can only act out instructions and suggestions he has difficulty comprehending. She keeps miming to him that he should leave the hut and get out of her way. Tormented by a jealous itch ever since she started showing, he is even tempted to ask Klara Isakovna about who the father of the child is as she squeezes his hand in her body-destroying pain. He is terrified, ashamed of his helplessness, and feeling guilty for wanting to know.

He steps out into a thick silence suspended among Osman, Moser-Ethering, and Eshan, thereby dispelling it. Osman finally makes a decision: Moser-Ethering will take the brichka and head in the direction of Kashgar as fast as possible; Pinto will stay here with Klara Isakovna, and go into hiding when—if—the child comes out; Osman will go back to intercept or misdirect the Bolshevik posse. Pinto objects—he thinks that Osman needs to be here, because Klara Isakovna is not doing well. Osman understands the reason for Pinto's objection—he fears, as does Osman, that if they separate they may never find each other.

There is no other way, Osman says. You have to stay. I have to go. Tsirul and his men are heading this way. We cannot all run away. They have to be stopped, or we will all have to answer to the revolutionary court.

I want to go with you, Pinto says.

Who is going to take care of Klara Isakovna?

The Kyrgyz woman will take care of her, will hide her and the child.

You don't know how to ride a horse. You don't have a gun.

What does that matter? Two heads are better than one.

Not when both heads can be lost.

I want to go with you.

No. Everyone has a better chance this way. I'll come back here, or catch up with you later. It will be fine.

No, it won't.

I don't understand the language you two are speaking, Moser says, but I presume the argument is whether the doctor should stay here or go back. I say, he should stay here.

Why? Pinto asks.

The woman needs you, Moser says. And it is easier for one man to hide or escape. Also, Doctor, you would get shot immediately.

No, I won't! Pinto says, and realizes that he sounds like a petulant child. Osman has won the argument. With tears in his eyes, Pinto asks to ride with him for a little bit, just so they can spend more time together.

Eshan has procured an exhausted, piebald nag for Osman to ride back toward Khodjent, Pinto holds the reins for Osman to mount it, and he leaps on the nag most gracefully. The possibility of their never seeing each other again is far too enormous and obvious for Pinto to say anything—his throat is clogged with sorrow. But instead of riding away, Osman extends his hand to Pinto and pulls him up on the horse. Pinto sits in front of him, like a child, and would remember that smell of smoke, sweat, and horseshit for the rest of his life. They ride in silence until they're out of Moser's sight, whereupon Pinto slips off the horse and drops into the dust to weep. Osman dismounts to hold Pinto against his chest, and wipe the wet dust off his cheeks.

I will never see you again, Pinto says.

Yes, you will. I promise.

He kisses Pinto's mouth, and for a while they cannot part their lips. The sun is setting beyond the mountain peaks, and all the shadows at the foot of the mountain are paling and disappearing in the twilight. Pinto cannot imagine the outcomes already laid down in their future like rails. There is a weak hollowing pain in his stomach, as if he was starving. Woe is me! our forefather Adam said when he saw the day gradually diminishing. Perhaps it is because I acted offensively that the world around me is growing darker and darker, and is about to return to chaos and confusion, and this is the death Heaven has decreed for me.

I have to go, Osman says. I cannot linger here.

Gently, he tries to extricate himself from the embrace. Pinto's grasp is unbreakable.

No, Pinto says. You are not leaving.

I will always be with you, Osman says. Always.

When Pinto walks back into the hut, it stinks of blood and shit and mortal perspiration. Klara Isakovna has bled a lot, all of her strength seems to have gone. The Kyrgyz woman's look tells him that it might be over soon; her face is wet but it is probably the sweat. Somehow, suddenly, Pinto knows exactly what to do: he demands the Kyrgyz woman help him scour his hands with hot water; he endures the burn, and while his hands are still warm he puts them inside Klara Isakovna, one at a time, to flip the child and rip it out of her womb. In his mind's ear he hears Osman's voice: "Ljubim te."

It is a girl, floppy and blue.

Pinto hands her over to the Kyrgyz woman and cuts the umbilical cord. The Kyrgyz woman smacks the child's butt a few times as if angry at her for being difficult and late, until the baby gasps, lurches, and produces a lung-full cry. Pinto then sits, collapsed, in a blood puddle already congealing on the floor, one of its agile streams cutting a little canyon in the dirt. He watches the girl being wiped off to emerge from the cocoon of red slime, as the Kyrgyz woman speaks to her in the voice of someone giving orders. She unwraps her headscarf to wrap the child in it and give her back to Pinto. The child is ugly, but has all the parts; when she opens her eyes for an instant, it is clear she cannot see him. She is very light, yet he can feel the warmth of her being alive emanating through the scarf. The Kyrgyz woman stuffs Klara Isakovna's groin with rags to stop the bleeding, and then pours fenugreek tea down her throat. The Kyrgyz woman's hair has streaks of grayness that reflect light so that it looks like there is an aura around her head.

Pinto sits amid the blood, considers the child, who is now asleep, its little lips now moving as if sucking. Her eyebrows are thin, her hair is dark and pasted to the skull. He has never before beheld such a small, soft child. He doesn't know what to say to her, so he sings, Nočes, nočes, buenas nočes, nočes son d'enamorar, ah, nočes son d'enamorar. He knows that the protocol requires that he kiss her forehead, so he does. She tastes like chicken liver. Was it you who made shade for my daughter? Klara Isakovna had decided that if she had a girl, her name would be Rahela. A boy would've been called Benya. He shows the girl to Klara Isakovna, who smiles with great effort, then closes her eyes.

In Freedom, Moser-Ethering lays out his subsequent escape. He bids goodbye and speeds in the brichka through the Ferghana Valley until the hastily reinforced wheel falls off. He is lost in a wild apple forest, gets covered with thorn scratches, eats the fruit off a tree, and considers the possibility that the Edenic apple Eve had picked was a wild one too, and therefore terribly sour—she might not even have enjoyed it at all, and here we all are now. He is sheltered by a Kyrgyz family, and is at one point lowered into a well, whence he watches celestial constellations enter and leave the circle above him, as hysterical nightingales rave all night long, forcing him to recall Keats (My heart aches, and a drowsy numbness pains / My sense, as though of hemlock I had drunk . . .), whom he now detests unconditionally. He scoffs at a story he hears from the Kyrgyz about Ak Khanum, the White Lady who flew planes around the Bolshevik positions, inflicting terrible losses upon the Reds. He gets caught in a freak mountain snowstorm (it is September), and when he wakes up he sees the plan of a city outlined in the snow by the wind, the whole streets, squares, house foundations, irrigation canals, black lines against white background, like a photo negative. He reaches the Irkeshtam Pass and gets through it at night. A few weeks after leaving Makhram, he safely reaches Kashgar. He will never return to Turkestan, except in his memory and writing, decades later. In his book, he does not bother to guess what might have happened to Osman, whose gratuitous courage he admires in passing, let alone to Klara Isakovna or the Jewish Doctor. His friend Charlie is no longer in Kashgar; in fact, there are no Europeans there, other than a few desperate Russians lingering, as it were, in the narrow space between two terrible centuries, including the wife of the Russian Consul-General, who has by now perished in vodka. At the end of the chapter, the wife has nothing but contempt for Sparky, so deep and obvious that it seems to have festered for years. In the last paragraph, he suddenly provides her name—Amalya Antonovna—but only to tell us that she died of self-inflicted wounds on the eve of his departure.

It was only some days later that Pinto could thoroughly comprehend the magnitude of the fact that Osman rode away and never came back, and, even if he did, would not be able to find him. At the time, Pinto was hidden in an alcove behind a mud wall that a Sart named Devlet and his son had built to conceal his presence. He recognized, with his entire body, that Osman might be absent from the world for good and that Pinto was more alone than he would be if he had been dead. He would have to get accustomed to Osman's absence, and the day he did, he would die. And then he cried for Klara Isakovna, who would never see Paris, or her daughter, who would never see her mother. Weep for the soul that cannot go home and not for the mourners hiding in a wall. The only source of air behind the wall was a hole close to the ceiling, through which the thinnest ray of light reached to cut an edge in the darkness.

He had no idea what might be happening on the other side of the wall, and, slowly, he slipped into a kind of fugue where there was nothing but his own breath and the crepitation of the drying mud in the wall. He understood that the darkness within which he was crouching was nothing else but la gran eskuridad. He spread his light like a candle, and then he was out like a candle. Where did he go? So strange, where did he go without me? His voice was gone. All of him was gone. Klara Isakovna's last exhalation was a weak hiss not followed by a breath. Pinto sat at her side, holding her hand, waiting to hear the sound of her next breath. But there was nothing; everything in the room, including the fire, went soundless. Because the sound of the soul leaving the body is silence.

Neither life nor death ask you if you're ready for what is next, Manuči used to say. Pinto and the child had traveled to Devlet's house on a cart, concealed inside a bale of hay, which made Pinto sneeze and Rahela wail. He consoled the child by humming a romansa Manuči used to sing: Ah ke ermoza kantika, ma la kero ambezar. Yasaman, Devlet's young wife, took Rahela into her arms to nurse as though she were her own child. Before the day was out, Pinto heard from behind the wall the enraged Bolsheviks ransacking Devlet's house, slapping Yasaman, as her daughter and Rahela screamed in unison; he was relieved to hear the screams and know that Rahela was alive. The Bolsheviks beat Devlet to a pulp, broke his arm and cheekbone. Yasaman eventually took the wall down and released Pinto, who after two days stank of sweat, urine, and feces, of hunger and despair. The first thing he saw, once he was no longer blinded by the light, were Yasaman's tears. He could speak no Tajik, but he understood that he had to leave as soon as possible, and that he should leave the child with Devlet and Yasaman. But after he washed up and ate some pilaf, Yasaman placed the sleeping child in his arms, and he held her like a lute, watching her lips purse to suck on an absent nipple, and it was then that he saw her cheeks and thick black hair. He understood that Rahela was Osman's child, and she thus became his daughter. Neither Klara Isakovna nor Osman had said anything about who her father might be, nor could he imagine a way or a time for Osman to have lain down with Klara. Yet in Rahela's narrow, hungry face he recognized Osman's: his kindness, his grimaces, his cheeks, his smile—the simultaneous uplifting of the corners, the wrinkling of the nose ridge. In his previous life, he would've been jealous; he would've been furious at Osman's betrayal, at his sleeping next to him, pretending to love him, after he fucked a woman. Now, Osman was with him as long as Rahela was with him. The Lord creates and destroys worlds, and those that preceded this one were like sparks that scatter and die away when the blacksmith strikes the iron with hammer.

Yasaman sat down next to him to nurse her daughter, who was older and already saying her first words, as if to show him how to love a child. She spoke to Pinto in Tajik, in a low, maternal voice, explaining something he could not begin to understand, until she put her daughter down on a sheep skin, bared her other breast, and grabbed Rahela from his arms to nurse her. Rahela sucked eagerly, committed to being in the world. Osman liked to declare, with that nod of his, that everything that lived wanted to keep living, and Pinto now knew it was his duty to take care of Rahela and make sure she kept living. And if Osman was still alive, Pinto was sure he would come looking for his daughter wherever they may be; he would not give up; he would come to retrieve the love that would be saved up in this child. The following night he dreamed Osman saying to him: "Thank you for making shade for my daughter."

A few days later he strapped the child to his back, and walked toward Kashgar. Yasaman had given him some sheep milk, some hardened mutton strips, and a farewell in the form of a song; she cried when kissing Rahela's forehead, but did not try to keep her by her side. Pinto never reached Kashgar, and never found out what happened to Devlet and Yasaman. Those who are kind to their fellow men are said to be paying their respects to His presence. Perhaps the Lord took care of them, or perhaps not.

* * *

On their way to Makhram, Osman had told him a story about the water horses that lived in those mountains. People said they looked strange: very fat, yellowish-green, and perfectly hairless. They were shy too, and dove into the water to hide as soon as they caught sight of a man. Perhaps, Osman had said, we shall be so lucky as to see one. Pinto had been too worried and scared to think about water horses and had asked Osman to shut up for once, which he had. For a long time, they had ridden not talking to each other, and now, hiding in a wall, everything in Pinto wanted to find a path of reasoning that would allow the possibility of Osman somehow returning, even if the Bolsheviks imprisoned him again. You cannot fathom my rules. But he would run into the indelibility of silence and he knew that Osman was gone. It must have been that it was after he had heard Osman say "Ljubim te!" to him that he had left this world; it must be those were his last words. He wanted to return to those hours of reticence on the brichka and spend them talking to the man he loved, even about water horses, but time flew only forward, leaving devastation in its wake. In the course of the endless hours behind the wall, Pinto's body was awash in ache, and he would drift into the visions of cutting his chest open with a scalpel to let it all out, to empty himself of everything inside, after which all that would be left in him was what was left of Osman. Even if the rings slip off, there are still the fingers.

PART III

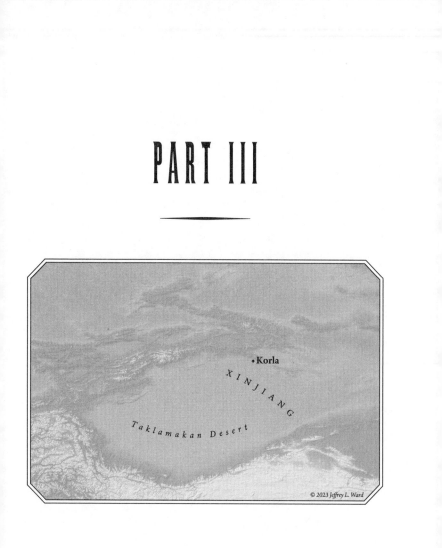

Korla

XINJIANG

Taklamakan Desert

© 2023 Jeffrey L. Ward

KORLA, 1922

PINTO'S STOMACH GROWLED. The wind is strong but the body withstands it. It was incredible that his body was still alive and demanding. The body is strong, and fear crushes it. Hunger too, and exhaustion and hopelessness, but it takes a long time, a lot of suffering. He couldn't start a fire, because there was no kindling to start it with, and all the wood had already been scavenged by other refugees, and the smoke would reveal their hiding place, and there was nothing to cook, and it was too hot anyway. The fire of a sick man is from Heaven—who could extinguish that? Nothing could extinguish that. The sun was scorching whatever was exposed to it, except for a patch of grass that managed to grow in the shade of one of the ruined walls where Rahela was presently asleep curled on her side, her back to the foot of the wall, her hand against her cheek to protect her from the rocks and dirt in the grass. Where did this grass get the water to grow? As a man makes a hedge for his vineyard, so He made the sand into a hedge for the sea. But where is the sea? It's all dirt, as far as can be seen. The grass was dry, the sandy soil beneath was baked into hardness and there was no way Rahela could be comfortable. Yet she slept in blessed oblivion, her lips pursed and throbbing barely perceptibly, as if she were dreaming of suckling. Now that I lie still, I am quiet; when I sleep, I am at rest. The child has not slept in a bed since she came into the world. Most of the time, she slept on his chest. She was born a refugee, never knew what being at home meant. She was tiny, a handful of skin and bones, her limbs like twigs, her eyes so large because her face was so narrow and small. It was amazing that she was alive at all. Nasrudin Hodža had taught his donkey to live without eating, and just as it learned, it died. She was learning how to live without food, and she was getting good at it.

Pinto sat down next to Rahela and leaned against the wall ruin; he put his hand on her naked calf; her skin was dry; weak as he was, he could have broken her leg with one hand. The night was created for no other purpose than to sleep. But the night turned out to be endless, la gran eskuridad lasted for days and years, only the amount of darkness changed. One day, if we live through this, I will sit alone in a fully lit room, untouched by death, lamps and candles everywhere, and just be. Here I am, I will say, to no one other than to Rahela and Osman. He will speak to me, tell me stories for hours on end, tell me what happened to him, promise me we will never be separated again. When I find him in Sarajevo, I will give him a handkerchief.

Osman sat down next to Pinto, leaned against the wall, and wiped his forehead and face with a handkerchief. His touch was as light as breath. If it wasn't for her, Pinto said, I would just quit living, just let myself die. I would just close the shop, turn off the light, say good night, and die, right here and now. He placed his head on Osman's chest. Soon enough there will come days, both long and short, when we will all have plenty of sleep.

"She looks beautiful when she's asleep," Osman said.

You look beautiful when you're asleep. She is your daughter.

"She is Klara's daughter."

Klara is dead.

"We all are," Osman said. "Rahela has been dead for days."

Pinto snapped out of his slumber so forcefully he slammed his pate against the wall, and a little avalanche of sandstone fell between his neck and filthy collar. His hand was still on Rahela's calf, and he dared not move it until he saw her chest quiver as she took a sob of air in.

"You must wake her up and hide," Osman said. "They're almost here."

Who is almost here? Pinto asked. What are you saying? Where should we hide?

A couple of Uighur men, in baggy pants and furry hats, with rifles in hand, raced past not even glancing at Pinto and Rahela. The men stopped to rise on their toes and peek over the wall, then ducked quickly, said something alarming to each other, and continued to run. Pinto climbed the wall, crumbling again, to see what they were looking at.

From afar the horsemen looked slow and tired, as if riding forth only because there was nothing else to do. Behind them the desiccated field flickered in heat, like a shimmering lake. There were a few dozen Cossacks on horses, and, in their wake, a herd of red-coated monks on foot rattling their bells, chanting half-heartedly, flags and banners fluttering above their heads. Gradually, the chants became stronger and clearer, as if they smelled more blood, and now the bells were screeching, and the horsemen straightened up, everything accelerated, and a cloud of dust suddenly rose, not only behind them, but before them too, as if they were pushing the wind ahead of themselves like a battering ram. They charged, and the Uighurs shot in their direction, which did nothing to slow the attack down, except that it woke Rahela. Peering over the mud wall, Pinto watched the galloping cloud of dust as if it were another dream that would not dissipate. Whereupon he picked up Rahela and ran. His felt boots were in tatters and one of them came apart, so he tottered and fell, twisting his body on the way down to fall on his back and shield Rahela from hitting the ground.

The Uighurs' desperate shots rang again. The thunder of the charge advanced undiminished, and now Pinto heard the shrieking of the horsemen too. He did not know where to go, just rushed forth clutching Rahela, the palm of his hand against her stick spine. He pressed her face into the curve of his neck, as if that could somehow protect her from the bullets. She whimpered, and he said, No tengas pinsar. Todo bueno.

The townspeople had hidden already, but Pinto saw a woman running, a refugee from the same caravan they came to Korla with; her headscarf unfurled and it now fluttered behind her like a banner. A dog with ribs clearly outlined under the mangy skin ran after her. Pur aki, pur aki! Rahela said, as if she knew where they needed to go, as if she knew this town. She didn't seem to be afraid, even if she must have understood they were in danger; she could always sense his fear and sorrow. She smelled of child sweat, her strawlike hair tasted like dust. Padri, she said, and tightened her grip. They turned off into a short and narrow street, and then into an even narrower one that became a dead end. The horsemen's roar and gallop were now inside the town, and everywhere there were screams, gunshots, shashka slashes. Pinto stopped before a wall and put his hand on it—it was warm—as if it could open upon his touch. What could he tell her? He didn't know what he was doing. There was a door to the right, so he opened it and entered the house, which was not a house but an empty room with scattered pieces of wood and a single small window glaring in the dark. It took him a moment to see a door at the other end, and he rushed to open it. The door was heavy and stuck on its hinges so he had to push it hard, with Rahela in his arms, before they stepped into a darker room, with an even smaller window that cast a beam of light before him, like a path to follow in a fairy tale. He heard the distant sounds of running, the boots on the dirt, a single shot, dogs barking and yelping. Somewhere near, a woman screamed, and then kept screaming, until her screams abruptly ended.

The room was a workshop. There was a row of upright barrels against the wall. On the workbench there were staves, barrel rings, a mallet, a pointed horn. Pinto grabbed the mallet, then changed his mind to take the horn, cutting his finger with the sharp edge of its root. The barrels had lids, but none was big enough for both of them. He could think of nothing else to do but to lower Rahela into the one farther from the door, as if that would make a difference. Silensijo, Pinto said. He placed the lid on the top of the barrel, then had to climb onto Rahela's barrel to get into his, and nearly toppled it over. He lowered himself into it, bending the knees to fit. Silensijo, he repeated, and placed the lid above himself so that it touched the crown of his head. Silensijo, he said once again, as if there could be a way Rahela would stay silent. The barrels stank of curdled milk and wood. He was grasping the horn like a rattle he could not let go of; its point was sharp too. "What is that thing?" Osman asked. The horn was a carpentry tool for scraping wood—Sinjor Papučo used to have one and pretend to the kids' delight it was a trompeta. It was all meaningless now, nothing could protect them from the Cossacks, or from anything or anyone who aimed to kill them. Just as he learned to live without dying, he died. The killing din was muffled now, but Pinto could sense that blood was soaking the town's streets and walls. War has a smell and sound, and everything and everyone is charged with it, your neck hair bristles, and there is less air, and what is left of it smells like blood and mortal sweat, and your fear is pain in your body, present, but not, like a memory of a previous life. The horn poked against his ribs, and slowly a point of pain emerged in his chest, and the pain became stronger until it felt as if it was entering and hurting someone else's body. Rahela was silent, but her silence now worried Pinto and he was about to call her, when the door creaked and he heard footsteps from the other room.

A century or so ago, the taking of Korla by Baron Teutenberg was a fabled massacre, but since then there has been so much killing all over the world it is barely remembered now. An odd sentence in an odd forgotten memoir (not least one of those written by Moser-Ethering), or a short chapter in a history book about the Russian civil war ripples in the territories beyond the Motherland, might mention Baron Teutenberg and his feared Asian Division. But even a nearly fictionalized account of the heroically roaming desert bandits would gloss over the inevitable waning of their savage notoriety, the last desperate days when the residues of the Baron's once indomitable Division disintegrated in a manner that exactly matched the steady dissolution of the Baron's mind.

Before they burnt and plundered Korla, the Baron's wild bunch had dragged themselves through the desert and dry wilderness for weeks, short on water, food, and sanity, tired of living off an alien, adverse landscape. Baron Teutenberg had decided that the Division should be heading to Tibet, thousands of miles away across the Taklamakan Desert, over the nameless, endless mountains. In Tibet, the Baron imagined, they would recuperate in the spiritual heights, get the blessing of the Dalai Lama, recruit more warrior monks, and return to waging war until the final victory. No one but the Baron, Andryonov the Yurodivy, and the monks, clad in their red deels with yellow epaulettes bearing the swastikas of Genghis Khan and the initials of the Living Buddha, had any desire to see Tibet, let alone perish on the way there, but few dared utter a word about it. When one Captain Smailov ventured to object, the Baron had him hanged by his wrists off a tree and beat him with a bamboo stick until the flesh on his thighs separated from his bones. The Yurodivy then disemboweled him for everyone to see what happens to those insufficiently committed to winning the war for the soul and the world. So that when the Division reached Korla, all the bottled-up murderousness erupted as the Cossacks punished for their own hopelessness whoever was in their way. They shot and slashed, ransacked homes and killed entire families, raping to catch a breath from the slaughter. A monk named Chinua had a penchant for boys but was not too picky to chase down any child he could find. Andryonov the Yurodivy was soaked in blood before noon, found time to change his clothes, and was soaked in blood again by two o'clock. The market was turned into a bonfire, and the monks threw into it all the unneeded worldly goods and all the creatures they could: people, corpses, meaningless money, tea, fur, animals, furniture, their own blood brothers unlucky enough to be wounded and unable to march on. Baron Teutenberg, his soul perpetually possessed, his eyes sparkling with passion, loomed over the fire on a white horse, like the Buddhist divinity the monks believed he had reincarnated. Hell, it was said, was the only place he could ever call home.

Inside the barrel, Pinto dared not breathe. When evildoers came upon me to eat up my flesh they stumbled and fell, even mine adversaries and my foes. One thing or another, my heart shall not fear; though war should rise up against me, even then shall I be confident. The merciful Lord would save us by providing peace to Rahela so that she wouldn't speak, cry, or make a sound. The footsteps now entered the workshop. Pinto begged the Lord to help them die quickly, without torture and rape, but the Lord said nothing, nor did He offer any comforting signs. "You might have to kill if you don't want to die," Osman said. Whoever entered the workshop was now rummaging and throwing things around, humming and groaning all along, as if shitting. "You will no longer be a melek if you kill," Osman said. "But you will still be righteous." Something smacked against Rahela's barrel and she yelped, and for an instant there was no other sound, no humming or groaning, and then the shuffling of the boots and the crunching of the dirt, and the man was now next to the barrels, Pinto heard him panting, then a knock on the other barrel with the blade of his shashka, the fullness of the sound, and the lifting of the lid.

Pinto pushed his way out of the barrel like a jack-in-the-box, screamed, and startled the man, who made a short step back and stood for a blink as if paralyzed, whereupon Pinto stabbed him with the horn in the eye before his next blink, tipping the barrel over. The Cossack screamed and grabbed the horn to pull it out of his eye; blood was spurting while he slashed blindly, hitting Rahela's barrel as Pinto rolled away in his, still in it up to his waist. He managed to wriggle out of it and snatch the stave mallet. Like a cat, he leaped toward the Cossack and imparted a ferocious blow. The mallet sank into the Cossack's forehead as if it were dough, and he grunted, surprised by his own death; he fell on his knees, down on his face; the tip of his left boot scraped the dirt floor as he twitched, until it finally stopped. Pinto stood above him, ready for another blow, but the Cossack made a sound as if gasping, followed by nothing. Only then did Pinto inhale some air, but just to pant and cough. A puddle of blood bloomed around the Cossack's head. His left boot had an eye-shaped hole in its sole. He did not wear socks, and had a raw sore on his foot. For a year, the body and its wounds and sores remain in existence while the soul ascends and descends. Then the body ceases to exist and the soul is gone forever. Why we live in this world, I'll never know, a foolish thing to do.

Pinto pulled Rahela out of the barrel; she gasped in shock and confusion. Todo bueno, he said. He held her in his arms, stroking her matted hair to console her; she was crying, scared. On his forearm he felt the warmth of her felt pants soaked with pee. When she saw the dead Cossack and yelped in fear, Pinto turned her to face a different direction, which meant he was the one now looking at the dead Cossack. The blood puddle was expanding toward Pinto, and the Cossack's eyes were now fully dimmed, his forehead grotesquely dented, the eyebrow above the destroyed eye vanished in blood. Pinto's heart was thundering, and he was weak-headed. He retched, but instead of vomiting he felt compelled to spit. And spit he did and his saliva dropped into the blood puddle, which rippled. I killed a man, Pinto thought. "You killed a man," Osman said. "Not an easy thing to do. Not an easy thing to live with. But you had no choice." I've stabbed a man in the eye and killed him. Rahela said something he could not understand, pointing at the window. Flame tongues were leaping toward it as the next house was on fire. The pane cracked, and the fire reached in. "Go!" Osman said. "Run!"

Baron Teutenberg was heir to a destitute and noble Estonian German-speaking family, whose generations loyally served the Russian Czar, had a knout named after them, and were known to have kept wolves in their house's attic. The Baron fought the Bolsheviks in southern Siberia, even after the White armies capitulated; his fearsome Division escaped to Mongolia, where he attacked and slaughtered the Chinese and restored the Bogd Khan to his rightful throne. Before and after the battles and skirmishes, he would berate the depravation of morals and the absolute licentiousness, intellectual and physical, that now prevailed in all of Russia and the world. Truth and honor are no longer admissible, he'd scream, the saber-slash scar on his forehead ablaze. Henceforth truth can be achieved only by merciless hardness. The evil that had fallen upon the land and was destroying the divine principle in the human soul must be extirpated root and branch. Our fury against the Jewish heads of the revolution, its devoted followers, must know no boundaries! Aroused as they were by his invectives, the Division's response failed to match his counterrevolutionary passion, as they had little idea what he was talking about, and were long exhausted by war. But the monks saw the Baron as the White warrior Buddha, reincarnated to exterminate the infidels and steel the faith. The lucky people who escaped the Division and joined the caravan of refugees told stories, all of which led to the same conclusion—it was

better to die than to be captured by the Baron's men. His standing order was that every man in a village under attack be killed
unless he joined his spiritual army; the women were raped before
being cut down, because they could not be taken along. Children
were tortured and destroyed so as to be given a chance to rein-
carnate as better beings in a better world. The Baron handed out
sweets to them, just before Andryonov the Yurodivy, his faithful
deputy, would do to them what he liked to do to terrified children. The Baron smoked opium to unwind after combat; in his
visions he was the new, greater Genghis Khan, marching triumphantly into the torched Moscow to cleanse its defiled streets
and palaces with the blood of Jews and the brains of commissars
and their families. He would summon Djambolon, his fortune-
telling monk, to divine what was ahead from the cracks in sheep
shoulder bones burnt in a bonfire. At least once, Baron Teutenberg's future was augured from a cracked human scapula. It did
not look bright, the future.

It began unraveling when Djambolon, reading chicken bones
while hungover, divined that the Bolshevik expeditionary force
could be defeated if the Division attacked it first. It was obvious
to all but the Baron and Djambolon that that would be suicide,
so an epidemic of desertion ensued, which could not be stopped
even with the most spectacular executions. A few of his officers
decided that murdering the Baron would increase everyone's
chance of survival. He escaped their assassination attempt and
ran off into the darkness on his white horse without a single fol-
lower. Still, those who had betrayed the Baron were more terrified of him than of the Bolsheviks and scattered in different
directions. No one knows how many escaped the Bolshevik
encirclement and subsequent slaughter, but we know that the
Baron eventually found himself in the center of a star of pointed

Bolshevik rifles, swinging at them with his shashka. When his saber shattered, he reached for an ampoule of poison that had always been attached to a button of his robe, but it had disappeared. The Bolsheviks, who knew the stories of the mad Baron and had waded through the aftermath of his monstrosities, would've preferred to rip him apart with their bullets, but the order from high above was to take him alive. The unnamed Soviet witness claims that he begged for mercy facing the firing squad, but that is probably just a propagandistic lie.

In the White versions of the Baron's end, however, he was executed as soon as he was captured, because the Reds just feared him too much; he refused to sing the first verses of "The Internationale" and thus save his own life. Moser-Ethering, in one of his many memoirs (*Flight to Shanghai*), claimed that the Baron had broken out of prison, reformed the Division as a gang of Cossacks and monks, and indeed ended up in Tibet, where he would die of the smallpox that decimated the monks who sheltered him.

Baron Teutenberg, sitting on an exhausted, sick white mare that hung her head as if about to be shot, did not appear divine or imperial to Pinto, but was no less terrifying for that. He was a scrawny, ragged, droopy man; the scar on his forehead was shaped like a minaret; his beard was wispy and auburn, his teeth yellow and rotten; he resembled a mangy goat. His faded blue eyes belonged to someone who had killed so much he grew bored with it but could imagine doing nothing else. He had a shashka on his hip and a gun at his very loose belt; the soles of his boots were shredded, and the rest, reaching his knees, were thickly coated in dirt. He wore a shabby yellow-red deel that might have been splendorous once, but was now encrusted with dried blood, gashed and ripped at the chest, where talismans and charms hung entangled on a bright yellow cord. A demon changes into many colors.

Holding Rahela's hand, Pinto stood before him numb with terror. He did not dare look in the Baron's direction. Rahela was staring at the Baron's entourage, the fierce Cossacks with their ammo belts and knives and guns, at the monks and their orange robes. Off to the side of them, there was a man leaning on a staff who looked like a straggler, his face sunken behind a thick reddish beard. Pinto didn't know if Moser had reached Kashgar or gone beyond it, but for a moment, he thought he recognized Moser's eyes. But the man looked away and downward when Pinto's gaze reached his eyes. Each and every one of us has a thousand demons at his left, and ten thousand demons at his right. What are we to do with those demons? The sun was high and relentless, burning everything exposed to it, including Rahela's face, so Pinto tried to make shade for her with his hand. The Baron smiled at them as if struck by a wistful memory, then slipped off the horse, which snorted, relieved. Demons don't have a shadow, only the shadow of a shadow. He knelt before Rahela, who turned away to hug Pinto's thigh. The Baron grabbed her hand and pulled her to face him, then gently removed a curl from her forehead. Ne boj se, Pinto told her under breath, but she did not hear him, or didn't dare to hear him, or didn't even understand what he said. She shivered as the Baron unfolded her hand and squeezed it in his.

You are so sweet! the Baron said in German, so strangely accented it sounded like a speech impediment. Have you seen what happened today? Did you learn something? Life, death, life, death, round and round. Very nice. This is the truth. People want to live, but they are fools. Life is death, death is life, round and round. It is a problem only if you are afraid. Are you afraid, little girl? What are you afraid of?

Rahela said nothing. She is afraid, Pinto said, but the Baron ignored him, still talking to Rahela.

People think that God should love them. But why bother with a loving god? A weak god loves. A strong god kills, destroys and remakes. It is the might that matters. Take Palden Llamo. Palden Llamo sacrificed her own children. She bore a crown of five skulls and a necklace of severed heads, snakes wound through her hair. She rode upon a lake of entrails and blood, clutching a cup made from the skull of a child born from incest, her thunderbolt staff ready to smash the unbelievers, her teeth gnawing on a corpse. Her horse's saddle was made from the flayed skin of her own child, who had become an enemy of the faith. Have you ever heard of her, little girl? I could teach you so much.

Rahela looked up at Pinto, as if asking what the Baron was saying, but Pinto's dry throat was now fully choked with fear. The Baron's entourage, stony men in weary uniforms high on their horses; the monks' orange robes splashed with blood, all bemused by the presence of an unkilled child, all watched the Baron kneeling in front of Pinto and Rahela.

I could tell you so many wonderful stories about all the other amazing divinities, the Baron said. About the fat, fiery Begtse, with his goatskin cloak, high boots, drawn bow, and garland of fifty freshly severed heads; or about Pehar, a god who rode wolves, bears, and elephants to battle. And then there was the Red Horseman, who trampled and speared the enemies of the faith. Or Mahakala, a tame demon who carried a cleaver to chop up those who strayed from the righteous way, and a skull bowl to mix their remains. Would you like to hear those stories?

Sie spricht kein Deutsch, Pinto said. I am about to die a horrible death, but I pray to you, Lord, that I die before the child.

The Baron stood up and stared directly into Pinto's burnished, dark face. Bist du ein Jude? Pinto could see the Baron's teeth, his asymmetrical incisors; he smelled his putrid breath. Nein, he said. The Baron touched Pinto's nose and pushed it up as if to look inside his nostrils. His hand smelled of urine and shit.

Mir sieht das wie eine jüdische Nase aus.

Nein, Pinto said. Ich bin ein Bosniak.

Ich kann einen Jude riechen, the Baron said.

Gut, Pinto said, aber ich bin kein Jude.

What gods do you worship then? The Baron slipped into Russian.

Ich bin ein Muslim, Pinto said. Ich verehre den Gott des Friedens.

Is that so? A Muslim who worships the God of peace? Well, your god is a stupid god. My god will destroy your god, because mine made war. To refuse war means to refuse divine epic life, to refuse a way to any eternity. Life is the result of war. So there.

Wir gehören Gott, Pinto said, und zu ihm werden wir zurückkehren.

Well, I am eager to speed up the return to your God for you, Baron Teutenberg said. My monks don't like your Muslim lot one bit.

The Baron grabbed Rahela's hand and ripped her away from Pinto, who reached for her as she screamed and then a gun smashed into his temple and he was out.

The rag smelled of plum brandy and was burning Pinto's temple. Osman took a sip from the bottle with the brandy, then soaked the rag again and cleaned Pinto's face with it until the rag was pink.

Is Rahela all right? Pinto asked.

"She will be," Osman said. "She's only a year and a half old, so she will forget all of this."

If she lives, Pinto said.

"She will live."

Am I going to live?

"It is not your time to go yet," Osman said. "And your daughter . . ."

Our daughter.

"And our daughter needs you still."

Needs me for what? What is the next thing?

"The next thing, as always, is staying alive."

When am I going to see you?

"You see me now."

Are you in Sarajevo?

"No. I am here."

Here? Where am I?

"You are here too."

When will I be able to touch you?

"Not in this world."

When am I going to die?

"Who can know such a thing? You'll die when it's time and you'll know it's time when it comes."

When he came to, Pinto was hanging on a rope tied to his wrists. Šalom, gran eskuridad. Terrible pain stretched along the length of his body, flashed against his forehead, though he could not open his left eye. It took him a few moments to comprehend that he was strung up high in a tree. His shoulders hurt, the skin was scraped off his wrists, and the rope was cutting into his bone now. Why didn't they just hang him, or plain kill him? It turned out he was wheezing and moaning, though there were lumps of something in his lungs and throat so it was possible he was not breathing at all. He was going to hang here until birds pecked his eyes out, and his arms were ripped out of his shoulders, and rotten flesh fell off his bones. Once his right eye adjusted, he could discern an entanglement of branches, and the moon like a ducat in the sky, and the dusting of stars above. Terror tore through him when he realized that Rahela was not with him, and then relief that she was not hanging next to him. It was obvious he was going to die, just as it was dark because it was night. Panic emerged in his stomach like the tip of a sword, made him turn and swing in an attempt to reach a branch, but he failed and was now twirling in the dark, like a skinned animal carcass. Oh Rahela! What would they do to her? He dared not imagine, he dared not even begin to imagine, what those monsters could do to a child. He closed his unclosed eye to block the images coming to him, he did not want to envision the horror, but there was no way to ward off the visions, and they were inextricable from the pain that was his body. God, full of mercy, who dwells in the heights, provide a sure rest, within the range of the holy, pure and glorious, its shining resembles the stars in the sky, to the untainted soul of my child. Protect her, the Master of Mercy, from behind the hiding of your wings, and tie her soul with the thread of life. Amen! They liked to torture because they wanted you to want to die while thinking that death was salvation. He swung again and the leaves rattled, and he wanted to keep swinging until he ripped his arms out of his shoulder sockets and fell off, or until he reached a branch with his feet. The pain was making him scream but he couldn't hear himself scream. Just as the branch the rope was tied to was beginning to crack, he heard shots somewhere near and shouting and orders in Russian, then more gunfire, cries, and horses galloping. God, full of mercy, come on, kill me, or save me. I cannot fathom your rules.

The tree shook, and shook again, and the rhythm of the shaking made Pinto understand that a shadow was climbing toward him. The tree could snap and topple over, or the branch could finally give way. Pinto didn't know what tree he was hanging from; he might die in the next instant, but he didn't know the name of this tree. He didn't know the names of any of those stars. Osman? Is that you? The shadow was now a body, and the body had a hand, and the hand had a knife and the knife cut the rope, and Pinto broke through the bottom of the tree crown and crashed with a groan to the ground.

The conspirators' plan was to kill the Baron and the Yurodivy at the same time. The sleeping Andryonov was shot in the head without problems, but Major Hopak hesitated long enough for the Baron to be awoken by the noise and slash Hopak's forearm with the shashka he always slept with, and then he slit his throat. He hopped on his white mare and galloped into the night as his former brothers-in-arms shot after him, not daring to pursue him. They feared he would find a way to come back, and were so overwhelmed with dread that they hopped on their horses and rode into the night every which way they could, figuring, without ever talking, that each of them would be harder to track down if alone. The monks raided what the horsemen left behind, and were gone by the morning, in search of another prophet warlord they could leech off. None of them knew that the Baron's thigh was shattered by one of those blind bullets, and that he rode straight east until he lost enough blood to fall off his white mare, which went on alone, shining in the night like a moonlit ghost.

When Pinto opened his eye again, the first thing he saw was the orange horizon burning through charcoal clouds. Then Rahela's face was looming over him: her cheeks were sunken and filthy but still glowed in the sunrise; there was a bruise under her left eye; her lips were chapped and gray with dryness; he could see her chin, small and pointy, and her scrawny neck. Padri, Rahela said, and showed him a pear, eager to share the news. Perhaps Pinto was dead and was now wherever people and children went when they died before living again. Perhaps Osman is here too. Pinto's back and hips hurt and when he tried to sit up he couldn't move his right leg or push himself up off the ground as his arms would not obey. Rahela was holding someone's hand. Osman? Pinto followed the arm up to the shoulder and the face bearded so thickly it took him a while to recognize it was Moser.

Your leg is broken, Moser said. Your shoulders are dislocated too. Tough night.

Padri, Rahela said again.

Would you like some tea? Moser asked. I would have to pour it down your throat, if you don't mind. And I'll give you a bit of morphine too to help with your pain.

TAKLAMAKAN DESERT, 1926

THEY MADE PINTO get at the head of the column to walk grabbing on to a camel's tail, while an Uighur woman named Arzu walked behind holding Rahela's hand, helping her stay up and not slip in the sand. The camel had been fed and watered in Jiuquan, so the beast farted with enthusiasm. Ahead and behind Pinto and the camel, people who had no shared language marched together, somehow deciding, without discussing, what direction to take, as if they were sharing a mind, like a school of fish. The Lord said: Let us go down and confound their speech, but people here found a way to get around His plan.

Pinto's boots were shredded, his feet had by now developed blisters and sores. He kept turning back every few steps to see if Arzu and Rahela were still there. There were no children in the tired refugee procession, and several women shared their food and water with the child, until their provisions diminished. He could not see much of Arzu's covered face, but the ease in her movement, her girlish voice, her smiling eyes, suggested she was still very young, probably not more than seventeen. When they paused to take some rest, Arzu would teach Rahela Uighur words: su, ata, apa; if Rahela repeated a word back to her, Arzu would give her a date, until she ran out of them. Pinto learned a few words himself just listening to Arzu and Rahela: tega, keche, qum. He would offer Arzu a sip of water from his waterskin, and say, Su. Arzu would bow her head in gratitude. One moonlit night, she lay on the other side of Rahela to buffer her against the cold desert, and sang plaintive songs that did not sound like lullabies but more like spurned-lover ballads or mourning songs. Rahela would wail along, trying to sing in the language she could not speak. He had sung some of the Manuči songs to her, and would choke up and tell her it was his dry throat.

After Padri Avram died, Manuči, her sisters, and their righteous husbands, descended upon Rafo, still fresh from Vienna, to get him properly married. What was he going to do? Pinjo the matchmaker was talked to and as soon as the long Šelošim was over il kuniser—a meeting—was arranged. Her name was Luna Kamhi, she lived in Logavina, she was eighteen and very shy. She kept looking at the tips of her toes before she sat down at the table to stare, without eating, at the tabaheja and kezus and all the other things. She kept touching the fruntera on her forehead, and the gold coins would tinkle. She was sickly and pale, unlikely to bear healthy children or survive the birth, and it was clear that her family was eager to offload her and willing to put up a rich dowry to grease the riddance. And his family was hoping that the vicious rumors of his being a kulu alegri would be properly dispelled.

Everyone came, all the tijas and teos, and all the neighbors and all the children from il hanizitju, so there were not enough chairs and tables. After the eating and drinking was done, Tija

Lea took a tambourine in her hands and everyone sang, and Pinto heard a high, clean, easeful voice, and only then looked up from the boiled beef tongue that stretched toward him as if to mock him. He saw Luna's face blushed with joy, and she was beautiful. Ken pensa di si namurar, ki fujga dil lunar, she sang. He smiled at her, and she said, This song is about me, Luna. She sang it to him, and by the end of the evening they sang together, Ke il lunar es mintirozo, I savi enganjar. He loved the song: If you want to fall in love, stay away from moonlight, for moonlight is fickle and it might fool you. Much later, he would sing the song to Osman too in their room in Tashkent, translating the words for him as the moon was peeking at them through the window. Luna thought they would get married, but he knew that he would do anything to escape it, though he did not know what exactly. Then God saved Pinto by killing Luna's father, so she had to wait for eleven months until Šelošim was over, by which time the Archduke and his wife were shot and Pinto was sent to war where he met the man he was born to love.

The leather-faced man Arzu was traveling with might have been her father or her husband, what with his grunting his orders, his two gray eyebrow clouds looming over the always scolding gaze. She lowered her eyes when facing him to obey, but otherwise he showed scant interest in her. He called her over gruffly to lie down next to him, or demanded to be served by her whatever food he still had in his satchel. He would drink water without offering it to Arzu, and she never asked him for it. Padri Avram had always been the one to distribute the food at the Pintos' table, always serving himself first, then the children, then Manuči, who never asked for more, or less, but would just take what was given to her. A good wife is a precious gift, he would say, ladling the čorba into his bowl. She is put in the bosom of the one who fears the Lord. Little Rafo sometimes wanted to give his čorba to Manuči, but he was to eat whatever was served to him to the last drop, so he did. If they live through and beyond this desert and make it to Sarajevo, Manuči will make her čorba and Pinto will make sure that she serves herself first. In fact, he will learn to cook and make it for her.

Rahela was exhausted and weak from eating only nangbing, which was so hard that Pinto had to soften it with his saliva until his mouth was so dry and sand-coated that he could no longer do so. But when she was with Arzu, she would laugh, watching her make animals and trees from straws and thread, and then trying to do it herself. Was it you who made shade for my daughter? Rahela seemed so happy, even in this heat, the sand scraping off layers of skin, that it was clear the child needed a mother, someone who would know how to comb her hair and bite her fingernails off, someone who could make her a hearty čorba, show her how to climb trees or kill chickens. If this caravan were ever to make it out of this predicament and get somewhere where a future could be feasible, he could perhaps bequeath Rahela to Arzu and go his own way, back to Turkestan to look for Osman, or, if he was not to be found there, all the way back to Sarajevo, where Osman might be heading. He could not know what and who was still there, whether Manuči or Simha were still alive, if indeed the city still existed. Cities come and go, as do worlds, as do souls. With Arzu, the child would have a better life, she would be taken care of, maybe even acquire some siblings. She would not remember him once she was grown up; she would never need to understand who he was and why he was the one dragging her through the desert, soaking her bread with his saliva; she would never find out who brought her into this world. And she might, one day, sleep in a bed, under a roof.

Presently, however, Pinto was facing a camel ass that smelled of long-fermenting dung, and he could not envision any viable future taking place a few hours, let alone a few years, from now. His feet were burning too; skin was shaved off the edges of his soles by the sand in his ramshackle boots; one of his toenails was cutting into the flesh of the toe next to it. Patches of sunburnt skin peeled off his cheeks and forehead, exposing raw flesh, making his scar swell. The last time he remembered not being in pain was with Osman at his side, his arm across Pinto's chest, his breath at Pinto's ear. He heard the voices of men shouting at one another somewhere ahead, but it was unclear if they were about to have a fight, or were just trying to announce something important. The camel suddenly stopped, and farted so loudly that Pinto was startled. El prinsipio de la sensija, temor del Dijo.

His memories were as clear as his hallucinations. He could recall the narrow streets of Bilave, the thickness of the world in the Čaršija, and he remembered Osman's stories of Hadži-Šaban's kahvana, about the Austrians' raids rounding up men who smoked afijun in the back rooms, some of them jumping out the window into the Miljacka. He had longed to return to Vienna, where there were friends, and the German language, and poetry, and a life so different from that in Sarajevo. No opium in Vienna, but there was morphine and Bayer heroin pills, and there were men and cafés and the newspapers on a reading stick, and it was all a dream now anyway. Who knows if Vienna still exists?

There once was an ancient city in the Taklamakan Desert that had been buried under the sand. But among the ruins of its towers, walls, and houses, gold ingots and lumps of silver still lay exposed, Moser had told him. All the explorers and bandits between Tashkent and Shanghai kept looking for this town but they could not find it, as it never stayed in the same place, moving around, riding on the ever-moving dunes, disappearing and appearing. Recovering in the apiary, Moser had eventually run out of his own adventures to narrate, so he unfurled rumors, myths, fairy tales, other people's stories, which he had collected on his peregrinations and then embellished them as he told them to Pinto. Just as he was in his febrile oblivion, he was silent only when asleep, as if talking were essential for his recovery, as if his long tales mended his bones. But if ever a caravan came across the vanishing city, Moser would go on, and discover the riches to load its camels with silver and gold, the drivers would become bewitched, and they would end up leading the caravan round and round in endless circles, till everyone collapsed and died. Only by getting rid of the cursed gold could they break the enchantment and be saved, yet no one ever did so, no one ever had the strength to let go of all the riches that could change their lives; they all thought that the imagined future could redeem their present suffering. There are many ghost caravans, Moser said, that are still wandering the Taklamakan Desert, all their people perished, the camels still unable to defeat the spell so they just keep roaming until one day they drop dead too.

There was no gold in this sorry caravan; they barely had food and water, yet it still seemed to be going in circles. Pinto had seen the same distant peaks more than once, and his only hope was that he was so exhausted and disoriented he could no longer tell the glorious mountains apart. Those who practice righteousness are like the mighty mountains, the teos in Sarajevo used to say to one another, while bending with age and gout. They only knew the Bosnian mountains, the exclusive measure of their righteousness— they had never seen any like the ones on the horizon, piebald with snowfields, jagged like saw teeth, closer to Heaven than this dirt and this life.

Like all refugees, they kept moving forward because they had nowhere else to go; being on the move meant being alive. Somewhere behind them, or ahead of them, or beyond those snarling dunes and distant mountains, the Chinese warlords were rounding up Uighurs, killing them, pilfering their homes, burning their mosques. They liked to put people up in the trees and keep them there until they fell off like ripe fruit, breaking legs and spines, only to be slaughtered in the end. Sometimes, they'd bend back a tree, then bind the traitor to be rent asunder by the branches when it was released. Where there were no trees, they buried people alive in deep holes, shot them to death, or just simply slit their throats. The necessity of killing Muslims was something just about all Xiang warlords agreed on. As the sun set upon the desert, the Uighur men of the caravan would face the burning horizon and pray, and Pinto remembered the rows of kneeling men outside the mosques of Sarajevo.

In daytime, the sun was ruthless. Arzu returned Rahela to him, kissing her forehead. The child's cheeks were pale and sunken, her hair brittle from heat and sand, her lips blooming with chapped skin, but she looked at him as if about to cry, her eyes dry. I'm thirsty, she said, but he told her to wait a bit; she whimpered, but did not whine. Can children cry in the desert? He had never taken care of any other child, in the desert or anywhere else. There was no precedent to any of this in his life, and there was no other life. Was there any in the Atora? Abraham carried Isak into the desert but that shouldn't count. Didn't Moses cross the desert as a child? Pinto could no longer remember proper stories, all of them infested with his memories and dreams, fears, fantasies, and hallucinations. He could not remember the last time he had seen an Atora, let alone read it. If he and Rahela survive, someday they'll be telling stories about their journey and suffering to somebody else, and they will not be believed.

Arzu went back to her father or her husband, so Pinto grasped Rahela's hand and walked. Her feet were small, wrapped in unraveling felt; they sank into sand, so he put her up on his back and trudged forth. At the beginning of their trek across the desert, she kept asking if they had much more to go, and then she stopped asking, as they never seemed to get anywhere and those who knew what was at the other end of the desert spoke a different language.

The men ahead were still shouting, and Pinto now clearly heard alarm in their voices. There were still at least a couple of hours left before sunset, before the caravan settled down for the night. The sun was burning his eyes, and his feet hurt. He would've already stopped for the day, but they had no choice except to stay with the caravan, abide by its rhythms and trajectories; he didn't know where to go, what to do, how to keep this child alive all by himself. Everything was still ahead of them; the only remnant of the past was presently fussing on his back. Pinto tried to grab the camel's languidly flicking tail, but it was too late, so he merely followed the animal. The beginning of wisdom, fear of God.

Both of the skinny dogs that had been running along with the caravan, occasionally snapping at the camel's feet or trying to steal a fallen piece of nangbing before Pinto leaped to save it from the sand, suddenly showed up with their bellies wet, and a tremor of excitement spread up and down the ragtag column. Pinto heard the word su—water—passed from voice to voice, and the caravan and his camel seemed to pick up its pace. It took an hour before they finally came across a sweet-water pool, limned by patches of reeds and young poplars rising to touch the wall of stone looming above the oasis. Arzu pointed up at what looked like a house buried in stone fifteen feet or so up on the cliff face, complete with paneless windows. When Devlet had closed the last hole in the wall and Pinto faced the darkness, he recalled that the Lord asked the prophet, What are you doing here, Elijah? But he could not remember what Elijah said. I don't know, You tell me, O Lord? Or was it, I am waiting for Your wrath to smite me? Or, I'm just trying to stay alive, could You help? No voice spoke to Pinto in the wall, no one asked him anything; and he was no prophet, just a Sefaradi from Sarajevo fully aware that his suffering would never be rewarded, on earth or anywhere else. When that which is coming arrives, Osman used to say, no one will be able to deny it has come. Until then, we do our best to stay alive.

In the lowering sun the water acquired shiny, shivering scales. Rahela drank it in small, slow sips, lest she get sick. When he stopped her from drinking, she cried and asked for more, and, again, he knew of no way to comfort her. Eventually, as the sun vanished, she fell asleep next to him on a patch of improbably soft grass. Pinto had drunk water too fast and was now having painful cramps and could not sleep. Above him the moon was round and shiny like Nono Solomon's medal, the desert stars like typhoid rash. He listened to the rustling of his fellow refugees and when they all settled down and fell asleep, another sound emerged from the silence and then it became gradually louder. It was a low hissing whistle, and when he opened his eyes he could see that the moon and the stars were dimmed. When Rahela woke him up at dawn, by touching his scar, which was what she did when scared and distraught, they were covered by a thin layer of sand, and he saw plumes fluttering from the crests of dunes, a yellow-red haze floating above the horizon.

Half of the caravan was already gone, including the camels. The pool seemed to have shrunk and changed shape, and the reeds wagged their sausage heads from side to side, as if in disbelief. Arzu was still there, hurriedly filling up a canteen with water, her bundle bulging on her back, her husband nowhere to be seen. Other than her bright eyes, her face was veiled. She offered the water to Rahela, who drank it voraciously, and then wrapped a scarf over the girl's face, laughing with her as if playing a game. Tebbad, she said to Pinto. She pointed toward the horizon whence a dust cloud was now advancing toward them like a cavalry charge. Then she pointed toward the cave openings above them and Pinto understood that they needed to get up there as soon as possible. Now he could hear the dull clattering sound of the wind pushing a mass ahead of itself, the air rapidly thicker and heavier, the sand scraping against his cheeks. Pinto asked Rahela to climb on his back so he could strap her, but she refused. I want to do it by myself, she said. I am a big girl. She was not big—though she was five now, she was tiny—she'd never had enough food to eat and grow. There was going to be an argument, as it was obvious that she could not clamber to the caves and might be blown back into the storm. But Arzu mimed that they should move urgently, and that Rahela should get on Pinto's back, and Rahela finally conceded.

Rahela was saying something to Pinto, but the words were erased by the wind, which lifted him as he gripped the sharp rock edges to pull up. The sand was washing against his face and eyeballs, coating them, so that he could barely discern Arzu's shadow climbing like a cat toward the caves. Rahela was choking on the sand, but he could not stop, nor go down. The howling wind kept pushing him off the rock face, and at one point his left hand slipped, and then his right one, and he slid downward, foreseeing in panic that if he were to fall on his back he would crush Rahela, but then he managed to grab a sharp slate sticking out at an angle, cutting his palm. He took a breath of relief, and with it a mouthful of sand. There was no point in spitting it out, so he swallowed as much of it as he could and found, gagging still, a crack in the rock to wedge his foot in and launch himself upward. The winds set forth in swift succession, violently storming, scattering far and wide, separating forcefully, to deliver a reminder: what you are promised will come to pass. Pinto could feel his hands bleeding, the sand getting into the gashes, but he kept going up. What you are promised will come to pass. What I was promised I cannot remember.

He hurled himself into the darkness of the cave, and it seemed as if the monstrous wind slammed the door behind them. The wind was now but an ongoing boom, as if the world outside, each of its particles, were being blown up, and the explosion was not going to stop until all of it was destroyed and nothing was left. He crawled deeper into the darkness of the cave, stopping only to vomit and spit out the sand. I thank You, O Lord, that You have brought me from light into darkness. Rahela was quiet, so he took her off his back and checked for her breath, whereupon she coughed into his cheek. He cleaned her throat and tongue with his uncut hand, but the sand was coating her teeth. She squirmed, cried, gagged, and vomited too; then he cleaned her nose—her nostrils so narrow that he could only use the very tip of his pinkie—until he could finally hear her wheezing. The tebbad shoveled sand into the cave's mouth, so he placed Rahela on his back without tying her; she held on to him as he crawled forth, advancing through a cold, damp air, redolent of skeletons and reptiles, until he had a sense that he had crept into a larger ventricle of the hill. Now it was as if they were inside a drum and the wind kept hitting the stretched skin. He rummaged through his satchel for the leather bottle, dripped some water onto her lips, while she grabbed it to squeeze out more. He had to take it from her hand, to have a sip himself and rinse his mouth. He could not waste the water on his palm wound, so he stuffed it with sand to stem the bleeding, and now his hand burned. He could not hear Arzu, and when he called her name, there was no response; all he heard was his panting and Rahela's coughs and the wind's bombardment. It became clear to Pinto that they might die inside this darkness as well. There wasn't much water left, and only a piece of flatbread. The tebbad could last for days, and it would cover all the tracks, and the caravan would vanish, and Pinto and Rahela would never be able to find the way. Arzu must have fallen off the rock face and into the sandstorm; she would never be found.

He who is in the dark can see what is in the light, whereas he who is in the light cannot see what is in the dark. Only the Holy One does see what is in the dark, because He sees everything, everywhere, including la gran eskuridad. And if He ever bothered to actually look into this particular lightless cave, He would see Pinto and Rahela, now sleeping on his chest, both breathing heavily, their noses, mouths, and throats still coated in sand and so dry they could not swallow, their tongues swollen and slowly turning dark. The Holy One would then be stuck in the cave with them, because even He would've been assaulted by a tebbad this mighty, even He would've been deafened by the wind barrage outside, even He would've found this dark void to be a comforting tomb. Whenever Rahela gasped and choked for an instant, Pinto would hold his breath and wait for her to catch up and breathe again, and when she did, he would exhale and stroke her hair, brittle from the dryness.

Once upon a time, he had thus stroked Osman's hair as he had lain with his cheek on Pinto's chest. His hair was thick and wiry, and Pinto would sometimes rake it with his fingers. In Galicia, before the onslaught, he picked lice out of it and crushed them between his nails. In Tashkent, he would wind his curls around his pinkie. Where is Osman now? If he left this realm of earth and water, where did he go? There had been no one who could tell Pinto what happened after Osman rode to meet Tsirul the killer. Pinto knew, but didn't want to know, that Osman might well be dead, because if he wasn't he would've been looking for the two of them and he would've probably already found them, for there was no other there in this world for him to go to. If he was alive, Pinto would still be able to hear his voice; this absence means death. An edgy rock was digging into his flank, so Pinto wanted to change his position, but he didn't want to wake up Rahela. Osman's absence was now as old as she. God has no needs and we are the needy ones. Pinto's injured hand throbbed with dull pain.

It took a night and much of the day for the wind to subside. Only after the howling abated did Pinto realize that there were other bodies in the darkness, because he heard their sandy snorts and rustling. He called Arzu's name again, but nobody responded. Someone might have been crying too, though it was more likely just wheezing. Someone else was drinking from a canteen—there was the pop of a cork and a gurgle or two, and then an argument in what sounded like Uighur. Pinto kept his leather water pouch under Rahela's cheek, like a pillow. When she woke up, she would be hungry and thirsty, but most of all tired and scared. Their breathing rhythms had synchronized and now he did not want to move, so as not to disturb her, for he was hoping that she would keep sleeping. What kind of a father would sacrifice his child because God's voice ordered him to do so? What kind of God would let a father kill his child to show that human life matters to Him only under the condition of absolute obeisance? This girl on his chest, this fragile life loaded with a future, this body that stood no chance alone in the world, yet somehow survived it, dependent on the love and kindness of others—the duty of protection fell upon Pinto and now a fear overwhelmed him, coupled with his hunger and the sand in his mouth, that he might not be able to do so. The bread was in his satchel, which was under his head, and he did not want to move. Abraham and Isak arrived at the place of which God told him, and Abraham built an altar there. He laid out the wood, bound his son, Isak, and placed him on the altar. The scorching heat of Israel, the prickly wood, the fear, and the ropes chafing at his wrists. Then Abraham picked up the knife to slay his son.

Under the linden trees aligned on each side of the street, Osman and Pinto rode their bicycles so fast that they reached the back of a car. Pinto could see the plume on the helmet of the man sitting in the back seat, and the white lacy hat of the woman sitting next to him, and he understood that they were in Sarajevo and that the people in the car were about to die, and that if they died, Osman would die too, so he wanted to warn the Archduke and his wife but they were speeding away from him, as if he were the one who would kill them, and that was just crazy and stupid, he yelled after them to stop, now, or they would die. But they laughed at him, they did not understand the language he was speaking, they called him a kulu alegri, and the car sped up. He wanted to say to Osman that these stupid people were going to die and they didn't even know it, but he was no longer next to him, so Pinto looked back and saw that there was a deluge rolling forward soon to catch up with him, and he pedaled faster, but the bicycle was not even moving, and then the water reached him, and he was carried by the flood, and Osman was right next to him again, and he said: Ken pensa di si namurar, ki fujga dil lunar.

Abruptly, someone lit a match, and then an oil lamp, and the darkness was extinguished, revealing the leather-faced man holding the lamp in the palm of his hand, as if he had just found it somewhere. He placed it before himself, and his face was swarmed by shadows, his eyes flickering, which made him look as if he had just returned from the underworld. Arzu was not by his side, and Pinto could not see whether she was hunkering somewhere deeper in the cavern. He sat up, still holding Rahela to his chest, though she began to stir. The leather-face said nothing, nor did he acknowledge Pinto's and Rahela's presence, busying himself with rummaging through his bag, as if perfectly accustomed to sitting inside a desert cave. The cavern turned out to be spacious, even if it funneled into nothing toward the far end. Rahela yawned loudly, and then said, Gladna sam. The child was five years old and spoke a mishmash of Bosnian, Spanjol, and German Pinto was using with her, with occasional words from other languages they picked up along the way. The leather-face raised the lamp above his head, not so much to see who it was making sounds as to show himself and assert that he was the ruler of this space. He glared at them, until he noticed that at the far end of the cave there was a pile of what looked like rolled rags. The leather man crept to the pile, the shadows dancing on the wall, on the drawings and writing in an alphabet Pinto could not identify. The leather-face picked up a roll off the top, held one end, and let it unroll, until it stretched all the way to the cave floor. It was a scroll, like a Sefer Torah, not a rag. The man moved the light closer to its surface and examined it, and Pinto could see the outlines of people and animals and writing in an alphabet he could not identify; the letters curled and sat in rows.

Pinto took some nangbing out of his satchel and rubbed it with a few drops of water, since his mouth was still full of sand and he could not chew it for her. He spat out sand residue and licked the palm of his hand, then rubbed her face, and she whined, too hungry to resist. A las prufunduras di la mar, li eču todu il mal, he said, without having decided to say it. Manuči would wash his face at the spout, splashing it with water, much too cold, and he would wriggle and frown, and she would recite, La kartija mu li lavu, il mal mi li saku, a las prufunduras di la mar, li eču todu il mal. With the water off his face, she would throw all the evil into the depths of the sea. There was no sea anywhere near this desert, but there was surely a lot of evil. Rahela put the entire piece of bread in her mouth and was now chewing it, her cheeks bulging.

The leather-face lit the bottom of the unrolled scroll on fire with his lamp, and it caught quickly, casting lively light on the rest of the cave—there was no one else there. It was clear from the hesitant way that the scroll was burning that it was old. The dark fire crept up the scroll, making the letters glow as they disappeared, and Pinto had no doubt that it was sacred. Ne! Ne! Rahela said, but the man paid no heed. The manuscript disintegrated in a shower of flimsy ash flakes. The smoke made Rahela cough and yowl, which must have been what stopped the leather-face from burning the rest of the pile. Instead, he took a couple of rolls and stuffed them in his bag, and blew his lamp out. Pinto sat with Rahela still in his lap, propping himself with a wounded hand that he could now barely move. In the sand on the floor, he felt with his fingers a round, smooth pebble, and with a certainty that he would later find ludicrous and terrifying, he decided that it could be useful in some future in which they ran out of water or food, and that he could give it to Rahela to suck on.

The leather-face dug with his knife through the sand wall at the mouth of the cave until the light burst and blinded them all. He slipped out without looking back, and Pinto and Rahela were now on the edge of a lambent narrow field stretching before them like a path. Pinto could not stand up, so he put Rahela on his back and crawled into the light.

Su, Rahela said.

Paz, he said.

Outside, the shadow shapes of the reeds all pointed in the same direction under the sand. The pool of water was now gone, except for a defeated, shallow puddle at which a camel knelt lapping the murky water. There was no one around to be seen, though some mounds looked like there might have been a body under the sand. The leather-faced man approached the camel from the back, carefully so as not to startle it and grabbed the reins while the beast continued to suck up all the water from the puddle.

Where was Arzu? The leather-faced man spent no time looking for her, though he did seek, the camel reins in hand, what he deemed could be useful. He excavated a staff, then someone's bag, from under the sand; he rummaged through it to find a canteen with water, from which he drank voraciously, draining the last drops onto his parched lips. He leaned his head so far back to drink that his hat fell off; he saw Pinto and Rahela but did and said nothing, as if they were not there. He dug, with the staff and then his hands, to the bottom of the camel's puddle, until he reached wetter sand, then deeper, until water rose up.

Su, Rahela said. The pebble was still in Pinto's hand. He sat

Rahela down on the ground to clean the pebble, rubbing off the already dried blood with sand. The pebble seemed perfectly round and had a wheel carved into it, surrounded by symbols or words in some alphabet unknown to Pinto. It was small enough to fit under Rahela's tongue.

PART IV

HONGKOU

CHAPEI

INTERNATIONAL SETTLEMENT

Huangpo River

FRENCH CONCESSION

© 2023 Jeffrey L. Ward

SHANGHAI, 1932

———

THEY SAY THAT when the Holy One rebuked the moon for its vainglory, the moon fell, and sparks flew from it into the sky—these are the stars. Now the stars sleep on the cushion of clouds, and we are under it. While from underneath we see only the darkness, there are entire shining worlds on the other side of the clouds. And one day they will all be gone, and the sparkling stars will come in all kinds of shapes, each a different world, and they will blind us with their beauty. Why can't the stars break through the clouds now? Rahela would ask. Why do we have to wait? Because right now they're where they're supposed to be, Pinto would say. Just fine where they are, so they don't know that we are here down below.

The clouds' underbelly was illuminated by the fires in Chapei. Los sjelos kero pur papel, la mar kero pur tinta. Except my sky paper is burning, and the sea is thickened with the silt from terrible rivers.

Rahela was asleep, her cheek against the side of Pinto's chest, her mouth open, cloudlets of her breath rising against the fire's glow. She was squeezed between Pinto and Lenka, insufficiently covered with his damp coat, the three of them lying on top of Lenka's, also damp, under which Pinto could feel dirt and stones. He lifted Rahela's head and slid his jute bag under it; her hair was thick and heavy with the dampness. The night was freezing, drizzle sparkling in the air. Every once in a while, gunfire cracked the hum of the distant flames. Then there was another explosion, followed, like an afterthought, by smaller ones. It was hard to imagine that anyone could sleep tonight, or anytime soon, yet Pinto had a sense that he was the only one awake. Now that you lie still, you are quiet; when you sleep, you are at rest. It so happens that I am not sleeping, and I am also not at rest; in fact, the rest might never come, not even when I die. Neither is Osman at rest, whether he be dead or alive. Even if he were somewhere, alive, in Sarajevo, or who knows where, or maybe even looking for me, there is no way that he could be at peace. The last time Pinto was at rest was in their bed in Tashkent, when Pinto's cheek pressed against Osman's chest, when his heartbeat sang a lullaby. Pinto had slept in many places since then, in many ways, except at rest.

Presently, he was trying to sleep next to an abyss, on the roof of a building crowded with refugees just like the streets below. His right hand was sticking out over the edge; he felt an updraft of the collective breath coming up from the desperate crowd on the street below. When by His command angels act as messengers, they are made winds. When angels are His ministers, they are fire. His ministers were now in Chapei, except for the few hopeless messengers breathing up at the palm of my hand.

The roof was full of people, as were the lobbies of the buildings along Avenue Edward VII, and whatever rooms and floors happened to be empty in them when the wave of refugees poured from Chapei and Hongkou to cross the Soochow Creek. God has no needs and we are the needy ones. They had followed the flow, until Pinto led them into a building in search of a place to hunker down, without even recognizing what or where it was. They climbed the stairs, up and up, because they couldn't turn back as the crowd kept pushing them from behind. By the time they reached the roof, nine or ten stories high, the only spots left for them to settle were at the far end, right at the edge. Pinto stepped over bodies and their possessions, dragging Rahela by the hand, to claim their paltry patch of space. They could barely fit; he lay closest to the edge. At least he could see as far as the flames in Chapei. Das Licht ändert die Welt und jedoch bleibt sie gleich, auf ewig warm unter Gottes Gewänder.

Lenka was now asleep too, or at least quiet and not moving, Rahela pressing close to her to keep warm. Wine and the sleep of the wicked are a benefit to them and a benefit to the world; wine and the sleep of the righteous are an injury to them and an injury to the world. But what if you're neither wicked nor righteous but just trying to survive? What then? Why punish those who already suffer? Is this the way the world is supposed to be? I don't know. This would be a crisis of faith, if I had ever had faith. Why do all these Talmudic thoughts float around in my mind? Chapei is on fire, the Japanese will burn all of it down, yet there is rabbinic chatter in my cursed head. Listen to me, Rabin Pinto, it is all because of loneliness. God was invented by the lonely people, by those who could not bear to think that no one would ever care about them, spend a thought on their loneliness. We are not chosen, what we are is terribly lonely and unloved. And all those righteous men who withdraw from the world to be with God— they're leaving us behind because they think they can spend their life with the only being that truly loves them. But I can't leave this world, there's nowhere else to go, no place of love available. God is love only if the world is depleted of love. God is the imaginary pantry where imaginary love is stored. When Osman spoke to me, God had nothing to say. A wicked thought if there ever was one. Padri Avram would've killed me if I had thought any of this around him, he would've seen the wickedness in me, the jetzer hara. But Osman is gone now, has been gone for ten years or so, and Chapei is on fire, as is much of this world, and whatever is beyond. I am free to do whatever I want, I can leap off the edge, dive into the human river below, because the world is what it is and there is no other one yet, until the Lord makes a new one and replaces this one. Where is Osman now? Where is my beloved? Where did he go?

Remember the future! I should be thinking about the future, about what we are going to do tomorrow. We had so little, now we have even less. How are we going to go back home? Although their shikumen was as much of a home as any other place in this city, or anywhere else, other than Sarajevo, if it still existed. Manuči had died, and Simha too. Simha had managed to send him a letter, but never responded to his response. Albert, her husband, whom he had never met, wrote back instead to tell him of all the people in the family who had died since, including his own young son and then Simha, crushed by grief. Albert also wrote to Pinto about his nieces, Laura and Blanka, whom he described as beautiful and smart young women, ready to be married and curious about the world, but now so motherless that their socks had holes from which their toes stuck out like potatoes from a sack. He seemed to think that Pinto had gotten rich in Shanghai; the gilded stories of Shanghai Jews reached even Sarajevo, and Albert begged him to share some of that wealth, as his girls had no dowry to speak of. They would be forever grateful to their uncle, and would receive him as their own whenever he came back home. Pinto could not wait to see his nieces, he wrote, and was so happy to hear that they were doing well. He was going to come back to Sarajevo sooner or later, though not anytime soon, as the ship tickets were incredibly expensive, and he had to save money for two, because he now had a daughter whose name was Rahela. It was true, he wrote, that there were people in Shanghai rich as kings, but Pinto was not one of them, he was a pauper like most of the people in this city. And even if he somehow scrounged up the money for his return, it wouldn't help him much, for he would find a place different from the one he had left, a country that hadn't existed back then. He didn't mention that in his letter, but he did write that to go anywhere, he would have to get traveling papers from that new country, Yugoslavia, which neither knew nor cared that he existed, so he was stuck here in Shanghai, because there was no one here representing the new country to give him a passport. He had been trying for years to get a Nansen passport, but, unlike the Russians, he came to Shanghai alone, when Rahela was seven and a half. He knew no one in Shanghai. He barely spoke English, which everyone speaks here. It took a long time for him to understand how this city worked, with all the foreigners running it from the top, while the Chinese go about their own business ignoring the foreigners, unless they kill them. He could apply for no documents until he had an address. But even after he had an address, he still had no money, so the haughty League of Nations representatives, expecting to be paid for their noble efforts on top of all the issuing fees, would not even deign to talk to him about a passport without an ample envelope of cash. He knew of no one who was as stateless as he was, other than Rahela. That aside, Rahela was happy to hear about her cousins, and had not stopped talking about visiting them someday, after she got a passport.

Pinto was not surprised that Albert never responded. At first he thought that he didn't care about Pinto and his passport problems, and hence he resented the brother-in-law he had never met. But then he figured Albert might have died, or was gravely ill; perhaps Sarajevo was burnt to the ground and everyone was winnowed around the world; perhaps he was now a refugee as well; perhaps he had made the journey to Palestine. Only for the anniversary of the Archduke's killing could Pinto find the city's name in the Shanghai papers he read in English, Russian, German, or French. He tried to tell Lenka about his witnessing the assassination, but she had no idea what he was talking about. She was too young, and her own misfortune—the war, the revolution, the escape via Siberia—was like a long-lasting storm, something that just came abruptly, destroyed her life, tossed her around, and finally deposited her, with a Nansen passport but sans family and money, on top of a building in Shanghai, two feet from the edge, ten stories above a river of refugees.

If Pinto were to roll over into the abyss and vanish, Rahela would find herself unprotected, with nothing between herself and the edge, and she could fall down too. Not so long ago, he'd had nightmares in which he would be prostrate on the rim of a void—sometimes there would be a churning sea below, sometimes just la gran eskuridad—untroubled by the danger, because he knew, in his dream, that he would avoid it since he could fly. So that he would let himself roll over the edge only to discover that he couldn't fly at all, whereupon he would be dropping for a long time, waking up just before he hit whatever was at the end of the fall. The last dream of that kind had not ended when his body hit the bottom, but when he felt an immense cold penetrating him, moving in, passing beyond his heart, beyond the marrow of his bones, beyond his soul, which in his dream was a small rag ball. After he had woken up, the cold stayed inside him, and he shivered, even if it was an August night in Shanghai, when the air is like molasses, when there was nothing within his reach that was not hot to the touch and coated with humidity. Now that cold was seeping into Rahela's heart and bones as well, and she didn't even know it, there was nothing he could do, except not let her roll over the edge. As long as I live, you'll never be cold again, Alija Đerzelez said to the hanuma. But Alija was a hero, and I am a nothing and a nobody.

O Lord, what are we going to do tomorrow? There was some money left in his pocket, but all their scarce belongings were left in the shikumen. When he decided to pack, he realized they had no suitcases. They'd arrived in Shanghai four years before with nothing; it had taken six years to cross the desert and make their way to the coast, trekking along with refugee caravans, begging for food in villages and hamlets, relying on the kindness of people whose language they could not speak. Rahela picked up some Gansu dialect, as they'd spent a winter in a remote hovel with two Chinese families, and a summer in a village outside Lanzhou. They spoke a different language in the shikumens of Shanghai, but it didn't take her long to pick that up too. She was a smart girl, but burdened with all that she had already seen in her life. And now the Japanese were shelling Chapei, and they were following the flow of refugees again.

Pinto only had a jute bag on his back when they arrived in Shanghai four years before. He had that same bag now; they hadn't needed suitcases as there was no chance of leaving Shanghai. There was no country to go to, no passport to get there. They couldn't sleep in the rain on a roof for another night. Neither was there another place in Shanghai they could go to tomorrow; the shikumen could be on fire for all they knew. Maybe they could go and stay with Lu and his family, but his wife wouldn't like that. Having a lover is one thing; having your lover stay at your home accompanied by his daughter and a Russian woman is another thing altogether. There are mansions in this town that are big enough to house all these displaced people, but they will be shot if they try to jump those walls. There is always a place for a refugee, yet they don't let them into such a place. Until there is somewhere to go to, or, who knows, even return to, all you can do is stay alive. Which might be hard here, in the cold drizzle, on top of a crowded building. Nothing ever gets dry in Shanghai. He has worn damp clothes since 1928; he's been coughing for years. Death is always growing inside you, like a nail growing on your soul. The fire in Chapei seemed to be receiving more nourishment, the flames and smoke blooming toward the sky. Who can he ask for help? Who in this city is a friend? Where can they go?

The effortless, joyous way in which Osman took care of him was what he recalled more than anything from their honeymoon time in Tashkent. Buenu komu il pan, Osman was. He made tea for him in the morning, and wouldn't let him drink it too soon so as not to burn his tongue, because, he would say, blowing to cool off the tea, he had plans with his tongue for later. He would kiss the scar on his cheek, invisible to others under Pinto's scraggly beard. He patched Pinto's pants and inspected the seams of his shirt and coat for lice. En kada dado un marafet. He would tell him stories about Sarajevo, about the funny and sad people he knew at Hadži-Šaban's, about the great Gazihusrevbeg and the man he loved, lived, and was buried with, and then he would slip from the past into the future in which the two of them were back and strolling in the Čaršija like a proper couple but pretending to be friends, and a wake of rumor behind them. The only thing Osman demanded in return from Pinto was that he scratch his back, gently, just before they fell asleep, and Pinto would oblige. And after Osman turned on his back in his sleep, Pinto's hand would end up on his chest, and if he tried to remove it, Osman would grab it and keep it there, and Pinto would feel the tapping of the heart, as if it were sending secret messages from its hiding place. If a man is liked by his fellow man, he is liked by God. When Pinto cried in bed in the morning because morphine made him desperate and despondent, Osman would stroke his hair, and sing to him that beautiful song: Bejturan se uz ružu savija, vilu ljubi Đerzelez Alija. And sometimes, he would just rip the blanket off him and force him to get up on his feet. Once, after Pinto had not eaten for days because he was going through withdrawal, Osman force-fed him, like a goddamn goose, and held his jaw shut to prevent him from spitting it out. Back then, he hated him for that, but now it all had a different meaning. Where is Osman now? Where is my beloved?

Carefully, so as not to awake Rahela, Pinto sat up with his feet dangling over the edge. What was on fire in Chapei was the North Station, and then also another, bigger building not far from it. The flames now streamed along the sides of the building, climbing toward the sky. Possibly the Commercial Press, or the Oriental Library, chock-full of paper, burning with celerity and bright flames. On this side of Soochow Creek, the lit oval of the racecourse was indifferent to the fire. Down on the street, the pavement on each side was thick with bodies and their bundles, loaded rickshaws moving through the murky mizzle. If he were to jump, the layer of bodies would soften the impact, as if he were landing on potatoes. Let us go down and confound their speech, so that nobody shall understand one another.

Once upon a time, Rabin Danon had busied himself with interpreting dreams. Once upon a time, in Sarajevo, now a dream unto itself. People would reveal their dream to Rabin Danon, and he would tell them what it meant, and then they would go around telling everyone else about what it meant, as if spreading gossip, until all of Bilave agreed on the right interpretation. A cock meant that a male child was coming; a hen meant joy in an abundant garden. A broken egg meant some gain. Also, nuts, cucumbers, glass, anything that can be broken meant gain—there were a lot of dreams about gain, because no one had enough of anything. He who in his dream entered a big city would have all of his wishes fulfilled. The old Papučo once dreamed that he was swimming in a vat of oil, and soon everyone in il hanizitju knew that he, just like anyone else who had ever dreamed of oil before him, was indeed hoping for the light of the Atora to burn forever. Those who dreamed of leaving their city, however, would soon die and leave this world. And if you dream that you are sitting on the roof, Rabin Danon claimed—and everyone in Bilave and all the way down to Mejtaš must have believed it—you were bound to attain a high position in life. But if in your dream you fell from the roof, you would lose your house, or your job, or experience some other kind of loss. There had been a time when Pinto's dreams were full of kissing. Once, when he was but a boy, he was touching Binjoki's pata, and woke up all messy and sticky down there. What does that mean, Rabin Danon? Pinto had grown convinced that the good Rabin had been making it all up as he went along, but once people took it all to be truth, it became so, and no one ever dared dispute it. There was God's word, and there were Rabin's stories, and both were what they were, no more, no less. Rabin's beard was enormous; the story went that one of his many daughters disappeared and could not be found for days, until she was discovered sleeping on his chest, under his beard, where she lived off the crumbs and morsels stuck in his thick hair.

Remember the future! Padri Avram used to say, with his finger of importance pointing up. The only memory that matters is of the world that is yet to come. Back then, Pinto had no idea what Padri was talking about. But in this Shanghai life, the possibility that his dreams might contain his future would keep him awake for nights on end. What if time didn't only flow forward but also backward? What if the past and the future streamed, creating, in opposite directions, a whirl in time that was neither past nor future, not even present? What if Osman had somehow been caught in that whirl and was not stuck in this shapeless time? If Osman was there, in that time whirl, Pinto would dive into it within a breath.

Presently, he had no doubt that if he fell asleep on the edge of the roof he would plunge; there was also a possibility of his dropping down even awake. So many people were on the roof, all the bodies touching other bodies, that if someone pushed any of those huddling in the middle, the luckless ones on the edge would spill over and down like sand. Our people, Padri Avram used to say, are like dust and like stars. When they go down, they go down to the very dust. When they go up, they reach the stars. What will happen to all these people, to any of us? You look into any of those faces and you can't know what happened to them before, let alone what will happen to them in the future, but you do know that it was not good and it will not be good. Let us not worry, it will not be good, Osman used to say in the trenches, and the soldats for some reason found it funny. It was past midnight, yet the refugee stream kept moving in the street, as if someone was assembling them up in a factory in Hongkou and sending them down here for storage in a nightmare.

Rahela, fidgeting, kneed him in the buttocks; he stiffened to resist her push. She turned over to throw her arm across Lenka's midriff, raised it again to drop her hand on the scar on Lenka's cheek. Lenka did not move, or react. Pinto thought she might be dead; if she was, there was nothing that could be done now, other than maybe wake up Rahela, and everyone on the roof. And do what then, exactly? Where would he take her dead body? There was little space for the living in this town, where people stepped daily over the dead, even on Nanking Road or the Bund—particularly on Nanking Road and the Bund. Pinto once saw an entire family dead, mother, father, and a baby still leaning against a wall; they fell asleep and never woke up. The endless dream. The meaning of life is not to be dead; you live so as not to die. That's it. Ask any soldier or refugee, anyone who has lived through a war, or any of those children still alive and begging for a handful of rice on Nanking Road. Ask Lenka. All we want from life is to keep living. It's that simple. Only the rich ponder a reason to live. Everyone else who is alive just wants to live. There is no meaning to it, any more than there is meaning to time. There is just life. When there is no life, there is no meaning. A thunderous series of shells dropped around the North Station, dust clouds assuming evanescent shapes against the screen of the flames. Now, what was the meaning of that?

Lenka wasn't dead at all, flinching as she was at the sound of explosions. Carefully, she lifted Rahela's hand and brought it down to her chest to hold it there. Rahela liked to touch Lenka's scar, which was much bigger and fresher than Pinto's. When Lenka first moved in with them, Rahela kept away. Lenka's presence exposed the absence of Rahela's mother, of whom Pinto had told Rahela stories—some true, some made up—featuring her birth, her mother's death, Pinto's escape from Turkestan, crossing the desert with her on his back, and making it to Shanghai. From the pebble with the wheel he'd found in the cave, he made a necklace for Rahela, which became the solid evidence that the improbable journey had taken place—there was nothing else he could show for it. He never told Rahela that he was not her real father; or that he had never in his life touched Klara Isakovna. He told her stories about Osman, her true father, the one who made shade for his daughter before he vanished. Pinto told her how beautiful and brave her mother had been, and how they had escaped the Bolsheviks, and how she had lost her life giving Rahela hers, and how she would've survived in some other time or place and would've been an amazing woman, and how Osman sacrificed his life to save them all, and how so much luck was required just to be and stay in the world. In any case, Lenka didn't quite fit into any of that mythology. To Rahela, Lenka looked slight, hurt, alone, devoid of power. Rahela kept away at first, contemptuous of Lenka's need for help, of her vulnerability, evident in the scar on her face. But then, slowly, carefully, she started approaching her. Eventually, Rahela asked her if she could touch the scar, and Lenka granted her access. Then Rahela grew so fond of her that she gave her the necklace with the pebble wheel. Lenka recognized it as the Samsara wheel, and was so touched she cried; she refused to take it, because Pinto had told her where and how he had found it. Rahela was a kind child, too good and kind for this world.

Now, like a brick from an oven, Rahela was warming up his back; her body generated heat, a little furnace of life. It was supposed to be the other way around; he was supposed to be the one who kept her warm and not hungry. She hadn't eaten much since they'd left their place. Pinto had only managed to shove a couple of buns, so old as to feel wooden, into his jute bag on the way out. He had forced Rahela, and Lenka too, to chew on them as they moved through the tributary alleys flowing into Haining Road, where they merged with the refugees heading across the Soochow Creek—Chinese, Russian, all sorts of the poor that lived in Hongkou and Chapei. Were Lu and his family among them? Lu was not poor, but the Japanese shells hitting Hongkou didn't care about the difference. Pinto and Lenka were grasping each of Rahela's hands, and her narrow, moist hand would every once in a while slip out of his, only for him to clasp it stronger. They were taken up by the stream, and had no idea where it was going, except away from the gunfire and explosions, to where the rich foreigners lived and the Japanese would not dare to bomb. The collective stench was incredible, for body secretions were triggered by people's aggregated fear and now all the sweat, shit, and who knows what was flowing out, greasing the streets for everyone to scurry in the same little-step rhythm like millipedes, humming and grunting and shouting and crying. People's bodies are full of noise, but everyone keeps it inside until they can no longer hold it in. Osman had once told him about Kasim, one of his characters from Hadži-Šaban's, who could never shut up: he muttered to himself ceaselessly, even while sleeping, shouting and crying and whimpering when drunk, a mill of noise inside his head never slowing down. Because you hear so many voices, do not imagine that there are many gods in Heaven.

Only when they had stopped at the Soochow Creek bridge would he realize that Rahela had been whining and that he was hurting her. He loosened his grip, then stroked and put his lips on her hand, eliciting a modest smile. Lenka was tired too, her feet were painful and cold, the scar patch on her cheek and chin now red. If they were to die right there, the refugee river would just carry them on, eventually dumping their corpses on some

Shanghai street whose name he had never known. But they didn't die, and the mass funneled to cross the bridge, so that the surge coming from behind pressed them forth. He dug in his heels to protect Rahela from being crushed, as did Lenka. The child was sandwiched between them, her head pressed against his solar plexus, while he and Lenka were nose to nose. Attending to Lenka's burn, he had seen her scar from close-up, the peeling skin and the raw flesh, changing the bandage as she recovered, until it looked like a relief map of some strange, painful country, what with its hills, vales, rivers stretching beyond the mountain chain of her small left ear.

Finally, they moved again slowly, shuffling their feet inch by inch until they entered the bridge and crept across, whereupon the space opened and the mass somewhat dispersed, and now they could stop and breathe the foul air in and out. Rahela was crying because her hand hurt so much from Pinto's squeezing, and because she was frazzled and scared. Pinto's face was coated with sweat and drizzle, his collar cutting into the back of his neck. Gospody, Lenka said. My zhivy. Before them rose the racecourse, vast like a ship.

Are we going to the racecourse? Rahela asked. Maybe we could all sleep there, with the horses? Maybe we can find something to eat.

They would not let us inside, Pinto said. They don't care what happens outside.

The child had been a refugee all of her life, and endured displacement without complaining. It made Pinto sad that she was so accustomed to marching aimlessly, always hungry and thirsty. The crowd thinned as people tried to disperse once they crossed the bridge. Pinto decided they should follow Bubbling Well Road, though he could not think of where to go or where they might end. A Sikh policeman stood in the middle of the street absurdly directing traffic while the crowd went around him like a creek around a rock, the stuck cars honked, and the rickshaws squeezed through. A single file of racing ponies with blankets on their backs was going somewhere, as the Volunteer Corps pushed people to part them for the ponies' passage. The ponies were anxious, snorting and neighing, terrified of the ruckus. A woman carried her wailing children and belongings in two rattan baskets hanging on a pole across her shoulders. A ruddy-faced volunteer, not older than twenty or so, shoved her with his rifle, and she tottered back, trying to keep the balance until she toppled over and the kids spilled with the belongings. A couple of ponies reared but were quickly tugged down. A Chinese man rushed through the space left open by the Volunteer Corps, grabbed a blanket from one of the ponies and ran off. Pinto could see the ruddy-faced boy raising his rifle to shoot at the thief, but someone stepped in front of him and the moment was gone. That edepsiz was going to kill someone, Pinto thought, and he couldn't wait to do so.

The Chapei fire lit up Lenka's face, which made her eyes dark holes.

Ya golodna, she said, merely stating a fact, whispering so as not to wake up Rahela.

There was nothing Pinto could say, no plan or hope to offer. He just nodded limply, and said: I can go down to the street and look for some rice balls.

The night is almost over, she said, offering no evidence. Let's wait for Rahela to wake up, and we can all go down. I don't want to stay up here alone. Someone might push me down.

No one is going to push you down, Pinto said, without conviction.

Before her face was burned with acid, Lenka had been a taxi dancer at the Majestic, where she cajoled men into buying expensive cocktails or bottles of champagne, earning a percentage of the bill they paid. Like all the other taxi dancers, she had to flirt and laugh and drink a lot to leaven the tab, submitting herself to much fondling and groping. Many other Russian girls— everybody called them Natashas—earned extra by providing services other than flirting and guzzling champagne; there were rooms in the back of the Majestic where they could fuck the patrons, sharing 50 percent of the proceeds with Halyapin, the vicious club manager. Pinto's job at the club was to dress knife wounds well enough to kick the bleeder out of the Majestic, sometimes take him to the hospital, sometimes to the morgue. On good nights, he induced vomiting; he made sure no one's heart exploded while trying to squeeze out an opium-hardened turd on the toilet; he provided ice or ointment to the girls beaten by their johns or Halyapin, or to the johns beaten by Halyapin; he waved smelling salts under the noses of the gentlemen obliterated by alcohol. After hours, he would administer Salvarsan or mercury cream injections to the girls infected with clap or syphilis. It was a job, and he was lucky to have it.

The first time Lenka came to him was because she was in pain and could not hear anything in her left ear. He shaped a small cone out of a newspaper, put the tip into her aching ear, then lit the cone's open side and made sure it burnt as far as it could before he took it out. It provided enough relief for her to tell him about her family's escape from Voronezh, then from Siberia, where both of her parents died; then a marriage to a young captain who took her to Harbin with thousands of other Russians. Soon she took a boat to Shanghai and left her husband behind, in an opium den. She didn't think he even noticed her absence. Pinto nodded along with her tale, as if he hadn't already heard scores of such stories from all the other Natashas who had once upon a time attended debutante balls and were now spun on the dance floor by inebriated American sailors, if they were lucky, or getting infected by them, if they were unlucky. Lenka never got infected, perhaps because, she said, she didn't sleep with the club patrons, although that was unlikely—even the fucking Natashas could hardly survive with what they earned.

Lenka would come to see Pinto at his office at the Majestic, a broom closet where the brooms and mops were still actually kept. She would complain to him about stomach cramps, and then about an infected skin tag in her armpit, and then about something else; once she complained about the roots of her hair getting gray. It was quickly apparent that she was coming only to talk to him. He had no choice but to tell her about his long arrival in Shanghai, and he kept mentioning Osman, his dear friend, whom he missed terribly; he also brought up Lu, his Chinese friend, with whom he was close, very close. It didn't take her long to understand what kind of friendships Pinto had with the men. She stood up and hugged him, awkwardly, as he stayed sitting in his chair; she kissed his forehead and laughed as though relieved. It made sense to her now why he never touched her, let alone groped her, never wanting anything from her, never angled to fuck her. Men, she said, are usually not like that. Men always want something from me. I am a man too, Pinto said. Do you want to know my real name? she asked him. It is Helena.

If she did sleep with men for money, she at least chose who

to go with, which was why she refused to succumb to Hovans. He came with an entourage of his thick-necked thugs and was throwing money around because he had found himself a golden goose in an American judge he was blackmailing for being a homosexual. Hovans kept ordering bottles of champagne and vodka for his gang, summoning the best house Natashas. He took hold of Lenka, groping and grabbing her crotch, pinching her nipples, biting her neck. He pulled her hair and told her that he was going to fuck her in the ass, so that when the rest of his party went to the back rooms, Lenka refused to go with him, and then he grabbed and pushed her down to fuck her right there, so she wriggled from under him enough to smash one of the champagne bottles on his head. Hovans punched her in the face, and would've probably killed her if he wasn't stopped by the bouncers and then escorted out. At the end of the night, Halyapin threw Lenka out without paying her and told her never to show up again at the Majestic or he would kill her himself. She didn't dare leave by herself to go back to her place, so Pinto took her in at his shikumen for the night. She stayed with him for a couple of days, Rahela monitoring her suspiciously, and jealously. When Lenka went back home, Hovans ambushed her and threw vitriol in her face. She was lucky he didn't blind her, or that her left ear didn't melt off her head. For everything God created, He created its counterpart.

Lenka sat down next to Pinto on the building's edge. She offered Pinto a cigarette, and lit up one herself, her feet dangling over the edge like his. Her left shoe was hanging on her big toe, and then it fell off her foot and spun downward to vanish. She didn't even wince, and it seemed that she didn't notice. You lost your shoe,

Pinto said, but she shrugged, and placed her head on his shoulder. The fires in Chapei appeared to have darkened, becoming redder, the color of an infernal twilight. They heard explosions, but they came muffled and there were no flashes.

What are we going to do? she asked.

Well, as soon as Rahela's up we will go down and find something to eat and then we'll see if we can go back home.

Home, she scoffed. We won't be going home anytime soon.

My mother used to say: Si los amijos kajeron, los dedikos kedaron.

What does that mean?

Even if the rings slip off, there are still the fingers.

Fine, but what does that mean?

I don't know, Pinto said. There has never been a time when there was nothing. We will go somewhere.

The night simply faded and turned into a dun day, the same nocturnal drizzle hovering in the diurnal air. More refugees amassed overnight, and the streets were even more crowded. The Municipal Council had managed to put up barbed wire along Avenue Edward VII, but that just made it impassable for cars as people took over the street. In the middle of it, a tent had already risen, opened to the sky, apparently offering a circus show, as Pinto recognized the sign 戏 on the banner above the entrance. From behind the curtain, a bamboo pole with a caged monkey emerged, then swung to attract attention while the monkey shivered and shrieked in fear. Before the curtain opening that was supposed to be the entrance, two skinny wrestlers in loincloths grappled and grabbed at each other's oiled bodies. They were like the Sarajevo pehlivans, who would oil up their naked torsos and legs on market days and strut like angry peacocks before they lunged at each other. Padri Avram never let him watch them, because he found half-naked men and their bodies disgusting, but to Pinto they were always beautiful. The monkey was screeching, obviously unhappy in the drizzle. Look at that monkey, Rahela! Pinto said. It's a circus. Do you want to go in?

Rahela shrugged. She didn't look too impressed. She had developed an anemic pallor that continuously worried Pinto, particularly when she seemed listless and tired. There had been a time, before he got the job at the Majestic, when they did not have much to eat. But now—that is, before the Japanese attacked Chapei—he made sure she had some fresh vegetables. Who wouldn't be hopeless and pale on a day like today?

What else are we going to do? Lenka said. There is nothing to do, no other place to go.

If you want to, Rahela said. We can go. Pinto excavated a coin from a pocket to pay for their entrance.

At the far end of the encirclement inside, four boys stood on each other's shoulders; the top one held a bouquet of sticks on which a flock of plates spun, dangerously close to the canvas wall. The audience was sparse, standing around with slouched shoulders, as tired and desperate people do. Everyone seemed to be Chinese, except for a man and a woman on the fringes of the crowd. The woman wore a tiara and a shabby velvet dress, incongruous in the drizzly drabness, and it took a moment for Pinto to recognize Bogolyubova. What was she doing there? He looked at Lenka to see if she recognized her too, but she and Rahela were mesmerized by the boys, who were dramatically close to dropping the plates or even falling.

Bogolyubova claimed to be a clairvoyant, performed at the Majestic more than once, under a different, more sorceress-sounding name, which he couldn't remember now. In a long black gown with a hood, only her hands and eyes visible, speaking English with an exaggerated Russian accent, and in a voice deeper than her normal one, she would call on someone from the audience and then tell them what she saw in their past and their future. Half of the time, the person was planted, likely to be her lover, a past, present, or future one. She had once been a lowly Natasha too, until she started performing in a club with another woman using a dildo stuffed with wood ear mushrooms that swelled in hot water, which made her famous all over Shanghai. So Halyapin said, and she never bothered to deny it. Once Pinto saw her in the public garden on the arm of a lover who looked like a Jardine Matheson comprador—handsome, confident, Eurasian. Pinto followed them to the door of the British consulate, where she kissed the comprador's forehead and dismissed him to enter the consulate as if returning home to her family house after a date. She had a penchant for popping up in strange places, accompanied by strange people.

Now she was in a street circus, talking to a white man in a tweed jacket with a flower in its lapel, a monocle, and a walking stick. The man reminded Pinto of Moser, what with his straight back and the chin slightly upturned in perpetual contempt. He had to be British; perhaps that was why he was reminiscent of Moser. The man was scanning the crowd without interest, but when his eyes met Pinto's, he flashed a feeble smile. Bogolyubova whispered something in the man's ear and he nodded slowly, still looking at Pinto. His eyes were as blue as Moser's. The man kissed Bogolyubova's cheek and walked away and out. He seemed to limp a bit, but it could also be that the stick made it seem so.

He hadn't seen Moser since he'd saved them in Korla. Moser had continued east beyond Kashgar, until he ran into the Baron and his Division. He had recognized the Baron's lunacy and potential in fighting the Bolsheviks and convinced him that he was not a Bolshevik spy but a British officer, who could help the Baron achieve his dream. Moser quickly understood that sooner or later the Baron would be disposed of by his troops. Had he tried to escape before the mutiny, he was sure he would have been, just like Pinto, strung up in a tree. Pinto and Rahela were very lucky that the Baron was deposed when he was deposed, Moser told Pinto. He was glad to be able to repay his debt by saving Pinto's life, and the life of the little girl. Afterward, Moser headed south to Tibet in the company of a few desperate Cossacks. Pinto and Rahela tagged along for a while, until their path crossed with an eastbound caravan's, just before they got into the deep desert. Pinto didn't even know if Moser made it to Tibet. It took Pinto and Rahela a few long and terrible years to reach Shanghai.

The boys were finally somersaulting off one another's shoulders, and Rahela gasped as each of them landed to receive the tepid applause. The boys were beautiful in their ragtag clothes, and ribbons on their biceps fluttered around them like feathers. They flew with ease, yet it seemed that they could crash and die any moment, and if that happened, no one in the audience, which was not at all awed by their performance, would care. Rahela was going to be interested in boys soon; she was almost twelve now. Part of Pinto wished she would turn out to be interested in girls, but that would not make it any easier for her; in fact, it would make it at least twice as hard. All you can do is make shade for the child and provide food as you fret about what might befall her.

I'm hungry, Rahela said.

Me too, Lenka said.

Don't you want to wait for the monkeys?

I don't think that monkeys are worth the wait.

Pinto remembered: Bogolyubova's clairvoyant name was Madame Pecher. She was now facing the audience and a couple of the boys were running around her in opposite directions to wrap her in a ridiculously thick chain, obviously not made of iron. Other than mushroom dildos and clairvoyance, she did Houdini-like escapes at the Majestic that were so un-Houdini-like that the patrons often laughed. He knew what would happen— she would spin around a few times, like the pirouetting ballerina she claimed to have been in Russia, and the chains would drop off, and she would spread her arms in triumph. The trick was so bad that Pinto wanted to see what the audience would do, whether they would laugh as well. She did not mention her Houdini name this time around. Why was she here? Lenka and Rahela were already on their way out. Pinto looked around for the man Bogolyubova was talking to, but he was gone. Bogolyubova did spread her arms in triumph, and Pinto headed out. But instead of tepid applause, he heard her deep clairvoyant voice.

Rafael!

He stopped in his tracks and turned around. With her arms still spread, she glared at him ominously from the low and shallow stage.

Rafael, I must talk to you.

Ludicrous as she was, a flutter of fear went through Pinto's stomach and he waited for her to walk over to him. A pipa player sat down onstage to face an even scarcer audience and plucked the strings and sang in a high-pitched nasal voice a song that sounded like a story.

Rafael, Bogolyubova said, that man wants to see you.

What man?

That man that I was talking to.

Why does he want to see me?

He wants to see you to talk to you.

Why didn't he talk to me now?

He wants to see you to talk to you.

What if I don't want to talk to him?

I am just giving a message. If you want to see him, go to Cathay Hotel this evening at seven. He will explain it to you. Ask for Mr. Nelson-Jones.

It was abruptly clear to Pinto that the man was no Nelson-Jones, of course, but Moser-Ethering, just as it was day and it was raining. After all these years, he had showed up in Pinto's life again. The years since he'd seen him last must have changed him, but back in Korla, he was sunburnt and bearded, his deel hanging on his emaciated body as on a rack. His cover here and now seemed to be proper Englishness. Pinto must've blanched, as Bogolyubova placed her hand on his forearm as if to hold him steady. Her hand was stacked with rings that could no longer be taken off because her knuckles were indelibly swollen with arthritis.

Do you know him? Bogolyubova asked.

No.

Are you going to see him?

No, Pinto said, and Bogolyubova shrugged. She was no clairvoyant, because she couldn't see that Pinto was lying and had already made up his mind to go see Moser, since he would surely be able to help in some way. Thou shalt not stand by the blood of a stranger, the Lord said to Moses.

Outside the circus entrance, the two acrobats launched themselves backward and landed on their feet, then they flipped forward and landed on their hands to stay upright with their toes pointing to the sky. Lenka emerged from the crowd limping in one shoe, stuffing her mouth with a rice cake, but Rahela was not by her side. A steel ball of unease stirred in Pinto's stomach and then started to grind his bowels.

Where is Rahela? she asked him, munching on a rice cake.

You're asking me? he shouted at her, scaring her—she had never heard him shout.

Wasn't she with you? Lenka said. I thought she was with you. She swallowed the morsel she had in her mouth, and its shape moved down her throat.

She was not with me. She was with you. Where is she?

I don't know.

Her eyes filled with fear and tears. Still she took another bite out of the rice cake.

Do you have to eat now?

I'm hungry, she said, and stuffed the rest of it in her mouth.

They rushed in opposite directions. He went toward the racecourse, ruthlessly pushing his way through the weak swarm. He ran into a cul-de-sac of bodies, then sidestepped it by following a brazen rickshaw, until it too got stuck. He barged through, squeezing past rickshaws and crawling cars. Children disappeared in Shanghai; they were tortured, raped, and killed; they were never found; they were sent down to the Hong Kong brothels. Whenever there was a sudden clearance in the street as the throng flowed and ebbed, he accelerated to running, but then was out of breath so quickly that he had to stop and retch. If something had happened to Rahela, perhaps the best thing for him would be to die here and now. There was no reason to go toward the racecourse any more than in any other direction. Where would she have gone? He turned around on his heel, the jute bag swinging like a tail, and pushed his way back toward the circus. Just last week, the decayed body of a child was fished out of the Soochow Creek, not far from the Majestic. Pinto tripped and stumbled forth to knock over an old man with a staff. The man fell down on his back to curse at him in Chinese, while stabbing at him with his stick. Pinto grabbed the end of the staff and pulled it, helping the man stand up, like a film run backward. The man continued to rail at him. His front teeth were missing so his tongue wiggled in the cavity as if about to fully hatch.

And then he saw Rahela, sitting on the curb, biting into a bun as if she had no care in the world; the sole of one of her shoes was peeling off. He hurled himself toward her with such force that she was startled and yelped.

What are you doing here? he vociferated. I was looking for you everywhere!

I'm waiting for you, she said. What does it look like?

Waiting for me?

For you and Lenka.

She had wandered up the street waiting for him to come out of the circus, she said, and when she turned around to go back everything was abruptly different and she was lost. She could not find him and Lenka, nor the circus, nor Avenue Edward VII, and all of a sudden she didn't know what to do or where to go.

The kneeling Pinto kissed her hair and forehead repeatedly. Mi fiža! he said. Mi fiža! The man with the staff walked on past them, still cursing at Pinto. Rahela's face, like his and everyone else's, was streaked with drops of rain. After they had crossed the most dangerous part of the desert, after they arrived in a village at the fringe of the Taklamakan, where they had food and water, and he could finally admit to himself that it was a miracle that such a young child could survive the trek and begin believing that she was exceptionally strong and resilient, she fell ill. For weeks, she could not open her eyes, let alone sit up. He sat at her bedside, staring at her face, as if his sheer will could erase her fever and unclasp her eyelids. He negotiated with the Lord and offered his life for hers, but the Lord neither said nor did anything. Pinto held her in his arms, draining soup or rice water into her mouth. He sang to her, and told her stories of Sarajevo and Osman, but she would not show any signs she might hear it. She became so thin and weak that when the earthquake hit, their host, the teacher of the village, tried to convince him to leave her in the house and let her die. But he grabbed her, and she was light as a handkerchief, and he ran out and one side of the house crumbled. He nearly passed out as he realized that they had almost died; but once he regained his breath and mind, it was clear to him that if she died, he would die too. He would just collapse on the ground and stay there folded until he was no more. But, once again, she survived, tough and resilient as she was.

Then a nice man stroked my head, Rahela said. He told me not to worry, because everything will turn out well. He was very handsome. Had a beautiful smile. A mustache too.

A nice man with a mustache? Rahela! You must never talk to strangers, particularly nice men with a mustache!

He said he knew you. He had a mustache. He liked my necklace, she said, and touched the Samsara wheel pebble that was the pendant.

Did he have a stick? Did he have a jacket with a flower? Did he wear a tie?

No, Rahela said. It was just a shirt. One of its collars was torn. His hand was a little crooked, like a claw.

A vast space opened up inside Pinto, as though all of his organs, including his soul, were swiftly annihilated. He sat down on the ground, in a puddle, and the water was warm.

Did he tell you his name?

No, she said.

Why didn't he wait with you?

I don't know, she said. He said that I should wait for you here and that you would soon come to find me.

What language did he speak?

I don't know.

Where did he go?

I don't know.

When did all this happen?

Don't yell at me.

Fine, Pinto lowered his voice. When did he leave?

Just a moment ago, she said. He gave me a bun and left.

Pinto lifted her into his arms and walked with her, unable to run as she was heavy. Once upon a time he carried her through a series of deserts, but she had grown bigger since without his really noticing. He had to put her down, grabbed her hand, and pulled her so hard that the bun leaped out of her hand and dropped on the ground. He did not stop for her to pick it up.

Tell me if you see him, he said.

No, she said. You are not nice to me.

He ignored her complaint, pushing through the crowd again, looking for that beautiful head of thick hair. Pinto would instantly recognize his smile, and his mustache, the smell of his body. Osman, you found me at the end of the world, in Shanghai! You were always going to find me, wherever I may have been. And where are you? Say something to me. Speak. Someone as tall and as Bosnian as Osman should be easy to spot here. His gait too, throwing his shoulders back slightly, as if always on the verge of dancing, or wrestling. Pehlivaning, they called that kind of demeanor in Sarajevo.

Who is that man? Rahela whined. Why do we have to look for him?

I will tell you later, Pinto said. Let's find him first.

He couldn't have gone too far ahead. He was limping too, Rahela said.

Who hurt you, Osman, my love? Who took care of you and helped you heal afterward? A surge of tears arrived to his face, burst out of his eyes, but he kept running. Everyone around him, this mass of people, was not Osman. Everyone except Osman was not Osman, everybody was someone he did not want or need. Everybody else was Osman's counterpart.

Rahela ripped her hand out of his and stopped.

What now? Let's go.

No.

Why not?

Who is that man?

I can't tell you now.

Why not?

Because I don't know.

Why are we chasing him?

Pinto could not answer. Because he might be the man I love and have not seen or had news of for eleven years? Because the man might be your father? If it was him, why did he walk away? Rahela would not move or go anywhere, stubborn as she was, but Lenka materialized again, so Pinto left Rahela with her and went on running up and down Edward VII, past the racecourse, up Tibet Road, around to Bubbling Well Road, back to Edward VII, then all the way to the Bund, where he stood on the bank of the Whangpoo, facing the river murk passing steadily around the Japanese Navy ships downstream, with all their turret guns pointed at Chapei. Osman would've spoken to him, he would not just show up to confound his daughter, then leave. That's what he used to do: Osman's voice, calm and loving, would guide him through all the difficulties and troubles. He would have been with him, inside him, telling him where Rahela was, placating him, dampening the thunder of his despair. He wouldn't have just deposited her on the street and left. But then, Osman hadn't spoken to him since Korla, not since Moser saved them from the insane Baron, not even while they were crossing China on their way to Shanghai, which took them years, many caravans, and stops in nameless towns and villages. Somewhere in Gansu, in a village destroyed by an earthquake, Rahela barely survived scarlet fever, but not even then did Osman speak to him. Later, it occurred to Pinto that Osman had maybe talked to him but did it at a time when Rahela was so overwhelmed by her illness, so close to dying, that he might not have heard him. Those weeks of no hope and no sleep, just the throbbing of love in his head for a child that was not even his. And it was in Shanghai, a few years later, when she was talking ceaselessly while munching on a tong youn, that he realized that Osman's voice had stopped talking to him just as Rahela had started speaking, and that maybe he was speaking to Pinto through Rahela's presence. But she was talking at the time about the straw doll Lu had made for her, and in a language she and Pinto used, a mixture of Bosnian and Spanjol and German, with many words they had picked up along the way from Tajik and Kyrgyz and Uighur, and the nameless languages and dialects they had absorbed while following various caravans—they spoke a language that no one in the world spoke other than the two of them, because no one had gone through the things they had. It could be that Osman was silent because he could not speak or share their language. Maybe he had come here with Moser, maybe Moser had found him and brought him here. Now he could be anywhere in Shanghai. Pinto darted around like a beheaded fly, looking for him all over town, until he understood that Osman would've surely found him if he wanted to, or he would have at least spoken to him, and that there must have been a reason for his not doing so, and the only reason that would make sense was that Osman no longer loved him. And there was another possibility, which Pinto denied and avoided and never wanted to believe: that Osman spoke to him for as long as he was alive, wherever he was, and then went silent after he had perished, and would therefore never speak to Pinto again.

I do not actually know how Pinto ran into Moser in Shanghai, but I do know that he did, because the Englishman writes about it in *A Foreign Devil in Asia*, his very last memoir before his death in 1974. In it, he mentions running into the Jewish Doctor he had met in Tashkent. Pinto scarcely occupies a short paragraph, wherein he is described as working in a shady club called the Majestic, hanging out with gangsters, prostitutes, and clairvoyants, and being involved with a male Chinese lover. Though Moser is quite tolerant himself of male love, not uncommon among his Oxford peers, he finds this kind of miscegenation quite bizarre. Moser also mentions Pinto's charming young adoptive daughter, with a tawny skin hue typical of exotic Jews like her father. The girl entered the world, he notes parenthetically, by way of killing her mother. He goes on to pity her for having to grow up in the poverty and debauchery of Shanghai, and casually mentions that he intervened to get her into the American school. He does not say what happened to her in the end: whether she had married a nice foreign man or ended up as a Natasha in one of Shanghai's many brothels, which he perceives as the two most likely possibilities. Later in the book, he casually mentions watching a certain Victoria Litvinoff perform her clairvoyant act, and meeting her afterward for reasons unclear. She is described as the grande dame of the Russian-speaking underworld in Shanghai, someone who started as a prostitute, graduated to a performer, and then invested her hard-earned money into a high-end brothel catering to more sophisticated and daring tastes. Madame Litvinoff—née Bogolyubova—was an invaluable source of intelligence and information, what with many a foreign diplomat, businessman, and player in the complex world of Shanghai crime and politics being a devout client of her house of deliciously ill repute. When some years later Moser comes back to Shanghai from Hong Kong to help facilitate the panicky evacuation before the Communist takeover, Bogolyubova, even if she collaborated with the Japanese occupiers, will be on the ship he had arranged for the British citizens and their families. At the peak of the summer, she will wear a thick fur coat because it is her most valuable possession. With a certain amount of whimsical nostalgia he also writes about visiting the Cathay Hotel before he boarded the ship never to return to Shanghai. It is empty, much of it looted, with filthy refugees camping in the lobby. Yet nothing can stop him from reminiscing about the marvelous parties orchestrated by the genius of Sir Victor Sassoon in the hotel's spectacular ballroom. He particularly enjoys recalling the circus party, when Sir Victor was dressed as a ringmaster, and the notorious *Titanic* one, where everyone was dressed as though they had just survived a shipwreck.

All along Nanking Road, the sidewalks were lined with refugees, except right outside the hotels: the Astor House, the Park, and the Cathay. Hotel security kept the sidewalks clear so that cars could drive up and unload guests and patrons. Refugees crowded along the perimeter of the clear space in front of the Cathay, creating a cordon of reeking bodies, through which Pinto had to push his way. With his clothes wet and worn and smelly, his jacket frayed at the cuffs, the seat of his pants still wet, and a knot in his tie that could not be untied without a knife, Pinto very much looked like a refugee himself. Even if he had worn clean and fancy clothes, being a refugee was legible in his frown, in his supplicant face imploring not to be thrown out of whatever space he happened to be in. He saw the reflection of his face in the door kept open for someone else by the porter, who despite the elaborate hat looked like he could work late shifts as a bruiser at the Majestic. When Pinto moved to enter, the porter closed the door and shook his head without saying a word.

I am here to see Mr. Nelson-Jones.

The porter shook his head.

Sparky Nelson-Jones, Pinto ventured. He is a friend of mine.

A friend of yours? No kidding. Where did you meet him?

We used to work together. In Turkestan.

Is that so? What did you do?

I was a doctor. I am a doctor.

And Mr. Nelson-Jones?

Maybe you should ask him, Pinto said. He'll be happy to know that you are very interested in him and his work.

The porter read Pinto's face for signs of bluffing or kidding, and then he opened the door for him and stepped aside.

It took the young man at the reception desk quite a while before he lifted his gaze to examine and subsequently detest Pinto, who had the temerity to place his hands on the counter, thus fully exposing the incriminating filth on his hands and frayed jacket cuffs. I'm here to see Mr. Nelson-Jones, Pinto said. Without saying a word, the young man lifted a receiver and spoke into it with a very English accent, only to laugh heartily at the end of the brief conversation. Indeed, sir! Indeed! he said into the phone. What does indeed really mean? It's never been clear to Pinto.

He will meet you at the Horse and Hounds in ten minutes, the young man finally said.

Where is that? Pinto asked.

The Horse and Hounds was in the lobby, which Pinto crossed carefully lest he slip on the polished marble floor. He had never been at the Cathay before—this was a place for the rich. He didn't dare sit down in the bar, worried that he might dirty the chair, that they might throw him out, or that the haughty server, moving deftly among the tables, would force him to have a drink he, a nothing and a nobody, could never dream of being able to afford. A group of tourists waiting for the elevator exchanged stories about their excursions to Suzhou just before the fighting started, and then complained about being stuck in Shanghai in the middle of a silly war. Pinto was detached from any part of the reality reigning in the hotel, from the marble floors, the stained glass, the bright lights, the casual joviality of the tourists, who were looking at him askance, as if at a stray dog. He had once met a man at a hotel in Vienna that had a red carpet leading to the elevator's mouth; he had been forced to sit in the waiting area as the receptionist called the room while emanating contempt for someone who met men in hotels as cheap as that one. Pinto had looked down instead of gazing back defiantly at the receptionist. After he had slept with the man—who was, Pinto suddenly remembered, from Zagreb—he was determined to meet the receptionist's eyes on the way out to show him that he felt no shame. But the man behind the desk was different, and he didn't even look up. This had taken place twenty-five years before, in a world no longer available. Only the past matters, because it is the only thing that outlives everything and everyone.

How do you do? Moser said, approaching Pinto with a clear limp, his hand extended for a shake. The nails were clean, its moons neat, so he must have noticed the contrast between their two hands. A pleasure to have finally met you! he said. I've heard so much about you.

Moser? Pinto said. Moser-Ethering? You are Moser, yes?

But Moser kept the unchanging smile lit up like a marquee, and would not show in any way that he recognized the name or Pinto himself. It was not impossible that Pinto was losing his mind, for the man was Moser, even with his hair cropped, his face shaven, and his mustache trimmed, with the nasal voice and his upper lip kept at the gumline in a cramped smile. The last time he'd seen him before today, his skin had been burnished, the beard sand-coated, lesions and blisters on his hands. In addition to limping, he wobbled, as those men who spend a lot of time on a horse do. The man standing now before him reminded Pinto of his anatomy professor in Vienna, who had his coffee at the Sacher Hotel and regularly read Karl Kraus columns to quote him in his classes. The Moser before this was a dream of a dream. But then what memory wasn't?

I beg your pardon? Moser said. I'm afraid you are mistaking me for some old friend of yours. Was it someone you knew in Russia?

He looked straight into Pinto's eyes in a way that did not match his words, keeping the smile in front of his face like a mask. You cannot fathom my rules.

I knew Mr. Moser in Turkestan, some years ago, when I lived there, Pinto said. Have you ever been in Turkestan?

Once, very briefly, Moser said. I was on my way to Korla, in Chinese Turkestan, where I was to serve as an adviser to a local potentate. So many things happened since then that I can barely remember those times, no point in revisiting any of that. Let's talk about the future. Shall we sit and take a drink? I am eager to get to know you better. By the way, friends call me Sparky.

Nice to meet you, Mr. Sparky, Pinto said.

Indeed, Sparky said.

Did you maybe run into my daughter earlier today, on Avenue Edward VII, and talked to her?

I'm afraid I haven't left my room at all until now, Sparky said.

Pinto was hungry, as he hadn't eaten anything since the day before, so the cocktail Moser ordered for them inebriated him within a couple of sips. He had a hard time following what Moser was saying about his recent arrival in Shanghai, about his need to make new friends, track down some old and dear ones. He was aiming to establish himself as a citizen of this amazing city and invest some money in its future, so to speak, which does not seem so bright today. The cocktail was called the Green Hat. Sir Victor Sassoon himself created it, and it was one of the many famous things about this hotel. Moser was in New York not so long before and asked the bartender at the Algonquin to make him a Green Hat and the poor sap had no idea what that was, so Sparky had to show him. I told him: two parts gin, two parts Cointreau, two parts vermouth français, two parts crème de menthe, a few drops of lemon juice. It is quite potent, isn't it? What do you think?

What Pinto thought was that this Sparky—who, after the Green Hat, may or may not have looked like Moser—wanted something from him, and would not come out and say it. And he also thought that if this man was in fact the Moser he remembered, then perhaps he could know what had happened to Osman and whether he was now here in Shanghai. Pinto wanted to ask him, but Sparky would not stop talking about how marvelous New York was, even at the time of the Depression, and how America, once it gets past its current travails, will dominate the world, offering a rather appealing alternative to the scourge of Communism. The banner of Western civilization, Sparky said, is now firmly in the hands of our American friends. Chicago will be the capital of the world.

Erinnerst du dich an Osman? Pinto asked.

Sparky stopped talking and Pinto could tell that he understood what he had said because he could speak German.

I'm sorry, I do not think I understand what you're saying, Moser said.

Ist er hier in Shanghai?

I'm afraid I don't speak German at all.

Du bist Moser. Ich weiß wer du bist.

Sparky looked around, as if to see if someone was listening. There was only one other man in the Horse and Hounds, and he seemed to be immersed in the China Daily News, putting it down only to take a sip of tea from his china cup.

Folge mir, bitte, Sparky said, and stood up.

Sparky Nelson-Jones wielded power at the Cathay Hotel, for he told the elevator operator to step out and get himself a bun or whatever, and handed him a few coins to do so. The boy was reluctant, but Sparky dismissed him and pushed him out. He moved the lever to eight and the elevator crawled up. Pinto smelled his cologne and the cleanliness of his attire, just as he smelled the stench of his own hunger and dampness, of having no idea what might happen next.

So, do not ever call me Moser around here, he said. That is a dead name. Call me Mr. Nelson-Jones. And if anyone has seen us here together now and asks you about me, tell them we had a mutual Viennese friend who implored me to look you up in Shanghai. We should not see each other in public after this.

In a blink, the man became a full Moser, speaking rapidly in his Moser voice, the stiff upper lip and the grin below it stored away for some later use.

How would our mutual Viennese friend know that I was in Shanghai? Pinto asked.

You wrote to our mutual friend, Moritz Ebner, asking for help. I am here now, eager and happy to help.

How are you going to help? Pinto asked.

Well, Moser said, funny that you should ask. Let me get you some better clothes first.

They reached the eighth floor, whereupon Moser pushed the lever back to four, and down they went.

Moser even let him take a bath. The more pleasant the feeling of warm water and sandalwood soap was on his skin, the more guilty Pinto felt. In fact, he decided not to mention it to Rahela and Lenka, although it was certain they would be able to smell his new cleanliness, since whole sheaves of dirt came off his skin and floated like frog spawn on the surface of the water. They would surely see his hands. He scrubbed his nails, clipped them, and his fingers now looked like they were transplanted from someone who was not poor, the numerous little cuts notwithstanding.

Moser gave him some clean clothes—the pale blue shirt was too spacious, and the pants hung loose on his hips. Pinto declined a new jacket, because it was so large that it swallowed him, and because he did not want to transfer all the pathetic things he kept in his pockets: coins, keys, notes, a hardened opium pellet. He stood in front of the tall mirror, in new clothes, and saw an old, tired, dark-skinned stranger. His neck rising from the buttoned collar, the way he slouched and sank into his own weakened body, his old misshapen jacket and the pockets weighted with the debris of his life made him want to cry. He was only forty-three and had already lived far too long and seen much too much. Not everyone gets the same amount of living in life. And the Lord will take away from you all that causes sickness, and give it to someone else, because He can, and someone else will have to take it because there will be no other choice.

Pinto was now clean and therefore different, so he asked:

Do you know what happened to Osman?

Who is Osman?

Osman, my friend, who got you out of Tashkent.

Karishik? Yes, well, as far as I can tell, he never made it out of Turkestan, but then, to be honest, I never tried to find out what happened. What happened?

He left and never came back, Pinto said.

Frankly, Moser said, I hadn't thought much about him until today, or about you for that matter. I'd be glad to send a telegram to London and see if there is any intelligence on what might have happened to your handsome friend.

My daughter might have seen him here, today. It was very strange.

It would be very strange and I'd be very surprised indeed if he somehow ended up here. I could check with my acquaintance at the Municipal Council to see if they have any record of—what's his full name?—arriving here. Of course, anyone could come in and out of Shanghai as they please.

A lump formed in Pinto's throat, and he could not say anything, aware that his eyes were filling up with tears.

I am sorry. It appears you were very fond of him, Moser said. On a different note, I am happy to see that your daughter grew into a remarkable young lady. I would like to help the young lady with her education. I think I can get her a spot at the American School.

Moser offered him a handkerchief, but Pinto refused, because he did not wish to acknowledge his wet eyes. He said:

We cannot afford that.

I can get her a scholarship.

She would need stuff. Clothes, shoes, books.

All expenses paid.

Only rich people's kids go to that school.

She will be fine. She is a sharp girl.

How do you know? You've never met her.

She will be fine, I promise you.

Why?

I beg your pardon? Why what?

Why would you help? What do you want in return?

Moser stuffed the handkerchief in Pinto's pocket.

Here, you might need it, he said. Now, let's go have some supper. I'll explain everything.

They stepped into the elevator and there were Madeleine and Henry Krantz, a newlywed American couple. They would not let a shitty little local war ruin their hard-earned honeymoon,

Henry declared to them before they reached the lobby. Henry was drunk already, while Maddy carried a picnic basket with canapés and a bottle of chilled champagne. They were going to check out what was going on across the creek, Henry said, see what makes the natives restless. It promises to be a lot of fun.

You should come along, Maddie said, drunk as well.

We were off to have supper, Moser said.

We got plenty of supper, Maddie said. I have a bucket of caviar inside this basket.

What do you think? Moser asked Pinto, who was surprised that Moser would even consider it.

No. We have to talk about something, yes?

We can talk about it later. It can wait.

I need to go, Pinto said.

It is going to be fun, Henry said. You wouldn't want to miss it.

Outside the Cathay, Pinto attempted to slip away from Moser and the Americans and merge back into the refugee mass, because he was ashamed, because he had a feeling that he was being lured into something sinister, because he did not want to be away from Rahela and Lenka. But Henry grabbed Pinto by the elbow and pushed him into the passenger seat of a Packard. Maddie and Henry flanked Moser in the back seat, passing the flask under his nose until he finally took a proper sip.

Their stout, bald driver, they would find out on their short drive to Szechuan Road, was a count and an artillery officer in the Russian Imperial Army. His unsolicited assessment of the military situation in Shanghai, delivered in an artillerious voice, was that the Japanese shelling of Chapei and the North Station was so far restrained and that they would soon unleash their full force, send in more ships, maybe even the airplanes, level Chapei, and thus quickly end this ridiculous little war. And I am all on their side, the Count said in his soft-consonant accent, for the Chinese are cattle. Fuck them. Fuck them all! Henry exclaimed, and offered the flask to the Count, who took a big sip while bumping into rickshaws to push through.

Maddie said they had gone up to Szechuan Road with some people they knew from the hotel a couple of nights ago, and had a fantastic time.

Everybody was out, she said. Drinking and watching the war.

The stupid Jap marines just marched in their knee-high white socks right down the street with all the lights on, Henry said, so the Chink snipers picked them off like bottles on a fence.

It was a bloodbath, Maddie said. We placed bets on which officers would go down first. Henry won a lot of money.

Yup, Henry said. Earned it fair and square.

Years later, sometime in the late fifties, in Saigon, Moser would run into Henry, deployed in Vietnam under cover of a *New York Times* reporter. In *A Foreign Devil in Asia*, Moser observes that Henry was quite hapless as an intelligence officer, behaving as if striving to get his cover blown. Moser recalls the drinks at the Continental Shelf, frequented by foreign correspondents and spies. Henry wore a toupee that looked like a beaver pelt and was quickly drunk enough to reminisce about their adventures in Shanghai and the serendipity of their meeting again. Moser, having become increasingly more philosophical with age, draws some profound conclusions in his book, featuring cosmic trajectories and the flow of destiny and the impenetrable logic of life and death, quoting Henry's inebriated quip: I don't need a perfect world, I just need to be in a perfect place. For his part, Henry never got to write a memoir. A few years after the meeting, he was embedded with a unit of the Green Berets in order to write a story about their heroism. On their mission in Cambodia, he stepped into a hole full of sharpened stakes and never came back out.

The Count was not a good driver. He kept hitting the brakes when unnecessary and not hitting them when necessary, cursing all along in sibilant Russian. He took a wrong turn and was now driving them in the opposite direction from Szechuan Road until Pinto pointed it out. Whereupon the Count exclaimed, Ah ydi na khuy! and then turned the car around in the middle of the street, blocking the traffic in all directions. Maybe we can walk? Henry said. Absolutely not, Maddie said. I have high heels. These feet were not made for walking.

In the course of the wretched trip, Henry told whatever he could to Moser, who listened to him silently, no doubt calculating how Henry's openness could turn out to be useful to him. Henry had recently graduated from Princeton, where his father had also gone, and his grandfather had taught until he followed Woodrow Wilson to the White House. Then Henry married Maddie, whom he had known since she was a girl spending her summers in Cape Cod.

He is my first and last love, Maddie said. I met him when I was twelve and he was seventeen.

Henry was going to start working for the government, as his older brother did, as soon as they were back from their honeymoon.

And I'll start popping out children, Maddie said.

I would like at least four, Henry said. Let's Krantz it up.

Pinto stopped listening, not least because Henry's fizzing American English would've been too hard to understand even if he cared about what he was saying. Pinto was still a bit drunk and so hungry that he thought he might faint. He would've liked to have closed his eyes to rest, but the Count was steering the car like a dinghy on a stormy sea. Is this your bodyguard? Henry asked Moser about Pinto at some point, and Moser said, You'd never be able to tell, but this man can be a cold-blooded killer. He stabbed a Cossack in the eye. The Count glanced at Pinto and scoffed derisively. Then he laughed, as did Henry and Maddie.

Padri Avram had once told a story of two brothers, one of whom killed the other. Their mother took a cup, filled it with the blood of the slain brother, and placed it on the east windowsill in her room. Day after day, as the sun rose, she would wake up and see the blood of her killed son. One morning, she saw that the blood was seething and she knew that the other son was dead too.

The car finally made it to the strip of the Szechuan Road where a few others had already pulled over. On top of one of the cars, a couple was dancing, foxtrotting to the music from the gramophone on the hood, which kept skipping, and to the shooting coming from Chapei. A group of men in black-tie attire and women in backless sequined dresses stood around, indifferent to the drizzle, chatting as if at a reception.

This is it, Maddie said. This is where the party is.

The Count stopped the car, and the three got out from the back seat, while Pinto stayed in the front. The Count said, Nu? but Pinto refused to get out, as disgust and fear swelled in his stomach. He sat in silence with the Count, who broke it occasionally to grumble something to himself. Pinto became even more determined to construct a solid lie so as to conceal from Rahela what he was doing this evening. His chest was throbbing with trepidation.

Szechuan Road was lit up to a point, beyond which there was

darkness full of gunfire. A waiter with a loaded tray crossed the street to deliver the drinks to the well-dressed group and pick up their empty glasses. Maddie got out and was about to unpack her picnic basket when Henry, who got out on the other side, stood with his feet apart and arms akimbo, like a general facing a battlefield, and declared, Don't get out! This is no good. There is nothing happening here. Let's go where the action is.

I do not think that going farther would be advisable, Moser said from the car. Either side could take us to be the enemy and shoot us up.

They won't shoot at us, Maddie said. They can see that we are all white here.

Not in the dark they cannot, Moser said.

We'll be fine, Henry said. We'll be just fine. God loves us. Let's go.

Even then, Pinto knew that he should've gotten out of the car, but he was so weak from the combination of hunger and the Green Hat that he simply could not make a decision to move. It would never be clear to Pinto why Moser decided to go along. Maybe because Maddie and Henry got back in on their respective sides, and making them get out was too uncouth. Most probably, in some incredible Moser way, he recognized that Henry, in his ambition and stupidity, would undoubtedly turn out to be useful. And we do know now that Henry would remain in Shanghai and that Moser would meet him whenever he came up from Hong Kong, for his American friend was in his garrulous verbosity a splendid source of information, just as he would be in Vietnam. Nevertheless, it did occur to Pinto, before the Count made the car lurch forward and drove it into Chapei, that maybe Moser did not want to let Pinto go alone with Henry and was worried about him.

The streets were empty now, except for the debris—a chair,

a basket, a dead civilian—but the Count was driving in a low gear and the engine was roaring. Turn off the headlights, Moser said, but the Count couldn't find the right switch to pull. It was quite possible, Pinto realized, that the Count had made the real driver give up the car so that he could do the job and pocket the money. Shut down the damn lights! Moser shouted. K chortu! the Count groaned, and flashed the lights before turning them off. There you go, Henry said. Suddenly, they were inside a thick darkness. La gran eskuridad, there it was.

Where are you from? Maddie suddenly said, and no one quite knew who she was talking to. Hey, you, in the passenger seat? Where are you from?

The Count leaned into the wheel to see ahead better and slowed down.

She's asking you something, Henry said, and only then Pinto realized that they were talking to him.

Pardon, Pinto said. You are talking to me?

Yes, you, Henry said. We know where everyone else is from. You are the mystery.

Pinto's mouth was shaping up to produce the sounds that would be the answer, when the Count switched on the lights again, and Osman said, "Head down!" and without a thought Pinto slid down the seat when the bullet shattered the window on his side and then the Count's head, and the car veered and smashed into a building wall. Maddie's screams were interrupted by more shots, the dashboard exploding, as did the windshield and the other windows, until it all stopped.

Nobody moved or said anything as the car was revving. Moser was the first one to stir, and when he did, he checked on Henry. I'm fine, Henry said, and leaned awkwardly across Moser to check on Maddie.

She is dead, Henry said calmly. Oh boy. I think she is dead.

The car smelled of blood. Pinto's knees were on the floor, the drizzle sprinkled his cheek through the shattered window. Osman whispered: "Easy! Don't be afraid. It is not your time yet. Rahela is waiting for you." That lavender voice, the timbre and rasp in his throat, the possibility of a chuckle always in it, the closeness of it, it was his home.

Well, Henry said, this is not good.

SHANGHAI, 1937

RECLINED ON HIS HIP, Lu detached the bowl from the pipe then scraped with the flat side of the needle the sand-like opium dross onto a little tray. Pinto was mesmerized by Lu's delicate, graceful moves as though he had never seen them before. Slowly, relishing the last seconds of earthly time, Lu counted off seven drops of chandu into the little copper wok and, pinching its slim ivory handle, held it over the lamp chimney, whose glass was adorned with a pattern of graciously swirling dragons. The sweet smell of opium delighted Pinto's heart, so it sped up a bit. The dragon shadows danced on the wall as the lamp flame flickered under the wok. Back when he was a student in Vienna, Pinto had once watched shadows of a waltzing couple, projected by a zoetrope onto a wall. He had never seen anything like that. He was having an affair with a man whose wife was away in the Alps with his son, because clean air and altitude were good for the boy's consumption, and her absence was good for the husband. Pinto had never met the man's wife, but imagined that the two of them had danced like that once upon a time. He and the man lay naked and sweaty in the couple's bedroom, watching the silent shadows glissade from the white armoire to the wall and back. He couldn't remember now if they had taken laudanum or not, but they watched the dancing shadows for hours. Gustav was the man's name, and he owned a store that purveyed complicated toys for rich people's children. Afterward, Gustav gave him a tin wind-up ringelspiel, which Pinto kept by his bed in his tiny student room. He took it back home to Sarajevo, but now couldn't remember what happened to it. Probably vanished, like everything else.

Lu's collection of pipes, lamps, and tools for opium smoking was neatly sorted out in the many little drawers of a teak chest between their smoking beds. Most of them were Lu's family heirlooms, from the days when only the noble and educated smoked opium. Pinto loved the smell of that chest, the opium and wood scent of caramel, of the loaded past. The chest looked like a little shrine, and Lu handled everything in it with careful reverence. Opium is the religion of the individual, Pinto had once quipped as Lu was rolling a pellet to be smoked. But Lu was far too seriously devoted to his task to acknowledge Pinto's cleverness. He was now just as dedicated to the thing at hand, his somber face reliably gorgeous.

Everything was so beautiful. The teak chest was beautiful, Lu was beautiful, the luminescent dragons dancing on his beautiful face. His fingers were delicate instruments, now that he was wrangling the opium paste with two needles, as if knitting, to make it into a pellet. Everything was about to become even more beautiful. With one of the needles Lu placed the pellet on top of the dross and rolled it with the tip of his middle finger, then stabbed it again and placed it into the bowl's mouth. It seemed that it was taking him hours to prepare the pipe, but every moment was full and resplendent and loaded with a certainty of oncoming pleasure—everything was going to happen the way it was supposed to happen and nothing could change its course, and that was exactly the opposite from the way everything in the world worked. The air was like sugar water, thick with humidity and sweet scents, everything coated in its inertia. Outside, it thundered, then thundered again, as though the Japanese were banging kettledrums and not shelling Chapei.

Pinto never learned to roll a pellet and prepare a pipe. Back when he'd smoked in the dens, before he met Lu, there had always been a pipe boy, who lived off the customers' tips and vapors. And then Pinto met Lu, and soon started smoking only with him. It wasn't just that Lu had the best chandu, which he handled like a jeweler priest, it was also that Pinto loved watching him perform the ritual. Much of his attraction to Lu had developed watching his serene concentration and the deftness of his hands, because he was fully present as he was doing it, undeniably in the moment, there and nowhere else. As soon as Pinto smoked a pipe or two, he wanted to go over to Lu's bed and touch him, and keep touching him. This was what he wanted to do right now too, but, of course, he was not ready to move, and would not move.

Lu reached across the tray to hand over the pipe. Pinto took it without feeling its weight in his hands, as if it had floated to his lips. He placed the bowl opening—the pellet in it neither too deep nor too far from the hole, just perfect—over the lamp chimney, and inhaled the vapor. The gurgling sound of the vaporizing opium must be the most beautiful sound in the world. Pinto had recognized it was so the very first time he'd smoked opium. After that, children laughing and birds singing were but noise. In the time to come the Holy One will make a covenant with all the wild beasts, birds, and creeping things, and with all of Israel, and rebuild Jerusalem with sapphire stones, and there will be no more anguish, weeping, nor wailing, and there will be no more death, and everything will be as it should be, there will be no thunder, and the world will be gurgling in weightless beauty and endless peace. Until such time, what we have to help us along is this excellent stuff rolled by the most beautiful man in Shanghai, maybe in all of China.

The first time Pinto had smoked opium with Lu, he was caught unawares by the purity and power of fine chandu, so he coughed, and Lu laughed, and then he started coughing as well so the two of them were then coughing and laughing, and Lu was beautiful, so that when the coughing and laughing stopped, Pinto got off his smoking bed and crossed to Lu's and kissed him. They did not make love then, because Lu's wife and his children were in the house, but they kissed and held each other in their arms. Lu's children were not allowed to enter the smoking room, and his wife would never enter it even if she could—she preferred not to know, Lu said, because she already knew everything she needed to know.

Lu used to write poetry in classical Chinese, but now he could no longer even imagine doing it. He would only recite his poetry to Pinto every now and then in his deep, chesty voice, as if remembering something that had happened long ago, in his previous life. While he could get by in Shanghainese, Pinto could not understand a word of what Lu was reciting, so that he could've very well recited someone else's poetry or grocery lists. But it didn't matter, as he could clearly hear the wistful music, the melancholy song made of consonant cadences and the sinuous rumble and hum of vowels and some kind of indelible sorrow.

And Lu had such a sonorous voice, always speaking from his depths—Lu was a spacious man.

His family was wealthy and influential enough to send him to college in America, but before his freshman year was over he was expelled for rolling chandu with some American girls, whom he had no doubt enchanted with his voice and his classical Chinese poetry, letting them take a peek into his vast and exotic interiority. They were surely smitten by his exteriority as well: the smile that contained both lust and melancholy, the promises and the disappointments lurking in what would begin with a kiss and a caress. In Lu's telling, it was the girls' appreciation of his poetry that had saved him from being lynched by a jealous mob—the girls managed to convince the boys that Lu was a sodomite, which, of course, was not all that untrue. After a long night of smoking, after many, many delicious pipes, Lu would deliver his poetry with Pinto's head on his chest, so that Pinto could hear his drawing breath, his muscles tensing—it was as if his body were dancing to the poetry without even moving. Lu then translated it in his splendidly accented English. A poet and his lover strolled by a lily pond in the evening. The moon watched the poet row across the swollen river to meet his lover. At twilight, a wistful poet recollects floating in a gurgling creek. The poet falls in love with his shadow. The poet and his lover saw a bee crawl into a peony and noticed only then that the spring was upon them and everything was in bloom.

And it was while listening to the peony poem that Pinto remembered a bee swarm hanging off a wild apple tree in the Ferghana Valley, years ago, after he and Osman escaped from Tashkent, riding into the future that had seemed uncertain and still far better than what would actually transpire, and he began to cry. The swarm was thick and shaped like a tear, humming and barely visibly trembling. It took Lu a little while to notice Pinto's sobs, but when he did he stroked his temple and reverted to speaking Chinese, as if it had been the English language that made Pinto upset. This too had happened a long time ago. Pinto would tell Lu only that Osman was a man he had once loved, but not much more. In fact, Pinto had never told Lu that he was from Bosnia—he let him believe he was Austrian. The Chinese poet loved a vagabond who imagined himself to be a Viennese prince.

Pinto did not know how long they had been in the smoking room, or how many pipes he had smoked—one or ten—but the meze layout was still untouched, and the tea was cold, then hot, then cold again, and the temperature in the room rose, then dipped, then rose again, and he sweated until he didn't, then sweated again. Now there was more thunder and the roaring of airplanes over their heads, which must have meant it was daytime again. Using Lu's ivory backscratcher, Pinto struggled to reach that exact cursed spot between his shoulders that itched whenever he smoked opium, and often when he didn't. He scratched his nose too. Attending to an itch was inescapably delectable. Sometimes he and Lu lay embraced, scratching, very slowly, each other's back, and it was better than fucking. Osman never cared about morphine or opium, but he loved having his back scratched, gently with the fingertips. En kada dado un marafet. Sometimes he would hum a song while his back was scratched, which would sound like he was purring.

Lu was cooling himself with his fan, adorned with a cherry tree in pink bloom, which a Japanese lover of his had once upon a time given him. Pinto watched the delicate fluttering of the fan until his eyelids slowly slid down his eyeballs. Abruptly, he had another pipe in his hands, and it gurgled and sang. Noče noče, buena nočes, the bowl twittered. Dando bueltas por la kama, komo l'peše en la mar, aj komo l'peše en la mar. Back in Tashkent, he had taught Osman the song, translated the words from Spanjol, and Osman sang it back to him, always hitting the wrong note at la kama. After a while Pinto could no longer remember what the right note was, what Manuči's voice used to sound like. The only voice he now had for the song was Osman's, presently accompanied by the gurgling bowl, so Pinto sang, hitting the wrong note at la kama the first time, exactly like Osman. But the note was right the second time, and the third time—it was just as it was supposed to be. Then he realized that he wasn't the one singing—there was another voice, doing it right. It perplexed him that Lu not only knew the song and the Spanjol words but also knew to hit the right note, and then it became clear to him it was Osman's hanino voice singing:

Salto la primera i dišo:
Gozemos la mosedad,
Ah, gozemos la mosedad.

And without opening his eyes, Pinto knew that Osman was sitting at the foot of his opium-smoking bed. This wasn't the first time he sat there—some days, or weeks ago, whenever it was that he and Lu had started smoking this time around, Pinto had sensed his presence, his weight on the bed, and then saw the concern in his frown, the kind of fear Pinto did not like and did not want to accept, because he was doing just fine, afijun was good for him, made him feel settled and not thousands of miles away from where his life was supposed to be unfolding, and it helped with all his pain too. He had said nothing to Osman, and Osman had stayed quiet, occasionally lightly touching his foot or knee.

Once, Pinto thought Osman leaned over him to kiss his cheek, but was too content to move or even open his eyes, and did not want to find out that what he felt touch his face was a fly, or dust, or death, and not Osman's mustache. But Osman was singing now, at the foot of his bed, and it was beautiful.

Salto la segunda i dišo:
Gozemos la novijedad,
Ah, gozemos la novijedad.

There he was, his ruddy hanino cheek, with his neatly trimmed mustache, the incongruous fez tipped rakishly to the side, the shirt unbuttoned, exposing his hirsute chest, wiping his armpits with a handkerchief. Pinto now wanted to sit up to kiss that cheek, touch that chest, put his head on Osman's shoulder, smell that sweat, but he didn't want to alert Lu or interrupt the singing, so he watched Osman's throat rising and falling as he inhaled and exhaled to produce the melodic voice, and his Adam's apple was bobbing.

Salto la mas čikitica i dišo:
Madre komo la voj a dešar,
Madre mija, komo la voj a dešar.

As he sang the last line, Osman nodded at Pinto, as if to confirm that he was in fact still there, alive. Pinto moved his head to the curve of the porcelain pillow to make space for Osman's cheek, but Osman remained where he was, even after he stopped singing. Instead, he put his crooked hand on Pinto's left ankle, and his palm was cold. When our love was strong, we could lie on the edge of a sword. Wherever we lie now, I still think of that sword. I miss the sword, I held your hand on the blade.

"This place reminds me of the back room at Hadži-Šaban's. It used to be the afijun room, before the Austrians banned it, where you could smoke for days or weeks. When I was working there, all the drunks who drank for weeks were kept in that room, and it still smelled of afijun."

Why are you talking to me? Pinto asked. Why are you here? His eyes were still closed but he could see Osman's shrug. His palm went up Pinto's calf, all the way back up to his knee.

"I missed you," Osman said.

You didn't miss me yesterday? Or the day before? Or a week ago? You haven't missed me for fifteen years, until now?

"I was always here. I miss you all the time. You did not want to speak to me."

I did want to speak with you. It's that you were not responding. And here you are.

"We have to go."

Go where? Why? I don't want to go anywhere.

"Do you love this man?"

What man?

"Lu."

I do.

"Do you really? Or do you love his pipe and opium?"

He is a good man. Buenu kom il pan. But that's beside the point. I am sick of going anywhere. I don't want to go anywhere. I want to stay here. And I do love his afijun.

"You cannot stay here."

Why can't I stay here?

"You need to be with Rahela."

Rahela is gone. She is with Henry. He's taking good care of her. She does not need me. She needs Henry.

"She is worried about you."

No, she isn't. I haven't talked to her in weeks. She doesn't even know where I am. I am a nothing and a nobody to her.

"It's been months since you've talked to her. And you've been here smoking afijun for weeks."

I will be where I want to be for as long as it suits me. She is where she wants to be just as well. With that American monster. As soon as she turned sixteen she left home and moved in with him. I have been relieved of my fatherly duties and I am here to celebrate my liberation.

"She loves you. She is your daughter."

She is not my daughter. I didn't fuck her mother. You did.

"No, I didn't."

Don't lie.

"Well, only once."

That once is Rahela.

"You saved her life. You raised her. You are her father."

She wants to be with her American, she does not want me anywhere near. She left me for that damn monster. He was her teacher! He made her read Shakespeare, then seduced her. He seduced a child. The smarmy widower. The smooth talker. The civilized piece of shit.

"She is a person. She's entitled to her mistakes."

You do not know Henry Krantz. Henry Krantz is much, much more than a mistake. He is an American. He is a monster. I never want to see him again. Or her. I chewed food for her when she had no teeth. I carried her through the desert on my back. I of- fered my life for hers when she was dying from scarlet fever. She is no longer my daughter, never was. And I told her so. I said it to her face: Good luck to you, I said. I never want to see you again.

"Have I told you the story about the paša who came to Sarajevo from Stamboul and set up his tent so that he could look at the city, at its minarets and sunsets, its beauty?"

You told me the story, Pinto said. Many times. It's an old story.

"One day, a wedding party was leaving Sarajevo, as the bride was to be married off to a man in some far mountain village. And the bride was weeping, while everyone was singing and beating their drums. The paša gave the bride a handful of ducats, because she had to part with her city, never to return."

So where are my ducats?

"Another time, another wedding, except the bride was going to Sarajevo to live with her groom. Except, this time around, the paša requested a handkerchief from her, because she was the lucky one who would spend her life in Sarajevo."

Why are you telling me this again? Pinto asked, but Osman was now quiet, his weight not on the bed. There was a handkerchief on Pinto's forehead now, soaking up the thick sweat, and it smelled of lavender.

Lu handed Pinto another pipe and as he turned to his side and opened his eyes to place the bowl over the lamp, he saw the silhouette of a woman standing in the doorway. The handkerchief slipped off his forehead and vanished in the abyss his bed was bordering. The woman wasn't Lu's wife, but someone taller, someone whose chestnut hair reflected the backlight and whose face remained dark as she advanced toward him. It was only when she moved into the flickering circle of lamplight that he recognized Klara Isakovna, who within a couple of steps morphed into Rahela.

Pinto looked small and frail on the bed, shrimped up and holding on to the pipe as if it were a flag of some defeated army. It was Lenka who had told Rahela that Pinto was at Lu's on an opium binge. But Lenka did not know where Lu's house was, so Henry spoke to his spy friends at the Special Branch. They were willing to go fetch Pinto for Henry's girl and a small fee, but when the fighting in Hongkou got more serious, all of them had to be on round-the-clock duty at the checkpoints that stopped the refugees from pouring into the International Settlement. Knowing that Pinto would never go anywhere with Henry, Rahela made Henry stay at home, even if he strenuously objected to her wandering alone around Shanghai at the time of war. This is not my first war, Rahela said. I grew up in war. War I can survive, it is peace that is too difficult.

When Pinto recognized Rahela, he said nothing, nor did his face change from its opium stoneness into some kind of expression—no anger, love, pain, nor disdain. He merely placed the bowl over the flame and slowly and deeply inhaled the smoke. Rahela hated that sugary, cloying opium reek, that horrid sound of a nightingale with its throat cut. Pinto rolled on his back and closed his eyes, and even in the murk she could see that he hadn't changed his shirt in a very long time, because a black line on its collar shone in the flickering light. The collar was now too big for his skinny neck; his Adam's apple throbbed as he cleared his throat. She hadn't seen him since she'd confessed to him that Henry was her lover, whereupon he'd kicked her out of their shikumen. She hadn't seen him for six months, and in that time he'd managed to ruin himself. This sick body was once her father.

Padri, Rahela said. Wake up. You cannot stay here. There is a war up and down the street, everywhere. We must go.

I am not asleep and I am not your Padri, Pinto whispered.

I don't care about whatever is down the street. I am not going anywhere. I am staying right here. Go away. Leave me alone. Lu, tell this woman to leave.

"It is not your time to die, and if you stay here, you will die," Osman said.

I don't care, Pinto said. Can you give me that handkerchief?

"Get up and go with her."

No. I am not going anywhere. I am not getting up. I aim to stay here for the rest of my life.

The August sun was high and blazing and Pinto could see nothing, except the sparkly volutes on the insides of his eyelids, tightly shut. He let Rahela pilot him, holding his biceps. He held the handkerchief in one hand, Lu's hand in the other. Lu discovered that his wife and children had left the house a couple of days, or perhaps weeks, before, so he came along with Pinto and Rahela. He took nothing from the house, other than a little silk pouch with his opium gear, including his Japanese fan and ivory backscratcher. Rahela guided them without a word through the stream of people, who smelled fetid and scared, along the clamorous streets of Hongkou, around obscure corners, through narrow shikumen alleys, wading through waves of new smells, each of which had the foundation of fire and smoke. Pinto's arm was light as kindling wood, shorn of muscles; he moved gingerly as if about to collapse, clutching the handkerchief like a widow at a funeral. He must not have eaten for days—the snack trays at Lu's were besieged by fat flies that all rose to meet her as Rahela had stepped forth. He was so meager she reckoned she could carry him if he was unable to walk. She could probably carry him on her back all the way to the river and the boat.

Lu forced them to stop every once in a while so that he could scratch his back, and then hand the backscratcher to Pinto without even asking him if he needed it, continuing to fan himself. Rahela snorted in disapproval each time they stopped for a scratch, but said nothing. There is nothing like an opium itch, Pinto declared, to no one in particular, passionately scratching the spot between his shoulder blades, his back slippery with sweat and the oily opium ooze. And there is nothing like scratching it. The relief was heavenly, so he just wanted to stand in the street with his eyes closed, like a tree in the wind, and scratch himself for as long as there was an itch to be scratched, and let everyone pass by him. I am the one who is seen but cannot see. Where is the one who can see but cannot be scratched?

An airplane roared above their heads, closer than before, and the human stream around Pinto and Rahela and Lu accelerated, carrying them forward. A rickshaw wheel ran over his foot, but he felt no pain. Someone poked his side with some kind of a stick. A hand touched his chest—possibly a pickpocket—but he had no money in any of his pockets. The clamor of people's breathing, gibbering, shouting, and moving, the feet trotting and shuffling, Rahela's panting, Lu chuckling at something behind Pinto's back. The airplane screeched above them again. He could not understand where and why they were all rushing— where could the safe place be if death was coming down from the heavens? He who is filled with the fear of Heaven, his words are listened to. Pinto felt no fear himself. Among the dead he would be free. A man in prison was told: Tomorrow you will be released and given plenty of money, and the man replied: Please just let me go free today and I will ask for nothing more.

Pinto and Lu had heard the explosions and gunfire and airplanes when the Japanese attack had begun, whenever that was, but they could see no reason to move or go anywhere, and they were right, since after a few pipes everything was very nicely elsewhere and distant. War will take care of everything, Lu said. There is no point in making any rash decisions. The airplane and its roar were far even now, somewhere in a different domain altogether, in the same remote world whence the sounds of the human flow and gunfire and artillery, and that particular, prickly, choral hum of many buildings burning in concert, were coming. The red and yellow stains bubbled up on the insides of Pinto's eyelids, beyond which there was all that noise. Meanwhile in his head, the song: Noches, noches, buenas noches, noches son d'enamorar. Ever since they left Lu's house, all through that noise, a voice sang Noches, noches in his head, and the voice was neither Manuči's nor Osman's, not even Pinto's. The song somehow sang itself, and it was all the more mellifluous for that, and Pinto knew that the song would vanish whenever he was able to open his eyes and see again. It would have been better for the wicked if they were blind, for their eyes bring a curse to the world. Rahela was not blind, she led him through this mayhem with her eyes open. In the land of the blind, a one-eyed man is king, and a two-eyed girl was his former daughter. The plane whined away once again and then looped to return and roar above their heads. Komo l'peše en la mar. Rahela pulled Pinto around another corner and in the course of that turn Lu's hand slipped out of Pinto's, and he was gone. Pinto opened his eyes to see where he was, but the light blinded him, and he shut his eyes again. The scratcher was in his hand, reliably real and present, like a sword. He had lost the handkerchief. The Lord is long in sufferings.

Wait! Pinto said. Where is Lu?

Fuck! Rahela said.

Since she'd been going to the American School, Rahela spoke

English to everyone, including him. But he had never heard her use that word.

Tu ke didjas?

She said, I am going to find Lu, you wait here! She pushed him against the wall of a building. Don't go anywhere!

Where would I go? Pinto said. There is no other place to be. Here is all there is or will ever be. I will wait just here. I will be here for as long as I am alive. Right here.

Rahela retraced their steps, for which she had to elbow her way through the deluge of refugees. The streets of Hongkou were crowded at the best of times, but now there was the glutinous terror flowing with the people. She yelled Lu's name, but it was crazy to think that he, or anyone, could hear her in this madness. She considered again leaving both of them to their devices. The American that he was, Henry would never let the two of them smoke opium around him. Nor would he let a Chinese man enter his house. Henry would also leave Pinto behind if he could, if she would; he did not want him in their life. She dreaded the moment of Padri facing Henry again—there could be a fight, which Henry would win with a pinkie punch. She yelled out Lu's name again to let out the tension and anxiety.

Lu stood in the middle of the narrow street, scratching his neck and fanning himself, as people shoved him in passing. The bag with his opium gear was no longer in his hand. His gaze was pointed upward, where a plane had been not so long ago, and he was shaking his head as if he had found some evidence for a supposition of his.

Let's go, Lu, Rahela said. We almost lost you.

There is nothing up there, Lu said.

Precisely, Rahela said. Let's go.

The wall Pinto was leaning on was warm and damp; when he touched it, the sandy surface crumbled, so he kept touching it, digging a hole in it with his fingertips, until he found some straws, which he pulled out. All the while, with the scratcher, he was addressing an incessant itch on the tip of his nose. Look at me, Manuči! I can rub my tummy with one hand and tap the top of my head with the other! Maybe Rahela would not come back for him, maybe she'd just finally leave him there, leaned against the wall like a shovel. If she didn't come back, he was intent on staying right there, pressing his itchy back against the wall, until it was all over, maybe even beyond the end. I will outlive this world and see the birth of the next one. First all the walls and buildings in Shanghai would dissolve, running out of themselves like sand in an hourglass, until the city turned into a desert. He scratched the scar on his cheek. You cannot fathom my rules. The sun was directly above Pinto, burning his face. So was the airplane that kept whining and caterwauling. Someone was up in that plane, looking down on us, seeing us small as ants. Go to the ant, you sluggard; consider its ways and be wise. Lu is lost inside an ant-hill. He did not know where Rahela was taking them. It didn't really matter. One moves in despair, and despair is all there is, plus chandu, if you're lucky, and the itching if you're not. He no longer had the handkerchief, a patch of God's garment. He had once tried to write a poem in German about God's garment. Das Licht ändert die Welt und jedoch bleibt sie gleich, auf ewig warm unter Gottes Gewänder. He could not remember at all what he meant, what that poem wanted to mean, but the words were in his head, like a memory of something that had happened in a previous reincarnation, and there was still light outside, a lot of it, beyond his shut eyelids. Im Inneren tragen wir das Licht, da wir, wann wir sterben, zurückgeben der Finsternis.

"Rahela will find him," Osman said, nodding. He stood next to him, leaning on the wall, one of his feet up against it, the fez still rakishly tipped, a straw like a cigarette in his mouth, his arms crossed like someone who had once stood on the Čaršija corners sipping boza, heckling the passersby and ogling the women. Osman did not seem worried. War was taking care of him as well.

I don't know anything anymore, Pinto said. I don't know her anymore. She just became someone else all of a sudden. She's speaking English now, all the time.

"She's still just a child."

That's not what she says. Once she turned sixteen, she declared herself grown up and independent, and decided to leave with that American. He was her teacher. I don't think she's ever coming back.

"What are you talking about? She's just come back."

Turning the corner with Lu in tow, Rahela saw Pinto speaking loudly in Bosnian with his eyes closed, banging the back of his head against the wall and scraping his scar, its ridge bloodied, as if trying to scratch off his face. He threw his other hand up and wagged his finger, shouting at someone she could not see.

Who are you talking to? Rahela asked him.

He's talking to his dead lover in their language, Lu said. He's been doing that for days now.

Are you talking to Osman? Rahela asked.

What is it to you? Pinto said. Leave me alone.

Now there were two or three airplanes howling in the sky up

over the Bund and the Whangpoo, going this way and that way, as if they were everywhere, as they probably were, and then there was an explosion, followed by another one, closer, shaking the wall on which Pinto and Osman were leaning.

"Let us not worry," Osman said. "Nothing good will happen."

Nothing good ever happens, Pinto said. But war will take care of everything.

Once more, Pinto tried to open his eyes, and this time he kept them open. He perceived the streaming shadows, and the scratcher that was in Lu's hand again, Rahela's whorishly rouged lips flaming under the sun; her frown, her eyebrows touching above her nose, resembling a drawing of a seagull in flight, or an airplane. Her eyebrows were beautiful, as was she. He hadn't seen her since the winter, since she moved in with Henry, and she was now someone else, older. He knew who she was, everything about her, yet she was a stranger who spoke a foreign language. She wore a necklace with the Samsara wheel as a pendant. He found that pebble in that cave, and gave it to her. There was nothing else he could ever give her. Osman was now squatting next to him, as if to hide from Rahela and Lu.

"She left you as a child," Osman said. "Came back as a woman."

Let's go, Rahela said, and grabbed Pinto's biceps again. He ripped his arm out of her grasp.

Where are we going? Pinto asked.

Out of here. Where you won't be killed, Rahela said.

Don't be stupid, Pinto said.

Rahela scurried ahead, parting the crowd for Pinto and Lu to come through, stopping every once in a while to see if they were still behind her. She wore khakis, and a buttoned-up man's shirt with her sleeves rolled up, the necklace strap entangled with one of the buttons. She looked like one of those sassy girls from

American movies, all movement and courage, no doubt to please Henry. She broke Pinto's heart. He had been too occupied with their survival in the insanity of Shanghai and had not been paying attention to her and she stopped being a child right before his blind eyes. He'd known nothing about girls, had never known any girls other than Simha, who was timid even by the standards of the Atora-abiding Sarajevo Sefaradim. He had known that Simha had bled once a month, because she had to keep away, but hadn't had any idea how the whole thing worked, not even when he went to Vienna to learn about human anatomy, which consisted of cadavers and Latin words. Simha never demanded anything. She didn't seem to think that she had a right to be herself, let alone love and sleep with whomever she wanted. Simha lived to serve the family, deliver children to the family, so that the family could keep existing in the world, which belonged to and was run by men, wise and otherwise. But Rahela had no family. Pinto was her only family—there were no grandparents, no elderly tijas and teos, no older cousins, no one who could speak to her with authority, or punish her, or provide dowry, let alone someone she could confide in; no one around her had gone through what she was going through. Pinto sometimes read the Atora to her, and he made her go to the Ohel Rachel temple, while he stayed as far away from it as he could. At the temple, she would hear that she had to obey her husband and have as many children as her womb could manage before it withered, as Manuči no doubt had heard, as had her mother, and all the other women, all the way back to Sara. That all the laws and rules and customs were suspended here in Shanghai had some good sides, but there was no city in the world where loneliness was thicker than here. Nobody in Shanghai was from Shanghai, nor at home here, not even the Chinese born and raised in the city, let alone

the Shanghailanders or the stateless dross like Pinto himself.
The Lord said, let us go to Shanghai and confound their lives.
Which was why everyone lived in the present, seeing the future
only as the material for the machine of the now. The past was
elsewhere, the present was always this—the masses of refugees
moving around the city looking for food and a place, for some
way not to die, or for opium, which was the best available op-
tion. He should have never come to Shanghai with Rahela. But
there had been no other place to go. They had no passports, no
money, no country, nothing. If she hadn't gone to the American
School, there would've been no real school. There were Natashas
of her age working as pheasants, hoping for a reliable job in a
brothel, or for a wealthy Western patron-lover who would take
care of them until a younger replacement appeared. Looking for a
Henry Krantz. It was the American School that delivered Rahela
into Henry's filthy hands. At the American School, she had been
taught that she was entitled to her freedom, that her goal was to
become herself, that no one had the right to tell her what to do.
All well and nice, except it was Henry Krantz who imparted all
that to her, grooming her for the moment when she would abandon the father who was not her father and who was thus helpless
to stop her. Henry lingered outside their shikumen as Pinto and
Rahela screamed at each other, and the old Russian and Chinese
neighborhood ladies formed a captive audience, and Pinto tried
to rip the bag with Rahela's clothes out of her hands and grab her
wrists to drag her inside. When he failed at that, he reached for
the Samsara wheel necklace to rip it off her, and she slapped him,
she slapped his face, the very scar on his face, and he stood at the
door in shock, his wound throbbing again as she stormed out and
walked away with Henry Monster Krantz, who had the temerity
to glance back at Pinto with a what-can-you-do grimace. When

Pinto went to the Municipal Police, they laughed at him—the city was full of sixteen-year-olds servicing men, they said, and if they were to try to retrieve them, they would need an army to do it, and the army would just end up keeping the girls for themselves. Besides, Pinto had no papers to prove his paternity, and the loud Special Branch plainclothesman suggested in his Australian accent that Rahela was in fact Pinto's baby doll, that he was merely jealous because she had ensnared a rich American for herself, and that he could easily find another girl, younger, maybe even a virgin, without a problem. Everyone in the Municipal Police knew Henry, the Australian said, and he knew everyone at the Special Branch. Henry was a good man.

Oh my Lord! Rahela said.

The Lord has nothing to do with any of this, Pinto said. Although, to be fair, all of this is His doing.

Four heads were stuck on tall poles, their mouths open as if about to croon out a song. Their faces were swollen with beating and death, their eyes frozen in insipid surprise. At the edges of their necks, where blood had crusted to make them look serrated, swarms of flies rose and landed again, buzzing in excitement. Rahela looked at Pinto as if to ask for an explanation while he just stared up at the heads, his eyes glazed with opiatic torpor, scratching his back slowly. Nočes, nočes, buenas nočes, the song started again in his skull. Unintelligible signs were nailed to the poles below the heads. Japanese spies, Lu said, fanning himself with his pink fan. At the foot of the stakes, a Chinese soldier with a fresh, bloody gash on his face stood swinging at and hitting the refugees with his rifle, as if protecting the poles with the heads. Pinto snapped out of his daze and pushed Rahela forth to start moving and she made the steps, her gaze still locked to the open mouths.

But when Pinto turned back to check if Lu was in their wake, he saw the soldier with a wounded face charging toward Lu, who didn't see him coming, and then smashing his rifle into Lu's neck, whereupon he dropped on the ground like an emptied sack. The soldier kept slamming Lu's skull with the rifle butt, releasing a flood of blood, then it cracked like a watermelon, and the soldier kept hitting until the watermelon was crushed. Just like that, Lu was dead. This did not happen, Pinto thought. This cannot have happened. The people around his body stopped moving to consider the crushed skull; they did think it had happened. It must have happened then, even though none of the onlookers showed they were in any way surprised. There were a couple of dogs squeezing between the legs of onlookers as if to see the dead man better. The soldier was panting, his gash now releasing a trail of blood to creep toward his chin. Rahela's eyes were wide in disbelief and she gagged, as if about to disgorge, and then screamed as Pinto had never heard her scream. The blood rapidly spreading from Lu's head quickly encompassed his pink Japanese fan, still in his hand. Pinto could not see his eyes, because Lu's face was pressing against the ground, but he must have been surprised. Death is surprising. A group of men, some with pistols, ran up to the soldier to check on him—one looked at the wound on his cheek—and engage in an excited exchange, pointing at Lu's body. Then they all came to some kind of agreement. Rahela was screaming still. A rivulet of blood advanced directly toward Pinto, as if it knew where he was. This did not happen, Pinto thought, but it will happen again any moment now. He stood at the horizon the blood was striving to reach, holding a scratcher in his hand like a sword. The handkerchief was lost. The men grabbed Lu by his feet and dragged him toward the poles, leaving a trail of blood and brains behind, while his garment climbed up his hips and back. A dog pushed its way through to lick the blood, and someone kicked it away. A man with a pistol in his hand pointed at Pinto and Rahela, whereupon all of them advanced in their direction.

It was Rahela who moved first, grabbing Pinto's hand and tugging him forward to run. She pushed people aside, banged into them, knocked a boy down so that Pinto had to jump over him, squeezed between an improbable car and a rickshaw, past another group of soldiers who were oblivious to the pursuit. The crowd closed behind them like a body of water, so that the pursuers had to part it all over again, or so Pinto imagined. Rahela was the engine of escape, finding cracks in the moving walls of people, because if it wasn't for her, he would just stop right there, sit down, and cry, until the spy-hunting men reached him and crushed his skull just as well. Then the Lord said to Moses, Hold out your arm over the sea, so that the water may come back upon the Egyptians, and upon their chariots, and upon their horsemen. If a man dies with his face turned upward, it is a good omen for him; if it is turned downward, it is a bad omen for him. If his skull is crushed, it is a bad omen for him; if he is dragged away by his feet, it is a bad omen for him. If no one knows where his corpse might end up, it is a bad omen for him. La gran eskuridad is a bad omen for him.

The Soochow Creek was red with blood, corpses of soldiers, dogs, and cattle clogging it. The access to the bridge was blocked by the people amassed at the Municipal Police checkpoint. Pinto had lost the scratcher too while running away from the gang; he noticed he'd dropped it and considered stopping, but by the time he was able to act, they were far away from it. He touched his face and it was wet, but only after he tasted the saltiness did he realize he was crying. That scratcher was Lu's scratcher. Lu and he would lie next to each other and take turns scratching each other's back. I demand from the Almighty to replenish my loss. The soldier crushed his skull and his brains spilled and left a trail as they dragged him. Lu didn't know that he was dead or that his brains were now sticking to the refugee feet already coated with Shanghai filth. The tears were getting into Pinto's mouth and they tasted saltier than sweat. There is no grief in the presence of Him who is everywhere. Rahela held his arm again, pushing him ahead of herself, but he did not try to escape her grasp, leading the way through the thickness of the crowd. She might have been crying too. There was no air to breathe, only stench and humidity, and Pinto was panting and gagging. A girl carried by a man and clinging to his shoulder looked at him in horror as he brushed past, her eyes enormous, probably from hunger. One day this same girl might be dragging her father along toward some hopeless escape. As the gardener, so the garden.

Where are we going? Pinto asked Rahela.

Just keep moving, Rahela said. We need to get out of here. We need to get across the bridge.

I don't have any papers, Pinto said. I lost the scratcher. I lost the handkerchief. I have nothing.

You don't need anything. Just keep moving.

Osman was now parting the crowd before Pinto and Rahela, as if advancing through a cornfield, and he was singing. Two parallel vines of hair climbed up his neck toward the thickness at the border of his pate and the fez. Osman was the only man in Shanghai wearing a fez, but no one in Shanghai knew that.

Bejturan se uz ružu savija
Vilu ljubi Djerzelez Alija

His voice was loud and breathy because he was moving force-fully, but all the richer for that.

Vilu ljubi svu noć na konaku
po mjesecu i mutnu oblaku.

Can you stop howling? Rahela asked.

I am not howling, Pinto said.

The mass was stopped at a barricade behind which stood a line of Municipal Force Volunteers, with their rifles at their chests, ready to be raised. At an opening, a couple of plainclothes were checking documents and letting people in, or pushing them back. The lined-up volunteers seemed angry, except for the ruddy-faced kid Pinto ended up facing, who was clearly scared, his blue eyes darting sideways as if looking for a way out, the hat strap under his chin nearly choking him. A woman was turned away by the officers and screamed at them, until one of the officers shoved her back into the crowd and she tottered backward and fell down on her ass, and then sat there crying. There is no grief in the presence of Him who is everywhere, unless He is absent from everywhere.

Stay close to me, Rahela said. We will get through here.

She moved toward the entrance with determination, Pinto holding her hand like a child. Behind the Munies' line, she saw Henry, wearing a light blue jacket with a yellow handkerchief sticking out of his chest pocket and a white shirt, as if he were on his way to a pony race, handsome as ever. He was scanning the crowd and when he saw Rahela his sweatless face brightened, his smile beamed, and she knew again that he loved her and she waved at him. Henry pushed his way through, the Munies stepped aside to let him through and he reached across the barricade to embrace her. They stood in a clinch for a moment, in the course of which Henry spotted Pinto.

What Pinto saw in Henry's eyes was not relief, nor love for Rahela, but something cold and brutally selfish; those were the eyes of the Henry who had once sat next to his young wife as she was dying and was now dressed up for pony racing. Yet when they unclinched and Rahela turned to Pinto to grab his hand, he saw the joy and love on her face. She loved him, she loved the monster, and there was nothing he could do about it. He had imagined dragging her home by her hair and locking her up, but he knew that that would not stop her from leaving again. Henry had her under his control.

Henry spoke to the officers who glanced at Rahela and Pinto, then stepped aside to let them in without even asking for their documents. Pinto resisted Rahela's pull and, once again, removed his arm from her grasp. Lu was dead, all that classical poetry, the magical hands, the languorous smile. *I am going to have to weep for Lu, beat my chest. When one sheds tears for a virtuous man, the Holy One counts them and lays them up in His treasury.* Behind him, the edge of the mob was pushing, and he resisted it too, until Henry grabbed his shoulder to force him into stepping across the line.

Henry Krantz was a spy, but not a great one, Moser-Ethering observes wryly in *A Foreign Devil in Asia*. Too airheaded, too lecherous, too much of a liability for being fond of very young girls, too committed to wishful thinking and arrogance, he was just about what one would expect an American to be. After his wife was killed in 1932, in a harrowing incident Moser described in the chapter entitled Trial by Fire, Henry decided to forgo the position waiting for him in his father's law office in Philadelphia, and remain in Shanghai. At first, it seemed he stayed to mourn, but in no time he was living it up, attending parties and frequenting clubs, ubiquitous at pony races and boxing matches. He charmed, and possibly pleased in some other ways, Mrs. Harriet Wexman, who was on the board of the American School, and thus got himself a job teaching English and literature. Other than his mandatory Princeton readings, he was no literature expert, nor did he particularly like it, but he knew his basic Shakespeare and smatterings of Shelley and Keats. Shall I compare thee to a summer's day, he would recite in his open-vowel American accent to his smitten students, some of whom in turn wrote their own verses about him, about the wanton curl on his forehead, about the shiny smile, about his sunny charm, and not as much about his groping them and sliding his hand up their skirts as they stayed behind the class to discuss poetry. There was a good chance, Moser-Ethering claims to have determined early in their long friendship, that a combination of Krantz's simplicity and charisma, which he sprayed around rapid-fire, combined with his energetic lechery, could be used as a resource for collecting intelligence. A lot of students at the school had fathers who possessed a lot of useful information. Even Borodin, Stalin's man in China, sent his children to the American School, though he did it under the name of Gruzenberg. One of Moser's rather clever ideas was to pack the classes Borodin's children attended with the children of Moser's assets, who would then surreptitiously milk information from the little Gruzenbergs. Henry taught literature to both of the Gruzenberg boys and, under Moser's guidance, gave them writing assignments that did yield some leads and intelligence.

But Henry was no natural spy, because he had a very hard time, by virtue of his Americanness, refraining from the pursuit of his own happiness and pleasures. He was incapable of reflection, a stranger to self-understanding, Moser writes, and was always hurling into a future to which he felt fully and unimpeachably entitled. Hence he was far less interested in stopping the advance of Communism in East Asia and the world than in sleeping with his most precocious students before motherhood ruined them. Soon, rumors started following him like a shadow, but this was Shanghai, where everyone dragged behind them several shadows of different degrees of darkness. Henry stayed employed by the American School longer than anyone expected, no doubt due to his influence on Mrs. Wexman, but once he started living with a student of his, whom Moser never names in his book, the school had to look for someone who would be less eager to compare his students to summer's days and less interested in touching the insides of their thighs.

Throughout his memoiristic oeuvre, Moser insisted that loyalty to his assets was one of the principles of intelligence work he always abided by. He was always good, he claimed, to the people who were good to him. When the bloody war of 1937 enfolded the Chinese section of Shanghai and it looked like it would spill over into the foreign parts of the city and hundreds of British citizens and families were shipped away from the troubles, Moser made sure that those who had worked for him were not forgotten. To his mind, loyalty to the assets was not only representative of the kind of gentlemanliness that could be bred only in Great Britain, but also pragmatic. In the chapter on the 1937 war in

Shanghai, entitled The Beginning of the End, he leaps forward by a few decades to tell us about the conversation he had with Henry Krantz in Saigon, over drinks at the Continental Shelf. You not only saved my life, the inebriated Henry, wearing the unfortunate toupee, would tell him, gushing. You changed its direction.

Henry carried two valises and used them to shove or knock over whoever was in his way. He progressed in long strides, Rahela in his wake hauling Pinto, who resisted like a petulant child. The HMS *Empress of Asia*, Henry said, was about to sail, and they needed to get to it before they pulled up the gangplank. What Pinto truly needed was another pipe, as he was reaching that horrid stage where the mind was beginning to clear but not becoming any less numb for that, and fatigue settled in the limbs, and itches spread all over the body like an army of voracious, furious ants. Henry was certain that the Japanese would sooner or later take over the International Settlement and the French Concession in one fell swoop, so the three of them would therefore be taking a British ship to Hong Kong, for which they already had the hard-to-obtain passes. Pinto understood that Henry did not want him to come along, and that it was Rahela who insisted. He did not want to go, and did not want Rahela to go. He wanted Henry to leave and never return. He wanted to lie down with a pipe and listen to the gurgling. God has no need, and I am the needy one.

Rahela felt the dampness of Padri's hand in hers, the opium stickiness coming through his skin. His hand was limp and slight, like a bundle of uncooked sausages. She tugged him forth whenever he'd slow down, and he did not care to follow them, even if it was quite possible he was too drugged to understand where they were heading. Henry was bludgeoning people aside with the valises. Rahela loved him for many things: for his beauty and intelligence, for his body and experience, for his burning need to be loved and for his appetite for life—but most of all, she loved him because he made her laugh, made her feel important, to him, to the world. He listened to her; he wanted to know about her, about her body, about her life, about her hopes and dreams. He believed in her, in her ambition and plans, even if they changed every so often. Still, there were moments when she could detect that there were thoughts behind his eyes he would never tell her about, that he had other lives she would have no access to—she understood that he did not need her as much as she needed him, and fear would reverberate through her body at the thought that Padri might be right. There were moments when Henry's clenched jaw and a dip in his nearly touching eyebrows bespoke a kind of determination that terrified her. It was precisely such determination that drove him to plow through the crowd, now slamming people with the valises to get through. He was determined to live, to be the last one alive if need be; if she were to fall too far behind, he would just proceed without her. She hurried her step and yanked Padri forward.

Pinto stepped into a pothole, twisted his ankle, and fell, extracting his hand out of Rahela's grip to break the fall. The pavement was grimy and sour-smelling, and his hand was instantly soiled, but it was also scraped and he could see a patch of blood on it. Feet and legs scurried past him, a bucket banged him in the head. The pain was fire and ice at the same time, but it belonged to someone else. I am going to sit right here until the conditions are right for me to depart from this shit. This looks like a good place to stop living. Weep for the desperate mourner, not for the soul that is going home to la gran eskuridad.

"You have to get up," Osman said, squatting next to him.

No, I don't, Pinto said.

"They will miss the boat."

What boat? I don't care.

"Do you want her to stay here for the war? It might last for years."

War is as good for her as Henry is, probably better. War will take care of everything.

"Whatever Henry is, he will not let her be killed."

You know nothing about Henry. Henry's women die. Henry doesn't care who lives or dies. Henry lives for himself alone.

Henry dropped the valises in exasperation to take a look at Pinto's ankle, as if he could do something about it, which he couldn't, so he lifted him without his cooperation. Pinto could not put weight on his right foot. Put me down, he said, and squirmed, but Henry ignored it. Rahela bent down to the valises and he saw the necklace dangling off her neck like a noose. She picked up the valises, while Henry grabbed Pinto around the waist, wedged his shoulder into Pinto's armpit, and then carried him forth. His cologne and hair pomade and clean clothes made Pinto nauseated. Henry's grip was strong, and Pinto was too light to slow him down as he rushed toward the *Empress of Asia*, or wherever they were going. Never in his life had Pinto hated anyone as much as he did Henry at that moment, squirming and wriggling to no avail, while all the pain of that hatred was now flowing toward his ankle. Hatred of his fellow men shortens a man's life, which is just fine with me. Let me see if I can hate him to death.

HMS *Empress of Asia* was heavy with people, women and children leaning over the railings to wave at the cordon of those who were seeing them off. The engine was already rumbling, the smoke coming out of the chimney, and the din of farewell and last words was unbearable. The right way to say your farewell is always silence. The nations of the world are like a ship, a sail from one place, a mast from another, a rumbling engine from the one that needs its might for war. Armed sailors guarded the access to the gangplank, pressing away the gang of the desperate with their leveled rifles. The noise of it all was enormous, like a creepingly developing explosion, and Pinto wanted to cover his ears, but Henry's grip shackled him. He could not see where they were going, while the American clearly had a goal and knew where it was to be found. Pinto was thirsty, his mouth parched, and his head loaded with dull pain, his ankle gnawed at by the injury. Another pipe would properly take care of it all. If Henry and Rahela made him board that ship, he would have to spend days without opium, and that would be hell. He had tried to quit many times before and never lasted more than two days, only until that moment when it was clear that he would die if he didn't smoke again. And then he would smoke again, and hate himself for not dying, for being a coward who wanted to live, if only so that he could smoke more opium. He wriggled again in Henry's hold, feebly. After Rahela had left, he wanted to end himself, and it was obvious that smoking to death would be far better than depriving himself of it until he was dead. He would not survive that trip to Hong Kong, and he did not want Henry to be the last man he would see in his life. Even if he made it all the way there, it was not clear how and when he would be able to smoke again, Rahela and Henry would be all over him, and he would die one way or another. She had told him many times that she did not want an opium fiend for a father. Good thing he wasn't her father.

"But she came back for you," Osman said.

She came back for her guilt.

"She loves you."

She loved me when she needed me. Now I am her burden, and she loves Henry. He made shade for your goddamn daughter.

Rahela put down the valises, and Henry finally released Pinto to sit on a valise. His ankle was swollen and throbbing on someone else's body.

Wait here, Henry said, and advanced toward the foot of the gangplank.

We made it, Rahela said.

I didn't make it, Pinto said. I don't want to have made it.

Listen, Padri, I am sorry for everything, Rahela said. I know that you think that I am just a stupid girl, that I lost my mind, that Henry seduced me and took advantage of me. I know you want to protect me. But I made my choice. Even if it is wrong, it is mine.

You are a child. Where I come from, you wouldn't be allowed to be in the room alone with a man until you were married to him.

We are not where you come from. Where you come from, I would've been married off at sixteen.

"She's right," Osman said.

You are my only family in this world, Rahela said. I don't want to live without you. We are going to Hong Kong together, as a family.

Henry is not my family, and he will never be. I was with him in the car when his wife died. I saw what he was made of, how stupid, callous, and careless. He will destroy you. He is reckless and selfish and he will abandon you as soon as he gets bored with you.

All the more reason for you to come along with me.

I am not your family, Pinto said. I am not your father. Osman was your father. And we are both dead.

Please stop saying things like that.

You came out of his loins.

Loins don't matter. You are my father. And you are not dead. I need you alive.

One way or another, you are going to live without a father.

Henry returned accompanied by Moser, pushing off his cane, wearing a tweed jacket and a fedora in the heat. No sweat showed on his face, as if he were a corpse.

I have got some bad news, said Moser. Only two of you can board the ship.

What do you mean? Rahela asked.

See? Pinto said. I am not going.

The third ship pass was revoked so as to be reissued to someone else. Someone was amply bribed. The *Empress* is now full. There is nothing I can do about it.

Fine, Rahela said. We'll wait for the next ship.

There might be no next ship, Henry said. And even if there was, the passes are only for the *Empress*.

Pinto understood immediately that Henry had given away the third ticket so as to prevent him from coming along, but he was not going to say anything about it.

"Among His signs are the ships," Osman said, "sailing like floating mountains: if He willed, He could bring the wind to a standstill and they would lie motionless on the surface of the sea."

Then we are staying, Rahela said.

No, we are not, Henry said.

No, you're not, Pinto said. I do not want to go with you anyway, not with this garbage of a man. There is no place for me in Henry's world.

You are going. I am not leaving you here, Rahela said.

I am old, Pinto said. I am done. I will be your burden. I will stay. And maybe later, after you settle, and this madness is over, you can come back to get me.

Absolutely not. I am not leaving you.

There is no place for me wherever you think you are going, Pinto said. Please, go.

No, Rahela said. Never.

SHANGHAI, 1949

THE ENGINE NOISE echoed in the empty plane, eradicating all the other sounds. Rahela imagined that was what it must've felt like to be sinking to the river bottom, complete with a pressure in her chest and piercing pain in her ears. Through the grimy porthole she could see the outline of the Bund in the distance, and was amazed that it did in fact exist and that her mind was not deformed enough to create figments of memory—the Bund's brutal geometric solidity was undeniable and eternal. Ever since she'd left Shanghai, her life there was like a story she had made up and then had to pretend was true, always expecting that someone would disbelieve her, accuse her of making it all up. It did not help either that Henry, the truth-loving American, would listen to her stories of trekking across China, from Kashgar to Shanghai on Padri's back, with a smirk of ironic skepticism. As for her Shanghai stories, he would never confirm or deny what she told others, letting her entangle herself in all the thin stretches and inconsistencies, which he was always quick to point out, until she herself questioned the inherent unreality of all retold stories. It took her a while to understand that it was his way of controlling her, of retaining the position of superiority he always claimed for himself, of acting like a serious and reliable man in charge of a child. In her new life, there were no witnesses, other than Henry, to who she had been in Shanghai. Neither were there any witnesses to the Rahela before Shanghai, other than Padri Rafo. All she herself could remember were the stories he had told her, and she wasn't always capable of believing they were true—they were like terrible fairy tales he was compelled to tell because he himself could never wake up from the long nightmare in which they had taken place.

The stories she had liked to hear were about Sarajevo, about Tija Simha and Manuči, about their strange and funny neighbors, about Binjoki the rascal, about the time Padri went with his whole family to see the first horse-drawn streetcar in Sarajevo, when he got lost in the crowd and it took him until nighttime to find his way back to the Jewish neighborhood up in the hills. And when he made it back Manuči beat him with a wooden ladle, then let him gorge himself on baklava. He was beaten blue, but that was the best baklava of his life. There were stories about Osman too, who was always good, handsome, and brave in them. The story of their escape from Tashkent, of Osman's last stand facing the evil Bolsheviks so that Padri and her mother could escape. All she knew about Osman came from Padri's stories, which he may have well made up. Osman was her true father, Padri had told her, he just took care of her for the love of Osman. He may have said that just to hurt her, but what she had never told him was that she had in fact imagined Osman as her father—this brave, handsome, clever man, so unlike the feeble, opium-smoking, melancholy, lonely stranger who had taken care of her for so long. The man whom she had understood and appreciated only in Hong Kong, when it was too late.

The plane flew low over the Yangtze, and then over a factory whose grounds were packed with soldiers in green uniforms, the multitudes of war teeming and milling among trucks and cannons. These were the Communist troops, and it was obvious they could easily shoot up the plane as it roared over their heads. A vision presented itself to her of the airplane bursting into flames and howling straight down to drop into the river and sink as the water broke through the windows and every hole and crack. She and her child would still be strapped to the plane's walls and would thus vanish into the muddy silted darkness below. That would solve a lot of problems. And there would be no witnesses.

But the Communists did not shoot, and the plane did land on the tarmac and then scurried to the airport building. When the door opened, she was blinded by the sun, and there were shadows right outside who then sharpened into American soldiers, their handguns drawn, their faces obscure in the stern shade of their helmets. When her eyesight adjusted, a smiling, shining man in a dark suit and tie was waving at her. You will recognize Jack, Henry had said, by his shine. His skin reflects light differently. He was the whitest man at Princeton and that means he must be the whitest one in the world. He could be a movie star if he chose to leave the foreign service. The camera would love him.

Beyond the gleaming Jack, there was a crowd of people with suitcases and bundles and screaming children, ready to get on the plane and get out before the Communists conquered the city. It seemed the refugees were standing under a cloud of despair, their faces pallid and fraught with the same frantic hope she had seen back in 1937. It was as though the same people she had once watched trying to leave the city were just transferred from the riverbank to the Lunghwa airport, lugging the same suitcases and the same children.

It is a matter of days, Henry had told her, before Shanghai falls. Jack owes me not just money but favors and he will be quick to help you. But there is no guarantee that he can get you out after the Commies take over, or that he will be able to protect you once they are there. He might have to leave in a rush himself. So if you go in, you might end up being on your own. Good luck! She was quite on her own now, walking down the narrow stairs, careful not to trip, followed by the two pilots. They said nothing to her before, during, or after the flight, not even as they pointed at a bucket fastened to the wall she was strapped to. When she asked what it was for, one of the pilots mimed barfing into it and laughed it up. She would barf into that bucket later; when the plane dropped in turbulence, the vomit splashed all over the floor and on her feet; she thought she would die, and she barfed some more, this time on the floor. It was nothing like the moderate disgorgements of her early pregnancy—on the plane, she purged herself until there was nothing left inside.

As soon as the pilots descended the stairs, the white-helmeted soldiers rushed in, as if to arrest or kill someone, except that now there was no one inside, just a few leather valises and wooden crates and Rahela's vomit. The tarmac was hot under her feet. It was only May, but she walked straight into the familiar heat—the everlasting thin soup of humidity, infused with the stench of swamp, sweat, and burnt straw. She had forgotten it; now it washed over her like a wave and she gasped in distress. In that moment, her life of the past twelve years since she'd left Shanghai was rendered a dream. Perhaps that was how people who actually had a place called home felt upon returning. I will never know.

Welcome to the end of the world, Jack said, and shook her hand, on which there were traces of vomit and airplane grime, although she did not tell him that. With a nod, he ordered a man who stood behind him, evidently the driver, to take Rahela's rucksack.

How was your flight?

It was many flights, Rahela said, all of them awful. I've puked my soul out.

Well, you've made it, Jack said. And here you are now.

They followed the driver to a black, banged-up car with all of its doors opened. They walked past the refugee crowd—a young Chinese woman wearing a wide hat with netting shouted Jack's name repeatedly and desperately but he ignored her. Rahela could tell he was practiced at ignoring others.

No one's coming into Shanghai anymore, Jack said. Everybody's hustling to get out before it's too late. Except it's already too late. People come to the airport and hustle to get a one-way ticket on Maybe Airlines, where your flight is always cancelled.

Jack liked his own joke, so he chuckled.

Where will they go? Rahela asked.

There're a lot of places to go to. Everybody ends up somewhere. The world's huge.

Another American, whom Jack didn't introduce and who said nothing, strode along with them, clearly listening. One of the man's eyebrows was constantly raised as if he were about to spot a subterfuge or ask a clever question. His socks were very white, his shoes very polished; his feet were enormously big. He was handsome in a sinister way, and his sweat shimmered like grease on the edges of his jaw. Only when they got to the car did Rahela realize that the soldiers were right behind them, carrying the leather valises, which they then deposited in the car's trunk.

The men went about doing what they had to do with a kind of American determination—with each move they knew exactly what their next one would be. Henry was like that too, born with his mind made up about everything, doubt-free. At any given moment, Henry could envision the next moment, and then the next one, and so on—he needed to live in a world reticulated with logic and manageable plans. Once upon a time, when Rahela was a child, she found such certainty about everything fascinating and seductively manly. It took her a while to realize that Henry actually had no idea what lay ahead, and was mainly pretending to know. He was improvising inside the vanishing time just like everyone else; he just never showed hesitation or doubt when considering the future, appearing clenched-jaw solid in his convictions and beliefs, in his love, in his lust, in his lies.

The raised-eyebrow man held the car door open for Rahela, waiting patiently until she squeezed into the back seat, uncomfortably. Her three-months belly was prominent enough, but Jack said nothing about it, even if she saw his glancing at the bump when he sat down next to her. The eyebrow man in the passenger seat had a gun in his lap that seemed to have appeared out of nowhere. The driver steered the car around a pack of nuns, their wimples stained with mud, or blood, or vomit. There were bundles of clothes abandoned along the road, by those, perhaps, who had made it to the last plane. The car scraped past a large piano, and a luggage trunk so big that a family could live inside it.

How's Henry doing? Jack asked.

I haven't seen him for a while, but he's fine, she said. He's Henry. He's always doing fine.

She could've told him that he had been gone on his reporting trips for so long that it had become clear he had left her and their unborn child, and that arranging for her to come to Shanghai was his parting gift at best, or, at worst, a way to get rid of her and the child. It was the worst, because he was Henry.

Henry's indestructible, Jack said. I miss him. When this is all over, I'll go to see him in the Philippines, do some serious drinking. If it's okay with you.

She could have told Jack that she would not be in the Philippines when he came to visit. Neither would Henry. But Jack knew all that, of course. He was just as skilled as Henry at lying.

By the way, Jack said, it could be that, if we're stopped on the road, we'll have to blow up the car and everything in it. There's a half a million dollars in those valises in the back. American companies here need to pay their employees, and the Chinese money is worthless, so we're lending them some. The last thing we want is for the suitcases to end up in the wrong hands.

The eyebrow man turned to look at Jack, his eyebrow finally appropriately questioning.

It probably won't come to that, the eyebrow man said. It is not something we need to get Mrs. Krantz all worried about right now.

I'm not Mrs. Krantz, Rahela said.

I've an idea, Jack said. How about Mrs. Not-Krantz and I take the money and run off together and live happily ever after?

He chuckled and turned to wink at Rahela, who offered no reaction to his tomfoolery.

We'd have to kill Marantz here, which wouldn't be that easy, Jack went on, enthusiastic about his unfolding joke. Unless Marantz wants to come along with us. We'll have so much money we'll need a bodyguard. We could all live like a bunch of Communists, but with a lot of money.

Okay, then, let's focus. Let's look at the road, Marantz said, and returned to looking straight ahead.

Anyway, Jack said to Rahela, your father is safe at the Broadway Mansions, snug as a bug in my office, waiting for you. I was told he was fine, if a bit weak. He's not really talking to anyone, other than himself.

How did you find him? Rahela asked.

Moser told us.

Moser? Moser-Ethering?

That one.

Is he here?

No, he's in Hong Kong. But he knows a lot of people here, and a lot of people Moser knows know a lot of stuff.

Where did you find my father?

It wasn't me, to be perfectly honest. I did look for your dad all over town after Henry asked me to, and he was nowhere to be found. I was becoming pretty sure that he may've in fact died. But Moser tipped us that Mr. Pinto was staying at a place—how to describe it?—of fairly ill repute.

Henry said it was a restaurant, Rahela said.

All kinds of services were provided, Jack said. The Natashas took care of him, and your father kept them clean and, you know, disinfected. When we went to fetch him, he didn't want to leave. This is my home, he said. The Natashas cried and kissed his cheeks. I wasn't sure it was him at first because he didn't look like a white person. He looked like, you know, an Indian, swarthy and all.

So how did you get him to leave? Rahela asked.

We, well, we had to carry him out a bit. Henry was clear: Find him, get him safe and wait for Mrs. Krantz to come.

I'm not Mrs. Krantz.

Whoever you may be, we did what Henry told us to do. So, Mr. Pinto's waiting for you.

Here and there, they passed packs of the Kuomintang without weapons, their uniforms unbuttoned, or torn, or absent, skinny-legged men in their undergarments, war sores maculating their bodies. The car crawled past abandoned trucks, stripped of everything, past turned-over mortars and field guns, empty wooden cases, the debris of a disintegrating army, of an ending world.

We gave them all this stuff, Jack said, and now they're either giving it over to the Communists, or destroying it. Turns out it was all perfectly pointless. Once the Communists get across the Yangtze, it'll be over in a blink. And no one gives a fuck, pardon my French. Everyone is ready for the end. Whoever can leave has left or is already packed. The war's well over; we just need the victor to arrive and take charge of the peace. It's funny how things don't just end, they have to die slowly before they end.

Two naked, bloated men lay dead in a roadside ditch. One of them grinned, as if the whole thing was amusing. A couple of dogs sat at the ditch edge, considering the possibilities. Rahela was nauseated, but she had emptied herself on the plane, and her mouth was now painfully dry.

God knows I'm ready to go home, Jack said. Are you going back to the Philippines?

I'll stop by, Rahela said.

They were stopped by a ragtag Kuomintang patrol—it seemed that only one man was armed, and he pointed his rifle at Jack and scanned what was inside the car. It was likely that there were no bullets in that rifle, but the driver showed the armed man some kind of a document. Rahela could see the tendons on the eyebrow man's neck tensing. The soldier looked surprised when he saw a pregnant woman in the back seat. Jack calmly spoke to him in Chinese and the man shouted what sounded like a threat back at him, but let them pass anyway.

Rahela understood what the man said, but still asked Jack: What did he say?

I told them, Jack said, that I was taking my pregnant wife to see a doctor because she was having, you know, woman problems. He said that it was crazy to be having children at a time like this. And he's not wrong. But then what time's a good time in a world like this?

Jack was lying, of course. The man had asked them for a ride, and Jack told him that the pregnant lady was the wife of a very big boss and that he wouldn't like it if his wife was disrespected.

One thing Rahela could never forget from the day when she'd left Shanghai in 1937 was the line of people along the wharf watching the *Empress of Asia* sail away, toward a place, and a life, unavailable to any of them. They stood right on the edge, shoulder to shoulder, teetering above the fetid river. She was on the ship and she looked for Padri's face in the crowd, as if that would make anything easier, or even different, clutching the Samsara pendant on her chest as if it could succor her. But she could not see him, maybe because he could not stand up with his twisted ankle, or because he did not want even to look at her sailing away with her lover. Rahela's last memory of Padri was his absence from the crowd. A girl then fell into the filthy water and a few men plunged in to save her. Henry pulled Rahela deeper into their new life, into a cabin he'd paid dearly for, where he would strip her naked before they even reached the sea and make love to her repeatedly, in a ravenous way that was new and much less gentle than before, as if his restraint had been left behind in Shanghai, as if he had been turned on by the possibility of the ship being sunk by the Japanese navy. Rahela cried all the way to Hong Kong.

She cried in Hong Kong as well. Henry tried to console her at first, convince her that she should be happy because she was now free. But then he gave up and would leave her alone for days on end to take a boat to Formosa or Vietnam and snoop around for his newspaper stories—he never bothered to tell her how he got the job as a *New York Times* correspondent. He urged her to meet with Nancy Sergeant, Rahela's schoolmate, whose family made it out of Shanghai to Hong Kong as well, but Rahela refused. She was ashamed, and not only because she was now their teacher's mistress, but also because Nancy would've heard that Rahela had left her father behind to escape to Hong Kong. Nancy was rich and had despised her at the American School, mocking her accent, her Nansen-passport life, her father who didn't have any kind of passport, not even a Nansen one, who would come to pick up his daughter in a jacket that had holes at the elbows, wearing shoes with worn-out heels. Years later, Rahela would realize that Henry had been sleeping with Nancy all along, even well before Hong Kong, well before they got married and Rahela started festering in her loneliness and sorrow.

Hong Kong for her was listening to melancholy jazz on the radio and reading thick, tragic novels all day behind the blinds drawn and about to catch fire from the relentless heat outside. She wrote letters to Padri, addressing them to Rabbi Brown at the Ohel Rachel temple, hoping that the rabbi would be able to find him. But she received only one response in which the rabbi told her that unfortunately no one had seen Mr. Pinto in a long while, and that it was believed that he may have perished in the opium den jungle.

Rahela had no friends in Hong Kong, no confidants, no one to talk to about her solitude, about her regret and guilt. Henry would be gone for weeks on end, and when he was home, all he wanted to do was fuck—in Shanghai they had made love; in Hong Kong they fucked. She would never write to Padri about any of that, of course; indeed she would not ever mention Henry, or her misery—she already heard his voice in her head, telling her: I told you so! What she mostly wrote about was a hypothetical future in which Padri and she would be together again. We can settle in Sarajevo, she wrote. I imagined the city, all of it, from your stories. I already know your family. In my dreams, I have already met Manuči. It would be like going back home. And I want to meet all of my cousins. Maybe Osman is there too. She asked Henry to help her get in touch with Padri's people in Sarajevo, and he said he would, and then he didn't, and then the war in Europe started. After a while, she was writing a letter a day to Padri, stamping them with her guilt. After a while, she stopped sending them.

One day, Henry came home and told her that there might soon be war in Asia as well, and that she was going to go to America, where a spot for her at Bryn Mawr was ensured by Mrs. Krantz, whose alma mater it was.

Where is Bryn Mawr? she asked. What is Bryn Mawr?

You're off to college, girl, Henry said. Education will turn you into a proper American woman.

They got stuck in a traffic jam on the Bund because the Kuomintang were holding a victory parade.

One way not to lose a war, Jack said, is not to fight it at all, so that just not being shot dead is a victory. Which works like a charm until you're shot dead.

Cars, pedicabs, rickshaws, and throngs of pedestrians crowded the street. Peddlers banged on the windows of their car, their faces distorted with hunger, or anger, or both. Some of the stately bank buildings were adorned with flags but had their windows boarded. Everybody and everything seemed to be involved in some kind of slow and stunted movement, glitching with helplessness. Everybody ends up somewhere, Jack had said. He will end up somewhere without becoming someone else, Jack the White Shining Man until the end of time. There was discordant music, the thundering drums and crashing cymbals, and the half-hearted but united shouts of the marching troops somewhere beyond the wall of the bodies blocking the traffic. People who stood on the stairs leading to the boarded-up Bank of China had no interest in the parade—they just stood there, as they had probably seen it all before, and had no other place to go and had to wait for something to happen, but couldn't know what it could be. There were flags and pictures of Chiang Kai-shek hanging from lampposts and windows. All of the events seemed to have been crushed into an uncomfortable synchronicity, as if time had stopped working properly.

There hasn't been the slimmest chance of a Kuomintang victory for a very long time now, yet they have their victory parades nonstop, Jack said. Chiang's forbidden speaking of defeat or thinking of surrender. The newspapermen get harassed if they dare write it's all over. Or if they mention that Chiang and his court are in Formosa already, have been for some time, and have no intention of coming back.

We can walk from here, Rahela said.

Walk where? Jack asked, as if just discovering the idea of walking.

To the Broadway Mansions.

They walked along the Whangpoo River, which was just as crowded as the street, throbbing with sampans and shallow boats and occasional foreign ships waiting to be loaded so they could leave. The river was the color of tea with milk, its smell muddy with more than a touch of rotten eel. When Rahela lived with Padri, they would never come down here, not even for a stroll—for him, the Bund was as far from Hongkou as Hong Kong. It was only after she moved in with Henry to a house off Avenue Edward VII that she sometimes came to the Bund, but seldom with Henry, who, she figured out much too late, didn't want to be seen in public with his adolescent mistress. What he said, though, was that he could not stand to imagine the things people would say about her. He always claimed he didn't care what people said about him, but that was all he ever cared about.

The Kuomintang parade turned the corner from Nanjing Road and now marched down the Bund. The parade was but a herd of desperate soldiers who seemed to have been randomly rounded up and forced to pretend that the victory made them proud and happy. Marantz pushed through the hungry and sweaty mass of people, who parted like seagrass. Rahela saw a woman in a velour coat with a fur collar, her face shimmering with sweat, some of which dripped off her chin, as off house eaves. The coat made it probable that she was Russian; she wore all of her possessions because she had no place to keep them. The woman must've sensed being watched, for she turned around and locked her eyes with Rahela, who suddenly stopped breathing, her head emptied of air and blood, because she thought she was now looking at Lenka. But the woman averted her gaze with a wince of disgust, and Rahela realized that Jack and the eyebrow man were nowhere to be found; she was now in the midst of a crowd hypnotized by the flags and the desperately victorious drum banging. She knew which way to go for the Broadway Mansions, she knew where she was, but what made her dizzy was that she was not supposed to be there, or anywhere else. She felt someone's hands on the curve of her belly, and a Chinese woman behind the hands said something to her in an alarmed voice, and then the rotten eels released their reek, and the sky was blue and spinning, and everyone was endlessly tall, and then they vanished and then everything was light as a snowflake and very dark.

Osman's eyes were like mountain lakes on a sunny day, wie die Bergseen, and could turn into a rusted sky when he was angry or distraught. And when his mustache overgrew in the camp in Turkestan it merged with his nose hair whenever he curled his upper lip to frown or cry, but the tips of his fingers were always soft; in the Bosnian language the fingertips are called jagodice, little strawberries, and now his little strawberries were on Rahela's forehead and his eyes were properly rusted, and she could see no mouth on his face, only hair and his nose and eyes peeked out from all that; when she was at Bryn Mawr they had to read Norwegian fairy tales, and there were hairy creatures in them, she would have nightmares, they read Shakespeare, what country, friends, is this, am I going to die, and when I do, will my child live without me, and if so, where, and will she ever remember me? and Osman sang to Rahela without moving his lips, because she could not see his lips from all the hair, and he was stroking her cheeks with his little strawberries, noches, noches, buenas noches, noches son d'enamorar, he sang, ah, noches son d'enamorar, and it was in Padri's voice that he sang, for he did that whenever she was febrile, he would tell her that the song was about love, dando bueltas por la kama, komo l'peshe en la mar, ah l'peshe en la mar, she should've never left Padri in Shanghai, she should've never left Shanghai, she should've never left with Henry, she should've stayed to be here, here is everywhere but there, Osman sang with his little strawberries, Bejturan se uz ružu savija, vilu ljubi Djerzelez Alija, vilu ljubi svu noć na konaku, po mjesecu i mutnu oblaku, what language, friends, is this, what is this thing in my throat, is it going to choke me, is it. I am going to die. It is not your time yet.

Jack declared that the elevator was too risky as it was prone to stopping at inopportune times, so Marantz carried Rahela up the stairs in his arms, pausing at landings to catch a breath. Her head was spinning, she was privy to Marantz's heavy breathing; when she opened her eyes, his cocked brow was looming right over her. Ahead, Jack's white face blazed in the staircase murk. There were maps on the walls, though they could've been stains of dampness, or of blood. Eventually, the eyebrow was gingerly lowered and Marantz put her feet on the floor and then she checked to see if her Samsara necklace was still around her neck. It was, so she walked, and although she felt conscious, everything still looked like a half-cooked dream: there were Chinese people everywhere, in the offices and the hallways, whole families waiting for something, pressing their backs against the walls, on which there were blurry pictures still hanging, to let her pass by as if she were a frightening hallucination. Somebody handed her a cup of warm tea but she tottered and spilled it. At the end of the hallway, in a large office, a Chinese woman was steaming something over a little stove that stood on top of a mahogany desk.

Are you okay? Jack asked. He seemed unfazed by the steady flow of nightmare around them.

Just got a little dizzy because of the heat, Rahela said.

I can get you some whiskey just to prop you up.

Whiskey? Where am I? Rahela asked.

The Broadway Mansions, Jack said.

Yes, but what city?

After the Japanese overran the Chinese part of Shanghai in 1937, refugees crossed over into the International Settlement, which was protected by the international law. Pinto must've been among the refugees, but his name cannot be found in the municipal or Red Cross records. My guess would be that Lenka took him along to stay with her Russian friends, but there is no way of knowing, as Lenka vanished from Shanghai, and Pinto's life, sometime in the late thirties. She might have died, or might have married a man who took her away from Shanghai—marriage was one of the ways to get out. Either way, I imagine Pinto struggling with his addiction in the company of strangers, having a hard time finding work, or even caring about staying alive. It probably didn't get better for him when the Japanese marines in tanks and armored cars brushed aside international law and drove down the Bund on December 8, 1941, the speakers blaring the obvious: all of Shanghai had been captured. The Americans, the Brits, and other allied-nation members who could escape were long gone; those who couldn't were told to report to Hamilton House, which became the Kempetai headquarters. The city was full of Jewish refugees who had over the years been finding their desperate way from Europe to Shanghai as no visa was needed to enter the city, most of them too helpless and unimportant to be tortured by Kempetai or interned in camps. But the Germans kept sending SS Colonel Josef Meisinger, the Butcher of Warsaw, to insist that the Japanese exterminate the Shanghai Jews, or at least let the Germans deal with the issue. One of Colonel

Meisinger's ideas was to send in SS units on Rosh Hashanah to round up the people in homes and temples across the city and load them onto ships slated for demolition, which would then be towed out to sea and sunk. Though the Japanese were happy to massacre the Chinese in the hundreds of thousands, they were disinclined, for whatever reason, to sink the Jews. Over the radio and on the newspaper front pages they announced that all the stateless refugees would have to move to the area of Hongkou known as Little Vienna, where ten thousand Jewish refugees already lived in abject conditions. Thousands of people trekked from the International Settlement to Little Vienna, with their children, bundles, furniture, and trinkets, to be crammed into the one square mile of the ghetto, surrounded by barbed wire and sentries at gates—Little Vienna turned out to be nothing like the Big Vienna. Pinto must have crossed the Soochow Creek yet another time, as his name does appear on the lists of Little Vienna's wartime residents. Many of them despaired and declared that the end of the road was now reached, but they didn't understand at the time that the ghetto protected them from Colonel Meisinger. Sergeant Kano Ghoya, who liked to refer to himself as the King of Jews, was put in charge of the ghetto. He enjoyed watching people stand in heat for hours on end to get an arbitrary piece of paper from his office; he would beat them for some random, incomprehensible infraction. There was a perpetual shortage of food; there were cholera and dysentery; there was a dreadful shortage of news from Europe; there was hopelessness. But there were no round-ups and killings; there were schools and dances; there were teahouses where German was used for gossip; there was worshipping in the temples; there were children coming of age, new ones were born. Pinto's name—as Dr. Raphael

Pento [*sic*]—shows up on the list of those who provided medical services, though it is hard to imagine what he could have done in a place rife with diseases and with no functioning hospital or pharmacies. There was no opium either, as the Japanese assumed tight control over the dens. They did let the Chinese poison themselves and pay for it too, but they lived on the other side of the barbed wire. Few in Little Vienna had money to spend on opium anyway, and it would've been hard to smuggle opium in without bribing the sentries. Pinto must have gone through horrible withdrawal; he must have reached the verge of death at least once. He must've been alone, destitute, devastated. From what I can guess, it is quite clear he never fully recovered.

Here he is, Jack said.

A shadow darkened the door; from the couch on which Pinto lay, the shadow looked very tall. The distant thunder outside must have come from the Communist artillery, but it still sounded like a major-key chord announcing the transformation of the shadow into a woman who had Rahela's green eyes and apple cheeks. She wore the necklace with the Samsara pebble. Yet her hips were wide and she was pregnant. Pinto had learned long before that he should never trust his eyes. But she wore the necklace and she smelled of lavender.

Rahela, Pinto said.

Padri, she said.

The woman's voice was also Rahela's, but much older, throatier. She knelt next to Pinto and put a hand on his cheek, layered with unkempt hair. He was all skin and bones, the edges of his jaw sharp like skate blades.

Jo, ken? Pinto asked.

Jo, Rahela.

Rahela, mi fiža.

Pinto closed his eyes. He felt the weight of her hand on his cheek and envisioned bringing it to his lips to kiss it, but he couldn't move.

Osman, do you see her too, or am I dreaming?

For days, weeks, months on end, Pinto would see and relive the moment Rahela was pulled by Henry into the crowd that was flowing up the gangplank to the ship deck—she stopped to look back with tears sparkling in her eyes, searching for him in the crowd, and the next moment she wasn't there at all, and just like that she was gone from his life. Back in the first Shanghai war, he had lost her in the crowd—it was the longest half hour in his life. Take me, Lord, he had muttered over her febrile body. Maybe this is the pay-up time. With his swollen ankle, Pinto limped around the Settlement, its streets taken over by refugees. The city was now fantastically different from before, yet to him exactly the same; he kept going in circles, down Bubbling Well Road, then Avenue Foch toward the Bund, the ankle throbbing at a distance from his mind, as if he were just receiving the news of the pain from afar. He discovered some American dollars in his pocket, probably stuffed in by Henry. He entered a maze of small streets looking for an opium den, and they appeared familiar but he had never seen them before, and for a little while he could not remember what the name of the city, let alone the country, was. Over his head airplanes wailed, dropping bombs into the river, and the boom of explosions reverberated under his feet. He kept walking, for hours, probably days; his ankle entirely disappeared into his numb flesh, which ached horribly for a pipe of opium. Eventually, exhausted, shaking, he sat down next to a woman and her three toddlers of varying ages, all sleeping on a straw mat across the street from the Wing On department store. His nose was running, but his mouth was parched, he spent the night shivering, and he drained himself—vomit, diarrhea—over the same leaky bucket the family used. The children constantly wailed, from hunger and thirst, from the stench and the itch. He offered them some dollars, but they did not know what kind of money that was, so they declined. He could not recall eating or drinking anything. He tried to get up, but his ankle was now a purple ball stretching his shoe, which seemed to have grown into his tumescent flesh so he couldn't take it off. He was looking up at the people around them, all of whom were very tall, and at the Wing On store beyond them, and beyond it there was a blue sky, across which an airplane screamed and left behind a dark dropping that slowly lowered itself onto the roof of the store. For a moment, nothing happened, and then he was hurled against the wall behind him by a wave of scorching smoke, and then glass and debris were raining, and something heavy smacked his cheek. There was no sound at all, and he could see nothing, still on the ground, other than the shifting billows of dust. He didn't know if he was dead, for he could see no one else, no sign of life, no sky, and there were no sounds. His mouth was full of dirt, then blood, and there was something warm and sticky and soft on his face; when he touched it he could not tell what it was, and then he understood, as the light penetrated the dark cloud, that it was a child's hand. He would've died, right there, if Osman hadn't lifted him into his arms and carried him out of that death cloud, away from the carnage, as he had done once upon a time, back in Galicia. "It is not your time yet," Osman said. "You are not going to die here."

Padri, Rahela said. I am taking you home. Andemos al Sarajevo.

For years—in Hong Kong, at Bryn Mawr, in Tokyo, in the Philippines—she had imagined this moment, the moment when she would finally face Padri Rafo again and tell him that she was painfully sorry, that she had been selfish and foolish, that she should've never left him behind, that she had been wrong about so many things, and that she had paid a terrible price for it. But now, seeing his closed eyes sunken into his face, the scar under the stubble, his moss-like hair, and the thinness of his neck with the folds of skin cascading over his filthy shirt collar, she could say nothing, and not because she changed her mind, but because no words could match the disorienting immensity of being here, in his presence. She always imagined that the Padri she had re-membered would be the one she would offer her penance to, and certainly not this husk of a man, this shrunken memory, a stranger who replaced the father she had left behind. His body gave off a yeasty urine stench, his clothes smelled of vomit, sickness, and smoke. Here was somebody else, somebody she didn't know, or recognize, and she had no one else in the world.

I am sorry, she said. I cannot forgive myself.

Pinto opened his eyes, reluctantly, as if coming to was too much. Rahela's face floated over him and he could see the tiny nick, like an apostrophe, over her right eyebrow which he had never seen before, and there were white spit dots in the corner of her mouth, and a birthmark on her left temple, shaped like a tear, which he liked to kiss when she was a child. The pebble was dangling over his face, twirling.

I thought I would never see you again, she said. My God.

She squeezed his hand, and it was cold and the bones in it felt weak, like bird bones.

Rahela, Pinto said. I thought I would never see you again. You came back.

Here I am.

It is too late. I should be dead. I will be dead.

Well, you're not. Andemos al Sarajevo, Rahela said.

Andemos al Sarajevo, he said.

I got a passport for Mr. Pinto, Jack said. The *Eclipse* is leaving tomorrow morning. It's a repurposed navy ship, so there're no cabins, just berths, but you'll be going only to Manila so you should be okay. You can be our guest here tonight. There's no other place to go to or sleep anyway.

Is that Henry talking? Pinto asked.

No, Rahela said. That's Jack.

Where is Henry?

Henry is not here.

Is he dead?

No.

Where is he?

I don't know. Last I saw him, he was in Japan.

Is he coming here?

No.

I don't want to see him.

You will never see him.

Please, don't leave me.

I will never leave you again.

She had earrings, tiny silver stars in her lobes. Lenka had pierced her ears when she was eleven, in defiance of Pinto's prohibition, behind his back. He was supposed to be angry about it, but then discovered that he didn't really care, and ended up buying her a couple of cheap earrings in the shape of a star.

Are we going to Sarajevo?

Yes, Rahela said.

Do you think it is still there?

Of course it is still there. Cities don't disappear or die.

Well, this one is dying right now.

No, it is not. It is just becoming something else.

Sarajevo is very far.

It is. But we're going there, however long it takes. We have no other place to go.

Is Henry coming with us?

No. Henry is not coming with us.

He is not a good man.

I know, Rahela said. It took me a while to figure it out. But here I am. It's just you and me from now on.

She wanted to tell him she was pregnant, but Jack was still lingering outside the office. More importantly, she didn't want Padri to think that she had come back because she was pregnant, because she needed him. She had come back because it was time to go home.

For a while after Rahela's departure, Pinto was spending on opium all the money Rahela had forced Henry to stuff in his pocket. He smoked so much in the Hongkou dens that sores spread and deepened on his right hip, and then on his left one. Osman would just lie pressing himself against Pinto, a wormwood around a rose, caressing his cheek, susurrously singing, Bejturan se uz ružu savija. Sometimes Osman would stop his singing to nag, to tell him that opium was turning him into a decaying plant, as if Pinto hadn't already known that. But then not even Osman could offer a better way for Pinto to be, nothing better to do, and eventually he stopped nagging him altogether. Pinto would tell Osman—again and again, as if he hadn't already heard them—the same stories. How Pinto hid from the Bolsheviks in a wall, where he could hear baby Rahela crying, and how he thought he would die inside that wall and Rahela would be an orphan yet again. And how he carried her through the mountains, and stabbed a Cossack in the eye, and how he carried her through the desert, trudging behind a farting camel, and how they almost got buried in a tebbad, and how he cleaned Rahela's mouth of sand and dripped water into her mouth, and how her tongue came out like a shy lizard to lick the water off her lips, and how he offered to the Lord his life for hers, and the Lord accepted the deal and tortured Pinto for many years to come, particularly after they reached Shanghai, where Rahela would go to the American School to be seduced by her teacher and leave Pinto here to die. Osman knew all that, there was nothing to hide, yet Pinto was riven with guilt and shame. Only once or twice did he unleash the full hatred he harbored for Henry, for his selfishness and arrogance and for his lechery, and in fury he would hiss: I've met killers and murderers and beasts, but I've never seen evil like that, evil so nicely smelling, so sunny, with his combed hair and clipped nails and cleanly shaven, always taking whatever he wants from other people, ransacking their lives, as if everything and everyone belonged to him, as if everyone else was just passing through the world given to him at birth. He stole our child, Osman. He stole her. The work, my love, the work that goes into just keeping a child alive, there is so much work, I never wanted to do it, I never knew I could do it, but I kept doing it and I kept her alive and I loved her. He is going to ruin her. He is going to make her miserable. He is going to hurt her, and she will be alone among strangers. He does not love her. Childhood is not a garland of roses. Life is not a garland of roses. The Lord is lazy, careless, doesn't have to look for food where there is none, does not hear the cry of a hungry, suffering child. He does not strive, like we do, to stay alive because something in Him hopes that one day—one day!—life might be worth living. Nor does He have to decide whether to end Himself or stick around to see what happens and whether He has survived. But that man, that Henry, he just wakes up in the morning, decides what belongs to him and takes it, every day he robs others, and he doesn't just steal, he soils everything too. If I had died a long time ago, back at home in Sarajevo, before we were sent off to war, or in the war, or in Turkestan, if I had died, I wouldn't have had to suffer, I wouldn't have had to see the horror, I wouldn't have worked so hard to stay alive to keep her alive, I wouldn't have to see how the world is now devoid of all that has ever mattered to me.

"If you had died," Osman said, "you would not have met me."

I would not have lost you either, Pinto said.

"Well, I am here," Osman would say. "You have not lost me. I am the only thing you have not lost."

Rahela slept on the floor, next to the sofa on which Padri lay, and her back hurt through the night. Jack did not offer her anything to eat, so the smell of food cooked in the offices down the hall made her hungry to the point of nausea. She got up and asked the Chinese lady who was cooking on the desk for a bowl of rice, which she gave her, chattering about her sons coming home with the

Communists. Too satiated to sleep, she listened to Pinto's steady snoring, occasionally interrupted by a gasp or a groan, as if he was being expelled from a nightmare. She finally fell asleep just as the dawn outside was beginning to make day noises: shouts, shots, boat engines grumbling, and that din of many things in a city moving at the same time. When she woke up and saw that Padri hadn't moved, her first thought was that he was dead, and for an instant she felt relief, immediately followed by a hollowing fear. She leaned in closer to see if he was breathing, if his chest was rising, but she couldn't detect anything. The gray hair of his face was smothered by the morning light already enfeebled by thick humidity. His hand was cold to touch. She pulled his right eyelid up and the white of his eye was yellow, but then he snorted, startling her, and opened the other eye, and it was clear that for a moment he could not recognize her at all—when he did, what came over his face was a wave of painful sorrow.

Mi kerida, he said.

Si, Padri, she said, but he didn't respond.

She let him go back to sleep, and stood by the window, looking out. The river stretched far, and across it were the expansive fields of Pootung, and there was the Soochow Creek pushing refuse and corpses into the Whangpoo. Back in her previous life, Padri had made her go to the Ohel Rachel temple, where she was often the only girl sitting among the women, ogled by boys and not a few middle-aged men. He'd never wanted to go, but had keen interest in what had transpired at the temple, and would interrogate her about what she had seen, heard, learned, and then he would proceed to argue with everything. If she was told at the temple that three creations—water, wind, fire—preceded the making of the world, he would say: It was spirit, not wind! Water gave birth to darkness, fire gave birth to light, and spirit gave birth to wisdom. Wisdom! They have none of it at the Ohel Rachel, he would shout. None!

There was a barricade with a couple of Kuomintang soldiers at the Garden Bridge. They looked so young, small, and helpless that, from above, they resembled pawns. One of them pointed his rifle in the direction of the river, but Rahela heard no shot. It was as if he was playing war, still practicing how to shoot.

Padri had a hard time standing up from the sofa, grunting as he pushed himself up, but when he did, Rahela was struck by how short he was, much shorter than when she'd left, diminished like a deflated balloon. He walked toward her at the window with difficulty, a decrepit old man. She did not really know how old he was, because there were no letters, no objects, no pictures from his previous life, no documents or evidence, no family or friends to remember him when he was a child or even young—for all she knew he could've been created out of clay, like a Golem. The only thing that confirmed that he was born a human child and had a family and a past were his stories about life in Sarajevo before the war. He had once told her that he was twenty and change when the war started and he had to leave his hometown, but what she remembered him saying might've been something she had imagined him saying. It could've been a conversation she had never had with him, but nevertheless replayed in her head many times in Hong Kong, at Bryn Mawr, in Manila and Tokyo. Presently, he smelled of piss and snot, his hair was flat on his right temple from lying on his side; he moved like someone who had misplaced his walking stick and was now apprehensive to be upright. She loved him so much at that moment, she loved his suffering and struggles, and the body that had paid the price, and all that he had loved and lost.

Padri, she said. I want to tell you something.

Have you talked to Osman? Padri asked.

Osman? What Osman?

Your father.

Padri, you are my father.

I raised you like a father, but you came from Osman's loins.

I know. You told me.

When did I tell you?

Doesn't matter.

I wonder where he is.

Where could he be? Rahela said.

He was here just a moment ago, Padri said. He was sitting on the floor over there, leaning on the wall, watching over you. All night long. He's worried about you. That's what he does; he has watched and worried over me every night ever since you've left. I wouldn't be alive without him. And now I don't know where he might have gone. Probably to find something to eat. But he'll be back. He wants to talk to you. He wants to look at you. He has missed you. He is your father. He wants to be with you. He wants to go back to Sarajevo with you.

With us, Rahela said,

We'll see, Pinto said. It might be too late for me.

No, Rahela said. It isn't.

It took forever to get down the stairs, because Pinto was feeble and afraid that he might fall. Jack and Rahela held him, one on each side. He was light like an empty suitcase. He slipped once, lost his balance, and Rahela tightened her grip to hold him, but she could not have stopped him from tumbling if it wasn't for Jack.

Is Osman coming? he asked.

He's right behind us, Rahela said.

Who's Osman? Jack asked.

My husband, Pinto said. Her father.

Jack glanced at Rahela as if to solicit an explanation but she offered none.

All right then, Jack said. Let's move along.

He's right behind, Padri, she said. He's coming along with us.

At the bottom of the gangplank, Rahela handed Pinto his passport so that he could hand it over to the grim customs officer. The passport was new, its pages cracking, as in a book just bought.

What is this? Pinto asked.

It's your passport.

I've never had one in my life.

Well, here it is. It will get us home.

The customs officer grabbed Rahela's backpack from her hand as if in a hurry, then rummaged through it cursorily—all he looked for was money or jewels, but what he found was her underwear and a Book of the Month copy of *Independent People* that she had carried since Manila. The customs officer smelled her underwear and flipped through the book to see if something might fall out of it, but it was empty, and he threw it back in and handed her the rucksack. The ship engine growled, and the stacks belched out smoke, and the gangplank was sagging under passengers shuffling upward toward a grizzled officer shouting in English, then in German, then in some other language she did not recognize. The ship looked rusted and grimy, ready for a scrapyard.

Where is this ship going? Pinto asked.

Manila, Rahela said. The Philippines.

You said we were going home.

We're going to catch another ship from there, to Cape Town.

That will take forever, Pinto said.

Well, Rahela said. Are you in a rush?

I am in no rush. Lay me on my side by the road.

What? What does that mean?

When the Messiah comes, I will be ready. And if he doesn't come, just leave me there.

They walked up to the top of the gangplank, where the grizzled officer glanced at their passports and waved them in without telling them where to go. Rahela followed a woman dragging a valise and two docile, tired children. The woman with the kids spoke Yiddish and seemed to know where they were going, but it turned out she was lost too, so they all stood and looked at the Bund, at its grimy marble and the pathetic aftermath of the victory parade and the flags fluttering limply in the hot breeze.

"I've never been on a ship before," Osman said.

Neither have I, said Pinto. I crossed the world on foot.

A seaman who introduced himself as Harvey and kept touching Rahela's back showed them to their double-decker berth in a dark corner of the lower deck. Pinto was out of breath from coming down the stairs, and sat down immediately to pant.

Osman and I will share this one, Pinto said.

Whatever you want, Rahela said.

She hadn't eaten much since she'd arrived in Shanghai and got dizzy herself coming down the steep steps and now got dizzier as she climbed to the upper bunk. The ceiling was low, and smelled of rust. The woman with the children settled in the far berth, but Rahela could still hear the children whimpering, their mother scolding them in Yiddish. She saw Padri's hand emerging from below, holding a bun.

Come on, she heard him rumble. Eat something. You need strength. A child is hard work.

She said nothing about her pregnancy to him, and he had said nothing to her. He must have noticed her bulge, her swollen knuckles and ankles and the heat hives on her face. She devoured the bun, which tasted bitter and crumbly, like Padri's pocket.

Padri, she said. I am expecting a child. It is Henry's child, but he is gone.

There was no response from below, so she said it again: I am expecting a child. Henry's child. He is gone for good.

I heard what you said, Pinto said. Go to sleep now. We have a long way to go. We have to take that child home.

They were not to go up on the deck, or even look out the portholes, until they reached the open sea, Harvey said, because the Communists are lined up all along the shore and they might shell or shoot at us. Not to mention the sunken ships and mines all the way to the mouth of the Yangtze.

Is there a way to get some food here? Rahela asked. I haven't eaten much in the past couple of days.

Not before the open sea, Harvey said. But I'll see what I can do.

"How long will it take us to get to Sarajevo?" Osman asked.

It will take a long time, Pinto said. Are you in a hurry?

"You can never get home fast enough," Osman said.

They would have to spend at least a week in Manila, Rahela

reckoned, before they could go on via Jakarta and Cape Town, all
the way to Genoa, then onward, or back, to Sarajevo. She would
give birth; her child would be born at home, and she would live
with Padri, and they would raise the child there, among their family, in il hanitzju. Some of the Sefaradim must still be alive. They
can't have all been killed. And even if they were all dead, she and
her child and Padri would start the family all over again, and the
Pintos would return to Sarajevo and never leave it again.

Presently she could hear Padri talking to himself, or to Osman, in the bunk below: Manuči will love you. Simha will cook
up a storm. Her children must be big by now. We will not live
in Bilave, we'll come down to town. We will reopen the Apotheke. We will take walks every evening, with our hands on our
butts. We will drink coffee under the linden tree. We will go to
the Čaršija for halva and boza, and bring back lokum for our
grandchild. You will sing songs to us. We will pick lavender in
the mountains.

"We will see," Osman said.

Rahela thought she heard bullets pinging against the ship's hull
but it was the ship creaking and groaning. She had fallen asleep
and it got dark. At the foot of her bunk, there was a piece of bread
wrapped in a rag, but when she bit into it, it was too hard.

Padri, she called. Are you hungry?

He must've been asleep, because he said nothing. In Manila,
they would both have to nurse themselves to strength, fatten
up for the long sail home. He could not be older than sixty, she
thought. People live to be a hundred. Jews are resilient. He survived many wars, he survived deserts and mountains, the deprav-
ity in the ghetto, he survived opium, so much sorrow. He survived

me. Padri, you have to eat something, she said. The child inside her suddenly moved, she felt a kick in her belly. The poor thing must be hungry. She bit into the bread, nearly cracking her tooth.

Pinto was on his back, his head on Osman's thigh, so that he could stroke his hair, slowly, parting the hair that knotted together. Osman's fingers smelled of lavender. The water carved by the ship's prow splashed against the hull. The sea was endless darkness, but above it there were so many stars that it looked like the Lord had spilled sugar in the sky.

Blessed be He who is everywhere, Pinto said.

Among His signs are the ships, sailing like the floating mountains: if He willed, He could bring the wind to a standstill and they would lie motionless on the surface of the sea.

I think my ship is coming to a standstill. I don't think I am going to make it back to Sarajevo. Or even to wherever we're going now. Manuči used to say, Let's see who lives and who dies. In a different world, we could've lived a different life.

"There are many worlds," Osman said. Now he was sliding his fingertips along Pinto's eyebrows, as if to make him frown, and then he touched his scar. "All you can do is hope you end up in the right one."

I remember the first time I saw you. You were washing yourself with water from a bucket outside the army barracks, you were splashing your armpits. A lot of hair on your shoulders, like fur. I could see your ribs, and you were squealing with joy.

"I remember that day."

You were squealing and yelping, as if the water was really cold.

"It was."

It was July.

"July or not, it was cold."

And I thought, I want to touch that man. I want to kiss him.

"Well, you did."

Not enough. No. Not enough.

"Well, here is some more," Osman said, and leaned down to touch Pinto's lips with his.

Rahela woke up to find that Padri was gone. She peeked in all the other berths, and saw the children piled up on top of their Yiddish-speaking mother, and he was not anywhere to be found. She could not imagine that he could climb up all by himself. When she came up on the deck, the moon was like a big, bright eye with a cataract and the wave crests shimmered and sparkled as they moved toward it. At the foot of a lifeboat wrapped in tarpaulin, leaning against it, a man was stroking someone's head in his lap. Instantly, she knew that the man was Osman.

"Rafo is gone," Osman said. "He's left us. I loved him more than anything in the world."

I know, Rahela said. I loved him too. I wish I had said goodbye.

"He wanted you to rest. It's a long way home."

I'll never sleep again, Rahela said.

She lay down next to Padri and embraced him. As soon as she put her head on Osman's thigh, he started stroking her hair and forehead, and his touch was gentle and familiar, and she remembered the times when she felt a touch on her forehead and temple and woke up in the dark to see nothing, and would hold her breath to hear movement, but the silence would be dense and solid. Padri's eyes were now closed, but not as when he was sleeping, but rather as though he was just about to open them and see her. She caressed his scar—she knew that skin ridge, the hardness of it, his skin was cold. His lips were slightly apart as though he was readying for a kiss. But no breath came out.

I haven't loved him enough, Rahela said. I wasted my life not loving him enough.

The sky was alight with stars, millions of them. Osman caressed her hair just like Padri used to do, slowly and gently, as if never intending to stop. Some of the stars up there were already dead.

"If you see them," Osman said, "they are not dead."

EPILOGUE

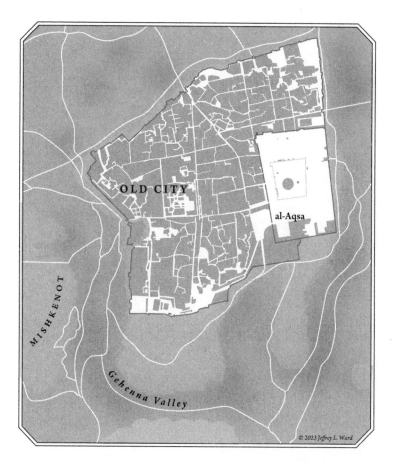

JERUSALEM, 2001

AFTER A GRUELING, LONG SUMMER, much of which I squandered in a cozy East Coast writer's retreat where every day I wrote about the difficulty of writing, only to throw it all away, I found myself at a literary festival in Jerusalem. This was just around the time my first book came out. I was eager to accept any and all invitations to readings and festivals so as to abscond from the idiocy of the Bushist America, a bad marriage, and the many inescapable and terrible decisions rolling down the steep hill of my future. It might also be pertinent to mention that the festival took place a week or so before 9/11.

It was finally and abundantly raining in Chicago when I departed, but in Jerusalem I landed into a dry, static heat, infused with ceaseless cicada choruses, and into a city in the throes of suicide bombings, including one on the very morning of my arrival. The festival van that had picked me up at the airport got stuck in traffic; sirens wailed and black buglike helicopters hovered in the distance. The grim driver, whose hair crawled up his neck in rich tributaries, listened to a discombobulated, hysterical radio voice that must have been calling in from the site of the bombing, but he said nothing to explain what might be going on, nor did I ask anything. I suppose I just unquestioningly accepted the reality into which I had landed, as it was not mine and was thus unalterable by me.

At the hotel, I could see in the lobby a TV nobody was watching. The split screen showed a reporter gripping a microphone, constantly pointing at something that was supposed to be behind her back and out of sight, but was shown with intercut footage of IDF soldiers armed to their invisible teeth breaking down a door and dragging out an Arab family: the crying children, the covered grandmother, the frail grandfather, and the rest. In the next shot, they knelt with their hands tied behind their backs. The other half of the screen showed an evidently important soccer game. With seven minutes left to play in overtime, the blue team was beating the white one 2–1. There is no world, it occurred to me, in which everyone wins or nobody loses.

I was staying in Mishkenot Sha'ananim, as were all the other writers. Back in those days, I was a smoker, but only when traveling—which was another reason I was so eager to travel—so I dropped my bag on the wrinkleless bed in my room to light up a cigarette on its balcony facing the walls of the Old City. I sometimes still miss smoking, still long for that certainty of pleasure made possible by addiction. Most of all, I miss how a cigarette could slow everything down—every little crack in time could be filled out by a burning cigarette, and you could do and think simply nothing, aim nowhere, just be as you were wherever you were, puff your sweet cigarette, and watch the world move around you like a river around a rock. And if you did it right, every cigarette tasted as if it was the last one, the final frontier of pleasure.

These days, if I have five minutes before doing something or being somewhere, I just joylessly fondle my smartphone, hoping for some good news that never comes. If you live long enough, you learn that nothing has ever been, nor will it ever be, the way it used to be.

Anyway, there I was on a balcony in Jerusalem, sucking on a duty-free cigarette. I envisioned the ancient armies of conquerors and crusaders charging at the Old City walls from below, blood running down the gullies, bodies tumbling to pile at the bottom of the valley, the roar of battle and death, the epic senselessness of it all. It is a common symptom of rank melancholy to keep imagining the past instead of a future, because the future feels both foreclosed and uncertain, whereas the past is all there is, infinitely reproducible. The Old City walls gleamed in the light of the late-afternoon sun; the air was suffused with the smell of lavender and sage and burning; somewhere beyond the cypress and olive trees, the cicadas were busy sawing through their steel cords.

I didn't know anyone at the festival's opening reception, and nobody knew me, let alone of me. I parked myself in the corner and stood shrouded in irrelevance, fortifying my discomfort with a glass of rancid sparkling wine, until a young woman with a lanyard tag that identified her as Caroline Staff approached me to inquire how everything was going. If it was any better, it wouldn't be any good, I said, at which she laughed and declared she was very glad that I made it to Jerusalem so that she could finally meet me in person. It was amazing to me then, as it is now, that anyone would ever want to meet me in person. But Caroline was Chicago-born, and her family had come to America as refugees from Hungary a generation or two before, so that my book resonated with her on a very personal level. She was very beautiful, with lively black eyes, asymmetrical eyebrows, and a reluctant smile that suggested deeply buried longing and sorrow. As for me, I am always ready to fall for longing and sorrow.

Hence I followed Caroline as she meandered through the crowded reception hall in search of writers and civilians she had determined I ought to meet. To each of them I had to repeat my name at least twice while offering my lanyard as if it alone proved that Caroline was not making shit up, that I was a fellow writer, if a minor one, and that I had official permission to mingle among the esteemed internationally renowned authors. For the life of me, I could not stretch the small talk beyond the dullest exchanges (And how was your flight?). I let Caroline steer me toward my next communication challenge with a light touch above my elbow, while I kept my arm in stiff obeisance. Throughout the ordeal (shaking hands, pronouncing my name, repronouncing my name, asking: And how was your flight?, moving on to the next indifferent target, and so on), which I endured with a complicit grin, I was devising plots that would ideally climax in my sleeping with Caroline. It was not that there was any reasonable probability of an intercourse taking place, nor would I ever dare actually do it. It was because what I did—and still do—when anxious and lonely was devise plots, my mind compulsively generating potential story lines to aid me in distress and in manufacturing a sense of control within a perpetual rush of helplessness. When people ask me what I do when not writing, I'm likely to say: I plot.

Blissfully unaware of the nefarious plot unfolding in my head, Caroline introduced me to an imposing woman with a thick mane of silver hair. I shook her hand before I recognized her—I do not wish to name her now, so I'll call her Doka here, because she reminded me of my elementary school language teacher known as Doka, who had the same silver mane, plus a scar across her gullet, and was just as scary and imposing. The Jerusalem version of Doka was a very famous author whose books I had burnt through in grad school, using them to buffer myself against the onslaught of poststructuralism, deconstruction, and other European intellectual gewgaws. My graduate-school notebooks, now lost, were full of random sentences from her essays, particularly the one on the embodiment of history and the ethics and aesthetics of autobiographical fiction. She had famously spent time in Sarajevo during the siege, staging a production of Marlowe's *Tamburlaine*; she refused to wear a bulletproof vest or a helmet in solidarity with all the Sarajevans who couldn't, and was said to be the first visiting foreigner to have done so. After Caroline's introduction, the Jerusalem Doka regarded me as if my very face were a lanyard and said, in a stern, teacherly voice: Oh, I know exactly who he is!

Naturally, her words and the manner of her delivery terrified me. In my stupefaction, I blurted: And I know exactly who you are, at which Caroline rewardingly chuckled. The Jerusalem Doka continued to stare at me coldly, saying nothing more, while I scanned my memory for the reasons she might know exactly who I was. It did occur to me at that moment that I myself didn't quite know who I was, nor why exactly I was whoever I was and not someone else. The doubt lasted as long as a sneeze, but it would be fair to call it a symptom of an ongoing ontological crisis. You cannot fathom my rules, the Lord said to some dope in the Bible.

Afterward, we did talk long enough for me to discover that the Jerusalem Doka and I shared a few friends. I had reasons to believe that the friends we shared would not have indicted me too harshly, but I could not know what history I might have embodied for her, nor who might have outlined to her my particular story. But at the time, I continued to panic and could not come up with the next thing to say to her, not even to ask about her flight. Declaring that I urgently needed to refill my glass with the bubbly, I finally bolted, leaving the fair Caroline to wrangle the great writer.

Instead of replenishing the bubbly swill in my flute, however, I hurried to my room, where I would subsequently spend the long jet-lagged night running up and down the list of reasons for the Jerusalem Doka's dislike of me, replaying obsessively in my head her stentorian voice as she said: Oh, I know exactly who he is! I kept considering what the Sarajevans might have in fact told her about me: that I missed the siege; that, safe in America, I wrote a book wherein the siege features, thereby putting myself in a position to represent and exploit other people's suffering, etc. I could hear their voices play out in my head whole scenes with my friends and enemies talking to her about me, telling her that I was absent from Sarajevo under siege, with or without the bulletproof vest, while she was there, proving that it was indeed possible, perhaps even necessary, to be present on the side of the victim. Eventually, I could see with 4:00 a.m. clarity what she might have perceived when she looked at me, and I was not in the least proud of that particular version of myself. I took Vicodin and fell asleep as stars fainted in the sky, and woke up—ashamed, with a headache and an ashtray mouth—only when Caroline called the room to tell me it was time to go to my event.

The event was a panel entitled Writing, War, Suffering; I was to discuss with an Israeli and a German the ways of writing about war and suffering, on which we were presumably experts. In the greenroom, the German writer told me, unprompted and indignant, that it was in fact he who had been the first foreigner in the besieged Sarajevo not to wear the bulletproof vest; and it was only because Americans invariably felt they were the best and the smartest in the world, and had the innate tendency to pirate what had already been discovered and developed by others—music, film, literature, whatever—that everyone and their mother now believed it was indeed an American woman who had taken off the bulletproof vest.

It was me, he said. I was the first one to take it off.

Congratulations! I said, and he didn't like it.

In the course of the panel, the brave German upped his game to rant against myriad Western writers who visit war zones on a self-indulgent whim, for a thrill, only to spend their time being driven in armored vehicles around the local hell, wearing helmets and bulletproof vests, and staging pompous theater shows in safe basements, never seeing, let alone experiencing, the true extent of other people's pain, and then some of them end up writing books lecturing the rest of us about suffering as if they actually knew anything about it. The auditorium was packed, vibrating with tension I could not trace back to anything I knew or understood. The Israeli writer picked it up from the German to rail against the continuous failure on the part of knee-jerk Western liberals to comprehend what was really happening in the Middle East. The Western liberals liked to bring the warring sides to the table thinking that their commitment to destroying their enemy was all a matter of some gigantic misunderstanding, he said, which misunderstanding could be worked out by way of empathy and conversation and a shared pot of herbal tea, or maybe even something stronger. Whereas the actual problem was that the warring sides desired and demanded the same thing, and the thing was not shareable and never would be, because that thing was a homeland. Few people in the world have a homeland, and those who don't have it want it, while those who have it are never sharing it, because they shed their blood and gave up their lives to live in it. It's all very simple, he said. Very simple.

A large number of people in the audience nodded at various points of the two writers' impassioned discourse. The intensity of their beliefs and convictions verily frightened me, particularly since it seemed that the audience was aroused by it. I ran through my head what I was going to say, and it was clear to me that none of it could match the uncompromising candor of the other two authors. Caroline's face in the front row was tight with a kind of desperate attention, as if the panel were the very last chance for everyone present to reach some solution for a horrible host of problems. She was using her lanyard as a fan, even if the space was air-conditioned to the point of refrigeration, which I interpreted as an expression of her anxiety about me and my oncoming vacillation.

In the seat directly behind Caroline, an elderly woman sat with her palms in her lap facing upward as if she were holding an invisible, delicate object. Her hands were gloved, and the whiteness of the gloves shone in the darkened auditorium. She wore a yellow jacket whose lapels were studded with badges and a black shirt on which CLOSURE read in English, Hebrew, and Arabic. Her gaze was directed at me, not at the other writers. She shook her head as if she could hear me think and was suggesting that it would be inadvisable to say what I was about to say.

But I had no other choice, so I started with offering my standard opening disclaimer: my personal experience was invalid and my opinion on the topic inadequate as I had not been subjected to war violence. I was in Chicago when Sarajevo came under siege, and all I had access to was other people's stories and testimonies, sometimes further narratively developed by my limited imagination. My friends told me what they had gone through, so that I could try to imagine what war was like, fully cognizant that the picture could never be complete or even accurate, that their experience would never be truly available to me, and that, in fact, that was how history worked. History leaves devastation in its wake. You can experience and understand history only when you're inside it, but when you're inside it you don't have time or gumption for understanding. All you want is just to stay alive, for which understanding is not necessary. You have no access to history's complex, catastrophic logic, which is indelibly overwhelming and incomprehensible, particularly as you're trying to survive. History has no limit in the exact same way my visual field has no limit, but the moment I write or speak about it, I place myself outside it, so it can only be experienced as a narrative. All I could ever do about the past, or any experience that was not immediately mine, was to imagine it and then dare tell stories about it, but only if I accept the inevitable failure of the project, because history is a matter of experience, of being, and not a structure, not a story. The German audibly scoffed, while the Israeli interrupted me to say that writers had been telling stories about the world for centuries, but the true task of writing was to change the world, and change it for the better. It was clear that neither of them thought that I had any chance of succeeding at that particular task, and I had to concur. Everyone clapped in enthusiastic approval, except for the woman in the white gloves, still fixated on me and shaking her head in vigorous reproach.

It took a lot of torturous time and refrigeration, plus a couple of bottles of rust-tasting water before we were done with our pointless debate, whereupon the moderator opened it all up to the audience. The first dreaded comment-and-not-a-question came from a man in the second row who wore a kippah and had a very challenging time disentangling his cane from the seat before him. When he finally stood up, he refused the microphone and triumphantly raised his finger to announce to all present, in English: Homer was blind. Blind! After that, practically nobody could hear him, but he kept talking nevertheless, and I kept watching Caroline fanning herself, hoping she would smile at me, which she eventually half-heartedly did.

Afterward, I sat at the table with stacks of my book's Hebrew edition in wait for the putative readers eager to have theirs autographed. It occurred to me that there was no way for me to confirm that what I had written was in fact inside the books, as it was behind the impenetrable glass of an alphabet illegible to me. Two long lines formed for the Israeli and the German, both of whom continued to speak in agitation to their fans and readers. Meanwhile, I brooded and doodled on the festival brochure with an ambitiously thick Sharpie. The clock on the wall was very ungenerously spending the ten minutes I gave myself before I could abscond from the nightmare.

And I almost made it—the brochure doodled up to the brim, the clock's second hand in its very last lap before my liberation—when the white-gloved lady appeared before me, flanked by a man in his fifties whom I had not noticed in the audience. She stepped forth while he stood back, placing his hands over his crotch like a hack bodyguard, his jaw taut, his eyes cold, his jacket spacious enough to conceal a cozy Uzi, or even a suicide vest. She put her gloved hand on the table right before me and leaned in so that her necklace pendant, picturing a Samsara wheel, dangled over my books like a plumb line. And then she sang:

> *Bejturan se uz ružu savija*
> *Vilu ljubi Djerzelez Alija*
> *Vilu ljubi svu noć na konaku*
> *po mjesecu i mutnu oblaku.*

She sang in a high-pitched voice, holding long notes and taking in loud breaths between the lines. Now it looked like she was shaking her head because she was moved by the song, and was draining her last drops of soul to express the sevdah in it properly. She had an accent, but only a slight one, like someone who knew the language but seldom used it. She stared at me while singing as if trying to get inside my skull and use the beauty of the song to clean up the torrid mess. I had no wherewithal to keep eye contact, so I read the badges on her lapel: End the Closure in the Territories. Remember the Future. Women for a Just Peace. After she finally stopped singing, I stupidly clapped, which allowed me to look away. The German and the Israeli, and their readers, were all considering us silently, like a tragic choir waiting for their turn to sing.

That's an old Bosnian song, I said. How do you know it?

I was in Sarajevo after the war for a while.

The last war?

No, the one before, the world war. My family was from Sarajevo, so I went to look for them, but they were not there.

I did not know how to respond. I was rapidly becoming uncomfortable, so I asked: Would you like me to sign a book for you? She shook her head again, and in a humbling deductive flash I realized that she was not expressing her disbelief, disapproval, or sevdah but that she had motor-control difficulties, possibly Parkinson's disease. I abruptly understood why her hands were trembling too, and why her bodyguard, or whatever he was, held her three-pronged cane in his overlapping hands. She said: I've already read your book. Maybe we take coffee together?

What could I do? We drank cardamom-contaminated coffee on the Mishkenot terrace as the Old City walls turned orange, then purple, then gray. I remembered that line from the Herbert poem: If we lose the ruins nothing will be left. Her bodyguard turned out to be her son, whose name was Avram. He wordlessly joined us at the table, proceeded to drink his Fanta straight from the bottle, and strenuously avoided eye contact with me, his gaze fixed instead on the neutral mid-space above the table. The woman's hand was shaking as she raised the coffee cup to her lips, but she did not spill a drop. She dabbed her lips with a very white handkerchief, adjusted her Samsara wheel pendant so that it was in the middle of her chest, and said: My name was Rahela Pinto, and both of my fathers were from Bosnia. I ended up in this country. It was new back then, a country of refugees, that created even more refugees.

She pronounced the word Sarajevo as a Sarajevan would, stressing the first syllable, so I didn't at first consider the value of her having two fathers.

It is a very long and difficult story, she said, but I must tell you a little bit.

By all means, I retorted. I could already hear the accelerated whirring of the plot machine in my head.

One of her fathers, Rafael Pinto, was Jewish, she said, and the other one, Osman Karišik, was Muslim. They were both Sarajevans, but they met serving in the Austro-Hungarian Army in World War I and loved each other more than anyone had ever loved another person before, or would ever after, and were together for the rest of their lives even when they were apart, even after Osman died. Her biological mother was a Russian Jewish woman from Tashkent, whom Rahela did not remember because she had died giving her birth. Neither did she ever meet Osman, except in Padri Rafo's stories about him, about his growing up in Sarajevo, about their time together in the war, in a POW camp in Tashkent, in the mountains of Turkestan, the deserts of China. She herself mostly grew up in Shanghai, where she and Padri Rafo ended up in the 1920s. She eventually left for Hong Kong with a man she loved, who turned out to be bad, and she regretted that mistake for the rest of her life. Padri stayed behind in Shanghai, lived through the war, and was there in 1949, when the Communists took over. She went to retrieve him and they headed to Sarajevo, because that's where Padri Rafo's family would have been and there was no other place for them to settle. But he never made it, and she had no choice but to continue without him, four months pregnant. When she got to Sarajevo and went looking for the Pintos she could find none. There were in fact very few Jews left in the city—most of those who survived the Shoah had already migrated to the newborn Israel. A whole world had vanished, like a dream. For a while she just wandered around the city in search of things she remembered from Padri Rafo's stories, his voice in her head guiding her. She went up to Bilave—Bjelave, I corrected her, but she ignored me—wandered around Mejtaš, asking about Avram and Rahela Pinto (she was named after her grandmother) and about his sister, his nieces Laura and Blanka, even his brother-in-law, Albert, who wrote him a letter she and Padri would read and reread as if it were the Torah. Even those who understood what she was asking knew nothing about them, or about any other Pintos, or so they said. She spoke a language she had learned from Padri Rafo and that no person in Sarajevo seemed to speak, a mishmash of Spanjol, Bosnian, German, and a dozen other languages his mind had been infected with between Sarajevo and Shanghai. It took her a while to understand that the language she was using was Padri Rafael's alone, and that she and he were the only ones who had ever spoken it. As for Osman, he, like me, she said, had never had any family. She asked all over the Čaršija, where, according to Padri Rafo's stories, he had grown up an orphan, but no one could remember anything about him, or if they did, they wouldn't say. She also asked about characters from Osman's stories, which Padri had told her since her childhood: Meho Kulampara, and Hadži Resko Šupak, and even the brave Alija Đerzelez. People thought she was crazy, speaking in some garbled language about characters from strange, old stories, and soon the Communist police were curious about her curiosity and she had to stop asking questions. They would've probably arrested her if she wasn't obviously pregnant. The city she had imagined from Padri Rafo's stories now appeared to have been annihilated, along with all its people and stories and spaces, as if an entirely different place had been built on top of it. There was little evidence that it had ever actually existed, even if her father's voice in her head kept talking to her, still telling her the same stories all over again.

She managed to find the apothecary that used to belong to the Pinto family. It was run by the state, and was presently closed. She lingered outside the apothecary in suspended despair, not knowing what to do. She knew no one who could tell her about the place, and no one knew anything about her. It was like she had landed on the wrong shore and all the ships were now gone and were never coming back. It occurred to her at that moment, and it was quite frightening, she said, that Padri Rafo might have made it all up. What if, she fretted, he hadn't been born in Sarajevo, and her mother hadn't actually died and was alive elsewhere? What if Osman had never existed, and Rafael Pinto had not been her father's real name, and he was someone else, perhaps not even a Jew? What if everything he had told her was but a collection of fairy tales and lies?

She wandered around the Čaršija for a while, just to calm herself down. Sometimes, life is like a dream, she said, and I agreed, that life was always involuntarily imagined and that everyone already knew that we might all wake up in a different world, as our own shadows.

And then, a strange thing happened, she said. Suddenly, Osman was walking next to her, she could not see him but sensed his presence just behind her, on her right side, she could hear his voice. He showed her where the old Pinto drogerija had once stood, and where he used to fetch coffee and halva for Sinjor Avram, who sometimes let him roll a cigarette with the tasty tobacco smuggled from Herzegovina. And he showed her where Hadži-Šaban's kahvana used to stand, and they sat on the riverbank and talked about the life that had vanished, and the life that might have been, and a world in which the apothecary belonged to Padri, and he and Osman took care of each other in their old age.

The following day, she went back to the apothecary, where a man saw her knocking on the door. The man spoke to her, told her that it would not open for a while. She perfectly understood everything the man said, but she could not remember and tell me in what language she'd been spoken to. The man was not young, but it was hard to say what age he was. His name was Blum, one of the few Jews still left in Sarajevo, she said he said, everyone else was dead or had departed. He did remember the Apotheke Pinto well: when he was a kid he'd come down here all the way from Mejtaš because his mother would send him to get the powders for her headaches or for some other malady. I remember the man who sold me the medicine—he had a beautiful smile shining on his swarthy face.

I will always remember that smile, he said. The Pintos were good people, a good family. As far as I know, there are no longer any living Pintos around. Are you family?

Yes, she said.

Well, the man said. I am very sorry.

He was as good as bread, Blum was, Rahela said to me. Buenu komu il pan. Blum helped her understand that there was nothing in Sarajevo for her and her child. He was a Communist and worked for the government, so he could help her get the necessary papers and within a couple of weeks she was on her way to Israel, where she did track down some other Sarajevans, who stuck together in their new land, still spoke the Sarajevo dialect of Spanjol mixed with their remembered Bosnian, and treated her as though she was always one of them. Some were old enough to remember the Apotheke Pinto and the young Doktor Rafael in his Viennese suit, with his tawny tan and crimson fez, his bright smile. After she gave birth to Avram, Rahela couldn't stop crying for days because it was then, she said, that his absence became fully real. She could no longer hear his voice, he was no longer speaking to her, and she could not tell him, or even write to him, about the life she had now, a life that he could never live or see. She understood what death meant—each death ends a life that can now no longer be altered. Only then could she mourn him, mourn his life and all the lives he could've lived in the world different from this one. She was the only one mourning him because she was the only one, other than Blum, who remembered him and Osman. Her heart had been broken since.

And they will die again when I die, she said. I will die soon too. Each and every one of the lives that has ever been lived will sooner or later be forgotten. You can be lonely in death as you can be lonely in life. That's why people believe in God. They think God takes care of them and will remember them and their lives, she said. But He won't. Everyone and everything will be forgotten. That is why it matters what we do now when we are alive. Remember the future, Padri used to say. Death is useless and worthless.

Her son put the bottle down on the table and wiped his mouth with the back of his hand; and then he burped. She was speaking to me slowly, shaking her head to the same internal beat, but what she told me only took as long as it took her son to finish his Fanta. I had read that when Mohammed dropped the water pitcher and went to Heaven, he came back before the pitcher hit the ground. The Al Aqsa was built on that spot, which was also the spot where the YHW created the world and Abraham almost slit his son's throat. And that spot was across the valley, behind those walls. If we lose the ruins nothing will be left.

I needed a moment to find something to say. I live for tales of displacement and oblivion. The plot machine was now spinning, and I was already imagining a story made from all that she told me, and then some more.

But what I said to her was in fact neutral: That is a lot of story for one life.

Many people don't believe me. Even my son doesn't believe me, she said, shrugging. So I stopped telling. But I thought, you are a writer, you have imagination, so maybe you will believe me.

I was just about to thank her for sharing, in the hope that she might say that I should be the one to write the story, when I saw Caroline advancing toward us, her high-heel stride so determined that the lanyard bounced on her chest—she was coming to escort me to some anguine pit of festival hospitality.

Do you believe me? Rahela asked me.

I do, I said, but mainly because Caroline was already beaming intentionality—it was evident she would not let me remain on the terrace and interrogate Rahela about her two fathers and her lost mother, her narratively deputed memories of Sarajevo, and the worlds in which she had spent her life and I knew nothing about—that, in short, Caroline would not let me acquire Rahela's story.

In the ten seconds I had before I was to yield to Caroline's indomitable will, I proposed to Rahela that we meet again, the following day perhaps, so that she could tell me more about her life and her numerous parents, because, as a writer, I admire and appreciate great stories, and hers clearly belonged in that category. She shook her head and nodded at the same time as I suggested that we pick a place devoid of other writers or people who took care of me and managed my itinerary (that is, Caroline). Rahela said something to her son in what might have been Spanjol, or, who knows, the Pinto language she'd talked about, and he—still safe from any eye contact—raised his hand and pointed toward the far end of the valley, where the last glints of the setting sun flickered on obscure windows.

There, how about there? he said, in English. Hell used to be over there. They used to sacrifice babies there, hurl them into the abyss. But you know what they say: Between the Garden of Eden and Gehenna there is no more than the breadth of a hand.

Ah! I said. Is that what they say?

By that time Caroline was looming over me, her smileful power undiminished. Rahela then said something to Caroline in Hebrew, who then told me in English that Rahela would meet me tomorrow afternoon at the Cinematheque, which she claimed I could see from there. Unless I get arrested at the protest today, Rahela said. Unperturbed by that possibility, Caroline endorsed the idea of meeting at the Cinematheque since it was very close to Mishkenot and had a lovely café and an even lovelier view of the Gehenna Valley. It's a good place for meeting because you will be safe there, since suicide bombers don't give a fuck about old movies, Caroline said.

The following day, I walked over to the Cinematheque where the movie being shown that afternoon happened to be *The Wild Bunch*, which once upon time I'd had recorded on a VHS tape to study obsessively. I could easily imagine some suicide bomber actually enjoying it, what with its massacres, explosions, bodies ripped to bloody shreds in slow-motion, but the café was totally empty, except for a dog stretched on the terrace floor not even looking up when I walked in. There was no one behind the coffee counter, nor was there any waitstaff. I considered a possibility that they were all being held hostage in the back room freezer, but I chose to let the situation resolve itself without me, and sat outside facing the valley that, according to Rahela's Fanta-nursing son, used to house Hell. Now that I think about it, I knew even then that Rahela would not show up, but I acted as though she would. I sat there fantasizing about her appointing me as the writer who would tell her story, successfully negotiating the acceptable amounts of narrative embellishment and restructuring. I outlined a scene with her submitting herself to my interrogation, to my fishing for vivid details, to all the emotion she would transfer to me. I had my Festival Moleskin ready, my reliable fountain pen; I was fully in my writerly mode. The valley opened itself up below me, the hillsides already trying out the colors for the sunset hour. I heard someone call my name—a voice deep and soft, pronouncing the soft consonants in my name as someone from Sarajevo would—but when I turned around, there was no one there, the place as empty as can be. And then the voice was singing that old Bosnian song, Bejturan se uz ružu savija. It was not Rahela's voice. The voice was male and warm, it sang hummingly, mumbling the words, as if the mouth was close to my ear. Bejturan se uz ružu savija, vilu ljubi Đerzelez Alija, Vilu ljubi svu noć na konaku, po mjesecu i mutnu oblaku.

It did cross my mind that somewhere around there a door between the worlds could be ajar, and that the voice I heard was singing to me from the beyond. Perhaps I would've stepped through that door and into the proper Hell, had not a waitress suddenly materialized to take my order. I slurped my cardamom-free espresso, and then another one, contemplating the fact that the world was a universe of stories that could only keep beginning and would never be finished, until a thunderous explosion some-where beyond what I could see burst all my thought bubbles and sent echoes to bounce around the Hell valley. A stork rose from one of the roofs and ascended into the darkening sky. There was a long beat of terrible silence before many sirens started howling and the noise of diffuse commotion came from multiple direc-tions, and then helicopters whirred overhead, and the valley sank deeper into itself. The waitress ran out onto the veranda with an expression of routine horror on her face, and then looked in the direction of the explosion as though she could will for herself a vision of what had happened.

It was clear that Rahela wouldn't come, and that I might never see her again, and never get any more of her story. I cer-tainly hoped she was not anywhere near that explosion. I had a choice now of returning to the hotel or staying here, maybe even watching *The Wild Bunch* for the thousandth time. I knew that Caroline would worry about me, but I also felt there was some-thing inappropriate and wrong about simply returning to where

I came from, as I could not imagine that it would be the same place now. I shuddered at the thought of all the other writers buzzing nervously around, sharing gossip, outrage, and speculation, offering opinions and staking out moral positions. I had no strength to face any of that.

I bought a movie ticket from the somewhat disbelieving waitress, who in the same turn took the ticket away from me to rip off its end and ushered me into a fantastically empty cinema. I picked the aisle seat in the fifth row and set out to wait for that great shot of a scorpion dropped by a herd of mean children on top of an angry anthill, whereupon the kids watch the poor arachnid being overwhelmed by an army of vicious ants. I heard again the same voice singing the Bosnian song, but before I could turn around to look for its source, the lights went out, and I found myself confronting a complete and utter darkness.

ACKNOWLEDGMENTS

First, I want to tell all of my readers that without them this book is a paper brick and I am nothing. Thank you, my reader, for choosing this book when millions of other books are available for reading.

I do not suffer when writing, but it has never been easy, not least because life, biology, and history inescapably intervene. A book always seems impossible until it is in the bookstores. It took me more than twelve years to finish this novel. Many people helped me get this thing into your hands. Therefore:

I would like to thank Lana Wachowski and David Mitchell (The Pit) for their kindness, friendship, and unlimited willingness to dance and make art. It is hard to exaggerate how much I've learned about storytelling, sharing, and collaborations from my fellow Pitians. It is hard to describe how much I love them.

Damir Imamović's singing voice has been in my head ever since he agreed to record an album inspired by *The World and All That It Holds*. (I highly recommend having Damir's singing voice in your head.) Without Damir's brilliance, Rafo and Osman's journey would've been different, not least because his album—also called

The World and All That It Holds—is an outrageous masterpiece. If a creative project expands and strengthens a friendship as ours did, there must be something right with it.

I continue to be grateful to Nicole Aragi, my fierce friend and agent, whose unconditional and mighty support has benefited my work since the end of the previous millennium. I look forward to our coordinated retirement and our subsequent time together in the upper circles of Hell, where I will DJ eternally and where, I hear, the food is excellent.

Sean McDonald, who has been publishing my work from the very beginning, is not just one of the best editors around, but also a cherished and steady friend. After all these years, he is still able to listen to my endless monologues in silence and seriously and productively consider my lopsided and crooked ideas. I wrote the book in your hands, but he made it.

For some decades now, Semezdin Mehmedinović has been among my closest literary and personal friends, as well as my favorite living writer. He helped me see Rafo, Osman, and Rahela with his discerning, generous eyes, and provided the comfort of Zoomed friendship throughout the loneliest months of the outbreaks of COVID and American fascism.

My comrades in art gave up their time and minds (temporarily, I hasten to report) to follow and love my heroes on their journey across the terrible, beautiful world and the twentieth century. I cannot thank them enough, so this must do: Thank you, Rabih Alameddine, Gary Shteyngart, Yiyun Li, Jesse Eisenberg, Charlie Finch, Gus Rose, Nami Mun, and a few others whose names escape me now—you know who you are, even if I don't.

John Freeman has been my friend, reader, interlocutor, and editor for decades now. I cannot imagine my writing life without him. One day, I'll make him dance. Until then we'll just talk literature for hours on end.

Vojislav Pejović kindly deployed his superbly persnickety reading abilities to nitpick through *The World and All That It Holds* and make it considerably better with his objections and suggestions. Vojislav is one of the best readers I have ever known, and he repeatedly does me an enormous favor by finishing whatever book of mine I ask him to read.

Indeed, if perfect readers exist, mine would be my Sarajevan friends and my fellow Bosnians/former Yugoslavs: Zrinka Bralo, Velibor Božović, Gordana Dana Grozdanić, and Amila Buturović, as well as Aida Hozić, Arnesa Buljušmić-Kustura, Emil Kerenji, Branko Rihtman, Elvis Bego, Aleksandar Brezar, Nedad Memić, Ervin Malakaj, Jelena Subotić, and Albinko Hasić (aka "Bosnian History" Twitter account). Infinite gratitude to all the other Sarajevans and Bosnians whose love and support for my work are now attached to me like a shadow.

I owe an enormous debt to Dr. Eliezer Papo, who helped me search for Rafo's Ladino/Spanjol voice, and to Dr. Iris Rachamimov, who generously opened the door for me to the vast world of Russian World War I prisoner-of-war camps in Central Asia, about which she seems to know everything. Dr. Sandra Bermann let me accompany her on long afternoon walks (commencing at the YES bridge), indulging me with brilliant conversation about the connections between language and displacement, between migration and translation. Sandie helped me understand my own book better.

Cielo Hemon, my electronic dance music project, has entirely coincided with the latter stages of writing *The World and All That It Holds*, so that the novel is somehow present in Cielo's tracks, and the tracks in the novel, in ways that would be neither visible nor audible to anyone other than me, but were crucial in creating both works of art. Thank you, Goran Markovi and Alan Omerović, for helping me make the music. Thank you, Harun Mehmedinović, Šejla Kamerić, and Zlatko Ćosić, for coming up with the images to match the music. I have learned so much and I aim to learn and create more with all of you.

Princeton University and its Creative Writing Program, my

intellectual-cum-academic homebase, have been incredibly patient with and supportive of my creative needs and demands. I hope to spend many years here and will always be grateful to my colleagues for putting up with the music blasting from my office.

Finally, my everlasting gratitude to Teri Boyd, the force that keeps catastrophe out of my/our life and loads it up with courage and abundant love. Forever, and beyond!

Now, let's go dancing.

A NOTE ABOUT THE AUTHOR

Aleksandar Hemon is the author of *The Lazarus Project*, which was a finalist for the 2008 National Book Award and the National Book Critics Circle Award and a *New York Times* bestseller, along with several books of short stories—*The Question of Bruno*; *Nowhere Man*, which was also a finalist for the National Book Critics Circle Award; and *Love and Obstacles*—and the novel *The Making of Zombie Wars*. He has also written the essay volumes *The Book of My Lives* and *My Parents / This Does Not Belong to You*. Among other accolades, he has received a "genius" grant from the MacArthur Foundation, a Guggenheim Fellowship, the PEN/W. G. Sebald Award for a Fiction Writer in Mid-Career, and the John Dos Passos Prize for Literature. He cowrote the script for *The Matrix Resurrections* and produces music as Cielo Hemon. He teaches at Princeton University.